The Winter Mantle

Also by Elizabeth Chadwick

THE CONQUEST
THE CHAMPION
THE LOVE KNOT
THE MARSH KING'S DAUGHTER
LORDS OF THE WHITE CASTLE

THE
WINTER
MANTLE

ELIZABETH CHADWICK

ST. MARTIN'S PRESS ✷ NEW YORK

www.stmartins.com

Library of Congress Cataloging-in-Publication Data

Chadwick, Elizabeth.
The winter mantle / Elizabeth Chadwick.—1st U.S. ed.
p. cm.
ISBN 0-312-31291-1
1. William I, King of England, 1027 or 8–1087—Fiction.
2. Great Britain—History—William I, 1066–1087—Fiction.
3. Normans—Great Britain—Fiction. I. Title.

PR6053.H245 W56 2003
823'.914—dc21   2002037027

First published in Great Britain by Little, Brown and Company
An imprint of Time Warner Books UK

First U.S. Edition: April 2003

10 9 8 7 6 5 4 3 2 1

ACKNOWLEDGEMENTS

I'd like to say some public thank you's to colleagues, friends and family behind the scenes. This is their moment of glory! As always, my gratitude goes out to my agent Carole Blake and everyone at Blake Friedmann for working so hard on my behalf. My thanks to my editor Barbara Boote for her continuing support and for always making time to answer my calls even in the midst of a very demanding schedule. Thanks too to Joanne Coen, my desk editor, and all the other friendly, approachable staff at Little, Brown. I should also like to say thanks to Wendy Wootton of Artemis Designs for keeping my website up and running.

Since the coming of the Internet, I have made many new contacts around the world. Teresa Eckford, founder of Medieval Enthusiasts, and Wendy Zollo, who runs my reader's e-list at Yahoo, deserve particular mention for their enthusiasm, knowledge and genuine warmth and friendship. Thanks guys!

As always, my family are an oasis of steadiness and love in a sometimes hectic and fraught world. My husband Roger understands that my writing is my soul and gives me the space I need. He also doesn't mind being tortured by read-outs of the first drafts while doing the ironing, so he is a genuine romantic hero!

Finally, I would like to say thank you to the members of Regia Anglorum, both those I have met in the flesh and those online, who have answered my frequent questions with patience, laughter and astounding knowledge – especially Andrew Nicolson for taking the time to answer my questions about eleventh-century coffins!

CHAPTER 1

Tower of Rouen, Normandy, Lent 1067

'I wonder what Englishmen are like,' mused Sybille as she laced the drawstring on her mistress's embroidered linen shift.

'Judging by the few we've seen before, more hair and beards than a flock of wild goats,' Judith said disdainfully to her maid. As niece to Duke William of Normandy, now King of England, she was intensely conscious of her own dignity. 'At least with our men you can see what lies beneath, and the lice are easier to keep at bay.' She glanced towards the window, where the sound of the cheering crowds swished through the open shutters like a summer wind through forest leaves. Below the lofty tower walls the entire population of Rouen crammed the streets, eager for a sight of their duke's triumphal return from England and his defeat of the crown-stealer, Harold Godwinsson.

Her maid's interest in Englishmen – and her own if the truth were known – was due to the fact that her Uncle William had returned to his Duchy laden not only with Saxon booty but accompanied by highborn hostages -- English lords whom he did not trust out of his sight.

'But it is nice to run your fingers through a man's beard,

don't you think?' Sybille pursued with sparkling eyes. 'Especially if he is young and handsome.'

Judith frowned a warning. 'I would not know,' she said loftily.

Not in the least set down, the maid gave a pert toss of her head. 'Well, now you have a chance to find out.' Fetching Judith's best fitted gown of blood-red wool from the coffer where it had been lying amidst layers of dried rose petals and cinnamon bark, she helped her into it.

Judith smoothed her palms over the rich, soft wool with pleasure. From the corner of her eye she was aware of her sister Adela being fussed over by their mother, who was plucking and tweaking to align every fold.

'God forfend that there should be a single hair out of place,' Sybille muttered and facetiously crossed herself.

Judith hissed a rebuke as her mother approached. Sybille immediately swept a demure curtsey to the older woman and busied herself with binding Judith's hair in two tight, glossy braids. A silk veil followed, held in place by pins of worked gold.

Adelaide, Countess of Aumale, studied the maid's handiwork with eyes that were as hard and sharp as brown glass. 'You'll do,' she said brusquely to Judith. 'Where's your cloak?'

'Here, Mother.' Judith lifted the garment from her clothing pole. The dark green wool was lined with beaver fur and trimmed with sable as befitted her rank. Adelaide leaned forward to adjust the gold and garnet fastening pin and swept an imaginary speck from the napped wool.

Judith restrained the urge to bat her mother's hand aside, but Adelaide must have felt the intention for she fixed her daughter with a frosty stare. 'We are women of the ducal house,' she said. 'And it behoves us to show it.'

'I know that, Mother.' Judith was wise enough not to expose her irritation, but behind her dutiful expression she was quietly seething. At fifteen years old, she was of marriageable age with the curves and fluxes of womanhood, but still her mother treated her like a child.

'I am glad that you do.' Adelaide frowned down her long, pointed nose. Beckoning to her daughters, she swept to join the other women of Duchess Matilda's household who were preparing to go out in public and greet their returning menfolk. Not that Adelaide's husband would be among them. He was part of the Norman force left behind to garrison England during the new king's absence. Judith had not decided whether her mother was pleased or relieved at the situation. She herself was indifferent. He was her stepfather and she scarcely knew him for he had seldom visited the women's apartments even when at home, preferring life in the hall and the guardroom.

A blustery March wind tumbled around the courtyard, snatching irreverently at wimples, mocking the meticulous preparations of earlier. Bright silk banners cracked like whips on the tower battlements and above them the clouds flew so swiftly across the blue sky that watching them made Judith dizzy.

Sheltering in the lee of the wall, she wondered how long they would have to wait. Her male cousins, the Duke's sons Richard, Robert and William, had ridden out to greet their father in the city. She rather wished that she could have joined them, but it would not have been seemly, and, as her mother said, when you were an important member of the highest household in the land, seemliness was everything.

The roars of approbation from the crowd had become a storm. Judith's heart swelled with fierce pride. It was her blood they were cheering, her uncle who was now a king by God's will and his own determination.

To a fanfare of trumpets the first riders clattered into the courtyard. Sunlight glanced on their helms and mail; silk pennons billowed from the glittering hafts of their spears. Under the rippling colours of the Papal banner, her uncle William rode a Spanish stallion, its hide the deep black of polished sea coal. He wore no armour and his powerful frame was resplendent in crimson wool, crusted with gold embroidery. His dark hair blew about his brow and his hawkish visage was emphasised by the way he narrowed his eyes against the buffet of the wind. A squire ran to grasp the bridle. William dismounted and, landing with solid assurance, turned his gaze on the waiting women.

The Duchess Matilda hastened forward and sank at his feet in a deep curtsey. Adelaide tugged at Judith's cloak in sharp reminder, and Judith knelt too, the ground hard beneath her knees.

William stooped, raised his wife to her feet and murmured something that Judith did not hear but that brought a blush to the diminutive Duchess's face. He kissed his daughters, Agatha, Constance, Cecilia, Adela, then he gestured the other women of the household to rise. His eyes flickered over them, a smile in their depths, although his mouth out of long habit and severe self-control remained straight and stern.

The courtyard was growing ever more crowded as William's entourage continued to ride in. Flanked by guards the English 'guests' arrived. Beards and long hair, Judith noted; her words to Sybille had been right. They did resemble a flock of wild goats, although she had to admit that the embroidery on their garments was the most exquisite she had ever seen.

A richly attired priest, whom Judith identified by the ornate cross atop his staff as an archbishop, was talking to two young men whose similarity of feature marked them as brothers. Mounted on a dappled cob was a yellow-haired youth with fine features and a slightly petulant air. He must be very well born, she thought, for his tunic was that rare colour of purple reserved for royalty and his hat was banded with ermine fur. She studied him until her view was blocked by a powerful chestnut stallion, straddled by a young man whose size and musculature almost equalled that of his horse.

He sported neither hat nor hood and the wind beat his copper-blond hair about his face in disarray. Outlining a wide, good-natured mouth and strong jaw, his beard was the colour of rose gold and made her consider Sybille's mischievous comment in a new light. What *would* it be like to touch? Soft as silk, or harsh as besom twigs? The notion both intrigued and disturbed her. He wore his costly garments in a careless, taken-for-granted way that should have filled her with scorn, but instead she felt admiration and a flicker of envy. Who was he?

In the same moment that she asked herself the question, Judith decided that she did not want to know. Her uncle's English hostage was sufficient to her needs. To think beyond that was much too dangerous. She lowered her eyes in self-defence and thus did not see the swift, appreciative glance that he cast in her direction.

Turning gracefully on her heel, she followed her mother and sister back within the sanctuary of the great stone tower and did not look back.

He was Waltheof Siwardsson, Earl of Huntingdon and Northampton. That he had retained his lands and titles was due to the fact that he had not fought against William on Hastings Field. It did not mean that the new Norman king trusted him or his companions, though.

'Whether or not William declares us his guests, he cannot disguise that we are prisoners,' declared Edgar Atheling, who was a prince of ancient Saxon lineage. His fine, almost effemi-nate features were marred by a fierce scowl. 'Even if our cage is gilded, it is still a cage.'

The English 'guests' were gathered in the timber hall that had been allotted to them during their stay in Rouen. Although the doors were not guarded, none of the hostages was in any doubt that an attempt to leave and take ship for England would be prevented – probably on the end of a sharpened spear.

Waltheof shrugged and filled his cup with wine from the flagon that had been left to hand. Captivity it might be, but at least it was generous. 'There is nothing we can do, so we might as well enjoy ourselves.' He swallowed deeply. It had taken him a while to adjust to the taste of wine when he was used to mead and ale, but now he welcomed the acid, tannic bite at the back of his throat. He understood Edgar's chaffing. There were many in England who thought that the youth should be king. His claim was stronger than either Harold Godwinsson's or William's, but he was only fifteen years old and thus more of a focus around which to rally men rather than a threat posed by his own efforts and abilities.

'You call drinking that muck enjoyment?' Edgar's light blue eyes were scornful.

'You have to grow accustomed,' Waltheof said and was rewarded with a disparaging snort.

'So you think that developing a taste for all things Norman will get you what you want?' This was from Morcar, Earl of Northumberland, his tone hostile and his arms folded belligerently high on his chest. At his side his older brother, Edwin, Earl of Mercia, was, as usual, absorbing all and saying nothing. Their alliance with Harold had been tepid, but so was their acceptance of William the Bastard as their king.

Waltheof pushed his free hand through his heavy red-gold hair and raised the goblet with the other. 'I think it better to say yes than no.' He met Morcar's stare briefly then strode to look out of the embrasure on the advancing dusk. Torches were being lit in the chambers and courtyards of the ducal complex. The rich smell of cooking wafted to his nostrils and cramped his stomach. It would be too easy to quarrel with Morcar and he held himself back, knowing how the Normans would feed upon their disagreements and take superior pleasure in watching them bicker.

'Have a care,' Morcar said softly. 'One day you might say yes to something that will bring you naught but harm.'

Waltheof clenched his fists. He could feel the burn of anger and chagrin flooding his face but he forced himself not to rise to the bait. 'One day I might,' he answered, trying to make light of the matter, 'but not now.' Deliberately he went to the flagon and, refilling his goblet, drank deeply of the dark Norman wine. He knew from experience that after four cups a pleasant haze would begin to creep over him. Ten cups and that haze became numbness. Fifteen purchased oblivion. The

Normans frowned on English drinking habits and King William was particularly abstemious. Waltheof had curbed his excesses rather than face that cold-eyed scorn, but still the need lingered – particularly with Morcar in the vicinity.

Waltheof's father, Siward the Strong, had once held the great earldom of Northumbria, but he had died when Waltheof was a small boy and such a turbulent border earldom required a grown man's rule. First there had been Tosti Godwinsson, who had proved so unpopular that the people rose in rebellion, and then Morcar of the line of Mercia, because Waltheof, at nineteen years old, was still judged too young and inexperienced to be given control of such a vast domain. Two years had passed since that time, and Waltheof's sense of possession had matured sufficiently to leave him resentful of Morcar's ownership – and Morcar knew it.

Further into the room, Archbishop Stigand was seated with Wulnoth Godwinsson, who was King Harold's brother and who had already been a hostage in Normandy for many years. A youth of Edgar's age when he had come into captivity, he was now a young man, with a full golden beard and sad, grey eyes. Quiet and unassuming, he was an insipid shadow of his dynamic brothers Leofwin, Gyrth and Harold, who had died beneath Norman blades on Hastings field. He was no more capable of rebellion than a legless man was of running.

Waltheof downed his wine to the lees and was contemplating refilling his cup when there was a knock on the chamber door. Being the nearest, he reached to the latch and found himself looking down at a slender boy of about nine or ten years old. Fox-gold eyes peered from beneath a fringe of sun-streaked brown hair shaved high on the nape. His tunic was of good blue wool with exquisite stitching, revealing that the sprogling was of high rank, probably someone's squire in the first year of his apprenticeship, when fetching and carrying were the order of the day.

Waltheof raised his brows. 'Child?' he said, suddenly feeling ancient.

'My lords, the dinner horn is about to sound and your presence is requested in the hall,' the lad announced in a clear confident tone. His gaze travelled beyond Waltheof to examine with frank curiosity the other occupants of the room. Waltheof could almost see his mind absorbing every detail, storing it up to relay later to his companions.

'And we must give "King" William what he desires, mustn't we?' sneered Edgar Atheling in English. 'Even if he sends some babe in tail clouts to escort us.'

The boy looked puzzled. Waltheof set a hand on his shoulder and gave him a reassuring smile. 'What is your name, lad?' he asked in French.

'Simon de Senlis, my lord.'

'He's my son.' William's chamberlain Richard de Rules arrived, slightly out of breath. 'I gave him the message and he took off ahead of me like a harrier unleashed!'

'Aye, we must make good sport,' said Edgar, speaking French himself now.

De Rules shook his head and looked rueful. 'That was not my meaning, my lord. My son may be as keen as a hound, but it is his passion that drives him, not his desire to make sport of valued guests.'

Waltheof admired De Rules' way with words – smooth without sounding obsequious. The Norman's face was open and honest with laughter lines at the corners of the grey eyes and he had the same sun-flashed hair as his son.

'Ah, so he has a passion for all things English, like most of your breed?' jeered Morcar.

The polite expression remained on De Rules' face, but the warmth faded from his eyes. 'If you are ready my lords, I will conduct you to the hall,' he said with stiff courtesy.

Waltheof cleared his throat and sought to lighten the moment with a smile and a jest. 'I am certainly ready,' he announced. 'Indeed, I am so hungry that I could eat a bear.' With a flourish he swept on his cloak, its thick blue wool lined with a pelt of gleaming white fur. He winked at the wide-eyed boy. 'This is all that's left of the last one I came across.'

'Hah, you've never seen a bear in your life unless it was a tame one shambling in chains!' Morcar snapped bad-temperedly.

'That shows how much you know of me,' Waltheof retorted and flicked his glance around the gathering of English nobles. 'I am going down to the hall to eat my dinner because, even if I am proud, pride alone will not nourish my bones and it would be churlish to refuse our Norman hosts.' And foolish too, but he did not need to say so. No matter how much they grumbled at their confinement, they dared not openly rebel whilst hostage in Normandy.

As they were escorted to the great hall, the boy paced beside Waltheof and tentatively stroked the magnificent white pelt lining the blue cloak. 'Is it really a bearskin?' he asked.

Waltheof nodded. 'It is indeed, lad, although you will never see one of its kind in a market place or at a baiting. Such beasts dwell in the frozen North Country, far away from the eyes of men.'

Simon's gaze was solemn and questioning. 'Then how came you by it?'

'Morcar's right,' Waltheof grinned over his shoulder at the glowering Earl of Northumberland. 'I have never seen other than the mangy creatures that entertain folk at fairings. But when my father was a very young man, he went adventuring and hunted the great bear that once dwelt inside this fur. Twice the height of a man it was, with teeth the size of drinking horns and a growl to shake snow off the mountain tops.' Waltheof spread his arms to augment the tale and the pelt shimmered as if with a vestige of the fierce life that had once inhabited it. 'He had it fashioned into a cloak and so it has come down to me.'

The boy eyed the garment with wonder and a hint of longing. Waltheof laughed and tousled the child's hair, the gesture boisterous and familiar.

Attired in their finery for the homecoming of their duke, the

Norman nobility packed the trestles set out in the Tower's great hall. The English hostages were placed to one side of the high table with William's kin and the Bishops of Rouen, Fécamp and Jumièges. A cloth of sun-bleached linen, richly patterned with English embroidery, covered the board. There were drinking vessels made from the horns of the wild white cattle that roamed the great forests of Northumbria, the rims and tips edged with exquisitely worked silver and gold. Goblets and flagons, decorated candleholders, gleamed in the firelight like the spangled pile of a dragon's hoard. All of it spoils of war, plundered from the thegns and huscarls who had fallen on Hastings field.

Surrounded by such trophies of conquest, Waltheof felt ill at ease, but he was sufficiently pragmatic to know that this was a victory feast and such display was to be expected. He and his companions were here because they were the vanquished and they too were part of that plunder. He supposed that in a way they should be grateful for Duke William's restraint. The legends of Waltheof's ancestors told of how they had toasted their own victories from the brainpans of their slaughtered foes.

Waltheof had an ear for languages. His French was good, if accented, and he was as fluent in Latin as he was in his native tongue, courtesy of a childhood education at Crowland Abbey in the Fen Country. He was soon engaged in conversation by the Norman prelates, who seemed both surprised and diverted by the ease with which he spoke the tongue of the church.

'Once I was intended for the priesthood,' Waltheof explained to the Archbishop of Rouen. 'I spent several years as an oblate in Crowland Abbey under the instruction of Abbot Ulfcytel.'

'You would have made an imposing monk,' said the Archbishop wryly as he broke the greasy wing joint off a portion of goose and wiped his fingers on a linen napkin.

Waltheof threw back his head and laughed. 'Indeed I would!' He flexed his shoulders. There were few folk in the hall to match his height or breadth, and certainly not on the dais, where even Duke William, who was tall and robust, seemed small by comparison. 'They are probably glad that they did not have to find the yards of wool necessary to fashion me a habit!' As he spoke he chanced to meet the eyes of the girl who sat among the other women of William's household.

He had noticed her in the courtyard on his arrival. Her expression then had been a mingling of the curious and the wary, as if she was studying a caged lion at close quarters. That same look filled her gaze now and made him want to smile. She was raven-haired and attractive in an austere sort of way, her nose thin and straight, her eyes rich brown and thick-lashed with deep lids. Her lips, for all that they were fixed in a firm, unsmiling line, held more than a hint of sensuality. For an instant she returned his scrutiny before modestly lowering her lashes. He wondered who she was: it might be interesting to find out. Certainly it would be a diversion to while away the tedious hours of captivity.

Following the various courses of the feast the women retired, leaving the men to the remainder of the evening in the hall. Waltheof watched them depart with interest. In her close-fitting gown of deepest red, the young woman was as lissom as a young doe. Waltheof imagined cornering her in the darkness of a corridor between torches. Thought of those dark eyes widening as he lowered his mouth to hers. The notion was unsettling enough to make him shift on the bench and adjust his braies. Perhaps it was as well that fate had not led him to monastic vows of poverty, chastity and obedience. He doubted that he would have been able to keep any of them.

Now that the women had departed the atmosphere grew more relaxed and, although Duke William was morally abstemious, he slackened the reins and allowed his retainers a degree of leeway. Under cover of raised levels of noise, Waltheof took the opportunity of asking Richard de Rules the identity of the girl in the red dress.

The chamberlain looked wary. 'She is the King's niece, Judith – her mother is his full sister, Adelaide, Countess of

Aumale,' he said. 'I would advise you not to become interested in the girl.'

'Why?' Waltheof clasped his hands behind his head. 'Is she betrothed?'

De Rules looked uncomfortable. 'Not yet.'

The wine was buzzing in Waltheof's blood, making him feel light-headed. 'So she is available to be courted?'

The Norman shook his head.

'Why not?' To one side an arm-wrestling contest had noisily begun and Waltheof's attention flickered.

'The Duke is her uncle, so her marriage will be of great importance to Normandy,' De Rules said, emphasising each word.

Waltheof's eyes narrowed. 'You are saying that I am not good enough for her?'

'I am saying that the Duke will give her to a man of his own choosing, not one who comes courting because the girl has caught his wandering eye. Besides,' he added wryly, 'you are probably best to keep your distance. Her mother has the Devil's own pride, her stepfather is prickly on the matter of his honour, and the girl herself is difficult.'

Waltheof's curiosity was piqued. He would have asked in what way Judith was difficult, but at that moment Edgar Atheling seized his sleeve and dragged him towards the wrestling contest. 'A pound's weight of silver that no one can defeat Waltheof Siwardsson!' he bellowed, his adolescent voice ragged with drink.

Men roared and pounded the trestles. Banter, mostly good-natured, flew, although there was some partisan muttering. Coins flashed like fish scales as they were wagered. Waltheof was plumped down opposite his intended opponent, a knight of the Duke's household named Picot de Saye. The man was wide-chested and bull-necked, with hands the size of shovels and a deep sword scar grooving one cheek.

His grin revealed several missing teeth. 'They say a fool and his money are soon parted,' he scoffed.

Waltheof laughed at his opponent. 'I do not claim to be a wise man, but it will take a stronger one than you to separate me from my silver,' he said pleasantly.

Hoots of derision followed that statement, but again they were amiable. Waltheof leaned his elbow on the board and extended his hand to the Norman's. The younger man's tunic sleeve gave small indication of the power of the muscles beneath. His hands were smooth, unblemished by battle, for although Waltheof had been taught to wield axe and sword with consummate skill he had never been put to the test.

Picot grasped Waltheof's hand in his own scarred one. 'Light the candles,' he commanded.

Either side of the men's wrists stood two shallow prickets holding short tallow candles. The aim of the contest was for each man to try to force his opponent's arm down onto the flame and extinguish it. In this particular sport Waltheof did have experience, although there was nothing to see. The evidence of his talent lay in the unblemished skin on the back of his wrist.

Waltheof kept his arm loose and supple as Picot began to exert pressure. Resisting the first questing push, he studied the almost imperceptible tightening of Picot's neck and shoulders. Humour kindled in Waltheof's eyes. The smile he sent to Picot was natural, not forced through teeth that were gritted with effort. Picot thrust harder, but Waltheof remained solid. Men began slowly to pound the tables. Waltheof heard the sound like a drum in his blood, but was only distantly aware of the watchers. Focus was all. The pressure grew stronger, and Picot's grip became painful. Waltheof started to exert his own pressure, building slowly, never relenting. He relaxed his free hand on his thigh and held his breathing slow and steady. Now shouts of encouragement pierced the drumroll of fists. Waltheof poured more strength into his forearm and slowly, but inexorably, started to push Picot's wrist down onto the flame. The Norman struggled, his face reddening and the tendons bulging in his throat like ropes, but Waltheof was too powerful, searing Picot's hand upon the candle and extinguishing the flame in a stink of black tallow smoke.

The roars were deafening. Picot rubbed his burned wrist and stared at Waltheof. 'It is seldom I am defeated,' he said grudgingly.

'My father was called Siward the Strong,' Waltheof replied. 'They say he could wrestle an ox to the ground one-handed.' He opened and closed his fist, the marks of the other man's grip imprinted on his skin in white stigmata.

'Cunningly played, Waltheof, son of Siward,' a gravelly voice said from behind his left shoulder. Waltheof turned to find King William standing over him, darkening the light with his shadow. Obviously he had been watching the end of the match and Waltheof reddened at the notion.

'Thank you, sire,' he muttered.

'A pity there is not much call for ox wrestling in my hall.' Despite the smile on William's lips, his eyes were dark and watchful. Here was a man who did not let down his guard for a moment, and who judged others by his own harsh personal standards.

Although Waltheof had just won the contest, suddenly the taste of victory was not as sweet as it should have been.

CHAPTER 2

A week later Duke William's court prepared to depart Rouen and celebrate Easter to the north at Fécamp. Countess Adelaide, suffering from a head cold, had opted to ride in one of the covered baggage wains, its interior padded with feather bolsters and thick furs to cushion the jolting of the cart and keep the occupants warm.

Judith hated travelling in such a fashion. The bumping and jarring was always wearisome, and the company no better. Her sister's voice had an irritating tendency to whine and their mother's constant scolding was enough to challenge the patience of a saint – and Judith did not possess such fortitude.

After much argument she finally persuaded Adelaide to let her ride her black Friesian mare instead. 'There will be more room in the wain,' Judith pointed out. 'I promise to ride where you can see me.'

Adelaide sneezed into a large linen napkin. 'Oh, go, child,' she flapped a weary hand. 'You make my head ache. Just have a care and do not give me anything with which to reproach you.'

Smiling with triumph, Judith curtseyed to her mother, and with a light heart instructed Sybille to tell the grooms to saddle her mare.

Outside there was chaos as the court prepared for the journey to Fécamp. Baggage wains were piled with household artefacts – beds and hangings for the ducal chambers, chests of napery, chairs and benches, cushions, candle stands, all the rich English spoils. Hawks from the mews, hounds from the kennels, a basket of flapping, squawking hens destined for her uncle's table. So saturated was the bailey with noise and smell that Judith nearly returned to the suffocating confines of her mother's chamber.

And then she became aware of his presence on the sward. Waltheof Siwardsson, Earl of Huntingdon and Northampton as she now knew he was named. She had seen him most days among the English party and had studied him circumspectly through her lashes, both fascinated and disturbed by the glow of his vitality.

As usual the chamberlain's lad, Simon de Senlis, was glued to his side, eyes filled with the boundless adoration of a pup for its new master. Waltheof's heavy copper-blond hair was bound back by a braid band and he was showing off with an enormous Dane axe for the boy's benefit and a gathering audience.

Judith gazed upon the effortless whirl and turn of the great blade. This was the weapon that the Norman soldiers had faced on Hastings field – that had held them at bay for hour after punishing hour and almost destroyed them. Watching the grace and power of Waltheof's movement, she had no doubt that God must have been on her uncle's side that day, for how else could he have prevailed against such a weapon?

Waltheof's laugh rang out, as huge and exuberant as the man himself. The axe blade glittered and was still as he grasped the shaft near the socket and presented the weapon to Simon's older brother Garnier to try. Judith felt a shiver ripple down her spine and centre in her loins. Filled with a longing that she had no point of reference or experience to identify, she walked swiftly away, distancing herself from danger.

They set out for Fécamp as the sun toiled towards its zenith. Approaching Easter, the weather was fine and the roads much improved from their winter mire so that the carts travelled dry shod. Judith enjoyed the gentle warmth on her skin and the pale green tints of spring covering winter's drab blacks and browns. Her mare bucked friskily and pulled on the reins, eager for more than just a sedate trot. There were plans to hunt along the way and Judith was looking forward to giving Jolie her head, for she too felt a quickening in the blood, a certain skittishness born of the spring warmth and the need to stretch out after winter's confinement.

A kennel keeper released the Duke's pack of harriers and the large golden dogs snuffled along the wayside, seeking scents to pursue. With one eye on the hounds, Judith did her duty and rode at a sedate pace at the rear of her mother's travelling wain. From within came muffled sounds of coughing and sneezing. Her sister said something in a petulant tone and Adelaide snapped curtly in reply. Judith was greatly relieved that she had been given her freedom. She could not have borne to sit within the stuffy confines of the cart with only a limited tunnel view of the passing spring day.

One of the harriers started a hare out of the lush grass growing beyond the rutted road. Uttering halloos of joy, blowing on their horns, the men pulled their mounts out of line and spurred in pursuit. Judith hesitated, but the temptation was too great. Ignoring the belated cry from her mother, she reined Jolie around and dug in her heels. Full of oats, keen to gallop, the mare took off like a crossbow quarrel. Throwing caution to the wind, Judith let her have her head.

She overtook several riders, including her cousin Rufus, who shouted an obscenity, his plump face flushed scarlet beneath his mop of straw-blond hair. The spring breeze filled her open mouth with its cold, pure taste and fluttered her wimple like a banner. There were other women riding with the hunt and their high-pitched cries of encouragement spurred her on, although she suppressed her inclination to yell at the sky. That would have been testing the bounds of seemliness.

The hare vanished into a sloping thicket of alder, ash and willow. Judith's mare took the incline in two strong strides but suddenly her gait chopped and shortened, almost jarring Judith out of the saddle. Clinging to the reins, the girl struggled to regain her balance while the hunt crashed on through the thicket and into the field beyond, leaving her far behind.

Hampered by her skirts, Judith struggled from the mare's back and saw that Jolie was favouring her offside hind leg. Without thinking she placed her hand on the injured limb. The mare's skin rippled, and she lashed out. Judith dodged and was fortunate only to receive a grazing blow from the iron shoe, although even that was sufficient to rip the soft wool of her gown and expose her linen undershift. Jolie plunged away then halted, reins trailing, leg held up off the ground.

'My lady, you are in difficulty?'

She looked up in surprise, and saw Waltheof Siwardsson riding back through the thicket towards her, his expression concerned.

Judith's heart began to pound and her mouth was suddenly dry. She glanced around but there was no one else in sight. 'My mare,' she said with a stilted gesture at the horse. 'She took the slope too hard.'

Dismounting with fluid grace for a man so large, he tied his own horse to the low branch of a tree. Softly, he approached Jolie from the side.

'Be careful.' Judith's voice rose, despite her attempt to keep it level and free of panic. 'she will attack.'

'No, no no,' he answered, his voice a low croon that set up a vibration in the pit of her belly, 'she will not. I like horses, and they like me. Ever since I was a small boy I have had a way with them. Prior Ulfcytel always said that I could have been a groom.'

He took a firm grasp on the mare's reins and stroked her sweating neck with his open palm. Judith had watched him swing a battleaxe with those hands, his precision and control deadly. Now she watched him gentle her horse, and felt her limbs melt. He murmured soft love words and breathed his own breath into the mare's nostrils as she had seen the stable hands do on occasion. Slowly but steadily he moved to the mare's hindquarters and eased his hand down her injured leg. Jolie flinched. So did Judith, fearing that Waltheof would be kicked and trampled, but after that single recoil the mare stood quietly for him.

'She will not be carrying you to Fécamp,' he said without altering the timbre of his voice so as not to startle the horse. His dark blue eyes were troubled as they found Judith's. 'There is much damage to the leg, I think.'

Judith moistened her lips. She looked from him to the horse. 'She will not have to be killed?'

He shrugged. 'Likely not, my lady. Even if she stays lame, she can be used for breeding.' His lips twitched. 'Of course, if it was a stallion it would be a different matter – especially with a hind leg.'

Judith's face flamed. She knew that a stallion could not mount a mare unless he had two sound hind legs to take his weight in the act of mating. Suddenly she was intensely aware of her vulnerability. She was Duke William's niece and she had committed the cardinal folly of being unchaperoned. How easy it would be for him to throw her down on the carpet of violets around their feet and rape her in retaliation for his captivity and her uncle's winning of the English crown.

'You need not be afraid of me, my lady,' he said, as if reading her mind.

'I am not afraid of you,' Judith answered boldly, although in truth she was terrified.

The curve of his lips became an outright grin. 'You are like me,' he said. 'It is impossible for you to lie, because your face betrays you.' His gaze dropped to her bosom. 'I am no ravisher of women,' he said softly. 'Much as I am tempted.' Turning away he untethered his horse from the tree, swung astride, and held his hand down to her. 'Best mount up, Lady Judith, if we are to catch up with the baggage train before it arrives in Fécamp.'

She stared at his hand while her stomach churned so hard

that she thought she was going to be sick. 'What about my mare?'

'You can send a groom back for her once we reach the others,' he said. 'She will have to be rested up in the nearest village until she's fit.' He beckoned persuasively. 'Come, you cannot stay here, and I promise to restrain myself.'

Against her better judgement Judith gave him her hand, set her foot over his in the stirrup, and let him pull her up. After an initial clumsiness and flurry of skirts, she managed to perch sideways on the chestnut's rump and clutched the saddle cantle to stop herself from falling off.

He glanced over his shoulder, amused that she should sit astride her own horse without a thought but consider it improper to straddle his. 'Warn me if you think you are going to fall,' he said through a grin. 'I would hate to bring you to your uncle across my saddle like a slaughtered hind.'

'I know how to ride pillion,' Judith snapped, stung by his teasing.

'Then that is well,' he answered, 'for otherwise I should have to dismount and walk at the bridle.' He clicked his tongue and, with a flicker of its ears, the chestnut broke into a smooth walk.

Judith gazed at the farmland and resisted the temptation to glance sideways at her rescuer's broad back. Her mother would be furious. She chewed her lip. It was not her fault, she told herself – or at least only in the sense that she had pushed Jolie too hard and caused the mare to overreach and strain her leg.

Waltheof Siwardsson was whistling softly through his teeth. She thought of him swinging that great axe in Rouen's court-yard. 'Did you fight my uncle in the great battle?' she asked.

'On Hastings field you mean?' He twisted slightly in the saddle to look at her. 'No, my lady, I did not.' His smile developed a sour edge. 'Mayhap I should have done.'

'What prevented you?'

'Ah, now that is a long tale, and I am not sure that I know the answer myself.' He was silent for a time, guiding the horse across the field where the wheat was beginning to form a shallow green carpet. Then he sighed. 'I owed neither allegiance nor loyalty to the Godwinssons. They had done nothing to advance my family. They took Northumbria from my blood-line and gave it elsewhere.' He shrugged. 'I do not expect you to understand.'

'But I do,' Judith said, thinking of her mother's constant lecturing. 'A man's birthright is his pride.'

He smiled. 'Well, I never thought that I had much pride, my lady, until I was led in silken fetters to board a ship for Normandy. And now it burns me and I wonder if I was wrong to hold back from Harold's last battle.'

Judith said nothing, for she knew she was out of her depth, but Waltheof answered the question himself with a shake of his head that sent a sparkle of light through the coppery tones of his hair. 'Even if I had fought, your uncle might still have won. And if by chance Harold had taken the victory, I doubt that I would be any closer to having my desire of Northumbria. Morcar is its earl, and Harold was his brother-by-marriage. There is no one to fight for the house of Siward, lest it be Sweyn of Denmark.' He sighed deeply. 'Sometimes I think that it would be better had I remained at Crowland and become a monk.'

'Indeed, I had heard you were trained for the Church,' she murmured.

He nodded. 'I was, but my older brother was killed in battle, and I was taken from the cloister to be educated as befitted the warrior son of a great earl. I had scarce been home two years when my father died too, and his northern lands were given into the hands of Tosti Godwinsson.' He crossed himself and suddenly he was not smiling.

'Would you have liked to take holy vows?'

'Sometimes I think I would.' He relaxed again. 'There was peace at Crowland and you could feel God's presence. It is harder out in the world to hear his voice – too many temptations.' He gave her an appraising look. 'Richard de Rules said that you were difficult, but I do not think you are.'

She raised her chin. 'I speak as I find. Surely that is being honest, not difficult?'

He inclined his head, conceding the point. 'Indeed, you are much like your uncle, my lady,' he said, giving the horse a gentle dig in the flanks so that it quickened pace.

They reached the main baggage train and a groom was sent back for Judith's mare. Waltheof delivered Judith to her mother's wain. The Countess Adelaide eyed him narrowly as he helped Judith within the stifling interior, aromatic with the smell of horehound and sage.

'Fortunate that you were on hand to come to my daughter's aid, Earl Waltheof,' she said, but not as if she were pleased at the notion.

'Indeed it was, my lady.' Waltheof gave her a broad smile and bowed. Adelaide inclined her head in frosty acknowledgement and then looked away, indicating that both her gratitude and the conversation were at an end.

'Thank you, my lord,' Judith murmured, feeling that she had to add something and that her mother's response was scant recompense. She was aware of the avidly staring maids, and of her sister hiding a giggle behind her hand.

'Think nothing of it, my lady. I enjoyed the pleasure of your company.' He bowed, regained the saddle with swift grace and reined away to greet the first of the returning huntsmen.

Adelaide gave her daughter a hard stare. 'The pleasure of your company,' she repeated in a voice nasal with cold. 'I hope that you did not encourage him, daughter.'

'Of course not!' Judith glowered at her mother. 'I have done nothing wrong. Why should I not converse with him when he is my uncle's guest?'

'Converse by all means, but do not encourage,' Adelaide warned. 'He is more and less than a guest, as well you know. You had no choice but to accept his aid just now, but I would rather that it had not happened. And I do not know what your uncle will say.'

'It is no concern of my uncle's!' Judith felt a quiver of apprehension.

Adelaide shook her head. 'Everything is a concern of your uncle. If you seem to favour one man above others, it complicates matters when it comes to settling a husband upon you. Granted, Waltheof of Huntingdon is handsome and pleasant, but he is not of high enough rank or quality to make a match with our house.' Her lip curled on the words *handsome* and *pleasant*, making it clear that she did not view such attributes with favour.

Judith flushed. 'Even though my grandmother Herleve was a laundress and the daughter of a common tanner?' she retorted.

Her sister gasped at the blasphemy. Adelaide reared like a serpent – no mean feat given the deep cushions and the rocking of the cart. 'I have not raised you to show such disrespect for your blood,' she said icily. 'My mother, your grandmother, God rest her soul, whatever her origins, died a great lady and you will not refer to her in such terms – is that understood?'

'Yes, Mother.' Judith compressed her lips and contained her resentment, knowing that if she continued to argue she would be whipped. Her mother was inordinately sensitive that Herleve de Falaise was indeed a tanner's daughter whom Robert of Normandy had encountered pounding washing in a stream and brought home to his castle. She had borne him two children out of wedlock, one of them Duke William, the other Adelaide, and when the attraction had paled she had been married out of the way to one of Duke Robert's supporters, Herluin de Conteville. Adelaide had set out to distance herself from all mention of laundering and tanning. As far as she was concerned, only the noble bloodline existed, and it was to be enhanced. Judith knew, although it went unspoken, that her mother considered matching her daughter with an English lord a step backwards for the family name – even if Waltheof Siwardsson's pedigree was better than their own.

Until her mother's outburst Judith had not really considered the notion of a match with the English earl, but now she did.

Sitting in the oppressive cart, beneath her mother's disapproving scrutiny, she thought of the journey she had just made on the rump of his horse. The copper flash of his hair against the soft dark blue wool of his cloak. The warm good humour. What would it be like to live in a household with a lord who would rather smile than frown? The thought was enticing and filled Judith with a feeling of restless excitement. She was accustomed to a regime of stern words and duty. Would it not be strange and wonderful to throw back her head for once and laugh with abandon?

'He won't give her to you,' scoffed Edgar Atheling, shaking his head at Waltheof in disbelief. It was the second day of their journey to Fécamp and they were close enough to see the smoke from the city hearth fires and inhale the occasional eddy on the sea-salt breeze. 'Not when he has as good as promised his own daughter to Edwin of Mercia. He is not going to marry off all the virgins in his household to English captives.'

'William has not said that he will give his daughter to Edwin, only that he will consider it,' Waltheof responded. 'It is as likely that he will give his niece to me as it is that he will give his daughter to Edwin.'

Edgar snorted. 'Mayhap you are right, Waltheof,' he said. 'Mayhap neither of you is destined for a Norman bride.'

Waltheof twitched his shoulders irritably and wished that he had not said anything to Edgar about his interest in Judith. He was annoyed at Edgar's scoffing, which reinforced the warning given by Richard de Rules that William the Bastard's niece was out of reach. She had not been out of reach yester afternoon, he thought. He could have abducted her across his saddle and forced a marriage by rape – a marriage that would have lasted about as long as it took the Normans to spit him on a lance. Waltheof grimaced. Perhaps Edgar and De Rules were right. Perhaps he should forget her and look elsewhere for a bride – a flaxen-haired English or Danish girl who would bear him enormous Viking sons. But it was not what he wanted.

What he wanted was travelling fifty yards behind in a covered wain, guarded by her mother like a dragon sitting on its precious treasure. What he wanted was to melt the ice and discover the fire.

'Don't be a fool,' Edgar said. 'She is comely, I know, but there are a hundred better women you could consider for a wife.' He made a thrusting gesture with his clenched fist. 'And a thousand in Fécamp alone who would welcome you to their private chambers for no more than the price of a smile.'

Waltheof snorted with reluctant amusement. The latter notion had already crossed his mind. Wooing and winning Duke William's niece was a matter for the future, albeit that how to do so was occupying much of his time. The tavern girls of Fécamp were accessible and would go a long way to cooling the heat of his blood – especially if he could find one with long, dark braids and sultry brown eyes.

CHAPTER 3

Sunlight splintered through the shutters and pierced Waltheof's closed lids. Groaning softly he rolled away from the stab of red light and came to rest against the hip and thigh of his sleeping companion. For a moment, he was disoriented by the sensation of another body beside his and then he remembered. He had been drunk, but neither to the point of oblivion nor incapacity.

Outside a rooster was crowing and he was aware that the sound had been threading through his slumber for some time. There were other noises too, the creaking of a passing cart and the gruff bark of a dog, the swish of a birch broom on a beaten floor and two women shouting to each other across a courtyard.

The girl at his side stretched and pressed back against him. Luxurious heat flooded Waltheof's groin. He was always receptive in the early mornings with the haze of sleep still clogging his senses. Rolling her over, he parted her thighs and, thinking only with his body, took his pleasure a second time.

She was lithe and petite, with dark hair tumbling to her waist and eyes as black as sloes. It was her colouring that had attracted him, and the sultry way she had looked at him in the tavern. The other whores had made a blatant play for his attention, sitting in his lap, stroking his beard, but he had been indifferent and they had sought customers more eager. Edgar Atheling had disappeared up the stairs with two of them. Edwin and Morcar had plumped for a pair of identical Flemish twins with plaits the colour of retted flax and complexions of new cream.

The dark girl's initial aloofness reminded Waltheof of Judith, and in his drink-blurred state it had been easy to close his eyes and imagine that the body he was possessing was that of the Duke of Normandy's niece. Now, in the sobriety of the morning light, he saw that apart from her colouring there was little resemblance. The sultry aloofness was contrived, as much a technique of selling herself as was the enthusiasm of her fellow whores.

She whispered words in his ear that he was certain Judith would not know, urging him on, clawing his spine. Waltheof groaned and gave himself up to the surge of climax. The whore gasped and writhed. That too, he thought hazily, must be an act. How could it be any other when she must have known so many men and her pay was dependent on satisfying her clients?

He rolled off her and lay regaining his breath, listening to the sounds of the city of Fécamp awakening and beginning to bustle.

'I please you?' She eyed him through the tangle of her hair and propped her chin on her hands.

'Yes, you please me.' Waltheof sat up and flipped her another silver penny from his pouch.

Clasping her hands at the back of his neck, she kissed him with enthusiasm. 'You will visit again?'

'Perhaps,' he said, not wishing to disappoint. Suddenly he wanted to be out of this room with its stale odours of wine, sweat and copulation. Easing away from her, he donned his shirt. Last night she had told him her name but he could not remember it – didn't want to.

She appraised him through her lashes, and sucked her index finger. 'Have you left a woman behind in England, my lord?'

'Why should you think that?' Waltheof asked with a side-long glance.

'The way you hesitated before you made your choice – as if you had a conscience or thought you should not be here.'

He gave a snort of grim amusement. 'You are perceptive.'
She eyed him questioningly.

Without bothering to lace his shirt Waltheof drew on his tunic. Braies and chausses swiftly followed. 'Are you always so inquisitive about your customers?'

'Only the handsome ones with large pouches.' She stretched sinuously like a young vixen and smiled at him. 'And I have seldom seen one larger than yours, my lord.' Her gaze rested suggestively on his groin.

Despite his irritation, Waltheof had to laugh. Leaning over, he slapped the girl's pert rump. 'I am glad to hear it.' Without giving her the chance to probe further, he went out of the door and quickly down the outer stairs.

Peering into the main room he saw it was empty save for a woman scraping old wax from the candle prickets and a couple of William's hearth knights seated at a trestle sharing a pitcher of buttermilk. Waltheof greeted them courteously enough but with a wry set to his mouth. He and his fellow Englishmen might be permitted to roam abroad, but a Norman guard was never far behind, ensuring that no one attempted to escape. The knights were brawny and, although neither of them wore mail, the swords at their hips were conspicuous.

Of Edgar, Edwin and Morcar there was no sign. Waltheof thought about kicking them out of bed and almost immediately decided against it. The pleasure of the deed would likely not compensate for the ensuing aggravation. Wandering outside he pissed in the midden pit beside the stable, and began a leisurely stroll in the direction of the palace.

Another Norman wearing the quilted gambeson of a man-at-arms rose unobtrusively from a bench outside the kitchen buildings and followed him into the street. Waltheof gave a rueful half-glance over his shoulder and considered evading his shadow among the warren of lanes leading away from Fécamp's harbour, but it went no further than a thought. Rather like the notion of kicking his companions awake, the strife it would raise was not worth the bother of the mischief. If he did attempt to lose his guard, doubtless King William would confine him to the palace and double the scrutiny.

As he walked, Waltheof noticed two merchants urging a string of horses towards the ducal residence and cast an appreciative eye over the animals. No common nags these, but livestock bearing the hot stamp of Spanish blood in their sharp ears, arched necks and elegant, compact build. They had lost their plush winter fells and their coats shone with the polished gloss of spring, bright bay, blue roan, grey and a dun the colour of sunlit sand.

Waltheof followed the traders into the courtyard and watched an official direct them to the stable compound.

'They're for Duke William. My father says so,' Simon de Senlis greeted him, a pile of tack draped over his shoulder. The star designs of worked silver on the buckles and browband of the bridle looked familiar to Waltheof, but he could not recall where he had seen them before.

'I suppose he lost many good mounts at the great battle,' he said.

The boy gave a dismissive shrug. 'Those horses are for riding, not war. Lady Judith is to have her pick because her mare is lame.'

Waltheof glanced down and met the lad's ingenuous tawny gaze. 'And just when is she to do the choosing?'

'Now.' Simon hefted the tack, which had begun to slip. As the sun dazzled on the silver mountings Waltheof remembered that he had seen them on Judith's black mare on the day of the rescue. Falling into step beside the boy, he was very glad that he had not lingered at the tavern to rouse his companions from their wine stupor. He was also suddenly conscious of his dishevelled appearance. While he was not well acquainted with Judith, he knew how much store she set by presentation.

He raked his hands through his hair, beat at his tunic and straightened his somewhat skewed leg bindings.

Simon eyed Waltheof's hasty attempts at sprucing. 'You

don't look as if you've been out in the town all night,' he said kindly.

Waltheof tried to frown but couldn't. His lips twitched. 'And how would you know where I've been?'

'I overheard you discussing it at supper last night. I don't speak English above a few words, but I heard one of you mention Madame Hortense's.'

Waltheof cleared his throat. 'I see,' he said.

'My brother goes there sometimes,' Simon said with a knowing look. 'It's a brothel.'

Waltheof did not know whether to laugh or admonish. 'At your age I did not realise such places existed,' he said somewhat grimly, wishing in part that he still had his innocence. 'But then I suppose I did not have an older brother to corrupt me . . . well I did, but he died.'

'I am sorry.' It was the automatic and polite response, but there was curiosity in the lad's gaze. It was probably that insatiable desire for information that had led young Simon de Senlis to find out about brothels amongst the more worthy subjects for study.

Waltheof shook his head. 'I never knew him. He was the son of my father's first wife and almost a man before I was born. He should have worn the bearskin cloak of the house of Siward. My father entrusted my own education to the monks of Crowland Abbey.' He almost smiled. 'So you see I have come rather later than you to the knowledge of brothels.'

'I don't know *everything* about them,' Simon said seriously.

'You don't want to,' Waltheof answered with an amused grunt. 'Keep your feet on the narrow path of righteousness. That way you'll have nothing to regret.'

'Do you regret going then?'

It was with relief that Waltheof saw the stables looming and the tethered selection of palfreys. 'Not at the time,' he said, 'but it is like drinking – the night's carousing has to be paid for by the morning's malaise.' He swatted good-naturedly at the lad. 'Now, stop bedevilling me. You don't need to know the answer to such questions until you're older – much older.'

He watched Simon disappear with the bridle into the stable's dark interior and, shaking his head, went to look at the palfreys that the coper had brought for Judith's inspection.

'I fancy the grey myself,' said an amused voice behind him.

Waltheof turned from examining a bay gelding and gazed round at the handsome young man who was leaning nonchalantly against the stable wall, arms folded. Ralf de Gael was a Breton lord whose father had settled in England during the Confessor's reign and acquired the earldom of Norfolk by peaceful means. Waltheof knew and liked Ralf; he was amiable, debonair and had an understanding of English ways missing in most Normans.

Waltheof shook his head. 'It has a mean eye,' he said.

Ralf unfolded his arms and came off the wall. 'My father was staller to King Edward,' he said. 'He could tell a good horse from bad just by glancing.'

Waltheof shrugged and grinned. 'That does not mean to say that you have inherited his talent.'

'Trust me, I have.' Returning the grin, Ralf sauntered to the bay. 'No grace,' he said. 'Whoever sits on this will resemble a sack of oats on a pack pony. The grey has by far the better breeding. Look at the way it carries itself.'

'That may be so, but it still has a mean eye,' said Waltheof, thinking that Judith could ride a woodcutter's scrawny donkey and still look like a queen.

Ralf clucked his tongue in disagreement. 'I am sorry to doubt your judgement, but I do.'

The horse coper, who had been half listening to their banter, suddenly dropped to his knees, snatched off his cap and bowed his head. Waltheof and De Gael turned, saw King William approaching with his sons and Judith, and quickly did the same.

'It seems that word has gone ahead,' William remarked, gesturing the young men to rise. His expression was good-humoured but sharp.

'I saw the horses arriving, sire.' Waltheof reddened as he

remembered that he had been returning from a brothel at the time. Judith stood with her cousins. She was dressed for riding in a gown of heavy green wool and carried a small whip in her hand. She looked so fetching that he could have devoured her whole.

'And I saw Earl Waltheof studying the horses and joined him, sire,' said Ralf smoothly. 'We were discussing their merits.'

'And do you have an opinion?'

'A difference of. I say the grey, Waltheof says the bay.'

'Reasons?'

As always Waltheof was struck by William's blunt economy with words. Not a shred of time was wasted in getting to the point.

'The grey's got breeding, the bay's a nag.'

'The grey is perhaps the finest animal to look upon,' Waltheof acknowledged, 'but I believe that the bay has a better temper. And none of them are nags.'

'Indeed not,' ventured the horse coper with a bow for Waltheof and a glare at De Gael.

William stepped forward to examine the horses. His sons followed, learning at their father's side how to judge soundness and conformation. Judith joined them, listening intently to their conversation, absorbing everything although it was not directly addressed to her. She cast her eyes over the bay, but it was the grey that she clearly favoured. The coper trotted the beast up and down the yard to show off its loose, fluid action, the muscles rippling like water under silk and the mane flowing like a black waterfall on the crested neck. The bay had a longer stride, more of a lope, and it carried itself quietly, without the high pride of the other.

Judith paused at Waltheof's side so close that his elbow almost grazed hers and he could see the individual strands of hair shining in the braids that hung below her veil.

'I admire spirit, Lord Waltheof,' she said. 'I like to ride a horse that knows it is alive.'

'Even if it bucks you off and cracks your skull against the stable wall?'

She slanted him an amused, slightly scornful look. 'I am as accustomed to riding as any of my cousins.' She indicated the Duke's sons. 'The last time I was thrown I was a babe of three years old upon my first pony. You need not concern yourself for my welfare.'

'It was fortunate that I did a few days since,' Waltheof said quietly.

She lifted her chin. 'I was not in danger.'

'Oh yes, you were,' Waltheof muttered and wrapped his hands around his belt because he was itching to span them at her waist and could not trust himself.

'But not from my horse.' She fixed him with a long, level stare in which he read challenge and invitation. Daring him. Holding him off. Then she turned to her uncle.

'I like the grey too,' she said in a clear, determined voice and smiled up at William. 'Can I try him?'

Simon de Senlis fetched the tack and her chosen mount was harnessed. It stamped the yard floor restlessly and kicked at its belly with a sharp hind hoof. Sometimes it was a sign of colic, but Waltheof suspected that in this instance it was irritation at the placing of a saddle.

Young Simon grasped the headstall while Judith set her foot in the stirrup and her cousin Robert boosted her across its back. She drew the reins through her fingers and commanded the squire to let go. The grey took several short, stiff-legged leaps but Judith swiftly brought it under control, using hands and heels to exert her authority. Waltheof watched with keen pleasure. She looked superb upon that champing, spirited horse, and as her eyes met his in triumph he found himself smiling in defeat.

Judith trotted the grey around the stableyard and, returning to the men, drew rein. Simon had caught the bridle and Judith was preparing to dismount when there was a sudden frenzy of yowls and two tomcats shot from the stables in a clawing ball of fur.

The coper and his attendant grabbed for the leading reins as the horses started at the commotion. The grey whinnied and reared, jerking the bridle out of Simon's hand. Its powerful shoulder sent the lad sprawling, and as he struck the ground the sharp forehooves came down across his leg. Simon's shriek rose above the noise of the fighting cats. White-faced, Judith strove to control the horse as it reared and plunged around the compound like a demon.

Waltheof was the first to recover from the shock of the moment. Bending, he scooped Simon off the ground and thrust him into De Gael's arms, then ran to intercept the plunging grey. Spreading his arms, he leaped in front of the horse. The shod hooves flashed, threatening death. Waltheof made a grab for the bridle and hung on, wrapping his fist around the leather, bringing the beast's head down and throwing his full weight against its forequarters so that it was unable to rear again.

'My lady, jump!' he roared.

Judith kicked her feet free of the stirrups, set her hands on the grey's sawing withers and half swung, half fell out of the saddle. Ashen with shock, she stumbled across the yard to safety then turned to stare at Waltheof in sick fear.

Slowly, with the same skill and pressure that had won him every arm-wrestling contest in which he had ever competed, Waltheof brought the grey beneath his command. Unable to raise its head, held in the vice of the man's grip, the fighting turned to the trembling, wild-eyed sweat of surrender and the grooms raced out to secure the horse with stout halter ropes.

Waltheof released his grip. The bridle had scored red weals across his palms and his sleeve was smeared with foam from the grey's muzzle. Wiping his hands on his tunic he hastened across the yard. 'My lady, you are unharmed?'

She swallowed and nodded. 'I am all right,' she whispered. 'Thank you . . .'

'You acted swiftly, my lord,' William said with a curt nod. 'My family is in your debt.'

Waltheof cleared his throat. 'It is a debt I do not acknowledge, sire,' he muttered, feeling awkward now that the heat of
the moment was cooling. 'I acted without thought of gratitude
or reward.'

'You might not acknowledge it, but I do,' William gave a
wintry smile. 'My niece means a great deal to me.'

To me as well, Waltheof wanted to say, but dared not. Head
lowered, he strode to the stall where Ralf de Gael had laid
young Simon. The boy's complexion was as pale and shiny as
new cheese and his fists were clenched against the surge of
pain.

'Broken leg,' De Gael said, looking somewhat green himself.
His eyes told Waltheof a tale that he would not speak aloud in
the child's presence. 'I'll bring his father.' He ducked out into
the daylight.

Waltheof knew it was an excuse. De Gael could have sent
one of the grooms to seek out Richard de Rules. Removing his
fine cloak, the English earl crouched to drape it over the shivering boy. 'I know it hurts,' he said gently, 'but help is coming.'

William's presence shadowed the doorway. 'You saved his
life too, Lord Waltheof,' he said. 'I have sent for my chirugeon.
Let us hope that he can mend the leg.' Entering the stall
William crouched across from Waltheof and lightly touched
Simon's arm.

'Courage lad,' he said, the harshness of his voice softer now
and holding a rumble of compassion. 'I know that you have a
deep well of it to draw on.'

'Yes, sire,' Simon answered through a throat that was corded
with the effort of resisting pain. Tears brimmed in his eyes and
he blinked them fiercely away.

William nodded with brusque approval and stayed until the
chirugeon arrived, with him an anxious Richard de Rules. 'Be
a good soldier,' he said to Simon as the chirugeon began to cut
away the boy's torn chausses in order to inspect the damaged
leg.

Waltheof grimaced to himself. The lad was but nine years

old, and however brave and courageous he must still be terrified and in pain. Mercifully, William rose and departed. The moment he had gone, Simon let out the breath that he had been holding on a long, pain-filled groan.

Richard de Rules leaned over his son. 'It will be all right, I promise you.' He smoothed the fair-brown hair. 'Once the bone is set, all will be well.'

'Yes, Papa.' Simon's eyes were huge with pain and so filled with trust that Waltheof could not bear it.

'Move aside from the light,' commanded the chirugeon, a grumpy young man, prematurely grey of hair. He scowled at Judith, who was standing in the doorway, her complexion little brighter than the boy's.

'Will he be all right?' she asked.

'My lady, I cannot tell until I have been able to see how much damage has been done – and for that I need the light,' the chirugeon said with laboured patience.

Gnawing her lip, Judith backed out of the stable. Waltheof rose to his feet and, murmuring an apology, went after her.

She was standing with her back against the wall, pleating her riding gown agitatedly between her fingers. 'It is my fault,' she whispered. 'If I had not been so determined to prove that I could handle that horse, it would never have happened.'

'You take too much on yourself, my lady,' Waltheof said. 'The horse bolted because it was startled, not from your mishandling. The rest is misfortune – or perhaps good luck, since both you and the boy are still alive.'

She looked at him, then down at her busy hands and shook her head. 'I should have listened to you and chosen the bay.'

'It has happened; there is no sense in lamenting over what cannot be undone.' He had wanted to comfort Simon. By the same impulse he wanted to pull her into his arms, smooth her braids and comfort her, but he knew that such familiarity was impossible – as matters stood.

'That is easy to say.' Challenge and bitterness clogged her voice.

Waltheof took a step towards her but stopped himself, knowing that he dared not come close enough to touch. 'Is not blaming yourself for everything a great arrogance when you should be accepting that it is God's will?' he asked.

A flash of anger sharpened her features. 'How dare you!'

He shrugged. 'Because I have very little to lose, and everything to gain.'

She stood her ground, and then, like the horse, the fight went out of her and she began to tremble. Uttering a gasp she gathered her skirts and ran from him. Waltheof watched her out of sight, a frown set between his copper brows. Eventually he returned to the fusty dark of the stable and sat with the injured boy and his father while the chirugeon did his best to mend the broken leg.

Damn him, damn him! Judith could not remember the last time she had wept. Her father had died and her eyes had stayed dry. Her mother had whipped her for childhood misdemeanours or lapses in behaviour and she had not cried. So why now? Why should the gentle reproach from an English hostage lord undo her? Judith sniffed and wiped her eyes with the edge of her wimple, but they only filled again with tears. She leaned against the wall, trying to compose herself, knowing that if she went within looking like this her mother would wring her dry with interrogation.

'What's wrong?' Her sister Adela had come out to look for her. 'Why are you weeping?' She gave Judith a look full of astonishment and surprise.

'I'm not weeping,' Judith snapped. 'The dust from the hay barn is in my eyes, that's all.'

'Have you chosen your horse?' Adela could not give a fig for riding. She much preferred to stay with their mother in the bower and sew. The fact that Judith was to have a new mount, however, had roused a certain amount of sibling envy. She had already begun to wheedle their mother for a new gown to compensate.

Judith shook her head and reached within herself to seal the breach in her control. 'Simon de Senlis has been kicked by one of the new horses and broken his leg,' she said, and was pleased to hear her voice emerge in its usual measured tones. 'He's being tended by Uncle William's chirugeon.'

Adela gasped with pity. 'The poor boy.' She bit her lip. 'Will the leg mend?'

'I pray so.' Remembering the suffering in the boy's expression, the twisted angle of his leg, Judith knew that, no matter what Waltheof of Huntingdon said, the blame was hers to shoulder whilst young Simon de Senlis paid the price.

CHAPTER 4

Ducking under the door arch, Waltheof entered the small wall chamber where Simon lay. There was space only for a narrow bed, a stone bench cushioned with bolsters and a niche in the wall for placing a candle. A thin window slit let in a waft of cool air and an arch of powder-blue sky.

Richard de Rules sat on a stool at the bedside, watching his son's restless slumber with paternal anxiety.

'How does he fare?' Waltheof asked softly.

The Norman sighed. 'Well enough for the moment. The chirugeon set the leg as best he could . . . but it was a bad break.'

'He has the best of care,' Waltheof said, trying to impart reassurance. 'God willing he will mend.'

De Rules' expression did not lighten. 'God willing,' he sighed and wearily rubbed his face. 'Jesu, he is but nine years old. He was to be trained to arms. What will become of him if he is crippled?'

'That won't happen, he is too tenacious,' Waltheof said stoutly. 'Even if he is lamed, he will still be capable of riding a horse, won't he? Nor will the injury affect the capacity of his mind.' He was aware of overprotesting, as if doing so would somehow make the situation more positive.

'That is what I keep telling myself.' The Norman offered his open palm to Waltheof. 'Whatever happens, I am indebted to you for saving his life. If you had not pulled him from beneath those hooves . . .'

'I only wish that I had been able to act more swiftly.' Waltheof clasped De Rules' hand, released it and stood up. 'I will come again when he is awake.'

'I will tell him that you were here.' De Rules gestured to the folds of fur-edged blue fabric on the bench. 'Your cloak, Lord Waltheof. Thank you for its borrowing.'

Waltheof lifted the garment and draped it carefully over his arm. 'I'm glad it was of use,' he said and went from the room, sombre and troubled. If William's chirugeon said that the break was bad, then what chance did that give the boy? Waltheof had not lived a soldier's life, but he had seen enough wounds treated at Crowland Abbey to know all the permutations.

Some broken limbs healed with nary a scar or discomfort, save to trouble their owners in damp weather and old age. On other occasions, however, the injury would swell and turn green, sending streaks of red poison through the patient's body, harbingers of an agonising death. Or the bone would heal, but in a manner twisted and deformed that left the victim crippled and in constant pain.

Suddenly very aware of his own sound limbs, Waltheof descended the stairs to the great hall. As usual it was bustling with activity. Scribes were busy at their lecterns, their business dictated by senior officers of the Duke's household. Petitioners and messengers arrived and left, or waited on the long benches edging the hall to be summoned. Two boys were stacking fresh logs by the hearth and replenishing the charcoal baskets for the braziers. A servant from the butler's retinue was decanting wine into flagons ready for the main meal later in the day, and nearby a young woman was transferring new candles from a wicker basket onto wrought-iron prickets.

'Lord Waltheof.'

He turned at the imperative note in the woman's voice and found himself looking down at Judith's mother, the formidable Adelaide of Aumale. The dragon guardian.

'Countess,' he inclined his head and regarded her warily. Judith had a darker version of her eyes and similar autocratic features. In Adelaide the bone structure was almost hawkish and he could see how Judith might look twenty years from now.

'I have heard what happened in the stableyard this morn,' she said stiffly. 'It seems that yet again I must thank you for coming to my daughter's aid.'

'I am glad I was present,' Waltheof replied graciously. 'I hope that she has taken no harm?'

'None – although I understand that it might have been different without your intervention.'

Waltheof thought that her face might crack if she smiled. He could see that she was doing her duty by thanking him – and hating every moment. He had often heard married companions make wry jests about their mother-in-laws, and had thought them rather harsh. Now he began to understand.

Adelaide inclined her head and moved on, her spine as straight as a mason's measuring rod. Her husband, Eudo of Champagne, was in England, keeping the peace. Waltheof wondered, rather uncharitably, if Lord Eudo had chosen to remain there above returning to his icy marriage bed.

One of the maids attending her paused at Waltheof's side for the briefest instant. She had a rosy complexion and merry grey eyes. 'Lady Judith is in the abbey chapel praying for the boy's recovery,' she murmured, giving him a meaningful look through her lashes before following the Countess.

Waltheof gazed after her in frowning bemusement. Then, slowly, he began to smile. Turning on his heel, he left the hall and walked purposefully towards the Abbey Church of the Holy Trinity.

The decorated arches had a pleasing symmetry and the pale slabs of Caen stone possessed a warm, butter colour in the sunshine. Tonsured holy brethren in their dark Benedictine robes were everywhere, their air proprietorial. Pilgrims crowded the front porch, their dusty appearance and travelling satchels marking them out from the general population. Some were here because of the Duke's presence in the town, but most had come for Easter week and to view the miraculous phial of the Holy Blood of Christ.

Waltheof joined their number and entered the incense-soaked greatness of the abbey's nave. He had worshipped here before at Easter Mass, but still the beauty of the carved and painted pillars filled him with delight and awe. He loved churches in all their forms, from the small wooden edifices no more than huts that served many of his Midland manors, to the towering dignity of great cathedrals such as Westminster, Canterbury, Jumièges and Fécamp. He could find God in any of them and tailored his worship to the surroundings. In the small churches he was humble and reflective; in the cathedrals he praised God in pleasure through the rich colours and ceremony. At Crowland in the Fens he yielded himself completely and received peace in return.

But today, although he was aware of God's presence, his seeking was of a different kind. Leaving the pilgrims, he walked down the great nave of the church, his calfhide boots making a gritty sound on the stone floor. Votive candles burned by the hundred on prickets and candelabra, tended by monks from the abbey. Before the alter knelt yet more pilgrims, praying, paying their respects, reverently touching the ornate box containing the phial of the Holy Blood of Christ that was held by a watchful priest.

Waltheof sought among the gathering of bowed heads and found her kneeling at the edge and just a little apart. Self-contained as always. Her head was bent towards her clasped hands and her eyes were closed, revealing a smoothness of lid lined by thick dark lashes. Squeezing amongst the pilgrims, Waltheof knelt in the space that she had left between herself and them.

She opened her eyes at the intrusion. The haughty stare she had been about to give him widened into one of recognition and then grew wary. Waltheof responded with a smile and bowed his neck, attending to the letter of worship if not giving the task his full concentration.

For perhaps a quarter candle notch they knelt side by side. Several pilgrims rose and departed, their places taken by others. The sound of suppressed coughs, of shuffling footsteps and the murmur of worship echoed against the stone vaulting.

'One of the maids told me where you were,' Waltheof said to his clasped hands.

'I came to pray for the recovery of Simon de Senlis,' Judith said stiffly.

'Indeed, that is my own reason for being here,' Waltheof replied, being selective with the truth. He was sure that God would understand.

The silence fell between them again, but it was communicative. Waltheof felt as if there was a high wall separating him and Judith, but that somehow he had managed to pull a slab out of the centre and could now glimpse her through the ensuing gap.

When she rose to leave he rose with her and escorted her out, one hand lightly beneath her elbow. It was indicative of the breach in the wall that she accepted his touch and did not draw away, but in the wide sunlit porch she turned to him. 'What you said earlier today, about God's will,' she said, 'you made me feel ashamed.'

'I am sorry, my lady, that was not my intention.'

'I know it was not. You were trying to offer comfort.' Her lips curved in a rare smile. 'And in a way, you did – after I had the time to think.'

Waltheof wanted nothing more than to pull her against him and kiss her, but he clenched his fists at his sides and reminded himself that he wanted to live. 'I suppose that is mete since I often speak my mind without thinking at all. Abbot Ulfcytel always told me that it was my greatest failing and my saving grace.' He fell into step beside her, reluctant to let the moment go. He sensed a similar mood in Judith, for as they left the abbey precincts she did not attempt to distance herself from him, although there were many witnesses to see them walking together.

'There has been one matter I have thought about ever since that first day in Rouen, though,' he murmured. 'And I have kept it inside my head until sometimes I feel my brains will burst with the effort of holding back.'

She lifted her head to him and he saw that she took his meaning, for her cheeks grew pink. 'If it is so important to your wellbeing, then you must approach my uncle and my stepfather for guidance,' she said adroitly.

'That I know,' he sighed. 'But perhaps it is better to bide my time until my feet are on more solid ground.' He paused in the shadow of a wall, aware that they were almost at the palace and in a moment he would lose her to the public space of the great hall. 'And before I make my bid, I need to know that I am not embarking on a fool's errand.' The hand that had been at her elbow now slipped down the inside of her forearm and sought her hand. Her skin was cool and dry, but he felt the sweat spring suddenly and heard her intake of breath.

'I want you to wife,' he muttered and turned her hand to look at the palm and narrow, smooth fingers. 'Are you willing?' Lust pounded through him; heat pulsed at his groin, as fiercely as if he had not lain with a woman for a year instead of only that morning. One gentle push and her back would be against the wall. One swift coil of his arm and her body would be pressed to his.

She was breathing hard. He could sense the response within her, wild as his own, and the control, pushing it down. 'I can give you no encouragement without the consent of my family.'

'But if your family were to give their consent – would you have me?'

Her throat worked as if she was parched. 'I do not know,' she said and pulled away. For an instant he tightened his grip, but before panic had time to flare in her eyes he let her go. She had not refused him, and he knew that she too was scorched by the reaction between their bodies. If she did not know, then it was up to him to persuade her until she did.

* * *

Simon stared at the wall beyond the end of his bed. It was a sight to which he had grown accustomed over the past fortnight. He knew every flake of plaster, every line of stone. He played games, making pictures out of the marks, a dog, a tree, a castle, until his eyes blurred with strain and he had to look away. The window embrasure yielded a cool draught and a narrow column of sky. Sometimes there would be the distraction of passing clouds, but today his window was the blank blue canvas of a perfect spring day.

What he would give to be able to throw aside the covers, leap out of bed and hurtle down the twisting stairs to the glorious morning outside his prison. But he suspected that he would never hurtle anywhere again. When people came to see him they smiled and said loudly that he would soon be better, but their eyes told a different story. And he had heard them mutter among themselves when they thought they were out of his hearing.

The break was bad. Even without the overheard conversations of his visitors, he knew that. The chirugeon had dosed him with syrup of white poppy before setting the limb, but the agony had been terrible – like white-hot teeth biting into his shin. The limb was now held rigid with ash splints bound tightly to his leg with linen bandages soaked in egg albumen. His task was to lie abed and allow the bone to knit.

The searing pain had been replaced by a dull and steady hrob. For the first few days he had been feverish and he knew that they had feared for his life. However that stage had passed and it was evident that whether the limb healed straight or crooked he was going to live. Thus he lay on his bed and waited out minutes, hours and days that seemed like years.

Early in his convalescence Lady Judith had brought him a box containing a sweetmeat made from crushed walnuts boiled in honey. She had sat with him for a while, doing her duty, assuaging her guilt. Then Lord Waltheof had arrived, bringing a tafel board and gaming pieces and Lady Judith's face had grown as radiant as a sunrise. Since then they had visited him regularly. One would appear and the other would follow like doves homing to the cote. Simon had swiftly realised that they were meeting each other rather than comforting him, but he had been glad of the company and enjoyed being a party to their conspiracy. Sometimes too Waltheof would send his personal skald, Thorkel, to entertain Simon with sagas of faraway lands inhabited by fierce Vikings, giants and trolls.

All that, however, was finished. As from today he was alone. Apart from affording him a glimpse of sky, the window embrasure also yielded up sounds from the courtyard below. The rumble of cartwheels, the shouts of soldiers and drivers, the clatter of hooves told him that William was preparing to leave Fécamp. By noon the last of the baggage wains would have rolled ponderously out of the gates, leaving the palace to its garrison and resident retainers. A fortnight ago he had been part of that vast, energetic tide; now he was debris, tossed above the water line. The thought made his mouth tighten with pain and misery. A lump came to his throat and his eyes began to sting.

Footsteps sounded on the stairs and he hastily wiped his eyes on a corner of the coverlet. It would not be manly to be caught crying, and he did not want any of them to think that he was a snivelling infant.

Waltheof flourished aside the chamber curtain and ducked into the room, his height and vitality immediately diminishing the small space. In the spring warmth he was wearing a linen tunic and had tied back his abundant copper hair with a strip of leather. Simon could smell the freshness of the outdoors on his clothes and wanted desperately to be able to go there.

'You've come to say farewell, haven't you?' he demanded.

'Yes lad, I have.' Waltheof looked slightly uncomfortable, but did not shirk the question. 'Where William goes, unfortunately I must go too.'

Simon scowled glumly at the coverlet, utterly miserable at the thought of Waltheof's leaving. Even if the Saxon earl had conducted his courtship with Lady Judith in this room, he had still stayed to play tafel once she had gone, had still made time to talk.

'I promise I will visit as often as I can while we are within riding distance,' Waltheof said, clasping his large, warm hand over Simon's on the coverlet. 'I won't forget.'

Simon gazed at the rings flashing on Waltheof's fingers. One was of gold wire, twisted into a rope, the other bore a large, blood-red stone and looked a little bit like one of the rings that he had seen Bishop Remegius wear. The lump of misery grew and solidified in his stomach until it was as heavy as a small boulder.

'As soon as you're better I'll take you out riding,' Waltheof said.

'But that's weeks away!' Simon burst out, unable to contain his disappointment and anger. 'And I might not get better!' He thumped the bedclothes and felt a sharp pain stab through the centre of his broken leg.

'Of course you will.' Waltheof fixed him with a piercing blue stare, forcing Simon to meet his eyes and not look away. 'It was a bad break, I know it was, and I would not belittle your suffering, but you will not be confined for ever.'

Simon eyed him mutinously. 'It seems like for ever,' he muttered.

Waltheof sighed. 'Yes, if I were your age I suppose that it would feel like for ever to me.' He gave a rueful smile. 'Indeed, I think that I would feel the same now. I cannot bear to be cooped up.' Ferreting beneath his cloak, Waltheof flourished a bone flute carved from a goose's wingbone. 'Thorkell fashioned this for you,' he said. 'We thought that perhaps you would enjoy making music.'

Simon thanked him, trying to sound more enthusiastic than he felt. It was not that he did not appreciate the gift, but it was no compensation for being left on his own for days on end.

Waltheof also produced several sheets of parchment bound in a roll and tied with a ribbon. This was followed by a leather pouch containing the ingredients for making ink, a small, sharp knife with a bone handle, several goose quills, and a small wax tablet and stylo. 'You can lessen the distance by writing to me,' he said cheerfully.

Simon flushed. 'I . . . I'm not well lettered,' he mumbled.

Waltheof spread his hands. 'Do you have anything else to do except lie here and mope? Duke William himself can do no more than read and write his own name with the greatest labour, but he values greatly those who are literate. It would be much to your advantage to learn, and besides, I would like to send you messages and receive them in return.'

Simon nodded rather dubiously. 'I will try,' he said, speaking more out of a desire to please Waltheof than out of any enthusiasm of his own.

'Good lad. I . . .'

More footsteps trod on the stairs, lightly this time. Simon knew them, and so did Waltheof, for eagerness blazed in his eyes as he turned expectantly to the door. The boy wondered what Duke William would say if he knew about these meetings between his niece and the English earl. Now that the court was moving on it would not be so simple for them to be alone.

'I cannot stay,' she said more breathlessly than the stair climb warranted. 'My mother is waiting below, but I came to bring Simon a parting gift.' She approached the bed. Waltheof moved aside, deliberately brushing past her so that her long, dark braid touched the back of his hand. She drew a swift breath and her colour heightened.

Simon looked at the coverlet. Lady Judith made him feel uncomfortable. She did not have Waltheof's easy manner. When she spoke to him it was always as if she was struggling to know what to say and her movements were stiff and unnatural. He knew that she felt guilty about his injury and all that really brought her to visit him was the lure of being with Waltheof.

'We were packing the chests to leave and I found this,' she said, giving Simon a rolled-up band of linen a little less than a foot wide. 'I thought that you might find it preferable to looking at the bare wall all day and we are not going to miss it among all the others.'

It was a hanging embroidered in wool and depicting the story of how the Normans had arrived in France and claimed the land for their own. Warriors and horses came to life in gold and green, scarlet blue and tawny. As he unfolded it, Simon was astonished and delighted. The first smile in days spread across his face as he touched the procession of figures and the scenes they created. He looked at Judith with genuine pleasure in his eyes, all resentment gone. 'Thank you, my lady.'

Her own lips curved in a stilted but no less genuine response. 'You like it?'

'Oh yes, my lady!'

'Then I am glad, and it was the least I could do. Next time I see you, I hope that you will be walking.' With a nod, she went to the door. Gesturing to Simon that he would return in a moment, Waltheof hastened after Judith.

The boy gazed upon the colourful pictures spread across his coverlet. He could almost smell the crisp autumn day of a boar-hunting scene, imagine the clash of spears as Frenchman met Viking, hear the hiss of the sea beneath a longboat's keel. It did not make up for being left behind in Fécamp, but suddenly life was that tiny piece more bearable.

Waltheof caught Judith on the narrow walkway to the stairs. 'That was very kind of you,' he said in a voice that was melting with pride and tenderness.

Judith faced him, her chin bearing a slightly defensive tilt. 'It was the voice of my conscience,' she said.

He shook his head and looked slightly exasperated. 'Why can you never admit to gentler emotions?' he demanded. 'Ah Judith, you're as fierce as a goshawk.' He raised his hand to stroke her face. 'I have never known a woman like you . . . never wanted one so much either.'

'You should not . . .' she began to say, but he set his fore-finger to her lips.

'I know what I should and should not,' he said, 'but knowing is not always the same as doing, is it? You realise that this is the last time we will be able to meet as freely as this.'

'Perhaps that is a good thing,' she croaked. 'It cannot be right without the consent of my uncle. If my mother knew . . . Oh!' She gasped, her words cut off as he pulled her against him and lowered his mouth to hers.

Twin strands of heat and cold prickled along Judith's spine as he kissed her. She knew that she ought to struggle, slap him, scream for help, but she did none of these things. She was overwhelmed to the point of intoxication by the scent of him, by the strength and gentleness of his hands, and by the disturbing but pleasurable sensations that the kiss was engendering.

The tip of his tongue lightly brushed her lips encouraging them to part. One hand slipped from her waist to lightly cup her buttocks and pull her in closer. Judith felt a hard pressure against her belly, and knew immediately what it was. Innocent she might be, but her maid Sybille was not, and she had not been slow to share her wisdom with her mistress.

'Just so long as your skirts stay down and his cock doesn't leave his braies, you're safe!' Sybille had giggled. Judith had pretended to be horrified, but behind her scolding had been avid to know more. Now the experience, the sensations were of the body, not just the curious mind. She knew that she was failing to resist temptation but found that she almost did not care. All that mattered was being closer still. Her arms slipped around his waist and her lips parted.

Waltheof groaned and the sound filled her mouth and throat, enhancing her sensations. She wanted to answer him, but held on to the impulse, afraid of what would happen if she let go. Nothing that Sybille had told her had prepared her for this. Nothing.

The kiss finally broke, leaving them both gasping for breath. Judith hastily took a back step, knowing that she had to put distance between herself and Waltheof while she was still capable.

'Perhaps it is time that your mother did know,' he said, his eyes bright and narrow. 'I must have you, Judith.'

She licked her lips, tasted him there, and felt a mingling of fear and pleasure. No man had ever made her feel like this before – but then no man had ever taken such liberties. 'I do not know if that can be,' she whispered.

'I will make it be,' Waltheof replied in a tone that was no longer light with laughter.

They both stiffened at the scrape of feet on the steps below. 'Judith?' Her mother's voice was querulous with impatience.

Judith gave a single, frightened gasp then steadied herself. Gesturing Waltheof to stay back and remain silent, she started down the steps. 'I am here, Mother,' she called. Her hands were shaking, her lips felt swollen. As she descended the steps, she was aware of slick moisture between her thighs and a dull ache in her loins, reminiscent of flux pains.

'Where have you been child?' Adelaide snapped. 'Anyone would think that you had had to stitch the hanging from the start instead of just giving it to the boy.'

'I stayed to speak a few words of comfort, Mother,' Judith said more calmly than she felt.

Somewhat awkwardly, Adelaide turned on the narrow stair and descended to the courtyard. Once in open daylight, she fixed Judith with a gimlet stare. Reaching a narrow hand, she pressed it to her daughter's brow. 'You look feverish,' she said with sudden concern in her eyes. 'I hope that you are not ailing.'

Judith jerked away from her mother's touch, feeling flustered and guilty. 'There is nothing wrong with me.'

Adelaide compressed her lips. 'Even so, it might be wiser if you travelled in the wain with me. I mislike the heat in your cheeks.'

'Mother . . .' Judith's voice rose with dismay, but Adelaide was adamant.

'Do not seek to argue,' she snapped. 'These past few days you have been granted more freedom than a girl of your status is usually allowed. You will travel with me, and you will be content.'

'Yes, Mother.' Judith knew that arguing was futile and with a supreme effort held her tongue. Behind her silence, however, her feelings churned as she imagined lashing out in rebellion. Suddenly she wished that she had not bade Waltheof remain out of sight until it was safe to come down. Suddenly she wished she had yielded to him, and smiled darkly at the notion.

'Take that smirk off your face,' Adelaide warned. 'You are not too old to be whipped for insolence.'

Judith lowered her gaze. Waltheof had said that he desired her to wife. Even if she was not sure that she wanted him, she was positive that life as his wife would be ten times better than dwelling beneath her mother's joyless rule.

CHAPTER 5

J udith threaded her needle with a single, fine strand of red-gold wool and, leaning over her embroidery frame, began to sew with swift, neat stitches. The design she was embroidering had been carefully sketched onto the linen ground in brown ink and depicted a scene of men and women riding out to hunt. Intended as a horizontal strip hanging to decorate a wall behind a dais, it was already about a third completed. The women of Duchess Matilda's household would work on the hanging when not occupied by other tasks. Since Judith was an excellent embroideress and as Adelaide had been keeping a close eye on her these past two months, much of the needlecraft was hers.

An unconscious curve to her lips, she worked upon the hair of one of the riders. It was long, unlike that of his companions who wore the shaven style of the Normans. She had outlined the man's beard in pale gold, and given him a gown of soft blue. The darker blue cloak flying from his shoulders showed a lining of white. At his side, a hawk perched on her wrist, rode a woman on a black mare.

'You like him, don't you?' Agatha, Duke William's middle daughter, joined Judith at the embroidery bench and tipped a silver needle from a cylindrical ivory case. She was small and rosy with fine, fair hair and dainty little features – so dainty that Judith thought them like the sketch on this fabric – nothing without the added boldness of colour.

Judith did not pretend ignorance of Agatha's meaning. It was obvious to the most casual observer that the figure was Waltheof. 'He saved my life,' she said, 'I want to remember him . . . and yes, everyone likes him.'

Agatha poked among the threads, finally selecting a dark green. 'Not everyone,' she sniffed. 'Edwin says that he should never have been allowed out of the cloister.'

Judith took several swift, controlled stitches and suppressed the urge to slap her cousin. It was no secret that Agatha and Edwin of Mercia were conducting a courtship. William openly encouraged the couple to sit together in the hall of an evening, and he had dropped several heavy hints about a betrothal, but the deliberateness of the suggestions had led Judith to wonder. Her uncle was not usually so forthcoming with his designs.

'Edwin would say that,' she retorted. 'He does not want Waltheof claiming Northumbria from his brother.'

Agatha began to outline one of the horses with neat stitches, revealing that she too was an accomplished needlewoman. Her small, pink tongue peeped at the corner of her mouth. 'Waltheof is not strong enough to displace Morcar,' she said scornfully. 'He's untried and he knows naught of governance.'

'That does not mean he is incapable,' Judith objected, 'and he is the heir by blood.'

Agatha flushed. 'My father is content to let the house of Leofric keep its lands,' she said, her eyes suddenly glittering with malice. 'He will agree to my match with Edwin of Mercia long before he agrees to a match between you and Waltheof of Huntingdon.'

Judith returned Agatha's look without yielding. 'Your father desires to keep Edwin of Mercia dangling on his hook,' she said coldly. 'You would be foolish to read too much into his suggestions I think.'

'I am more than just bait on a hook,' Agatha preened. 'Edwin's well born. My father will give me in marriage to him.'

Judith said nothing but raised one eyebrow in a way that said Agatha was entitled to believe as she chose but was deluded.

'Anyway, Edwin said that Waltheof should have stayed in the cloister because he hasn't got the wit to be out in the world. He's a big, dumb ox.'

In and out went Judith's silver needle, stab and draw, stab and draw, filling in the marigold brightness of her horseman's hair. 'A dumb ox who can read and write and cipher,' she said quietly. 'A dumb ox whom our Norman courtiers like well, and who has proved his worth twice over. I have yet to see Edwin do more than pose in his fine clothes and show off.'

Agatha scowled. 'You won't be allowed to have him,' she said.

Judith shrugged as if she did not care. 'I may sew his image in an embroidery, but that does not mean I am ready to become his wife.'

'Are you not?' Agatha's gaze was hard and shrewd. 'I have heard it whispered that your mother keeps you closeted in the bower because you grew too familiar with him in Fécamp.'

Judith drew herself up. 'Then you must listen to whispers in some foul corners,' she snapped and set her needle aside, afraid that her anger would cause her to spoil her stitches. 'I have done nothing to cause reproach.'

It was Agatha's turn to raise a knowing eyebrow. 'You have never been so charitable towards the sick before,' she said. 'You seemed very concerned for the wellbeing of Simon de Senlis.'

'He was injured in my sight. Of course I was concerned for him,' Judith said irritably. 'I still am, for I do not think he will ever walk a straight course again.'

'And it had nothing to do with the English earl's visits to the boy.'

Judith sprang to her feet, unable to bear being near Agatha a moment longer. Her cousin was a bitch. 'Of course it didn't.' Her sudden movement dislodged the silk basket and spilled a riot of colourful hanks on to the floor. With a hiss of exasperation she stooped to pick them up and untangle them.

Agatha was silent for the course of several stitches but there was a satisfied curl to her lips. 'Waltheof has a mistress in

Fécamp you know,' she announced spitefully. 'She's a brothel whore from Madame Hortense's near the harbour.'

'I suppose Edwin told you that too.' Judith kept her back turned so that she would not have to bare her expression to her cousin's scrutiny.

'No,' Agatha said. 'It was my brother Robert. He went there with some of his friends and saw Waltheof with her. He says she's got the reputation of being willing to consider all manner of unnatural deeds for a silver coin . . . and that she has hair just like yours.'

Very carefully indeed, Judith set the basket of silks back on the bench. 'And I think that you would say anything just for the pleasure of casting a stone in a pool and watching the ripples,' she said glacially. 'The Earl of Huntingdon's private affairs are of less interest to me than they are to you, Agatha. You weary me with your prattle, and I will listen to no more.' Head held high, she walked across the room to join her mother and sister who were sewing a tunic for her absent stepfather.

Adelaide gave Judith a thoughtful look but said nothing and merely handed her a seam to stitch. Judith was glad of the silence, which gave her time to compose herself. Agatha's gossip was unsettling. Men seldom made permanent mistresses of girls they met in brothels, she knew that, but they did make regular assignations. The mention of Waltheof's whore having dark braids had been made deliberately by Agatha to disturb her, but Judith wondered if Waltheof's choice had been deliberate too. Did he imagine that he was bedding her when he paid for the whore's services? She reddened at the thought, torn between embarrassment, anger and a shameful melting between her thighs.

The silence was broken by Adelaide, who sighed and laid down her sewing. 'You may as well know that a messenger arrived from your stepfather this morn,' she said. There was anxiety in her light brown eyes. 'I was wondering whether to tell you, but I can see no point in keeping it to myself. It will be common knowledge soon enough. There is trouble in England.'

'Mother?' Judith's needle poised between stitches. Adela looked up. Neither girl was particularly close to her stepfather, but he was family, and they both felt a jolt of fear.

'Lawless thieves and rebels are banding together and causing dissent. Your stepfather says that the men your uncle William left to govern the country are hard pressed to keep order. He says it is like sitting on the lid of a boiling cauldron.' Adelaide pressed the palm of her hand over the fine linen fabric of the garment she was stitching as if by smoothing it she could make everything well. She would not say aloud that she feared for her husband's life, but Judith could sense her alarm.

'Uncle William will send aid,' Judith said quickly.

Adelaide nodded. 'He is already making plans to cross the water and put an end to it once and for all.' Fierceness glittered in her eyes. 'He will make them pay dearly.'

Judith moistened her lips. 'Will my uncle take the hostages with him?'

'That I do not know, although I hope so. They do naught but drink us dry and live lavishly off our tables. I for one am tired of the sight of them, and their habits are a bad influence on our own young men.'

Judith bent her head over the needlework so that her mother would not see the irritation in her expression. 'When is my uncle to leave?'

'As soon as he can gather troops and ships,' Adelaide said. 'Your stepfather has heard a rumour the Northerners have been appealing to the Danes . . . The English cannot be allowed to join with them.'

Waltheof was half Danish. Judith wondered where his loyalty would lie if it came to the crux. With the rebels, or with her uncle at whose feet he had knelt in homage. Was he aware of the news, and if so what would it mean to him. A chance to raise rebellion, or the opportunity to prove himself a loyal vassal and then mayhap ask her uncle for a Norman bride? She did not know which way he would step, because despite their meetings at Simon's bedside in Fécamp she did not know him.

The rumours of a return to England received a mixed response from the hostages. There was pleasure at the notion of going home, furtive hope that the rebellion would succeed, and continued resentment at the knowledge that they would be bound closely to William's side and watched like naughty children.

'If William does not give me Agatha to wife by the end of the year, then I will find a way to join the rebels,' Edwin muttered, sloshing another measure of wine into his cup and passing the flagon along. 'I am not a tame dog to constantly trot to heel for the promise of a bone that is never produced.'

Waltheof refilled his cup with wine. No one was sober and the talk had turned dangerous. He had no doubt that whatever was said would get back to William, but for the nonce no one seemed to care.

'You think you can fight William?' he asked. 'You think you are a better warrior than Harold Godwinsson?'

Edwin's pale complexion darkened. 'I am still alive,' he slurred. 'Harold chose the wrong time and the wrong place.'

Morcar nodded in vigorous agreement, as did Edgar Atheling, who had been listening to the fighting talk with bright eyes.

'All of the North Country will rise up,' he declared, striking a pose. 'William has never set foot across the Humber. If Sweyn of Denmark sends a fleet then we can shake off the Normans like a dog shakes water from its pelt.'

Waltheof had held aloof from the fighting talk thus far, but the mention of the Danes brought him into their circle. He was half Dane himself and the tie of blood was strong. What would he do if Sweyn of Denmark sailed into the Humber – join him, or profess his allegiance to William? The wine buzzing in his head made it difficult to think. Kinship and belonging were important. Often he felt that he possessed neither. Parents and a brother he had scarcely known before death took them, lands that had been snatched from beneath his boyhood feet. All he had were the tales of his father's great deeds, and in strange contrast the quieter chanting of monks, drawing him through simple faith into the heart of their community. The way of the warrior or the way of peace: he had a foot in each territory and knew that he was in danger of falling down the chasm between.

He staggered to the coffer and picked up a fresh flagon, knowing that if he could down it to the dregs he would find the comfort of oblivion. He would not have to listen to the plans of his companions or the contradictory voices arguing back and forth in his mind. He gulped the potent red brew, felt the overflow trickling through his beard, and thought of Judith. If he took the cowl she was lost to him, the same if he chose the Danes. Only by becoming William's man did he stand a chance – and that was a slim one.

He knew that everyone liked him because he was good-natured and always prepared to laugh at his own expense. Never angry, always patient, even when bedevilled by such trials as small children, vicious dogs and cantankerous old folk. Unfailingly polite despite his rustic English manners and his propensity for drink. Oh yes, he knew his worth in the eyes of other men. But tonight, in the murky light of dark plans and sour wine, the laughter had deserted him and he felt danger-ously close to tears.

'I've brought you another gift,' Waltheof said, his breath steaming in the dank November air.

Simon watched Waltheof produce a walking stick from beneath the bearskin cloak. It was made of ash wood – a cut-down spear haft by the look of the thickness and length, fantas-tically carved with a sinuous design of hunting dogs pursuing a stag towards the smoothed and polished top. He and Simon were seated on a bench in the courtyard of the palace at Fécamp where King William was making final preparations to sail for England.

Waltheof was studying him from beneath his lids with an expectant expression.

Simon hated the stick, but he managed to smile. 'It is very fine, my lord, thank you.' Very fine if you were an old woman, but not a boy of ten years old desiring to run across the sward with the fleetness of a wild deer.

Waltheof nodded and looked pleased. 'I thought it would help you now you are able to bear weight on the leg.'

Simon nodded. 'Indeed it will,' he said tonelessly. To prove it he took the stick, levered himself to his feet and walked several steps across the courtyard. Fog was rolling off the sea and smothering the town. Heavy, damp, clinging. Waltheof's coppery hair was hoar-grey and a cobwebby mist dewed his cloak.

There was biting pain every time Simon set weight on the leg. The break had healed reasonably well, considering the seriousness of the original injury, but the limb was still twisted out of true. His walk was no longer an unthinking bounce but a slow, lop-sided progression. The situation was not helped by his weakness. Lying abed for weeks on end had caused his muscles to waste and he had no strength to support the damaged limb.

He had seen the beggars at the abbey gates with all manner of wounds and deformities, had watched men pity them and toss a coin, or walk past in the arrogance of their own power and manhood. He had observed them beg crusts and other leavings from the monks who came to dole out food at vespers. Now, but for the grace of his noble birth and his father's position at court, he would be one of their number.

Waltheof studied his progress with folded arms and a slight frown. 'You should do this every day,' he said. 'And go further each time. Only then will you build up your strength.'

'It hurts,' Simon answered, knowing that he sounded churlish but unable to prevent the all too familiar black misery from flooding over him.

'I know.'

'But you don't feel it,' Simon snapped. His fist tightened around the carved stick. Suppressing the urge to cast it across the bailey he continued to limp towards the open ground where the squires did their training. It was empty this morning, the straw archery sheaves standing like ghosts beyond the quintain post that reared out of the mist like a gibbet.

'Perhaps not, but I see it,' Waltheof said and walked beside him, shortening his own long stride to blend with Simon's. 'If you do not fight, lad, it will destroy you.'

Simon said nothing, but his lips compressed petulantly.

'I have never thought you short of courage,' Waltheof murmured, 'But it will be to no avail if your self-pity is the stronger.'

Simon had been about to stop but Waltheof's words goaded him across the practice ground until he stood at its centre. The pain stabbed through his damaged leg in excruciating waves and he clenched his teeth so hard that his jaw began to ache too.

'Much better.' Waltheof clapped an approving hand on Simon's shoulder. Simon staggered, as the accolade almost felled him. The man did not move to steady him, but left him to find his own balance.

'Come the spring you'll be walking three times as fast, riding a horse, and back in full weapons training – I mean what I say. I am not feeding sops to an invalid – or at least I hope I am not.'

Simon jutted his jaw. Waltheof's words had stung his pride. Even if he died of the pain, no one was going to accuse him of wallowing in self-pity. Pivoting on his good leg, he made his way back towards the hall. Half smiling, Waltheof accompanied him.

They were halfway across the courtyard when Ralf de Gael joined them, his thin features bright with the relish that always lit them when he had gossip to impart.

'You're doing well,' he said with a pleasant nod to Simon.

Simon nodded gravely back. He knew many folk disliked Ralf de Gael. They said that he was smooth and shallow and not to be trusted. But then Normans frequently disparaged men of Breton birth. Simon liked De Gael because he was amusing and he took the time to speak to him without patronising. That De Gael was a good friend of Waltheof was also no small part of the boy's approval.

'Very well, considering the severity of the break,' Waltheof said with a wink at Simon.

The gesture warmed a smile from Simon. He strode out a bit more, showing off despite the increased pain.

'There's news from England,' De Gael said as they walked.

'Oh yes?' Waltheof's tone was suddenly cautious.

'The trouble has escalated. Exeter is in full revolt and there is a rising in the West Country that has spilled beyond containment. We're sailing on the morrow's tide. You had best hone your battleaxe – for whichever side you choose.'

'You know for sure that we are to sail?' Waltheof demanded.

De Gael nodded. 'I look through the right keyholes,' he said with a feline smile. 'And listen at the right doors.' With a pleasant nod and a ruffle of Simon's hair, he moved on.

Waltheof halted and stood gazing into the fog, his head turned in the direction of the harbour. Simon thought that he looked like a hound testing an elusive scent.

'What is England like?' he asked.

'What?' With a bemused shake of his head Waltheof focused on the boy.

'England,' Simon repeated, resting on his stick. 'What is it like?'

Although Waltheof smiled, the expression was wry and sad. 'I am not sure that I know any more,' he said, and after a moment began slowly to walk. 'Changed for ever. Nothing will ever be the same again – no matter how we wish it to be.'

Limping along beside him, pain stabbing through his leg, Simon knew exactly what he meant.

*   *   *

Judith crossed herself, rose from her knees, and with downcast eyes and modestly folded hands left the church. Sybille followed a few paces behind, her pose echoing that of her mistress.

From the edge of her eye, Judith was aware of Waltheof rising too, signing his breast and following her out. His presence loomed behind her, large as a bear in the porch. Without looking round she stepped out into the swirling, dank air. The fog had thickened as the day progressed and now it was like wading through a fleece.

She heard his footfall and it sent a shiver down her spine. The instinct of all creatures to fear shadows from behind. Then he fell into step beside her and the threat changed its form.

She had not seen much of him since their encounter on the stairs. Her mother had been suspicious and shrewd enough to confine her to the bower. Although Judith had chaffed she had also found relief within the safe walls of the women's quarters. Rules were rules, and, while she was tempted to break them, the orderly domesticity of her surroundings and her own strict sense of duty kept that temptation within bounds.

It was only in church and beneath the eyes of others in the great hall that she and Waltheof exchanged words. He had made no approach to her uncle concerning marriage or even courtship. She would have heard. Perhaps he did not have the strength of will or courage to take the necessary steps. Perhaps he was all words and no intention.

She slanted him a glance, aware that she should not be speaking to him. 'So you are to sail to England with my uncle?' Her breath clouded in the air and mingled with his.

'I do not have a choice, my lady,' he said. 'Where he goes, so do I – until he chooses to release me.'

'Will you help him put down the rebellions of your countrymen?' she challenged.

'I will act as my conscience dictates,' he replied evasively.

'If you are not my uncle's ally, then you are his enemy. There can be no middle path.'

'I would rather make friends than enemies,' Waltheof said quietly. 'But it is difficult to know which is which.'

'Is it?' Decisive herself, Judith felt a surge of impatience. 'If you cannot see what is before you, then you might as well be blind.'

'Stumbling in the mist you mean,' he said with a grin to which she did not respond.

'You are foolish to make light of the matter. My uncle can fulfil your ambitions, or he can cast you in the abyss. But the road you choose is your responsibility.'

He looked slightly taken aback, chagrined almost, and it was a strange expression to see on the face of so large and vital a man.

Waltheof cleared his throat and stooped slightly, bringing his height closer to hers. 'Judith . . . are you wroth that I have held off from asking for you?'

She tightened her lips. 'Why should I be wroth?'

'Because perhaps you thought I was reneging on a promise.'

'In truth the matter has dwelt little on my mind,' she said. It was a lie, but pondering the matter had led her towards her mother's viewpoint. 'I may be innocent, but I do know that a man's words are often driven by his lust.'

'Not mine!' He looked indignant.

'Indeed?' She gave a scornful toss of her head. 'And what have you told your dark-haired whore at Madame Hortense's who will do whatever you desire for a silver coin?'

She expected him to bluster and deny her accusation, but although his complexion grew as red as his hair he answered her candidly. 'Nothing of late,' he said gruffly. 'I have not seen her in many months. Besides, Edwin has her now.'

Judith was taken by surprise. 'Edwin?'

He spread his hands in an open gesture. 'I lay with her no more than two or three times, so she had to find custom elsewhere.'

Judith almost smiled, imagining Agatha's expression could she be listening now. 'I was given to understand that she was your permanent mistress.'

He made a face. 'No. I went to her in lust and the aftertaste was bitter because she wasn't you.'

Judith drew a sharp breath through her teeth. She was affronted, but at the same time his words excited her.

'I meant no insult,' Waltheof said quickly. He reached for her hand. 'If I have not asked your uncle for permission to be your suitor it is because I have been waiting the right moment.'

'Then perhaps you are one of those men who will wait for ever.' She snatched her hand from his for they were close to the ducal apartments now and could not afford to be seen thus.

'It is not that . . .' He gnawed his underlip. 'I am afraid that he will refuse me . . . and then the matter will be finished.'

'Unless you ask, you will not know, and he will bestow me on someone who does have the courage to approach him,' Judith said scornfully.

He recoiled at the remark as if she had struck him. 'I may lack many things, my lady, but do not missay my courage,' he growled.

She saw that she had wounded him but lacked the ability to conciliate. The words stuck in her throat, refusing to be born. 'Then do not insult my pride,' she said, before sweeping on into the apartments.

Usually after attending prayer she felt calm and refreshed, but now her hands were shaking and there was a pounding ache at her temples.

'You were harsh with him, my lady,' Sybille said.

Judith rounded on her maid. 'When I want your opinion I will ask for it!' she spat. 'You think I was harsh? You do not know the meaning of the word.'

'Neither does he, my lady,' Sybille murmured, not in the least set down by her mistress's fury. She had long since grown impervious to the cold words and hauteur, aware that there was a softness within Judith's brittle shell. 'He is truly gentle, and such men are as precious as gold. You should treat him with more care.'

Judith's eyes narrowed. 'Hold your tongue if you would keep

your position with me. That is a command. One more word and I will have you whipped and dismissed.'

'Yes, my lady,' Sybille said in a tone that told Judith precisely what she thought of such tactics.

Judith turned her back on her maid and paced swiftly into the hall. Someone had put damp wood on the fire and the billows of smoke seemed no less thick than the fog she was leaving behind, but Judith walked with relief into the pungency. Waltheof disturbed her. She wanted to lay her head on his broad chest and listen to the thud of his heart, and at the same time she wanted to repudiate him. Torn between the two, she made up her mind that he was not worth the turmoil and decided that she would forget him. With the decision came a feeling of relief, coupled with a sudden, inexplicable urge to weep.

CHAPTER 6

Exeter, Winter 1067–1068

Waltheof handed Osric Fairlocks a cup of mead. 'Drink this,' he said with sympathy. 'It will warm your blood.'

The young man took it hesitantly and raked his free hand through his flaxen hair. He was not old enough to grow a beard and his face had the tender smoothness and bloom of late adolescence. There was fear in his eyes, although he was doing his utmost to conceal it. That afternoon he and eleven other hostages had been brought to the Norman camp in token of Exeter's promise to acknowledge William as king and cease hostilities. Osric, whose father was a prosperous merchant, was the youngest hostage and Waltheof had taken him under his wing.

Outside the tent the January day was as raw as a battle-pitted blade. Nightfall was closing on the horizon and rain had begun to spit in the wind. 'William is harsh, but he treats his hostages well,' Waltheof reassured the youth and led him to a large brazier burning in the centre of the room. 'You will not want for anything.'

'Except my freedom,' Osric said, his complexion reddening.

Waltheof nodded, 'There you have it. That is indeed the hair shirt we all wear. But if the city yields on the morrow, you at least will be free to go home to your kin.'

The young man regarded him out of pale blue eyes, startling in their clarity. 'Are you free to go home, my lord? Could you leave here on the morrow and not be hunted down?'

Waltheof twitched his shoulders as if shifting a burden that chaffed. 'Not yet,' he said, 'but I hope to do so very soon.' William had bestowed on him the full titles of Earl of Huntingdon and Northampton and confirmed him in his lands before the entire court at the Christmas feast. The freedom to take charge of those estates had not been forthcoming, though. Instead William had bidden him join this campaign in the West Country. It was the same for Edwin and Morcar; they too had been confirmed in their lands and then forced to stay at William's side. Edgar Atheling had been left in London under guard, but he had no lands from which to rally support and he was still little more than a boy.

He gave Osric a glance filled with wry warning. 'No one crosses the lines that are drawn by King William.'

'And if they do?'

'I have never met a man so sure of himself, or so ruthless.' Waltheof finished his mead and replenished his cup. 'He is feared, and rightly so.'

'You know that King Harold's mother and his sons are in the city?' Osric said with nervous defiance.

'I had heard the rumour. If they have their wits about them they will make shrift to leave tonight before the gates open on the morrow.'

'And if the gates remain closed? What will happen then?'

Waltheof shook his head. 'You do not want to know, lad,' he said bleakly.

'My father and the elders say that we should open the gates to William rather than see the city burn, but many others say we should resist.' Osric's jaw jutted with a hint of challenge. 'We have stout walls, good fighting men and plentiful provisions. William may find that he is king in London, but not king here.'

'And yet, knowing the danger, you agreed to be a hostage?'

Osric gave him a pained look. 'I had no choice. As my father's firstborn son, it was my duty.'

Waltheof said nothing, for there was no point in frightening the lad and he knew from his experience with Judith how overriding a sense of duty could be. He hoped for Osric's sake that sense prevailed and the citizens of Exeter opened their gates on the morrow.

Waltheof swirled the mead in his cup and watched the reflections break and shimmer on the surface. What would he do if this were Northampton or Huntingdon? Would he yield to the invader, or fight to the last drop of blood in his body. 'I am William's man now,' he said aloud, the remark intended to bolster his own resolve rather than make a bold statement for the pale-haired youth at his side. 'For better, or worse.'

In the morning the Norman army gathered before the walls of Exeter in full array and William demanded that its citizens yield their town into his hands. Upon the Roman walls, outlined in the red winter dawn, a soldier lifted his tunic, turned his exposed backside towards the Normans and waggled his hips. As William's jaw tightened, missiles began to fly over the battlements – cabbage stalks, clods of dung, rocks and stones. Horses skittered and shied. The Norman ranks developed ragged holes as men fought with their mounts and drew back out of range.

'Ut, ut, ut!' surged the English battle roar, a sound not heard since the October confrontation on Hastings field. 'Ut, ut, ut!'

Amidst the chaos William sat as still as an effigy on his black Iberian war horse. He stared expressionlessly at the walls, and the more the volume of the shouting increased the greater became his control. At last he tugged on the bridle and urged his horse out of danger's way.

Watching from the back of the line with Edwin and Morcar, Waltheof swallowed. Something bad was going to happen. He could feel it all the way down his spine.

'A pity one of their slingers didn't get him while they had the opportunity,' Morcar said softly.

'Hold your tongue, fool,' Edwin muttered, glancing round.

'There is no one to hear except sympathisers,' Morcar growled. 'Is that not so, Waltheof?' His eyes gleamed with challenge and malice.

'Indeed, I have great sympathy for the people of Exeter,' Waltheof said grimly. 'Judith told me a story about William as a young man. The people of Alençon taunted him by waving hides from their walls, reminding him that his grandsire was a common tanner. Some lived to rue the day and the rest were butchered.' He lowered his voice. 'That slinger could not afford to miss, any more than that fool on the battlements could afford to bare his arse.'

He drew back as a dozen Norman soldiers arrived and shoved their way through the ranks. Their mail gleamed like dull water, reflecting the steely dawn. Waltheof's gut clenched. Moments later the men returned, escorting the hostages that had been given by the city's elders in token of their good faith.

'Dear, sweet Christ,' Waltheof whispered and crossed himself. There were ten men, including Osric who was the youngest and yet to reach his majority, and five women, high of rank and gowned in deep-dyed wool, rich with embroidery.

Waltheof nudged his horse forward, intending to follow, but more Norman soldiers swiftly barred his way.

'No, my lord earl,' said one of them and grasped Waltheof's bridle close to the headstall. 'You cannot go.'

It was Picot de Saye, the Norman whom he had defeated at arm wrestling on that first evening in Rouen, and it was obvious from the look on his face that he was enjoying the moment. Waltheof was tempted to dig in his heels and ride the man down, but knew that he would not live much beyond the deed.

'But you can watch,' Picot added lazily and shifted his fist to the cheekstrap, the force of his grip preventing Waltheof from wrenching his horse around and riding away. 'So are all traitors brought to justice.'

Waltheof swore in English at the Norman. De Saye absorbed the insult without a flicker. 'Watch,' he said, his lip curling. 'Watch and learn your lesson.'

King William was staring dispassionately at the clutch of hostages. Raising his mace, he pointed it with brutal decision at Osric. 'Bring him before the walls and put out his eyes,' he commanded.

Without demur, two of the escort plunged among the Saxons, seized the youth and manhandled him towards the towering city defences. Osric's expression was pale with fright, but he knew no French and thus did not understand the portent of William's words.

De Saye might have had a tight grip on Waltheof's bridle, but he had no control over Waltheof's voice. 'No, my lord king, you cannot!' he roared. 'In God's name, have mercy, I beg you!'

William turned his head. The sharp eyes appraised Waltheof and they were impassive. Neither pity in them, nor anger, nor irritation. Nothing but a brown so dark that it was almost black and merged with the pupils. 'Save your pleading, Lord Waltheof, and be thankful that I have not ordered the blinding of all,' he said icily and, reining away, rode off to see the sentence carried out.

Osric screamed like a hare in a trap. The sound, high-pitched and keening, went on and on until it wound itself permanently into the coils of Waltheof's brain. His gorge rose and it took all his will not to unman himself and spew over his mount's withers. From Exeter's walls came a response of angry yells and a renewed barrage of missiles. The Normans sheathed their bloody knives and retreated out of range, leaving Osric to groan and writhe in the wet, reddening grass.

From the Norman camp the sound of Osric's moans continued long after the early winter dusk had fallen, growing gradually more sporadic and faint as blood loss and cold took their toll. Finally, not long after Compline, the sounds ceased. Waltheof had spent the time on his knees in prayer for Osric's soul. There was nothing else he could do for William was as implacable as granite. No one was to go to the hostage's aid. Any breach of William's command and a second hostage would be blinded too.

'Not so fine now, your Norman lord,' sneered Morcar in passing. 'What price now your desire to be a Frenchman?'

Waltheof's hands clenched on his prayer beads as he fought the desire to round on Morcar and use his fists to pummel away his grief and anger.

'Leave me be, Morcar,' he said raggedly. 'I cannot pray to God while you disturb me.'

'You think prayer is the answer?' Morcar mocked. 'Truly you should not have strayed from your cloister, "Brother" Waltheof.' Wrapping his hands around his belt, Morcar sauntered off to join his brother.

Waltheof bowed his head and whispered the Psalter over and over, seeking the path through and between the words towards communication with God. But tonight it was difficult, the way stumbling and strewn with lurid, bloody images that tripped and felled him.

The morning dawned and still the citizens of Exeter howled defiance at the Normans. Under cover of darkness a handful of them had crept out and brought Osric's body back into the town, leaving only a depression in the grass and dark bloodstains on the pallid winter blades.

William summoned Waltheof and brought him before the walls. In the early light, sappers were toiling to undermine a section of the massive stone battlements. Screens of wattle hurdles protected the men and Norman archers kept the defenders on the walls pinned down. William's half-brother, Robert, Count of Mortain, was supervising the activity, the harshness of his voice carrying on the frosty morning air.

Waltheof bowed stiffly and then stood at William's side to watch the industry. 'They did not open their gates, sire,' he said, making oblique reference to yesterday's atrocity. He wondered why William had requested his presence. Was he going to be forced to view another blinding in order to 'learn' his lesson?

'They are stubborn,' William replied. 'It is because they are harbouring the remnants of the Godwinsson family. They would not be so ready to defy me if they had naught but their own hides to defend.' He slanted Waltheof a dark look. 'You think me harsh, Earl Waltheof?'

'I could not have done as you did, sire. It would fester on my conscience.'

William gave a contemptuous grunt. 'A king cannot afford to have a conscience when his lands are threatened. Sometimes a single act of savagery saves time. I destroy one man for the sake of saving others. If the people of Exeter had opened their gates yester eve, they would have spared themselves a deal of pain.'

Waltheof could not prevent a shiver of foreboding. 'What will you do when you have broken down the walls, sire?' There was no doubt in his mind that Exeter would eventually fall. There was not an Englishman left in the land who could match William's iron discipline and military leadership.

'You suspect I am going to order a massacre?' William said dryly.

'It had crossed my mind, sire.'

'That depends on how swiftly they learn their lessons. What I did yesterday was not from anger but necessity. If I had let their defiance go unpunished they would have seen it as a weakness and it would have bolstered their resolve.'

'But they did not open their gates to you, sire,' Waltheof pointed out again.

'That would have been a weakness on their part. But when the sappers bring down their wall and my soldiers ride through the breach I doubt their boldness will continue. No one wants to see their child maimed, blinded or trampled beneath the hooves of a warhorse.'

Waltheof could not prevent the shudder that rippled down his spine. William's words had brought to mind the memory of Osric's screams and he was filled with a revulsion so strong that he felt sick.

'This is the way of a leader, Waltheof,' William said, nailing the young earl with a shrewd and ruthless stare. 'You have to make harsh judgements and overrule all other men with your will. Even if your choices burden your conscience, you do not cry out but shoulder them without sign of weakness.' He took up a bullish stance – planting his feet wide and folding his arms. 'I am not justifying myself to you, but explaining the role of a leader in wartime.'

'Why should you do that, sire?' Waltheof asked stiffly.

'Because you are an earl and the son of an earl. Because you have never been blooded in battle or had your abilities tested to the limit.'

Waltheof flushed. 'I have been your hostage for a year. How can I be tested when I kick my heels at court?'

William looked at him steadily, his eyes obsidian dark. 'It is all a matter of trust, is it not?' he murmured. 'If I take my fist off the leash and let you go, will you be loyal, or will you muster an army and make war against me? I have small doubt that your companions would whet their swords the moment they were out of my sight.'

'You would release me, sire?' A note of eagerness entered Waltheof's voice.

'I did not say that. I said that it was a matter of trust. How trustworthy are you, Waltheof?'

'I gave you my oath at the Christmas Gemot in Winchester, sire.'

'As did the others. I did not ask about your oath, but about your trustworthiness.'

Waltheof swallowed. How loyal was he? Could he follow a man who would blind a youth for political expedience? If he couldn't, then he faced worse than blinding himself. If he could, then perhaps William might let him have Judith. 'I am trustworthy, sire,' he heard himself croak. 'Only let me go from court and I will prove it to you.'

William rubbed his palm across his jaw, considering. Finally, he nodded. 'Stay with me until Exeter is taken, and then I give you leave to depart until the Easter feast at Westminster.'

Elation coursed through Waltheof, sweeping aside all other considerations. It was only later that he remembered Osric and felt ashamed that the gift of his own freedom should so easily have overwhelmed his revulsion at William's deed.

Exeter fell, the mined walls rumbling down and an initial charge of Norman cavalry pouring through the breach to terrorise the citizens into capitulation. Following hard upon that first warning assault, William sent in his most disciplined troops. There was to be no looting, no burning, no harassment. A Flemish mercenary caught in the act of rape was summarily hanged.

Waltheof watched the masterly taking of Exeter, the way the population now pleaded with William for mercy and how he gave it. Not only that, but the orderliness of his troops and his implacable attention to discipline gave the people an anchor. They were not going to be butchered in their homes, everything was going to be all right. William might be a Norman conqueror, but he had won the right to be their king.

The remnants of Harold Godwinsson's family escaped by boat at the last moment, but William was sanguine about the matter. There was no one to truly challenge him from that clan. Their best had died on Hastings field.

He gave instructions for land to be levelled and a castle to be built. That this involved the destruction of several English houses and garths was the only damage wrought on Exeter apart from the broached wall.

True to his word, William gave Waltheof leave to depart the city and return to his lands. Edwin and Morcar were furious, but impotent. Threats to leave William of their own will were met with courteous but firm counter threats. The promise of marriage to Agatha was dangled before Edwin's eyes together with the insinuation that Mercia would suffer if William had to go chasing north in pursuit of renegades. Perhaps later, he hinted; perhaps after the Easter feast.

'You must have had to lick his arsehole all the way to his

throat for this,' Morcar sneered as Waltheof mounted his chestnut stallion and prepared to leave the city. He had a safe conduct
in his pouch from William and an escort of Norman knights
and English mercenaries.

'My lands are not as great as yours,' Waltheof answered. 'He
risks less in letting me go than you or Edwin. Besides, this is
only a trial. If I renege, William will throw me in the deepest
dungeon he possesses.'

Morcar fixed him with a look of utter loathing and turned
away. Edwin stepped forward and looked up at Waltheof
through sun-narrowed eyes. 'Enjoy favour while you may, son
of Siward,' he said with a curled lip. 'It will not last.'

There was nothing more to say. Waltheof knew that if he
extended the hand of friendship, he would be shunned.
Clicking his tongue to the horse, he reined about, heading for
Exeter's city gates and the road home.

He had to pass the remnants of the burned-out houses that
were being flattened to make way for the castle. Under the
watchful gaze of Picot de Saye, English labourers toiled with
shovels, their expressions wearing a blank neutrality that
Waltheof was coming to know too well. More eloquent than
resentment, more subtle than resignation. He averted his head
from the sight and the acrid stink, fixing his gaze instead on
the ragged blue sky and the pale sun, forerunners of the spring.
He promised himself that in his own earldom no man should
ever look upon him thus.

CHAPTER 7

Dawn streaked the sky and sea with pearl and silver. A brisk wind mined the seams of light and bellied the sails of the Norman fleet, thrusting it towards the smudge of England's shoreline.

Simon stood on the deck of his galley and watched the land drawing closer. His leg was aching, but he was so accustomed to the sensation by now that it only bothered him when his mind was unoccupied. For the moment, he was too full of exhilaration to give the pain much heed. He had scarcely slept at all during the night – just a couple of hours rolled in his cloak. Most of the time he had lain awake, gazing at the stars as they appeared and vanished behind fine tresses of cloud. His mind had turned with the turning of the heavens, dwelling on the adventure to come.

Duke William had put down the rebellions in England; the Danish threat had been avoided by diplomatic negotiation, and he had summoned his family to come to him. This Eastertide Duchess Matilda was to be crowned Queen of England in King Edward's great abbey of Westminster. Simon had pleaded with his father to be allowed to make the crossing as part of the entourage, promising vehemently to be a help, not a hindrance. He could walk, he could ride, he never complained. When his father had frowned doubtfully, Simon had started making plans to stow away on a supply vessel, but it had not come to that; his father had finally agreed to let him come. 'If only to prevent my ears from being nagged off,' he had said with a reluctant smile.

De Rules had found Simon light fetching and carrying duties within the household. When his leg grew tired he was made to sit and keep tallies of the goods being transported, or given employment greasing armour and mail ready for the voyage.

Yester eve they had sailed from the port of Dieppe and headed out into the Narrow Sea. Simon had been boarded on the Duchess's galley, its strakes painted a moon white and rows of overlapping kite shields protecting the deck from the exuber-ant salt spray. The ladies had recourse to a canvas deck shelter and had spent most of the time inside it, the flaps pulled tight. Duchess Matilda was not fond of journeying across water, although for her husband she would have braved sailing over the edge of the world itself.

It was Simon's first sea voyage. His stomach was queasy, but he had not succumbed to outright seasickness. On the galley that held the Duke's sons he had several times seen Rufus puking over the side. There was no mistaking the pale sandy hair and thickset body. Simon felt sorry for Rufus and was glad that he was not sailing on that particular ship. Jeers from the Duke's older sons and their companions floated on the wind, laced with the malice of too much wine. The ringleader however, was not of William's brood, but Robert de Bêlleme, a son of the great Earl Roger of Montgomery. The youth was extraordinarily handsome and outwardly of a charming and debonair mien, but Simon knew from bitter experience that De Bêlleme's deeper nature was twisted and cruel. Inflicting pain and humiliation were favourite pastimes of his, and Simon, with his damaged leg, was often on the receiving end of pranks and taunts. Today he was safe, but Rufus, with his lack of grace and his stammer, was not.

Simon inhaled the salt tang in the air and watched the band of dawn widen and spill across the sea like the glitter from an open treasure chest. Turning slightly, he saw the Lady Judith had emerged from the women's shelter. She nodded to him without speaking and went to look out on the approaching land.

Simon knew that she did not like him much. He would always be grateful to her for giving him that hanging when he was confined to the tiny wall chamber in Fécamp, but he knew she had done it from guilt, not kindness.

Lord Waltheof was smitten by her. She seldom laughed or smiled, and Simon thought that the Earl pursued her in the hopes of making her do those things. He was hoping that Waltheof would be at court. He wanted to show him how far he had progressed since their last encounter. From halting steps to strides, from blotted scrawl to fluent script, and from uncertain notes on the bone flute to twinkling tunes.

He had been standing in one place for too long and as he moved vicious pain stabbed through his leg, making him stumble. He stifled the instinctive cry of pain and managed to grab a stay rope and remain upright. Lady Judith half glanced, then swiftly averted her head.

Turning his back, pretending he had not seen her look, Simon limped stiffly towards the red-faced sailor at the steerboard. The man greeted him with a grin and let him try his hand at operating the large wooden rudder. Simon's discomfort immediately diminished as he tackled the challenge of learning a new skill. The wind tangling his hair, a mist of salt droplets narrowing his eyes, he became a bold sea-reaver with the blood of the Vikings surging in his veins.

Judith hated crossing the Narrow Sea. The knowledge that all that lay between her and fathoms of drowning green water was a flimsy layer of wood was terrifying. She would not disgrace her blood by showing her anxiety, but within her, that blood ran as cold as the ocean beneath the keel.

She wished that Simon de Senlis had not been assigned a place on the women's vessel. The sight of his stiff gait was a permanent reproach to her conscience, and the way he looked at her with those knowing fox-coloured eyes made her want to shriek at him to go away and leave her alone. She wanted to bury that moment in the stableyard and forget it had ever happened. And she could not do that with the evidence always before her eyes.

Judith was relieved when the boy went to join the steersman and left her line of vision. She made an effort to banish him from her mind by concentrating on the matters uppermost in her mind. England and Waltheof.

Her mother muttered privately and out of the Duchess's hearing that England was occupied by a gluttonous, uncivilised rabble and that given a choice she would rather remain in Normandy. Judith suspected that half her mother's grumbling was caused by the journey itself, since Adelaide hated travelling and disruption of routine with equal amounts of vehemence. Even the grand prospect of a coronation had not sweetened the vinegar of her mood.

Judith turned her thoughts to Waltheof. In the three months since his leaving, her memory of him had both faded and clarified. She could not recall his features clearly, but his vibrancy and vitality had stayed with her as surely as the memory of his glossy red-gold hair and the touch of his mouth on hers. Those things were indelible, no matter how she strove to obliterate them. She would wake in the night from dreams that were sweet and heavy with a longing she had no experience to name, but which set her on edge and brought the uncomfortable dull ache like menstrual pain to her loins.

There had been no word from England to indicate that he had pursued his declaration to have her. Judith knew that for her own sake she should stay as far from the fire as possible. Only a fool stepped too close and risked being burned. And Judith prided herself on her pragmatic common sense.

The fleet docked in Southampton and, after the royal entourage had rested there overnight, they travelled on to Winchester and thence to London. Gazing upon the April landscape as they rode, Judith thought that England was not much different from Normandy. The same pastoral scenes in the countryside; the

same industry in the towns. The only signs of unrest and struggle were sporadic – charred marks on the ground where a building had burned, a farmstead worked solely by women whose
husbands had not returned from the great battle, the rising
earthworks and palisades of motte and bailey castles, dug by
the English and supervised by the Normans.

She could almost see the peace, laid down as heavily as slabs
of stone between lines of mortar. No one dared rebel lest they
were crushed beneath a mailed Norman fist, but Judith could
feel the resentment. It was there in the way that folk bowed to
her, concealing their hostility beneath downcast lids and
making obscene gestures under the cover of their doffed hoods.
She rode past with a raised chin, her shield one of Norman
hauteur, but it was not sufficient to protect her entirely from
the pierce of their side-cast glances.

They arrived in London just before dusk of the second day
and travelled by barge up the Thames from the wharves at
Queenhythe to the royal palace at Westminster. Sequins of
sunset dazzled on the water and turned the sky to molten gold
beyond the towers of King Edward's abbey. Judith folded her
arms within her cloak, glad of the fur lining, for it was cold on
the river and the water was choppy with a glittering cold spray.

'Are we almost there?' her cousin Agatha demanded petulantly. 'I feel sick.'

Judith regarded her with dislike. Agatha was convinced
that her parents were going to announce a betrothal between
her and Edwin of Mercia at the coronation celebrations.
Throughout the journey to England she had been primping
and preening, her eyes aglow with anticipation. Although
Judith would not admit it to herself, jealousy was a potent
ingredient in her antipathy towards her cousin.

The barge bumped along the side of the wharf and the barge-
master secured his craft with a stout mooring rope. Willing
hands reached down to help and steady the occupants as they
disembarked.

'My lady,' Waltheof said and, taking Judith's hand in a sure, warm grip, he pulled her onto firm ground. The sunset burnished his hair to fire. He was wearing a tunic she had not seen before, of sky-blue wool richly embroidered, and the famous bearskin cloak was clasped at his shoulder by an enormous ring-brooch set with chips of lapis lazuli.

'Lord Waltheof!' Her greeting was a gasp.

'Why so surprised?' He flashed her a smile. 'We are all here to swear our oaths of fealty and witness the coronation of Duchess Matilda. I thought I would be the first to bid you welcome.' Leaning in closer, he breathed against her ear. 'I also intend to ask your uncle for you in marriage.'

His words shook her, as did the danger of being so close to him in public. She took a back-step.

So did he, and at the same time he bowed. 'Countess,' he murmured.

Judith's mother inclined her head in a tepid response and as she swept past him beckoned Judith with a terse forefinger.

'Waltheof!'

He turned at the cry and Judith saw his smile widen until it split into a broad grin.

'Well look at you, Simon de Senlis!' he cried. Striding forward, he clasped the lad in an exuberant embrace. 'I told you that you could do anything if you set your mind to it. How's the leg?'

Adelaide swung to look at the scene and gave a cluck of irritation. 'I am reminded of the dogs your father used to keep,' she said contemptuously. 'Huge, enthusiastic and tiresome.'

Judith gnawed her lip. She dared not tell her mother that Waltheof was intending to ask for her in marriage – at least not while Adelaide's mood was tetchy from travelling. Glancing over her shoulder, she saw that Waltheof and Simon were walking together, the former tailoring his pace to the latter's uneven gait. The boy was chattering and Waltheof was leaning to listen with every indication of interest. She felt a surge of jealousy and, opposing it, feelings of tenderness and pride. Her mother had disparagingly compared Waltheof to one of her father's dogs, but Adelaide had omitted to mention the unconditional love and loyalty of which such animals were capable. Such traits, surely, were worth their weight in gold.

The evening meal served an hour after their arrival was a relatively casual affair. No one had known the precise hour at which the Duchess would arrive at Westminster and so no formal arrangements had been made. Agatha and Edwin were permitted to sit side by side and share their portions of squabs in wine sauce. Their blonde heads leaned close and Judith could almost hear them cooing like lovebirds.

Judith was seated next to her mother, her sister and her stepfather, Eudo of Champagne. He was stocky and robust, balding, but still handsome with a determined cleft chin, high cheekbones and shrewd blue eyes. Adelaide had married him out of political expediency. There was little love or attraction between them, but there was pride and unity of purpose, and the ever present bonds of duty.

Waltheof sat at the same trestle but at some distance from Judith, separated by various magnates and their families. Judith noticed how confident he was amongst them and thought she perceived a change in him. To say that he seemed more responsible or more of a man was wrong. His ready laugh still rang out with too much exuberance and his tongue still ran away from the governance of his mind, yet, something was different. Assurance? Authority? Perhaps it was because he was now on his own soil instead of being a hostage in a foreign land. Whatever the reason, it was a change for the better.

The meal finished, the company broke up into smaller groups, men gathering around friends and acquaintances to exchange news, play dice and tafel, or listen to the bards sing tales of praise for whichever lord they served. Her mother prepared to retire to the small chamber that Eudo had secured for them, but Judith begged permission to linger awhile and listen to the tales.

Adelaide raised her brows. 'You are not usually so fond of song,' she said suspiciously.

'The English music is different, and I'm not tired.'

Her mother frowned and began to shake her head.

'Yes, stay,' spoke up her stepfather with a brusque gesture. 'And your sister too. I scarcely think that listening to a few tales in the open hall will compromise your virtue.'

'I don't . . .' Adelaide began, but her husband squeezed her hand in his strong, swordsman's fist.

'Peace, wife,' he said brusquely. 'Let the girls have their pleasure, and let us have ours.'

Adelaide's face flamed at his implication, made all the more obvious as he began tugging her purposefully towards the stairs. 'Do not be too long,' she said somewhat desperately to Judith.

'But not too soon either,' Eudo said with an eloquent eyebrow and a swift smile. 'Your mother and I have much to talk about.'

Judith's own complexion reddened. She knew that their activity would not involve much talking. At least if she and her sister were in the hall they would not have to lie on their pallets and listen to the stealthy sounds of coupling coming from the main bed.

Sybille chuckled and folded her arms. 'It is not often that your mother is bettered,' she remarked.

Judith sniffed and pretended not to hear.

The maid considered her charge with shrewd eyes. 'I wonder why you want to stay, mistress,' she murmured. 'I do not think it is out of consideration for your mother and stepfather, and you no more enjoy listening to bards than I'm the Duchess of Normandy.'

'You are impertinent,' Judith said haughtily.

Sybille shrugged. 'I speak the truth as I see it,' she said, not in the least chastised. She fell into step behind her mistress, her grey eyes mischievously sparkling.

Judith ignored her maid and glanced around the hall. Adela had darted off to join her royal cousins Agatha and Constance, who were in the company of Edwin of Mercia. Waltheof, by his height and the brightness of his hair, was easy to locate. He was standing beside Ralf de Gael, and his arm was around young Simon de Senlis as they listened to one of the several bards in the hall. Judith's brows twitched together at the sight of him with the boy, but her hesitation was a brief one. Drawing herself up, she went to join the group. As always she could not bring herself to take that final step but stood just a little aloof.

Waltheof must have seen her approach from the corner of his eye, for he turned with a widening smile of welcome and beckoned her closer. Judith stayed where she was and, fixing her gaze on the bard, pretended to give him her full attention, although she could not understand a word that he was singing. The English tongue was foreign to her, and the man's pronunciation was different again from the English she had heard Waltheof speak.

With the smirk of a conspirator Sybille stood aside, making room for Waltheof next to her mistress. He grinned at the maid and winked, then stooped to Judith's ear.

'What do you think of my skald?' he asked.

'Your skald?' His breath tickled her and the rumble of his voice set up a vibration low in her stomach.

'My bard,' he gestured to the singer. The man's hair was the dull gold of new pinewood and his beard was striped with the silver of early middle age.

'I did not know that you had such a man in your retinue.'

He shrugged his wide shoulders. 'I did not bring him to Normandy with me. Why should I clip his wings as well as my own? He is a free spirit and he serves me for pleasure, not duty.'

Judith eyed the man who was accompanying himself on a small but beautiful lyre. Whether or not the sound was true she could not tell for she had no flair for music. 'His accent is strange.'

'Thorkel comes from Iceland. He speaks English well, but it is not his mother tongue.' He looked at her. 'It is the same with me for French.'

They stood in silence for a while and listened. Waltheof seemed to be enjoying the ballad, whatever it was about. There was a gleam in his eyes, and his lips were parted in pleasure. 'It is the story of a great warrior who held a bridge single-handed against all comers,' Waltheof said. 'And through his action his country was saved, even though he died of his wounds.'

Judith was less than impressed. Most songs were of that ilk. She had nightmares sometimes about the tedium of the Song of Roland, which was a favourite of her uncle's own bards. The songs were all for men, she thought, and women of a martial frame of mind. But then she was not sure that she would have the patience for love ballads either.

The skald finished his lay on a haunting cry and a rippling shiver of notes. Judith guessed that the hero had tragically died, surrounded by a massed heap of enemy corpses.

Applauding loudly, eyes moist with a suspicion of tears, Waltheof drew a gold bracelet off his arm and presented it to the musician. 'Well sung, Thorkel,' he said gruffly.

'Your belief in my craft is worth more than gold, my lord, but I thank you for the gift,' the Icelander said graciously. His dark grey eyes flickered between Judith and Waltheof and he coaxed a gentle, stepping stone of notes from his lyre.

'Perhaps a tune for the lady?' he suggested.

Judith started to refuse, but Waltheof overrode her. 'Yes, Thorkel, a tune for the lady.'

The skald nodded and eyed Judith thoughtfully. 'A wood in springtime,' he announced. His gaze went past Judith to Sybille and he drooped his eyelid at the maid in what might just have been a wink. Then he started to play. No words, just sweet cords and cascades of notes that mimicked birdsong and the rill of meltwater down a hillside.

Judith surreptitiously moved her feet as they began to grow heavy with standing. She knew that many folk found music almost as essential as breathing, but she was not one of them. The skald's head was bent over his lyre but now and again he glanced up. His eyes pierced Judith as if he could see through her and she wanted to squirm, but after the first couple of looks he turned his attention to Sybille, and it soon became obvious for whom he was playing.

The tune ended on a clamber and fall of notes reminiscent of a skylark's song. 'That was beautiful,' Sybille sighed, her eyes misty. 'I could feel the leaf dapple on my eyelids.'

Thorkel smiled with pleasure. 'You have a rare imagination, mistress. It is not given to everyone to be so gifted.'

Judith narrowed her eyes, but the musician's attention was upon her maid and there was no sign of mockery in his expression. 'You are very skilled, Master Thorkel,' she murmured.

He bowed and she met a glint of ironic humour in his eyes. 'I am pleased you think so, my lady.' He excused himself to fill his drinking horn. Sybille lingered, obviously smitten.

Waltheof laid his hand on Judith's sleeve. 'Thorkel is not the only man of my retinue here at Westminster,' he said, and proceeded to introduce her to some of the other warriors who had been listening and whom she had earlier seen seated at one of the lower benches in the hall. Their names all ran one into the other, harsh and guttural: Hakon, Toki, Guthrum, Siggurd, men of Huntingdon and York, whose grandfathers had been Danes, tall and square-boned with the same vital air as their lord. She felt engulfed by their presence and was glad when Waltheof drew her out of their company and into a quieter corner.

'Your uncle released me to my lands after Exeter fell,' Waltheof said. 'And for that I have been grateful.'

Judith's gaze sharpened. 'He truly let you go?'

Waltheof nodded with enthusiasm. 'He said that he put his trust in me to return to court for this feast, but otherwise I have been my own man, free to deal with my estates as I see fit.'

The implications of his words sent a jolt of excitement through her. 'But he did not release Edwin of Mercia or his brother,' she said, determined to be practical.

Waltheof looked almost smug. 'He released neither of them. They and Edgar Atheling have been held in London ever since our return from Normandy.'

'So, he favours you.'

Waltheof pondered. 'I hope he does,' he said, 'because after the coronation I am going to ask him for you in marriage.'

'You said you were going to ask him before.'

He grimaced and rubbed the back of his neck. 'I know I did, but I could not. Your uncle confirmed me in my lands on the feast of Stephen. After Exeter, he let me return to them. To have asked on top of that would have seemed greedy.' His expression brightened. 'Now I have brought the men of Huntingdon to court and fulfilled my vow to come to him at the feast of Pentecost I am in a better position to make an approach. My loyalty is proven.' He stroked her cheek and his voice softened. 'I want you, Judith. I ache at the thought of you.'

She smiled, but drew away, aware of how many eyes there were to see and report. 'You have been spending too much time in the company of your bard.'

'And you in the company of your mother,' he retorted.

'My duty is to her . . . until you make it differently. I must go.' She made to push past him and he caught her hand in his.

'Is that all you want? If I gain the consent of your uncle, you will be content to wed with me?'

She was aware of the danger of his hold, that people would see and she would be compromised. The urgency in his voice spoke to her, the language exciting, dangerous and frightening.

Giving him a stiff nod, unable to dare further, she snatched her hand out of his and hurried away.

CHAPTER 8

In the great abbey church of Westminster, William's duchess Matilda was crowned Queen of the English before a vast array of witnesses, both Saxon and Norman. At William's coronation two winters since the English had rioted outside the church, resulting in the burning of several houses and many English deaths. This time all was peace and decorum, if not love and harmony.

Waltheof had been present at both ceremonies, the first time as a full hostage, his breath emerging as white vapour in the stark winter chill and his blood freezing as the houses burned. Now, still under Norman scrutiny but free of his leash, he witnessed the transformation of William's duchess into a queen. The green scent of May filled the air and touched his heart with optimism. Spring was burgeoning around him. Matilda herself was fecund, her belly swelling with the child conceived in Normandy shortly before William's departure. Perhaps now all would be well. He imagined Judith as his wife, her own womb ripe with a child of their mingled blood, English, Dane and Norman. The thought warmed him and he glanced sidelong to where she stood in attendance behind the new queen, her eyes modestly downcast. Her dark braids were glossy, reflecting the candle flicker, and crowned by a veil of gossamer silk. She would be his queen, he thought, and he would cherish her all of her days. She would lack for nothing, least of all his love.

As if sensing his scrutiny, she looked up. The slightest flush tinged her cheeks and the almost curve of her lips sent a flash of desire through him. His own smile in return was bright with the warmth of his love.

'You seek audience with me, Waltheof?' William beckoned his visitor to enter his private chamber and with another flick of his fingers dismissed the guard.

'Sire.' Waltheof bowed and advanced into the room, his footfalls crackling softly on the new green rushes that strewed the floor. William was seated in a curule chair before a charcoal brazier that had been lit to take the evening chill from the room. Two large fawn hounds lay at his feet. Both had been dozing, but now they raised their heads to watch Waltheof's approach.

Matilda sat across from him, some embroidery in her lap. Here in the private chamber she had removed her wimple and her sandy-blonde hair hung to her waist in two thick braids woven with ribbons of blue silk. Her rounded belly pushed against the fabric of her gown.

'Sit.' William indicated a folding stool with a leather seat.

Waltheof did so. The stool was slightly too small for his great frame and he hunched over uncomfortably. Matilda looked at him and he thought he detected a gleam of sympathy in her gaze, perhaps even a twitch of humour. He fondled the head of the nearest dog and it beat its tail on the rushes.

'Wine.' A clap of William's hands brought a lad from the corner of the room where he had been burnishing the Duke's helm.

'Sire.' With a show of great dignity Simon de Senlis poured wine into two drinking horns and offered the Queen a daintier goblet.

Although he felt sick with apprehension, Waltheof managed to find an encouraging wink for the boy and something approaching a smile. 'I see that you are training your chamberlain's son to follow in his footsteps,' he said.

William grunted. 'He's a good worker,' he conceded. 'I take on merit as much as breeding.' He nodded to Simon in dismissal and the boy returned to his work. The limp was noticeable but controlled. 'I know that you take an interest in him, my lord. Be assured that his talents will grant him a good and permanent position in my service.'

'I am glad, sire.' Waltheof took a swallow of the wine and almost coughed as it slipped down his parched throat. William was looking at him expectantly. Waltheof knew how impatient he was with petitioners who did not come straight to the point.

'Sire,' he began, paused to cough again into his clenched fist, and made himself speak. 'I know that you have shown much favour to me in vouchsafing my lands and granting me permission to dwell on them . . .'

'But you want more . . .' William said. His dark stare was hooded and impassive.

'Sire, I . . .' Stumbling would not help his cause. William would see it as weakness. Waltheof thrust out his jaw. 'Sire, I ask your permission for the right to take your niece Judith to wife.'

William neither spoke nor moved but studied him with the eyes of a hawk. Beneath the scrutiny, Waltheof felt as vulnerable as prey in the grass.

It was Matilda who broke the terrible silence. Leaning forward, she fixed him with a gaze no less piercing than her husband's. 'Has my niece endorsed your suit, Lord Waltheof?'

'She has, madam . . . but within the bounds of propriety,' he added hastily as he saw her expression grow pinched.

'One contradicts the other, my lord,' Matilda said severely. 'If my niece has given you encouragement of any kind, she has been very foolish.'

'No more encouragement than to say that I should seek your permission if I desire to court her.'

'And why should you "desire" to court her?' William's voice was quiet but terrifying. 'Because the sight of her inflames your lust, or because the thought of marrying into my bloodline inflames the lust of your ambition?'

Waltheof's complexion darkened. 'It is naught of lust or ambition,' he declared in a congested voice, furious that William was making his motives sound obscene and grasping.

'Then you should have been a monk indeed,' William sneered. 'All men are driven by their lusts and their ambitions. All men,' he repeated, thumping his chest to emphasise the point. 'It cannot be love, since you do not know the girl well . . . unless of course you are lying to me, and you and she have been conducting a liaison behind everyone's back.'

'I do not lie, sire,' Waltheof said hotly, feeling increasingly angry and humiliated. 'I came to you in honesty and good faith to seek your permission.'

William's eyes narrowed. 'I have given you much, Waltheof. Do not seek to strain the bounds of my generosity.'

'Then you refuse?' Waltheof began to tremble and a red mist crept across his vision.

'I refuse,' William said brusquely. 'You have my leave to go.'

'Will you tell me why you will not give your consent?' Waltheof's voice was hoarse with the effort of control.

'You would be wise not to push me,' William growled. 'Suffice to say that I have already been more than generous to you, my lord. You ask for too much.'

'So seeking your niece in marriage is too much?' Waltheof's upper lip curled back on a sneer. 'Is my English blood not to your taste?'

William looked him coldly up and down. 'It is naught of blood,' he said. 'But of merit and suitability. That is my last word on the matter. I hope I do not have to summon my guards.'

Waltheof swallowed and clenched his fists. Some final thread of self-preservation prevented him from using them. Turning on his heel he managed to leave the room with a modicum of tattered dignity, but once outside in the cold corridor he smashed his knuckles against the wall, tearing the skin, bruising to the bone, and let out a roar of anguish and rage so wild that it might have belonged to the white bear whose pelt lined his cloak.

'Last word!' he snarled in English. 'I will ram his last word down his throat until it chokes him!'

He strode into the hall where folk were preparing to bed down for the night. Waltheof should have been amongst them; he had his own sleeping space near the dais. Already members of his retinue were rolling out cloaks and blankets. 'Do not bother,' Waltheof snapped. 'We are not staying.'

'My lord earl?' His shieldbearer Hakon looked up at him in surprise.

'Go and tell my grooms to saddle our horses. We're leaving.'

'But . . .'

'But nothing!' Waltheof snarled. 'Do it!'

Waltheof's behaviour was so out of character that Hakon stood his ground. 'My lord, there is a curfew. No man may go abroad after dark, and the horses are bedded down for the night. Should we not wait until dawn?'

'I have William's leave to go,' Waltheof ground out. 'I will not stay a moment longer than I must.'

Still Hakon hesitated. He was almost twenty years older than Waltheof and had known his father well and served him with loyalty. Such credentials gave him the leeway to ask, 'Does this bode ill for us? Have you quarrelled with him?' He looked pointedly at Waltheof's bleeding knuckles.

Waltheof bit his lip, his restraint precarious. 'No to both questions,' he said in a choked voice. 'I'll tell the grooms myself. See that everyone else gets the order.'

Without giving Hakon further opportunity to argue, Waltheof strode out.

The air was moist and mild, a night for lovers. A night for fools. Cursing, Waltheof drew deep breaths filled with the almond scent of May blossom. Perhaps at the back of his mind he had known that William would refuse. Perhaps that was what had made him hold back for so long. Without having the brutality of the answer, it had been possible to dream. He knew in his heart that Judith would not fight the decision. Her uncle's word was the rule by which she lived, and, although she was strong-willed, that will was devoted to serving her family.

The red tide of his fury and disappointment dissipated in the gentle, scented air, leaving a weight of dull misery. Sucking on his grazed knuckles, Waltheof turned towards the stables. The grooms came sleepily from their loft, and with looks askance and much wordless grumbling kindled lanterns and set about the task of harnessing the mounts belonging to Waltheof's entourage.

Waltheof set about saddling Copper, his chestnut. It gave him something to do other than wallow in dark thoughts. His work was interrupted by the sound of rustling from a nearby stall, and on investigation, he discovered his skald and Judith's maid Sybille lying in a lover's nest of piled straw. Her light brown hair tumbled around her shoulders in disarray and her lips were red and kiss-swollen.

Usually Waltheof would have laughed, but tonight all humour had flown. 'Does Lady Judith know where you are?' he demanded grimly of the girl.

Sybille faced him squarely. 'No, my lord, and there is no reason to tell her since it is no concern of hers.'

'It would be if she knew. You do her reputation no good by sullying your own.' He scowled at Thorkel, who was looking at him with wounded astonishment. 'I am going home to Huntingdon tonight. Go or stay as you choose.' He led his chestnut out of the stall into the open air. Christ, it was so easy for them, the minstrel and the maidservant. Envy was a crimson wire in his chest.

The grooms were swiftly harnessing other beasts and his men were beginning to arrive from the hall with their travelling satchels and accoutrements. No one spoke, but their expressions were eloquent.

From his eye corner, Waltheof saw Thorkel murmur to Sybille before the girl slipped away through the darkness.

'William refused you then?' the skald asked, coming to Waltheof's side.

'It is none of your business.'

'When you are an earl, it is everyone's business,' Thorkel contradicted, his words dovetailing with Waltheof's thoughts of a moment since. 'Whatever has caused your anger, it will be all over Westminster come the morrow.'

'Well, I won't be here to listen,' Waltheof said savagely. He glared at Thorkel. 'William says that he has shown me enough favour. He says that I fail on merit and suitability.' He spat the last word as if it were poison.

'Ah,' said Thorkel.

'And since he is of that opinion, I am of no mind to stay.'

'You do not believe he will change his mind in time?' Thorkel asked. 'Sometimes when men have surprises sprung upon them, they react as if they have been thrown a live rat.'

'I doubt that William will change his mind between night and day,' Waltheof said bleakly. 'Better for us both if I leave.' He glowered at the Icelander. 'Stay if you wish. I am sure that Lady Judith's maid will continue to give you all the "comfort" you need.'

Thorkel shook his head and smiled wryly. 'Mistress Sybille is indeed engaging, but I have no mind to stay at court. Doubtless Earl Edwin or Morcar would offer me places in their retinues, but I would rather ride with you to Huntingdon than dwell in lust and luxury here.'

Slightly mollified, Waltheof gave a brusque nod. 'As you wish,' he said and swung into the saddle.

Overlooked in his corner, Simon hardly dared to rub the oiled cloth over the surface of the helm lest the slight whispering noise recall his presence to William and Matilda. Moments ago the King had summoned an older squire and sent him to fetch Judith. The air bristled like the atmosphere on the edge of a thunderstorm. Something bad was going to happen.

'Did you know about this attraction?' William demanded.

His wife shook her head. 'If I did, I would have quashed it at once,' she said. 'And I am sure that Adelaide would have done so too. I know that she was in Earl Waltheof's debt for saving Judith from that bolting horse in Fécamp – we all were – but it went no further than that.'

'Obviously it did,' William contradicted grimly.

'Certainly not in my sight,' his wife said on an indignant note. 'Adelaide is the most conscientious of mothers – you know she is. It could be that Waltheof has overstated his case – perhaps mistaken a word in passing as proof of a deeper interest.'

William grunted and chewed on a thumbnail. 'Perhaps,' he said sceptically.

In his corner Simon remembered the clandestine meetings that had taken place between Judith and Waltheof in Fécamp. The tales he could tell if he chose. Almost as if fearing the words would spill out of their own accord, he tightened his lips.

'So you would not consider a match between Waltheof and Judith at all?' Matilda asked into the heavy silence. 'Do you truly believe that he is unsuitable?'

William stared into the brazier and said nothing for a time. Then he looked at his wife. 'Waltheof is young and rash – acts before he thinks. I like him, but he is untried in battle and in diplomacy. His heart rules his head, and that is not a good trait for a man of authority.'

'Indeed not . . . my lord.' Matilda's voice held a note of amused irritation and Simon was surprised to hear William chuckle gruffly in response.

'I do my best to hide my single weakness,' he said. 'And I am glad that you aid and abet me.'

'And if I did not?'

'I think you know the answer.'

There was another silence, ended by a knock on the chamber door.

'Enter!' William raised his voice to command, thereby sparing Simon the need to rise and show himself.

A guard opened the door and ushered Judith, her mother and her stepfather into the room. Judith was as white as a new cheese. Adelaide looked impatient and irritated, Eudo of Champagne bewildered.

'Why have you sent for me at this late hour?' Adelaide demanded of her brother, and gave him such a perfunctory obeisance that it was almost an insult.

William gestured her to a bench positioned near the brazier. 'Perhaps you should ask your daughter that question.'

Adelaide refused the offer of a seat and her gaze darted between William and Judith. 'I do not know your meaning.'

Leaving her mother's side, Judith knelt before her uncle. 'Waltheof of Huntingdon has asked your permission to seek me in marriage, hasn't he?' she said.

'What?' Adelaide's voice started low and finished on a new octave. Her eyes widened and blazed. Leaving her astonished husband, she crossed the room and stood over her daughter with hands on hips. 'Have you been conniving with him behind my back?'

'Peace, Adelaide.' William raised his right hand, palm outwards. 'Since it has reached my ears, let me be the one to deal with it now.'

Dusky colour heated his sister's cheekbones. She prided herself on running an orderly household and her brother's terse comment suggesting that she had been lax was galling. 'If you have brought shame on this house, I will see you confined to a nunnery,' she hissed at her daughter.

Judith swallowed and raised her chin. 'I have done nothing of which to be ashamed.'

William narrowed his lids. 'And yet you knew without my speaking of the reason why I have sent for you. Does that not suggest that you and the Earl of Huntingdon have already made your own arrangements?'

Judith held her uncle's gaze. It was the hardest thing she had ever had to do. She knew that if she relaxed her spine for one moment, she would melt in a boneless heap of terror. 'There were no arrangements, sire,' she said, and wondered what Waltheof had said to William. Waltheof had no skill at dissembling. She could only pray that he had not mentioned that interlude in Fécamp.

'So why should he come to me with hope in his eyes?' William demanded.

Judith gazed at him mutely, not knowing what to say.

'Answer me, or by God, I will indeed do as your mother suggests and see you closeted in a nunnery!' William thundered, slamming his fist on his thigh.

'I . . . .' She chewed her lip. 'I know that Waltheof had a certain regard for me, but I did not encourage him. He . . . he did broach the subject of marriage and I said that he would have to approach you . . .'

'And how long ago was this?'

'He first spoke of the matter in Normandy. I thought perhaps he had forgotten, but when I saw him again he said that he still intended to seek your permission . . .' She clasped her hands together until the knuckles showed white. 'I have kept my distance and obeyed my duty.'

William grunted. 'And if I had agreed to his request, what would you have said?'

Adelaide spluttered, the sound declaring without words what she thought of the notion.

'I would have been bound by the decree of your will, whatever your decision, sire,' Judith murmured and felt herself wilting beneath the blaze of his stare.

'So you have no especially fond regard for Waltheof of Huntingdon?'

Her stomach churned. 'I am grateful to him for saving my life.'

'But it goes no deeper than that.'

'No, sire.'

There was a long and thoughtful pause. 'It seems then,' William said at last, 'that the young man was building a mountain out of no more than a heap of soil. I do not doubt your virtue, niece, but I hope that you will not make a habit of sending me young men of whom you have passing acquaintance to ask for you in marriage.'

'I did not know what else to do,' Judith said.

'Well, the dilemma is easily solved,' Adelaide spoke out angrily. 'From this day forth you do not leave the confines of the bower lest I be at your side.'

Judith was not quite swift enough to conceal a grimace and Adelaide seized upon it. 'Yes, my girl, I have clearly been too lax with you, and that slut of a maid is no protection.'

'I have done nothing wrong,' Judith reiterated, and pushed from her mind the remembrance of being kissed and kissing back at the foot of the stairs in Fécamp.

'Let matters rest, Adelaide,' William said. 'Waltheof has either left the court or is leaving on the morrow, and I made the situation plain to him. He knows that I will grant him no further privileges above those that he has. Judith has received her warning. I know that she will be more cautious in future.'

'So will I,' Adelaide said grimly. Judith's heart sank.

As Judith followed her mother and stepfather to the door there was a clatter behind them. Whirling round Judith saw young Simon de Senlis picking up the banner that his elbow had dislodged and sent tumbling. Judith met the youth's foxbrown eyes and saw the knowledge in them. If he spoke even half of what he knew the scandal would burn her alive. She thought that she could trust him, but she was not certain. At least he was fond of Waltheof. Blurting out his knowledge would not help his hero's cause. She could only hope that he was more discreet than she had been.

As the door closed, William beckoned to Simon. 'I have no need to tell you that what goes forth in these chambers is not to be discussed outside that door,' he said tersely.

'No, your grace.' Simon returned William's dark stare before looking down as custom demanded. 'I know when to hold my tongue.'

William's mouth twitched. 'And when to be as quiet as a mouse so that you are overlooked,' he said.

Simon flashed a glance from beneath his brows, so innocent that William's almost smile became a grunt of amusement. 'I hope that you have not been paying so much attention to your ears that you have neglected your other duties,' he said and held out his hand. 'Bring me that helm.'

Simon duly fetched the King's helm from the corner where he had been oiling and burnishing it. The metal shone with all the colours of the forge, an iridescent bloom of blue-gold on the iron surface.

William examined the work and nodded with thoughtful satisfaction. 'Large ears, quick hands, a close mouth. It seems, young man, that you will go far.'

Simon reddened with pleasure.

'The trick is of course,' William said, still turning the helm in his hands, 'to know when to stop.'

'Who is Waltheof of Huntingdon?' Eudo of Champagne demanded of his wife. His stepdaughter had retired to her pallet, pleading a headache, and Adelaide had let her go without demur – more, he thought, from wanting her out of the way than from compassion. They were standing together in a corner of the hall. It was draughty away from the braziers, but relatively private.

'You must have seen him,' she said impatiently. 'The tall one with the red hair and white bearskin cloak.'

'Ah, yes.' Eudo nodded with a slight narrowing of his eyes. 'A friend of Ralf de Gael of Norfolk to judge from the manner they were laughing together.'

Adelaide sniffed disparagingly. 'They are of an ilk,' she said, 'and neighbours.'

Eudo's lips twitched. His wife obviously had a wasp in her wimple over the Earl of Huntingdon. 'Whoever knew a tall man who was wise or a red-haired one who was faithful?' He flippantly quoted the old proverb.

'Precisely,' Adelaide snapped. 'And it is no cause for amusement.'

Eudo grimaced. His wife had brought him the prestige of an alliance with the house of Normandy but she was a shrew of the highest order. Putting her in her place was not an option when her brother was Duke of Normandy and King of England.

'Has Judith truly been indiscreet with him?' he asked.

'Enough to form an attraction, but not sufficient to cause a scandal. However I should have been more vigilant. There are always foxes prowling around the henhouse in search of a victim.'

'I do not doubt your vigilance,' Eudo murmured and glanced across the hall at William's three sons, who were chasing each other boisterously in and out of the aisles of the hall. Queen Matilda was swelling with yet another pregnancy. All he had thus far of his own marriage were two stepdaughters resembling their mother and the prestige of the bond with the house of Normandy. It would be a fine thing to set a son in his wife's womb. She was not barren, just reluctant. Perhaps a new child would lessen her intensity over her daughters too.

'What of this Waltheof's lands? If he is an earl, might not the match be suitable?'

'You would see your stepdaughter wed to an ignorant Viking?' Adelaide's bosom heaved with indignation.

Eudo shrugged. He was not going to remind his wife that her own mother was the daughter of a common tanner. That would have been tantamount to treason. 'I would see her content,' he said.

Adelaide gave him a scathing look. 'I doubt that Judith could be content with such a man,' she said glacially. 'He has no sense of what is fitting.'

'But she would be a countess. Mayhap we should investigate how large and prosperous his earldom is.'

His wife raised a scornful eyebrow. 'We can do better for her than Waltheof of Huntingdon,' she snapped.

Eudo inclined his head as if conceding the point, but he was not taken in by her dismissal of the notion. There had definitely been a spark of interest in her eyes. He was a patient man and the notion of adding an English earldom to his family's concerns was an attractive one.

Across the hall there was a loud commotion as William's eldest sons Robert and Richard caught their brother Rufus, flung him to the ground and sat on him while Robert de Bêlleme attempted to stuff floor rushes into the victim's mouth.

Eudo watched the ensuing struggle with folded arms and did not attempt to intervene. He was fond of the older boys, who were high-spirited, boisterous youths, but he had never been able to warm towards the third son. William was considering Rufus for the Church and the boy was being educated at Saint Stephen's in Caen, although he had been released from his lessons to come to England and see his mother made queen. Rufus was a plump, unprepossessing child with sandy-white hair and lashes that put Eudo in mind of a pig. He seemed to squeal like one most of the time too.

'Christ, someone send that boy back to the cloister,' muttered Robert of Mortain, coming to join Eudo and Adelaide. 'He screams like a girl.'

Eudo gave a pained smile of acknowledgement. Robert of Mortain was a maternal half-brother to William and Adelaide. Eudo did not particularly like him, but he respected him, and they shared antipathy towards their youngest nephew. Both were content to stand by and watch his brothers bounce on him as if he were a cushion while de Bêlleme attempted to prise open Rufus' tightly clenched jaw.

However someone else was willing to step in. One of William's senior pages, who was passing through the hall carrying two sharpened spears, approached the fracas, stooped, and murmured to the bullies. Looking irritated and petulant, they got off Rufus and let him go, although De Bêlleme gave him a sharp kick in the ribs. The older youths swaggered from the hall, leaving their victim choking and blubbering on the floor. The page stooped to comfort Rufus and after a moment helped him to his feet.

Mortain lost interest and turned away. 'If he cannot fight his own battles now, he will never amount to anything,' he growled.

Eudo nodded agreement and turned away too. He had promised to buy Adelaide some gold strap ends for a girdle she was weaving, and he could tell from the look in her eyes that she was growing impatient.

Gasping for breath, his complexion blotched, Rufus looked up at his saviour. 'Did my father really want to see them?'

Simon shook his head. 'No, my lord, but it seemed the best way of stopping them without provoking a fight.'

'You should have st . . . st . . . stuck them in the ribs,' Rufus said, his grey-flecked eyes bright with vehemence and tears. 'They'll be after y . . . you when they realise you've tricked them.' He dragged his sleeve across his nose, leaving a shiny trail on his cuff.

Simon shrugged. 'I can take care of myself,' he said with more confidence than he felt. He had no particular fear of William's older sons, but Robert de Bêlleme was a different cauldron of pottage entirely. 'Best not linger here though. I'm going to the armoury to get these spear tips honed – if you want to come?'

Rufus nodded. 'Thank you,' he said. 'I won't forget this.' Giving another loud sniff he extended his hand to Simon. His fingers were heavy and soft to the touch, still clammy with the cold sweat of fear and struggle, but Simon betrayed not a twitch of distaste. He knew what it was like to be viewed as flawed. Rufus might stammer, might be an ugly and clumsy child, but for all his awkwardness he had a swift brain and a generous heart. If he said that he would not forget, then it was true – both in matters of friendship and enmity. His elder brothers, for all their outward strength and boasting, did not have the staying power of a pair of grasshoppers.

Companionably, side by side, one lame, the other walking with his customary clumsy wallow, they headed towards the armoury, and Rufus insisted on carrying one of the spears.

CHAPTER 9

The fenland stretched away to the horizon, grasses bleached to shades of gold by the blaze of the early September sun, the meres and pools glinting like eyes as they caught the light. The song of reed warblers drenched the air and flies hovered in the ripples of heat rising from the reeds and sedges. Through the shimmer Waltheof watched Crowland Abbey's herd of white cows graze the rich pasture. Autumn might be on the horizon, but it was still no more than a distant speck and the sun still had power to burn.

'You are content, my son?'

Sweeping his hair off his brow, Waltheof studied the small monk standing at his side. Abbot Ulfcytel looked no older than he had done fifteen years ago when Waltheof had entered the noviciate, but he must be at least three score by now. The skin was still smooth, and, although the existing lines had deepened with time, there were remarkably few new ones.

'I wish that I could say that I was,' Waltheof murmured. 'Indeed, I sometimes wish that I were one of those cows with naught to concern me but the grazing of the meadow.'

'You would still be bedevilled by the flies,' Ulfcytel said shrewdly. 'And before winter you would be in danger of facing the poleaxe.'

Waltheof sighed. 'You are right,' he conceded. 'I do not suppose that life as an ox would be much different to the life I lead now . . . although perhaps less knowledge would be a boon. I know that I should have the grace to accept what is to be, but recently I have found it hard to come by.'

Ulfcytel said nothing and turned back the way they had come, following the dusty path towards the cool, grey stone of the abbey. Waltheof paced beside him. Usually a visit to Crowland and time spent with Ulfcytel would help to settle his restlessness – like the hand of a ploughmaster on the yoke of a favoured ox, he thought wryly. But today there had been no such peace. News had arrived that precluded such a possibility.

Since returning to his lands, he had visited the monastery often, a part of him yearning for the spiritual grace that had been his as a young oblate learning his Psalter at Ulfcytel's knee. That yearning was strong today. For two pins he would have exchanged his rich tunic for a simple Benedictine habit.

'All around me I see people struggling beneath William's yoke,' he said as they toiled along the path, the late summer's blaze making their limbs heavy and bringing a glisten of sweat to their brows. 'And I do nothing. I bury my head, I feign ignorance.'

Ulfcytel made a sound of acknowledgement and doubt. 'Has your own lot been difficult?' he queried. 'Are your people not contented and your lands peaceful?'

Waltheof grimaced. 'It is true that my lands are peaceful,' he said 'and that my lot has been easier than many. But the King's hand is heavy. It seems to me that he takes all and gives very little back.'

'But if you rise against him and you fail, it may be that he will take all and give nothing at all back,' Ulfcytel murmured. 'Others have tried and failed this last year, have they not?'

Waltheof paused to look at the abbey buildings. The church was dedicated to Saint Guthlac, and had been raised above the marshy ground on oak pilings with additional soil brought from Upton, nine miles away. While his gaze admired the toil of man in the cause of God's glorification, he pondered the Abbot's warning.

Filled with discontent, Edwin and Morcar had fled the court and tried to raise rebellion but William had put it down as easily as swatting a couple of flies. Once again the brothers were hostages at court and castles were being built in the English heartlands to quash any further notions of revolt. Edwin was still being promised a royal bride, but Waltheof thought the Earl of Mercia had little chance of seeing that promise kept. The Normans appeared not to think that English husbands were good enough for their daughters – or nieces.

'Edgar Atheling has made his escape to the Scots court with his mother and sisters,' he said.

The older man exhaled heavily. 'And so could you, if that was your desire, but I do not think that it is. If you stay here then you have to accept the burdens laid upon you by the Normans. Complaint will only sour you.'

Waltheof's lips twitched. 'You mean either shit or get off the privy.'

A down-to-earth, unaffected man, Ulfcytel was not in the least perturbed by the robust language. 'That is exactly what I mean. It is no use bemoaning your lot. Either accept it with a smile or set about changing it.'

Waltheof felt a rush of affection for the small monk. Ulfcytel was very different from Waltheof's sire, the magnificent Siward of Northumberland, but the bond between the Abbot and Waltheof was as powerful as that between father and son. 'That is why I came to speak to you. I have had news today and I do not know what to do with it. I need your advice.'

'Ah,' said Ulfcytel, rubbing his jaw where tiny spikes of silver stubble glinted in the sunlight. 'I thought there was more to this visit than the spare time a man has when the harvest is all but gathered in.'

'A messenger came to Huntingdon two nights ago,' Waltheof said. 'From Earl Gospatric in the North Country.'

'Ah,' said Ulfcytel again, rubbing harder, making a rasping sound.

'King Sweyn of Denmark has sent his fleet into the Humber – two hundred and forty ships filled with warriors ready to fight the Normans.'

'And you want my advice whether to join him or abstain?' Ulfcytel saw the eagerness and doubt written clearly in the young man's deep blue eyes and was troubled.

Waltheof folded his arms, tucking his hands into his armpits as if putting temptation out of his way, but a moment later he lowered them and clutched unconsciously at the hilt of his dagger. 'It is perhaps the last chance that Englishmen will have to be rid of the Normans,' he said. 'My father was a Dane; I have blood ties with the men in those ships. I do not believe I would have stirred from my lands for the sons of Harold Godwinsson, but this is different. I can almost smell victory on the air.'

'To a man of the Church, victory and defeat both smell suspiciously of blood and burning,' Ulfcytel said, turning round to look at the peaceful scene they had just left.

Waltheof turned too, but his gaze was looking inwards. 'If I go north and lend my arm to the uprising, then perhaps I will be able to regain all the lands that my father held and that the Godwinssons denied to me.'

'Morcar might have something to say about that,' Ulfcytel murmured.

'Morcar does not have the advantage of my tie with the Danes.' Waltheof's good-natured expression was replaced by one that was narrow and stubborn.

Ulfcytel shook his head. 'I think, my son, that whatever I say will make no difference. You have made up your mind, and rather than asking me for advice you have come to tell me of your intention to join this uprising.'

'You disapprove?'

'I disapprove of all warfare,' Ulfcytel said. 'The Norman king has proven himself repeatedly in battle. You came to me with your nightmares of what you witnessed at Exeter. Has it all faded from your mind so swiftly?'

'No,' Waltheof said grimly. 'It has remained with me every waking moment.'

'Then why risk the same happening to your own lands?'

Waltheof sighed. 'Because I stood back at Hastings. Because the Danes and the English are my people – not the Normans. Because . . .' He made a gesture to show that he could not explain what he was feeling.

'Because your heart rules your mind,' Ulfcytel said almost sorrowfully, 'and it has always been so.'

'Surely a man must be guided by what is in his heart?'

'But curbed by the rein of his reason.'

Waltheof tugged on his moustache as if in thought, but Ulfcytel could see that his decision was already made. He would join the Danes and march with them because they were 'his people', because kinship mattered when kin were few.

'Father, will you give me your blessing?' Waltheof went down on his knees in the dust before Ulfcytel and bowed his head, his copper hair falling forward to expose the tender white nape of his neck. The sight reminded the Abbot of how much a boy Waltheof still was – and likely would be all of his life.

Gently, with a paternal ache of tears behind his lids, Ulfcytel laid his hands upon Waltheof's sun-hot hair. 'God be with you,' he murmured softly, 'and bring you through all trials with grace.'

Fires twinkled in the night, hundreds of them, lighting the spread of the Danish army and the English who had flocked to their banners. The surface of the River Humber seethed with longships, lanterns lighting the carved prows and sending shimmers of gold across the dark water.

Drunk on mead, camaraderie and hope, Waltheof feasted with the sons of King Sweyn of Denmark and roared death to the Normans with the rest of them. These men were his kin. He recognised himself in their joyful fierceness. Here he did not have to be abstemious and guard his tongue. Here he did not have to curb his laughter. He arm-wrestled with Viking warriors and his strength was acclaimed. He was a true son of Siward Digerra, accepted, fêted and treated as a hero, not a green boy.

Come the morning the Danish army, its ranks swollen by Northumbrians and Scots, by the men of Holderness and Lindsey, by Saxon rebels from every corner of England, would march on York, the old Norse capital of England. Hopes were high, and increased with each swallow of mead. The Normans would be driven from the land and their hated castles torn down.

Waltheof ceased drinking before he reached a state of help-less intoxication. He did not want to go mead-witted into battle on the morrow. While such a state might enhance his courage and daring, it would numb his responses. To go up against a sober Norman would be intense folly. The Danish leaders seemed to think the same way, for they curtailed the feasting early and commanded men to seek their slumber so that they would be ready to advance with the dawn.

Waltheof slept with his axe for company and thought that, had matters been different, he would be lying in a feather bed at Huntingdon with his dark-haired Norman wife at his side – perhaps even a child of their mingled blood in the cradle. The notion was too sweet and sad for a battle eve. He closed his eyes and prayed, the Latin words filling his head in drink-muddled snatches, echoing as if they were being chanted in a church.

He dreamed of battle, but instead of the physical effort of wielding his axe he was trying to muster arguments in his head. He found himself engaged in a contest of wits, but the more he racked his brains, the closer he came to defeat. He could hear himself shouting, and a woman's voice shrilling in furious reply. She had all the strength; he was powerless. As the argu-ment drained him, she forced him to his knees and he saw that they were in a courtyard, surrounded by accusing faces, none of them friendly. On the edge of the crowd a child gazed at him out of solemn, dark-blue eyes. As he looked at her, she turned away and Waltheof knew that in some way he did not understand, he had failed her. He bent his head; there was a scything pain and then nothing.

.He awoke in a cold sweat, his heart thundering and the sharpness of the pain transmuted into the dull assault of a drink-induced headache. The shouting continued outside of his dream, but there was no anger now, just the exhortations of men eager to march on York and drive the Normans out.

As the massed English and Dane army approached the city the smell of smoke gusted at them, reminding Waltheof of Exeter and turning his stomach. The scouts who had gone ahead reported that the captains of the Norman garrison had burned down the houses immediately in front of the castle so that the English would have to cross open ground in order to lay siege to the keep. The flames had spread from the initial burning and had engulfed much of the city, including the cathedral itself.

Waltheof gripped the haft of his axe and prayed as they advanced into York. Those townsfolk who had not fled hastened to join the invading army, cheering, waving brooms, pitchforks, or spears that had been kept well hidden in the rafters. Elation and pride united with the roil of emotion in Waltheof's belly. Tears prickled behind his lids, some the result of wind-blown smoke but most caused by the welcome of the crowd. He was entering the city that had been the Norse capital of England for over two hundred years, a settlement that had been familiar to his father as Earl of Northumbria, and to his dead brother. Now their mantle was his and he felt the pride coursing through him with each beat of his heart.

A thick drift of smoke gusted across the advancing army and suddenly the cheers became screams and shouts of warning. The Norman commanders were sallying from the keep using a charge of cavalry and heavily armed soldiers to try to scatter the invaders.

Without warning, without time to realise and assimilate,

Waltheof's section was confronted by a conroi of mounted Normans. Hakon screamed and went down beneath the trampling hooves and the thrust of a lance. The razored steel punched through his throat, killing him instantly. The knight withdrew the lance with a jerk of effort and turned on the gaping, horrified Waltheof.

Waltheof's mind ceased to function and instinct took over. As the spear thrust at him he brought up the axe, whirling it round and down to chop off the haft beneath the socket. The knight groped for his sword and Waltheof struck again, and again, his lungs filling with a howl of rage and denial. Horse and knight went down, and so did the footsoldier who ran to defend them. Waltheof licked his lips and tasted the sweet saltiness of blood. The edge of his axe ran red, and he felt a terrible exhilaration. No more demonstrating his skills and strength for the paltry entertainment of his Norman captors. This was the reason why he had sweated on the training ground. This was *his* entertainment now, and when he had finished there would not be a single Norman left in the city of York.

Morning mist wove between the trees of the Gloucestershire forest in milky ribbons and a red sunrise filtered through the turning leaves. Simon rode his mount along the edge of the woodland, glad of his cloak, for although the day was set to be fair there was still a chill in the air this early. The King had decided upon a day's hunting and the court was gathering in preparation. He could hear the shouts of the kennel keepers calling the hounds to order and the boisterous laughter of men keen for a day's sport.

Simon was eager too. Since breaking his leg and enduring months of convalescence followed by the painful struggle to return to his duties, he valued such days as these. They allowed him to test himself to the limit, to force his will through the pain and keep up with or even exceed the other squires. In the saddle his handicap was minimal. He had to ride with his left foot at an odd angle in the stirrup, but he had learned to adjust to that, and the high pommel and cantle on the saddle gave him additional support. He was never going to make a jouster, but that did not matter. His slight, wiry build was meant for reconnaissance and scouting, for nimbleness and travelling light. Besides, to be a good battle commander Simon knew it was better to have an overview of the fighting rather than be in the thick of it.

He slackened the rein and let his pony pick its way along the edge of the trees until they came to the track that led back to the hunting lodge. William would want him soon to carry his spear or hold his cloak.

Two gossiping women, walking down the track towards the lodge, carried rushwork baskets laden with freshly picked mushrooms and fungi. Simon eyed the bounty as they drew level. He was very fond of the mushroom pasties that William's cook made when the ingredients were available. Served with the best bread and tart blackberry sauce, there was no finer dish in the world.

Remembering the English that Waltheof had taught him, he greeted the women pleasantly in their own language.

They looked at him, startled, muttered a response, and heads lowered, wimples drawn across their faces, hurried past.

Simon was wounded, but not surprised at the rebuff. The English had acknowledged William as their king, but grudgingly – because they were forced to do so. They yielded deference with hatred in their eyes and it was not going to change for the sake of a single greeting.

He turned his pony to follow the women. Behind him, hooves thundered on the track and a messenger hurtled towards the lodge on a sweat-foamed courser. The man bellowed at the women to get out of his way and they leaped for their lives with screams of shock. A basket of mushrooms went flying and scattered the efforts of one woman's toil far and wide. She shook her fist at the horseman's dust and cursed him. Then her glittering eyes fixed on Simon and her voice fell to a low mutter. There was nothing Simon could do. If he dismounted to help gather the scattered mushrooms his lameness would be a hindrance and he would be vulnerable to attack. Besides, the messenger had been riding so swiftly that his news was clearly urgent and Simon wanted to know what it was.

Abruptly he reined his pony about and galloped in the messenger's wake. He could almost feel the women's glares burning his back and knew that they were calling him a Norman whoreson.

The messenger had dismounted outside the hunting lodge and was on his knees before William. Simon arrived in time to see the King's brows draw together and his colour begin to darken in response to what was being said. In the three years since Simon had come to court he had never seen William in a rage. Angry on occasion, it was true, but always a cold anger, held down with iron control. William was scorching now, though, his complexion almost purple.

'It is true, sire,' the messenger panted, his head bowed and sweat dripping from his forelock. 'The North has risen against your rule. The Danes have anchored in the Humber and marched upon York. Lord Malet begs that you come with all haste.' He coughed and someone stepped forward with a cup of the wine the hunters had been drinking. The messenger took several grateful gulps.

'All the North?' William repeated. His own voice was dry and husky, but when he too was offered wine he thrust it aside.

'Maersweyn, Gospatric, Edgar Atheling,' the messenger said, 'and Waltheof of Huntingdon. It was he who led them into York, and he and his men who caused the most damage. North of the Humber there are naught but English and Danes.'

Simon's stomach plummeted. He had been hoping to visit Waltheof in his earldom. He thought that Waltheof liked the Normans, that he was prepared to be part of their rule . . . but perhaps he too was like those women with their mushrooms, serving because he was forced and hating every moment.

William's eyes had narrowed at the mention of Waltheof's name. 'Splendour of God!' he rasped. 'Once and for all I will show the English who is their king, and I will write the lesson so large and in so much suffering that no one will be in any doubt!'

The hunt was abandoned; the hounds were returned to the kennels but the horses remained saddled. The messenger was ordered to change his mount, refresh himself and be prepared to take to the road again with instructions to William's commanders.

Simon helped to load baggage wains with William's effects, which were to follow in the wake of the rapid cavalry advance. No concessions were made to Simon's disability and he fetched and carried with the rest of them. Stools, hangings, caskets, lamps and candle prickets, trestle legs and boards, spare cups and flagons, a set of gaming counters and a tafel board. Then he aided the grooms harness the cobs to pull the wains and the pack ponies to carry more immediate supplies such as food and bedding and the royal tent. His leg ached ferociously, but he forced himself through the pain. If he stopped, he would have to think. Toiling like a demon helped to keep his anger and distress at bay.

As he struggled to load a sack of oats onto a pony's back, his arms burning with effort and his legs in danger of collapse, the load was taken from him by his father, who heaved it the rest of the way across the pack saddle.

'Ants work together,' said Richard de Rules, 'so why should you think you can do it all on your own?'

'I can manage,' Simon said defensively, but his legs had begun to tremble, giving the lie to his words.

'So can we all, but a little help makes things easier. I've been watching you from a distance and you've been working like a slave with a whip at your back.' From his shoulder he unslung a small leather costrel and handed it to his son.

Simon pulled out the stopper and drank. It was the King's best wine, potent and smooth. Usually the nearest he got to it was pouring it into goblets when he was on duty in the private chamber. The warmth of the drink burned into his stomach and fortified his limbs.

'What's wrong?' De Rules placed a perceptive hand on his son's taut shoulders.

Simon shook his head. 'Nothing.'

. His father's gaze remained steady. 'It's Earl Waltheof, isn't it?'

Simon swallowed and felt his eyes begin to burn. He turned within the shelter of his father's embrace and fiddled with a buckle on the pack pony's bridle. 'I thought that when Lord William refused him Lady Judith he would turn against us, but he didn't . . . he just went and stayed on his lands. So then I began to think everything was all right . . . and that I could go and visit him . . .'

De Rules sighed. 'Perhaps everything would have been all right if the Danes had not arrived,' he said. 'Even if the King had given Lady Judith to Waltheof, I do not know that he would have remained loyal. He is half Dane after all, and his father is buried in the city of York. His heart must surely lie in that direction.'

Simon shook his head. 'He is our enemy now.'

'Yes,' said his father gently. 'I am afraid that he is.'

CHAPTER 10

I t was the shortest day of the year, and the darkest. Lowering clouds and heavy drizzle had drawn a dark curtain across the land, so that the space between dawn and dusk was little more than twilight.

In the antechamber of the Queen's apartments in Winchester, Judith directed a maidservant to lay more charcoal on the brazier. Rain spattered against the shutters like tiny stones. Over the hills of the North Country it would be falling as snow, she thought. They heard sporadic reports of the hard-fought skirmishes between her uncle's troops and the English and Danish rebels. Bitter, bloody, no quarter given. Reports said that all the land north of a town called Stafford was now a smoking, ravaged waste, that wherever her uncle went fire and sword were his terrible companions. There were rumours about Waltheof too. How he had slaughtered a hundred Normans single-handedly at York in a battle frenzy the equal of any berserker in a Norse saga. She had known that he had grudges to settle, but the depth and wildness of his rage had frightened her. Perhaps it was as well that she was not to be his wife.

From behind the closed door of the main chamber, Judith heard her mother give another low moan. The soothing voice of the midwife followed, with the sound of water splashing from pitcher to bowl.

'Surely the labour should not take as long as this.' Her sister

Adela moved from the window embrasure where she had been standing, supposedly spinning fleece, although there were scarcely two yards of thread wound onto the drop spindle from the distaff stuffed through her belt. 'Queen Matilda only took from matins to prime to birth Prince Henry, but Mama's been labouring twice as long as that.'

Judith shrugged. 'I know not,' she said, her tone short because she was worried. The infant her mother was struggling to birth had been conceived during the coronation festivities, the result of deliberate strategy. Eudo said that he was entitled to try to beget an heir. Adelaide, a stickler for duty, had been forced to agree, and in her forty-first year, with daughters old enough for marriage, had found herself with child again. Throughout the pregnancy she had been ill. Judith and Adela had done as much fetching and carrying as the maids, massaging their mother's swollen legs and feeding her slivers of expensive imported ginger to aid her querulous digestion.

'What if she dies?' Adela's lower lip quivered.

Judith rubbed her hands together. In spite of the fresh building of charcoal, the sealed shutters and the two gowns she wore over her undershift, she was cold. 'She won't die,' she said tersely. 'The midwives would have sent for the priest by now if that was the case, and Sybille would have been out to us. Don't you dare start snivelling!'

'I'm not.' Adela gave a huge sniff and folded her arms beneath her breasts in a defensive gesture.

Judith folded her arms too, keeping herself to herself, even though she could tell that Adela wanted the comfort of a hug.

A fresh burst of rain peppered against the shutters and the wind rattled the catch so hard that for a moment it seemed as if the wild afternoon would burst into the room. The wind died, and in the lull that followed a baby's wail pierced the heavy wooden door between the main chamber and anteroom. Thin as a reed, sharp as an awl.

The girls stared towards the sound, transfixed. Judith's stomach churned. The door flung open and Sybille came out to them, her face flushed as if she had been labouring too and her sleeves pushed back up her wrists. 'You have a brother,' she declared with a half-moon grin. 'A fine boy.' She stood aside so they could enter the birthing chamber.

Adelaide was propped against a pile of bolsters in the great bed. Her dark brown hair, usually secured in two tight braids, was loose around her shoulders, since to have any bindings or knots in the birthing chamber might have impeded the delivery. A statue of Saint Margaret, patron saint of women in labour, stood in a niche, two candles burning either side of her image. Swaddled in Adelaide's arms was a small, pucker-faced bundle with a quiff of golden hair.

Adelaide looked up at her daughters. There were bruised smudges beneath her eyes and her lips were bloody where she had bitten them in her attempt not to give vent to her pain. But beneath the suffering there was glittering triumph and a love that was as fierce as fire, a love that had never kindled for the labour of bearing female children. Seeing that look, Judith was filled with a huge and jealous resentment. It took every ounce of her determination to approach the bed and look at the newborn intruder.

'How is he to be named?' she asked.

'Stephen – it is one favoured by Eudo's line,' Adelaide said. 'Let the best wine kegs be broached and let everyone drink a cup to honour his birth. I trust you to see to it.' Her gaze swept briefly over Judith then dropped again to the new treasure of her son.

Adela leaned over her baby half-brother and extended a fore-finger so that he curled his minute hand around it. 'He's beautiful,' she said, her expression utterly besotted.

Judith's stomach heaved at the betrayal. 'I'll do it now, Mother,' she said in a choked voice, and fled the stench of the birthing chamber before she was sick.

Seated on his campstool, Waltheof listened to the mourning of gulls and drew his bearskin cloak around him, seeking warmth and knowing that the gesture was fruitless. The cold came from within and had little to do with the bone deep chill of the January morning outside his tent. No longer did the fire of battle burn through his bones. The conflagration had been too fierce, too intense to last, and Waltheof did not have the nature for coddling a flame once the initial blaze had died down.

York had fallen. That part had been bright and glorious, although he could remember little enough of the battle. They said that he had fought like a hero; that it was as if the great Earl Siward himself had returned to wreak vengeance on the Normans who had dared to violate his slumber. Thorkel had composed stirring battle songs to honour Waltheof's prowess: there had been huge rejoicing, and every man, woman and child in York had rushed to tear down the hated keeps that the Normans had erected to control the city. Those moments had been dazzling – a great blaze of triumph and exultation. The Norman usurpers would be driven from the land. Waltheof had been so certain, so sure, so filled with burning enthusiasm. Now it was all ashes blowing in the wind.

Rising from the campstool, he swept his lank hair off his brow and went outside into the chill morning air. A fine drizzle was falling, so cold that it was almost sleet and the land was lost in a misted grey haze. They should never have torn down the castles at York, he thought. It had been a mistake. They had no fortifications to bolster their position when William came raging to the North.

Allies had melted away like butter off a hot griddle. The Scots, the Northumbrians had plundered and scattered. The Danes had returned to their ships, feeding off the land like migrant geese but showing small commitment to stay and fight.

Toki brought him a cup of hot mead and Waltheof took it gratefully, holding the cup in his hands like a small heart. There had been no stopping William. Organised, determined, cold as iron, he had pushed northwards, destroying everything in his path. Waltheof was still ashamed that he had retreated, but there had been no alternative. The fortresses were burned, their army of its own volition scattering to gorge on the delights of victory and plunder. Whatever was visited upon them was their own fault.

They had heard terrible tales of William's wrath. That entire villages had been destroyed – the livestock slaughtered, the young men executed, so that never again would the North be able to rise in rebellion. On Christmas Day William had sent to Winchester for his regalia and had worn it in York's devastated ruins, setting the stamp of his rule upon the city.

Now, too late, Waltheof understood the true power of the man to whom he had given his oath of allegiance and then reneged. The ruthless, single-minded determination, the skills of leadership were beyond anything that the rebels could match. What use was personal courage against the inexorable force of disciplined Norman troops?

A figure emerged out of the mist – Earl Gospatric, lord of lands on the Scots borders. He and Waltheof had retreated together with each advance of William's army until now they were camped on the banks of the Tees, unsure of their next move. Toki brought mead for Gospatric too. The Earl took the cup, drank deeply and gazed morosely into the drizzle without speaking.

'We could take the road to Chester,' Waltheof volunteered after a moment.

'We could,' Gospatric said, but without any great enthusiasm. He knuckled red-rimmed eyes.

'Likely we would be safe there for the winter at least. I am told that the walls are well manned and strong.' The safety of Chester also happened to lie on the other side of the Pennine Mountains. A January crossing of the passes was a prospect that neither man relished, but it had to be considered. They did not have the resources to fight the Normans at this point unless they could muster their scattered army. And the likelihood of that was the same as the drizzle ceasing this side of the morrow.

Waltheof was aware that they needed someone to tell them

what to do, to imbue them with the fire and confidence they had possessed at York. He didn't have it; neither did Gospatric.

Their brooding was interrupted by the arrival of one of their scouts, who had been out reconnoitring the Norman position. Now he came before Waltheof and Gospatric. Behind him, bearing a banner of truce, rode Richard de Rules and his two sons, Garnier and Simon.

Waltheof stared. Then he leaped to his feet and strode forward. His heart was hammering like a fist against his ribcage.

'My lord, I bid you welcome,' he cried and gestured a hovering soldier to take their horses.

De Rules dismounted. Although Waltheof had smiled at him, the Norman did not return the gesture, just inclined his head gravely, as did his eldest son. Simon's face was expressionless and he looked not at Waltheof but at the ground. Waltheof noticed that the boy dismounted smoothly and balanced himself well. A space at the back of his mind found time to wonder how many hours of practice that move had taken.

'You will drink mead?' Waltheof gestured towards his tent.

Again De Rules inclined his head. 'I am sorry to greet you in such circumstances,' he said as Waltheof led them into the relative dryness of the canvas shelter. Gospatric followed and dropped the flap.

'And I am too,' Waltheof responded. 'We hear grievous tales of the harm being visited upon the people of the North Country.' He turned to Simon and pointed to the cups and mead jug standing on the chest at the side of his camp bed. Wordlessly, eyes still downcast, the boy set about pouring drinks.

'A harm that they have brought upon themselves by giving succour to Danes and rebels,' De Rules said sharply.

Waltheof flashed him an angry glance. 'But Danes and rebels have more in common with these people than you Normans ever will,' he said. 'My own father is buried in Jorvik under the care

of Saint Olaf, and its people abhor your keeps and your fortifications. They are symbols of captivity.' He had clenched his
fists. Looking down at the skin stretched taut across his knuckles,
he saw again the battleaxe in his hand and remembered the
mingling of exhilaration and revulsion as he wielded it.

'They are symbols of the order that King William would
bring to the land,' De Rules said softly. 'He will brook resistance from no one. You stand in his way not only at your peril,
my lord, but at your death.'

Waltheof took the cup that Simon gave him and saw that
despite his attempt at a neutral visage the boy was trembling.
He felt much the same way himself. 'I am not afraid to die,'
he said with a curl of his lip.

De Rules' look pierced straight through the bravado. 'Then
you are a fool, Waltheof of Huntingdon,' he said, 'and I speak
as a friend now, and a man who is grateful for the gift of his
son's life, not as my king's messenger. You should be afraid to
die because you will be squandering more than just your life.
You say you have heard what is happening to the people of the
North because of their defiance. What then will happen to the
people of your earldom? Under whose yoke will they be put to
labour if you die? Your responsibility is to them first, not your
own selfishness. You cannot hold out against William. He will
cross the river with his army and you will retreat – where, to
Chester?'

Waltheof was wrongfooted. He stared at De Rules, a jolt of
panic surging in his gut.

'It is obvious,' the Norman said with an impatient wave of
his hand. 'The last English resistance is gathered there. William
will advance and break it as surely as he has broken all defiance. Do not make the mistake of believing it impossible at this
time of year. He is capable of moving mountains, let alone
crossing them.'

'So what are you offering?' Gospatric spoke for the first time,
his voice a dry whisper. He remained standing near the tent
flap, as if ready to take flight.

De Rules took a drink of mead then rested the cup on his knee. 'The King will give you your lives and allow you to retain the lands you held when you swore your first oath of allegiance,' he said, 'but you must surrender to him now, and your surrender must be absolute.'

Waltheof exchanged glances with Gospatric.

'You will not find succour with the Danes,' De Rules added. 'William has bought their loyalty with gold. Those who have not taken it and sailed away are pinned down and dying even now beneath the swords of Mortain, Taillebois and Eudo of Champagne.' He shook his head. 'The Danes came like kites for plunder, and they mind not whether it comes from English or Norman pouches.'

'That is not true!' Waltheof was stung to retort.

'True or not, they are no longer here to back your cause. They have had their victory of battle and they have their plunder. Why should they stay to face a hard winter fighting the Normans when they can go home with their booty and feast in their own mead halls with their wives and bedmates?'

Waltheof rubbed his beard and suddenly felt as weary as an old man. Their cause was hopeless. The only spark of light was the fact that William had sent Richard de Rules to the parley and that he should have brought the lad with him – a sign that the road to discourse was still open.

'You can go home too,' De Rules murmured. 'All you need do is surrender to the King.'

Waltheof smiled grimly. 'This is my home,' he said. 'And William may indeed be the King, but that does not mean that this land will ever truly belong to him.'

The Normans took their leave shortly after that. Gospatric had departed to his own tent, but Waltheof accompanied De Rules and his sons to the horse lines. Simon had still not spoken beyond a monosyllable and his eyes had not met Waltheof's once.

'I know the reasons why you took up arms against the King,'

De Rules murmured. He fiddled with the bridle, seeming reluctant to mount up and ride away.

'Do you indeed?' Waltheof folded his arms across his body like a shield.

'Mayhap in your position I would have done the same.'

'And what would you do if you were in my position now?'

The Norman set his foot in the stirrup and swung his leg across the saddle. 'I would throw myself on the King's mercy and renew my oath of allegiance.' Gathering the reins, he rested his hands upon the carved pommel. 'William knows your reasons too,' he said. 'If your yielding is complete, he may be prepared to change his stance on certain matters.'

The words hit Waltheof like a punch in the gut, taking his breath. For a moment he could only stare, then somehow he managed to gather his scattered wits. 'And dangle me like Edwin of Mercia?' he snarled. 'You think I am so cheaply bought and sold?'

De Rules' horse plunged and circled and the knight swiftly shortened the rein. 'You saved my son's life. I may be William's messenger but I am my own man and would not say you false. The King is camped across the river and you have fourteen days in which to make your surrender.'

'And if I do not?'

'Then God have mercy on your soul,' De Rules said sombrely. He extended his hand in a pleading gesture. 'In the name of Christ, my lord, I ask you make your peace with William before it becomes the peace of the grave.'

Waltheof's jaw tightened. 'I doubt if I made my grave now that I would lie in any kind of peace,' he said. 'Tell William that I will come when I am ready.'

De Rules nodded. Simon swung up into the saddle and took the lance of truce into his hand.

Waltheof looked up at him. 'How is your leg?' he asked.

Finally the boy's eyes met his and Waltheof saw that they were filled with wariness and reproach. 'It serves me well, my lord,' he said.

His voice had deepened, although it still bore the pure bell tones of boyhood and it would be a while yet before it broke. But some of the eager innocence had gone and Waltheof felt saddened, not least because he suspected that he had a part in it. Heroes were not supposed to be traitors, and explaining the motivation was too difficult when he did not understand the half of it himself.

'It is good to see you again, and I think you have grown,' Waltheof said, taking refuge in the mundane.

Simon's gaze was direct now, the light brown eyes almost the shade of Baltic amber. 'Do you not hate us?' he asked.

'Hate you?' Waltheof was nonplussed. 'God's love child, of course I do not hate you! Why should you think that?'

'Because of York . . . because of what has followed.' His voice faltered slightly. Waltheof wondered how much of the devastation Simon had seen. Probably more than he could stomach, given that he was squiring in William's household. And in York, in the heat of battle, Waltheof had personally slaughtered an untold number of Normans. Walking among the corpses in the aftermath, he had emptied his belly at the sight of so much blood and destruction. He had confessed his bloodlust, had been absolved, but to him it felt as if the taint still remained on his soul and would never wash clean.

He shook his head and grimaced. 'Ah lad,' he said, 'you always bring me questions I cannot or should not for decency's sake answer. There are many things I might hate about Normans, but you are not one of them . . . and never will be.'

Simon pondered this, a slight frown knitting his brows. 'Does that mean I can visit you . . . if you are pardoned?'

Waltheof found a pained smile. 'You and your father will always be welcome at any of my manors,' he said. 'Whatever has gone before, whatever comes afterwards, I would never turn you away.'

Simon's expression gentled in response, the frown vanishing. 'I hope it is soon,' he said.

'So do I,' Waltheof replied, and meant it. If there was one

good reason among all the less noble ones for bowing his head to William, then the boy's trust was it.

The Norman camp was orderly and disciplined. Riding into it with his troop, Waltheof felt like a brigand or a common pirate. His white fur mantle, the gold bracelets on his wrists, the rings on his fingers seemed garish in comparison to the spartan garb of the soldiers who watched him ride through their ranks. Their short hair and clean jaws added to the impression. Waltheof had washed his hair and combed his beard before setting out to the parley, but still he felt like a barbarian at the gates of Rome.

The drizzle of two days ago had been replaced by a bone-deep cold and the ground had begun to freeze. Waltheof had stuffed his boots with extra fleece and wore his quilted gambeson as much for warmth as protection. Any last shred of hope that the Norman army might turn back from a serious winter campaign was destroyed as he rode through their camp. Seeing the industry and discipline, he realised how naive he had been in ever thinking that he could pit his abilities against William's.

Waltheof dismounted and handed the reins to his groom. Richard de Rules arrived to escort him to William's tent. 'I am glad you came, my lord,' he said with relief in his eyes.

Waltheof shrugged. 'I had no choice, did I?'

De Rules cleared his throat. 'I must take your sword and your knife,' he said apologetically. 'They will be restored to you when you leave.'

Waltheof handed his belt and scabbard to the chamberlain and turned to lift his axe from its strap behind the saddle.

'That too,' De Rules said, eyeing the weapon sidelong.

Waltheof shook his head. 'That I will yield only into the hands of the King.'

'You cannot go into his presence so armed. I have seen your skill with that thing, and heard of your prowess at York. One blow and no one could stop you.'

Waltheof flushed. 'You doubt my integrity?'

'No,' De Rules said quietly, 'I do not, but I would be failing in my duty if I did not see foremost to the safety of my liege lord.'

Waltheof clenched his fists around the smooth ash wood of the haft. He had spent hours cleaning the blade and honing out the pits and nicks scarring the steel from its contact with wood and mail and bone. Now the edge gleamed with silver fire. 'I will yield this only to the King in token of my surrender,' he said. 'It is my pride. I will let no other man do so.'

Richard de Rules had not become the King's chamberlain by chance alone. Quick wits and tact formed a large part of his usefulness. 'I understand your reluctance, my lord,' he murmured. 'But you must understand my responsibility. Perhaps for your pride you will let no other man carry your axe – but what of a boy?'

'A boy?' For a moment Waltheof was nonplussed, but then he saw Simon standing in the background and took De Rules' meaning. 'Very well,' he said. 'Let your son be my axe bearer.' He beckoned Simon forward. Wide-eyed, the lad came to him, his stride awkward but controlled.

Waltheof presented him with the weapon. 'Bear this as if it had been in your family since the time of your grandfather's grandfather,' he said.

Reverently Simon gripped the haft, holding it as Waltheof had shown him, one hand immediately beneath the socket, the other halfway down. His fingers were thin and fine but possessed a tensile strength that made them competent to the task. 'I will not let you down, my lord,' he promised, and set his mouth in a resolute line.

'I know that you will not,' Waltheof said. Drawing a deep breath to sustain himself, he gave his attention to De Rules. 'I am ready,' he said, and gestured Simon to go before him like a standard bearer. It seemed entirely fitting to Waltheof that his axe bearer should be lame for the entire campaign had been flawed from the start.

William's tent was little different from the others pitched

along the banks of the Tees. It contained only a campbed, a trestle table and a travelling chest. Austere, functional, much like the man himself. A ceramic hanging lamp was suspended on chains from the wooden support running across the top of the canvas and the ground was covered in a thick litter of clean straw.

William sat at the trestle table, his broad shoulders swathed in a scarlet cloak lined with sables, and beneath that a quilted, embroidered gambeson. Surrounding him were his senior battle commanders and they were obviously in the midst of planning their campaign.

On seeing Waltheof William rose to his feet and pushed aside the wax tablet upon which he had been sketching diagrams. Men turned and stared, eyes narrow in speculation and hostility. Feeling as if he had stepped into the lair of wolves, Waltheof fell to his knees in the heavy yellow straw and bowed his head.

'My liege, I yield myself to your mercy,' he said formally. 'And in token of this, I give to you the axe that was my father's and his father's before him. My life is yours.'

Beside him, Simon knelt too and held out the weapon on the palms of his hands. Waltheof imagined himself seizing the axe and arcing it round and down to cleave William from crown to breastbone like a flesher splicing a bacon pig. The vision held such clarity that he was sure the others must see it. His palms were suddenly slick with sweat and his breathing shallow; nausea churned his gut.

He was on the verge of breaking, of snatching the axe and leaping to his feet, when William stooped and took it from the boy, setting his own firm, square hands to the haft and taking up the stance of an executioner.

'You yielded once before,' William replied coldly, 'and you swore me your oath of loyalty. When a man puts his hands between mine and promises to serve me, the vow is binding unto death.'

Waltheof swallowed. 'I know that, sire.'

'Then why did you turn oath-breaker, Waltheof Siwardsson?

It seems to me that all of your countrymen are faithless.'

'I had no choice but to take the oath to you,' Waltheof said, a hint of resentment creeping into his voice. He wasn't faithless, no matter that it seemed that way to William.

'But you had the choice to hold to it or break it,' William said silkily. 'And you chose the second way.'

'The Danish people are my kin. I have no blood in common with Normandy. I thought . . .'

'You thought that if you could shake off my rule that the Danes would embrace you as one of their own and give to you the lands and riches that were your father's,' William said scornfully. Hefting the axe, he turned it contemplatively in his hand.

'No!' Waltheof's eyes flashed. 'It was a matter of kinship . . . of belonging. You made it clear that you desired no such bond with my blood.'

'And if that were to change?'

Waltheof met the hard, dark eyes. Devoid of warmth, they probed him and he dared not ponder their purpose. 'Sire, a blood bond is the most binding of all.'

William continued to grip him with his stare. 'How long will your loyalty last this time?' he demanded. 'If I bid you renew your homage, how do I know that you will keep the faith?'

Waltheof bowed his head. 'I have seen the way you lead your men, sire. To go against you is futile. If Sweyn of Denmark had truly desired the North Country, he would have come himself rather than send his sons.'

'Perhaps he thought that the taking would be easy. Like you, he knows differently now.' William raised one fist and clenched it on the statement. His upper lip curled with contempt. 'At least you had the courage to come to me and submit to me yourself. Your companion Gospatric has chosen the Danish way and sent proxies to submit in his stead.'

If he had hoped for an indignant response, he was disappointed. Waltheof knew Gospatric's shortcomings, even as he knew his own.

'I have no intention of giving an opinion when I have my own lacks,' Waltheof said quietly. 'What Gospatric does is for his conscience and manhood to decide.'

William gave a disparaging snort. 'What manhood?' he said, and thrust the axe into Waltheof's surprised grasp. 'Go in peace, Waltheof Siwardsson. Tend your lands, stay out of trouble . . .' he paused to give his next words significance. 'Mayhap I will after all consider that bond of blood.'

Waltheof's breath caught. He did not know whether to be filled with joy or irritation. How often had Edwin of Mercia had the promise of 'good news' dangled before him without a royal match ever materialising? Waltheof had just sworn to be William's man whether he was rewarded or not. But if that choice should bring him Judith . . .

He thought he saw wintry humour light in William's eyes, as if the King could read his thoughts.

'Thank you, sire,' he said, and bowed out of William's presence into the raw January morning. The ashwood haft of his axe felt warm under his fingers. He had his lands, he had his life, and the hint of more than such sustenance to come. He felt wildly euphoric and deathly sick and it was all he could do not to vomit against the side of William's tent.

De Rules emerged, a paternal arm curved around Simon's shoulders. When the baron made to approach him, Waltheof thrust out a hand to ward him off. 'Let me be,' he said in a choked voice. 'For the nonce, I can stomach neither your comfort nor your company.'

'I think I would feel the same,' De Rules said, and then, mercifully, walked away, his arm firmly guiding his son.

Simon looked over his shoulder at Waltheof, his stare filled with question and anxiety.

Waltheof swallowed. 'That does not mean I hate you,' he said. 'But my wounds are bloody and you would only rub salt into them.' He spun on his heel and strode towards the horse lines.

Simon watched him leave, then looked up at his father in perplexity.

De Rules' fingers tightened upon the curve of his son's narrow shoulder. 'Let him be,' he said. 'If we were in his place and he in ours, do you think we would desire his companionship of this moment?'

Simon's dark tawny brows drew together. 'No,' he said doubtfully. 'But I wish it wasn't like that.'

'It is the way of the world,' De Rules said, and when Simon looked up into his father's face he saw that his expression was grim and tired.

'So, you will give him Judith?' asked Eudo of Champagne, rubbing his thumb across the cleft in his chin. The notion of bringing an English earldom into the family gnawed at him, the more so since his son had been born. His own lands were negligible, for although he was the son of the Count of Champagne he was living in exile on his brother-in-law's sufferance.

'I am considering it.' William drew the wax tablets towards him again and turned the bone drawing tool end over end. 'He is young and malleable still. If I can anchor him to me, then well and good.'

'And yet before you would not have him.'

William shrugged. 'He burst in upon me with the demand when I had already given him more rein than any other Englishman. He was like a child begging for one more sweet-meat . . .'

'And who then had a tantrum when you refused,' pointed out Robert of Mortain with a scowl.

William pushed his thumb against the side of the stylus and looked at his half-brother with a brooding dark stare. 'Perhaps that was part of his rebellion, but not the whole I think. Nor do I believe that his request for Judith was one of overweening ambition.'

Mortain snorted. 'A man who follows his cock is unreliable.'

'Perhaps,' William nodded, 'and again perhaps not. I bind men to me with the tools I have. Judith is of an age to wed and

Waltheof harbours as much desire for her as he does for her connections. She has a strong will to compensate for his weakness and powerful family ties to bolster her. I may have denied him before, but it would be folly not to reconsider.'

'And dangerous,' said Mortain.

'No more dangerous than him run loose.'

'Why let him run at all?' Eudo asked. 'Why not confiscate his lands and bestow them elsewhere?'

William gave him a piercing look that made Eudo check and hold his breath, wondering if he had been too eager.

'That would only cause more rebellion and we are stretched enough as it is. Chester is my goal, and ridding the land of the last of Godwinsson's supporters. I do not want to chase my tail back to Huntingdon, and I need your presence here, Eudo. For the granting of a small grace, I have peace with Waltheof. His lands are prosperous. Judith will be a countess and you will be Waltheof's father-by-marriage. I cannot give you Huntingdon outright. I hope you understand that.'

Eudo nodded stiffly and swallowed his disappointment. He had not really expected William to give him Huntingdon, but it had been worth planting the idea. And as William said, he would be Waltheof's father-by-marriage. Likely he could bring some influence to bear.

CHAPTER 11

Caen, Normandy, Autumn 1070

J udith sat near the embrasure so that the light spilled onto the hem of the wine-red tunic she was embroidering. It was to be a Christmas gift to her uncle William from his wife. Since Matilda was acting ruler of Normandy in her husband's absence and did not have the time for embroidery, the task fell to the other women of the household.

Judith's needle flew in and out, laying down a lozenge pattern in shades of emerald and sapphire on the background of Flemish twill. An hour since a messenger from England had arrived and was now closeted in the Duchess's private chamber unburdening his news. Judith wondered what tidings he had brought in his worn leather satchel.

There had been several uprisings in England during the past year, all of them swatted down by her uncle like bothersome flies. The most serious had been the rebellion in the North around the time that her brother was born. Waltheof had been amongst the leaders. She had braced herself to hear that he had fallen in battle, but learned instead that he had surrendered to her uncle and had been pardoned. Her relief had sharpened the knife-edge along which she trod until it was impossible to be at peace with herself.

She and her mother had returned to Normandy with the Queen. Waltheof, so Judith gleaned, had stayed firmly on his lands whilst fresh surges of unrest disturbed the country. Agatha had been inconsolable when Edwin of Mercia had been killed whilst hiding out with rebels in the fenlands. His brother Morcar had been captured and thrown into prison. Waltheof, however, remained free.

.Sometimes she would think of him while engaged in needle-work. She would wonder what he was doing, how he was faring. Was he the same? Had he found an English wife to comple-ment his estates – her uncle's conquest must have left many bereft heiresses – or did he remain unwed? She had knelt with a distraught Agatha to pray for Edwin's soul, and had been ashamed to discover a secret well of pleasure. Now that Edwin was no longer a contender for a Norman wife, perhaps there was a chance for Waltheof.

The notion filled her with restlessness. Suddenly the sewing, which she usually enjoyed, was tedious. Setting the needle in the fabric, she rose and went to the open shutters. Outside it was cold and overcast, the window arch yielding a vista of dull, grey cloud. Placed where he could obtain the best of the light, but out of the draught, her small half-brother Stephen gurgled in his cherrywood cradle. He had Eudo's cleft chin and blue eyes and all the women doted upon his plump rosiness. All but herself. She turned from his gummy smile with tightening lips, refusing to be wooed. In the eleven months since his birth it had become clear how much more value Adelaide set upon her son than she did on her daughters.

The curtain rings clattered vigorously across the doorway and her mother stalked into the room. She was breathing heavily and her fists were anchored so tightly in the fabric of her gown that the skin was bleached across the knuckles.

'Cease your daydreaming,' she snapped, her voice so harsh that it could almost have been William's. 'There is news from England and your aunt Matilda wishes to speak with you.'

Judith touched the sudden swift pulse at the base of her throat. 'What about?' she asked as she turned.

'That is for your aunt to say,' Adelaide replied stiffly. 'I am only your mother. My word evidently means nothing.'

Judith lowered her eyes and moved away from the window.

Passing the cradle, she gathered her skirts so that the hem did not so much as flick the glossy wood. A wail rose from the depths and a small arm flailed. At once a maid rushed to pluck the baby from his bed and jog him in her arms. Adelaide gave a brusque nod of approval and for a moment her eyes softened. Then she recalled her purpose. Heeling around, she stalked from the room, leaving Judith to follow her to the Duchess's chambers.

Judith made a deep curtsey to her aunt, who sat on a cushioned bench before a glowing brazier. Nearby a nurse was dandling Matilda's youngest child, the two-year-old Prince Henry, in her lap. It galled Judith that wherever she went in the ducal chambers she had to endure the sight of adored boy babies.

Matilda patted the bench, indicating that her niece should come and sit beside her. The Queen's fair complexion bore the pinkness of recent anger, making Judith wonder what had happened between her mother and Matilda, who were usually firm allies.

'Child, you are to go to England.' The Queen placed her hand over Judith's in a proprietorial gesture that subtly excluded Adelaide.

'England?' Judith's gaze widened. 'Has the Du . . . King sent for us?' They were to spend Christmas at the royal court, she thought. That was why her mother was so agitated; she loathed sea crossings. It also meant she would have to join her husband, whom she tolerated much the better for the distance between them.

Matilda shook her head. 'Not for all of us, child,' she said, 'but certainly for you and your mother. Your uncle has arranged for your marriage to Waltheof of Huntingdon on the feast of Saint Stephen.'

Judith was aware of staring at her aunt and being unable to move, as if a huge hand had pinned her down. 'My marriage?' she repeated in a stunned voice.

Matilda snapped her fingers and one of her ladies fetched a

goblet of wine and pressed it into Judith's numb fingers. 'Drink, first.' Her aunt gestured to the cup.

Judith raised a trembling hand to her mouth and sipped. She barely tasted the good red wine, but when it reached her stomach it burned. 'I thought . . .' she swallowed. 'I thought Earl Waltheof was considered an unsuitable match.'

'It seems that your uncle has changed his mind,' Matilda said neutrally. 'He wishes to reward the young man's loyalty.'

'Loyalty!' Adelaide spat. 'After what happened in York?'

'He has not been involved in the uprisings since – and some of them were perilously close to his borders,' Matilda said flatly with a narrow glance at her sister-in-law that warned her against speaking out. 'The King feels that Waltheof is owed a reward – that binding him more closely to our house will ensure his future co-operation. Your stepfather is in full agreement.'

Adelaide made a strangled sound that told without words what she thought of such an endorsement.

Matilda locked stares with her. 'If William deems this match with Waltheof of Huntingdon to be provident, then nothing will stand in his way. Neither you, nor I, nor a winter sea crossing,' she said with iron finality. She looked at Judith and there was the slightest softening of her mouth corners. 'I do not think your daughter will be displeased by her uncle's decision.'

Judith shook her head, certain that she was going to wake up and discover that this was all a strange dream induced by eating too many cheese wafers close to retiring. What was she supposed to say? What was she supposed to feel? Marriage to Waltheof. Once she had dreamed of it, but now the memory was as distant as the summer on this raw November morning. 'It is my duty to do my uncle's will,' she heard herself say.

'Pah!' Adelaide folded her arms tightly beneath her bosom. 'Your uncle thinks that wedding you to an English earl is a worthy ploy, but he will live to rue the day he did not marry you to a Fleming!'

'Adelaide!' Matilda said in terse warning.

Judith's mother compressed her lips. 'You will need cloth

for a wedding gown,' she said without pleasure, 'and warm robes to keep out the winter chill.' She clucked her tongue. 'I suppose you will have to take linen for sheets and napery too.' The tone of her voice suggested that she thought Judith would be living a primitive existence bereft of all comforts.

'I will send for the mercer this very day,' Matilda murmured soothingly. 'As Judith says, it is our duty to do my lord's will, and we must fulfil it to the best of his expectations. Let her go in the full array due to the niece of a king and the daughter of a countess. She shall have the best of everything, and you must have new robes too.'

Adelaide's lips remained pursed but her posture relaxed slightly.

Judith looked at her aunt. 'Did . . . did Earl Waltheof say anything?'

Matilda reached to the ivory casket on the coffer beside her and threw back the lid. 'Your uncle says that Earl Waltheof agreed readily to the contract. He awaits your arrival in England with eagerness and in token has sent you this ring.' She held out to Judith a small circlet fashioned from plaited bands of gold.

With shaking hands, Judith took it from her aunt. Waltheof had one the same; she had often seen it gleaming on the middle finger of his right hand. Aware of the older women's scrutiny, she slipped it on her own right middle finger. It fitted perfectly and shone with a dull lustre against her skin.

Matilda nodded and smiled. 'He has chosen well,' she said. 'My own betrothal ring hung off my finger like a quintain hoop.'

'We shall see,' Adelaide said darkly. 'Rings that fit a young girl at the start oft grow too tight in the wearing.'

Matilda frowned at her sister-in-law and sighed with irritation. 'Making doom-laden predictions serves no purpose,' she said curtly. 'We must be practical. Travelling chests need to be packed and arrangements made.' Leaning over, she gave Judith a dry kiss on the cheek. 'I am happy for you, niece.'

Adelaide made no move to embrace her daughter. Instead she swished over to one of the clothing chests, banged open the lid and began to sort through the linens within.

Matilda gave Judith's newly beringed hand a sympathetic squeeze. 'All will be well,' she murmured. 'A little time to grow accustomed is all that is needed – for us all.'

Judith nodded and finished the wine. The first numbness of shock was beginning to wear off. It was true. She was going to England. She was going to marry Waltheof and become Countess of Huntingdon and Northampton. But the thought that blossomed most brightly amongst the several that began to chase around her mind was that she was no longer going to be ruled by her mother but was now able to make rules of her own. She would be mistress of the household and able to do as she pleased. Without stifling, without censure.

A tinge of colour returned to her cheeks, and her eyes began to sparkle as she realised that this news meant her freedom.

CHAPTER 12

S hears in hand, Waltheof's chamber attendant Toki hesitated. 'You are sure about this, my lord?'

Waltheof grimaced. 'I am not sure at all,' he said, 'but
do it. It is not as if the results will be permanent if I change
my mind. Make haste. It would be unseemly to be late for my
wedding.' His laugh shook slightly. He could still not quite
believe that William had granted him Judith in marriage. For
a month he had been pinching himself. But it was true. This
morning was the feast of Stephen, and before the hour of prime
their marriage was to be blessed by Lanfranc, Archbishop of
Canterbury, and celebrated with a mass inside the abbey
church of Westminster.

Behind him he heard Toki sigh heavily and felt the crunch
of the shears as they came together. Seated on the bench, his
hands braced on his thighs, his head held very still, Waltheof
watched the locks of hair fall around him like tongues of flame.
His father had been flax-white of hair, his mother plain brown,
but the copper trait had run in her line and she had bequeathed
it to him. Perhaps tonight he would in turn bequeath it to a
child of his own. The thought made him shift restlessly on the
bench and caused Toki to swear.

'If you do not remain still, my lord, you will go to your
marriage with a missing ear and a resemblance to the Earl of
Norfolk's dogs,' he said, referring to Earl Ralf's deerhounds,
which had recently been affected by a serious attack of mange.

Waltheof laughed, then, because that made him shake too, swallowed the sound.

'You're going to feel the cold,' Toki warned as he started on the beard.

It was a statement already borne out by the truth. Waltheof's bare neck did indeed feel the draught from an ill-fitting shutter. His beautiful golden beard, which had grown stronger over the last two years, had caused him more agony of decision than his hair. As an Englishman it was an immediately identifiable sign of his manhood, something to toy with in times of anxiety, to hide behind, and a symbol of authority. With it gone, his face was naked to the world.

Toki stepped back and eyed his handiwork dubiously. He stroked his own thick beard as if for reassurance. 'Splendour of God,' he declared, using King William's favourite oath. 'You surely do look like a Norman, my lord.'

Waltheof ran his hand over his smooth jaw and then through his cropped hair. Toki had sheared it in the Norman style, baring the entire back of the neck and up the scalp so that the hair began on a level just up from Waltheof's ear lobes and was shaped above the ears and round to a fringe. 'I want to do Judith proud,' Waltheof said softly. 'I want to surprise and please her.'

Toki clucked his tongue. 'You'll do that for certain,' he said.

Waltheof looked hard at Toki but the manservant's expression was bland. He wondered if he had done the right thing. It was too late to worry.

The bath was the next order of proceedings, to remove the tickle of cut hair and ritually cleanse himself for the coming marriage. The wooden bathtub was somewhat small for his large frame and he had to bend his knees and keep his elbows in. Although the water was hot, it quickly began to chill and Waltheof did not linger at his ablutions.

He had just stepped from the tub and another manservant was drying him with linen towels when there was a knock on the chamber door and Simon de Senlis entered the room. The lad wore a tunic of russet-coloured wool that enhanced his fox-gold eyes and dark tawny hair. A beautifully tooled sheath hung from the belt at his waist and a hilt of cunningly worked antler stood proud of the top.

Waltheof flashed a grin at the sight of him. 'You're not supposed to outdo the bridegroom!' he remarked.

Simon did not respond to the jest for he was staring at Waltheof in open-mouthed astonishment.

'What do you think?' Self-consciously, Waltheof ran one hand through his hair. 'Do you think Lady Judith will approve?'

'You look very different,' the boy said.

Waltheof made a face. 'You're as diplomatic as your father.'

Simon frowned. 'No . . . It suits you, but you no longer look like yourself. But I think that Lady Judith will be very pleased indeed . . . and Countess Adelaide too.'

Waltheof snorted at the observation, admitting to himself that young Simon was as sharp as a bradawl. 'Come, help me dress,' he said. 'I presume that your father knows where you are.'

'Yes. He said not to linger if you wished to be alone.'

Waltheof shook his head. 'No, lad. I like my solitude for prayer, but I need company as some men need bread.' He tousled the boy's hair. It was slightly longer than his own new crop, the rich-brown strands nudging the boy's brow-bone.

While Toki set about emptying the bath water Simon helped Waltheof to don his wedding clothes. First came the shirt of soft embroidered linen, then braies of the same, held up by a waistband of plaited cord. Chausses of dark blue wool were fastened to the braies with leather ties. Kneeling at Waltheof's feet, Simon carefully wound decorative braid from ankle to knee. Filaments of gold thread twinkled amidst the red and white wool. Waltheof's tunic was of a lighter blue than his chausses, a summer-sky colour with the same red and white braid trimming the hem, cuffs and deep neck opening, the latter pinned by a large gold brooch. The sword belt came next, the solid gold buckle cunningly worked in the shape of a serpent coiling round to swallow its tail.

. Waltheof hesitated over donning the several gold bracelets that adorned his wrists. The fashion was somewhat outmoded, but his father and brother had always worn them, using them as gifts for songs well sung and services performed. The Normans, he knew, saw the habit as barbaric and outmoded. 'Yes, or no?' he said to Simon.

The boy considered. 'You cannot give up everything of you that is English,' he said. 'Everyone will be too busy looking at your naked face to have time to notice your wrists.'

Waltheof grinned at the lad's perception. 'Aye, you're right.' Waltheof slid the bracelets onto his arms, but all the same pushed them a little beneath his sleeves. The final touch was the bearskin cloak. He had thought about discarding that too, but had swiftly quashed the notion. More than anything this was his heritage, a symbol of who he was. No one else owned a cloak lined with the fur of an Arctic bear.

'So,' he said, 'will I do?'

'You look magnificent, my lord.'

There was more than just diplomacy in the boy's tawny eyes. The gleam of admiration bolstered Waltheof's courage. Turning to a coffer, he took his battleaxe from its waxed wrappings and presented it to Simon.

'Here,' he said. 'You were my weapon bearer when I surrendered to William. Now be so again in pride as I go to my marriage with his niece.'

Simon flushed with pleasure and he took the weapon reverently.

With heart beating fast, Waltheof went to the door. For a moment his hand seemed stuck to the latch. He had deliberately made his men wait outside while he took the traditional bath and the less than traditional drastic barbering. He knew there would be consternation. What he hoped would carry him through was the approbation of his bride. It mattered that

Judith should be proud of him and show to all that she was marrying a man worthy of her love.

Jutting his naked chin, he raised the latch and stepped outside. The gold bracelets jingled on the movement and slipped down over the bones of his wrists.

Seated in the great hall, granted a place at the head of the high table because it was her wedding feast, Judith glanced between her lashes at her new husband. She could not believe the transformation that the barber's shears had wrought. He had been handsome before, in the unkempt way of the English, but now his features were clear and sharp, etched in Norman austerity. So changed was his appearance, she was unable to keep her eyes from him; quite simply, he was stunning. Women, who had ignored him before, now cast him languishing glances. Men, who had disapproved of his English abundance, clasped his hand in gruff approval. Even her mother had been impressed by Waltheof's changed appearance. Since his French was so fluent, she said, one could almost mistake him for a true Norman. If only it weren't for those vulgar bracelets jangling on his wrists.

Judith had noticed them too, and dismissed their presence as a matter of small importance. She would have care of his clothes and his dressing now that she was his wife. It would be a simple enough matter to persuade him to set them aside.

Some of the English guests had been less fulsome in their praise of Waltheof's shaven looks, but they were common thegns and counted for little. Any Saxon with a pitkin of sense these days was doing as Waltheof had done and adopting Norman ways.

Waltheof caught her looking at him and smiled. It was an open expression, full of honest joy. Judith blushed, unable to return the emotion before so many onlookers, all assessing and judging the couple's every response.

'I am the most fortunate of men,' he said huskily, laying his hand over hers, his thumb caressing the two bands of gold that now sat side by side on her middle and ring fingers.

'And I am the most fortunate of women,' she replied, her voice barely audible.

Ralf de Gael noticed Waltheof's gesture and raised a rowdy toast. Judith pursed her lips at his conduct. He behaved like an Englishman, she thought – always the first to disappear under the table, but not before making himself sick and objectionable with drink.

'Then our children will be doubly blessed,' Waltheof leaned closer to murmur, his breath scented with the spiced wine that had been served with the last course of honeyed figs, cheese wafers, and small crisp, flat cakes cooked on a griddle.

The mention of children made Judith's breath catch. She was trying not to panic about the wedding night, but with little success. She was not ignorant about the act of procreation. Her mother could not confine her to the bower all the time. She had seen dogs in the hall, cats in the stables, and had once come across one of the grooms taking a kitchen maid in the heaped straw beyond Jolie's stall. At the time she had stared at the heaving white buttocks and straddled thighs with a mingling of shock and fascination. Sybille, on being told of the incident, had chuckled knowingly and assured Judith that the groans she had heard were of pleasure, not pain. Now, tonight, she and Waltheof would adopt that same position and she would find out. The notion of crying out beneath him was one that filled her with shame and curiosity, eagerness and fear. She shivered slightly.

'Are you cold, my heart?' Waltheof asked, 'or does the notion of our children unsettle you?'

She forced a smile. 'A little of both,' she admitted. 'Last night I slept in the women's hall, as I have done for all the years of my life. Tonight I must lie in a different bed and perform the duties of a wife.'

'Ah,' said Waltheof. A smile lit in his eyes making them shine lapis blue. 'So bedding with me is going to be a duty?' His voice was warm and teasing as he signalled the attending squire to refill his horn.

'That depends upon how drunk you become,' Judith said with a pointed look at the brimming vessel. 'What price your dignity and my pride if you have to be carried to your wedding bed?'

Waltheof's smile broadened into a white grin. 'Not twelve hours wed and already you are scolding me.'

Judith blinked and bit her lip. 'You make light of the matter, but everyone's eyes are upon us. If you are drunk they will remember and think less of you.'

'And that matters to you?' The humour left his face.

'Of course it does.'

Waltheof shook his head gently. 'You have enough pride for both of us, my love,' he murmured. 'But you may rest assured that I will not tumble it in the mire. I sheared myself close as a May sheep for you this day. Remaining sober is small enough coin compared to that. Besides,' he added, his smile returning with an incorrigible glint, 'I have no intention of ruining my wedding night with a surfeit of wine. I want to remember this occasion for the rest of my life.'

The couple had been allotted a fine chamber on the upper floor of the hall, with thick arched windows looking out over the moonlit glint of the River Thames. Fresh rushes had been strewn on the floor and scattered with aromatic herbs so that each footfall aroused the scent of lavender, rosemary and cinnamon. Charcoal braziers burned in each corner of the room, keeping the cold at bay, and a jug of wine had been set on a cover over one of the braziers to warm through.

Judith sat in the bed where the women had placed her and watched Waltheof bolt the door after the last guest, predictably Ralf de Gael, who at one point in the merry jesting had offered to take Waltheof's place in the great, fur-covered bed. The notion had nauseated Judith. Once she and Waltheof were more familiar with each other she thoroughly intended discarding certain of his friendships along with those garish bracelets.

There were small, damp spots on her chemise where Archbishop Lanfranc had sprinkled her with holy water as he blessed the union between her and Waltheof. Waltheof's shirt was damp too. At least they had not been made to strip totally naked, as sometimes happened. She could not have borne the thought of standing before the entire court clad in naught but her hair.

Waltheof turned from the door he had just barred. 'I would not put it past Ralf to listen outside and then burst in on us at the crucial moment,' he said with an embarrassed laugh and rubbed the shorn back of his neck, which had turned a rich pink.

'Neither would I,' Judith replied somewhat grimly, 'although I think that my uncle and my stepfather will keep him in hand.'

'I suppose so, or your mother will know the reason why,' Waltheof grinned wryly.

Judith did not want to talk of Adelaide. The closing of the door marked a barrier between her former life beneath her mother's roof and her new one as Waltheof's wife and countess in her own right. No longer was she subject to her mother's rule, although she knew that there would be some struggles on that score. Adelaide was nothing if not tenacious. 'Do you remember your own mother?' she asked to divert her thoughts.

Waltheof went to the heated jug of wine, poured a scant measure into one of the cups set to hand, and came to the bed. 'Only a very little,' he said. 'She died when I was small. I remember that she wore her hair in long braids twined with red ribbons. She was very fond of her garden and would spend hours tending the plants. She was much younger than my father – she was his second wife, and it was not a match made for love.'

'Matches never are.'

Waltheof looked at her and the expression in his eyes melted the flesh from her bones. 'Maybe not,' he said softly, 'but sometimes the spark is there. Sometimes men and women are fortunate enough to make an arrangement that brings them their heart's desire.'

Judith swallowed. Her throat was dry. As if sensing her need, he handed her the cup of wine. Their fingers touched and he raised his index one to rub it gently along her knuckles until she shivered at the sensation.

'I desired you from that first night in the hall at Rouen when I asked Richard de Rules who you were,' Waltheof murmured. Folding his hand around hers, he brought the cup to his own lips and drank from the place where hers had touched. 'And now I have you and I swear that for the rest of my days I will want nothing and no one else.'

'You are not ambitious, my lord?'

'I have seen what ambition does to men . . . and what you do to me is far more important.'

Judith licked her lips, nervously. Waltheof moved closer, angled his head and kissed her. She was passive, struck by fear and uncertainty. His mouth tasted of wine and sweetness. He pulled gently away and looked at her.

'Drink,' he said, returning the cup to her keeping.

She shook her head. 'I have had enough.'

'Trust me, you have not,' he said.

'You mean it will be easier for me if I am insensible?' Her tone took on a waspish note.

Waltheof laughed, and bouncing from the bed, went to refill the cup. 'No, of course not. You would be missing a deal of pleasure, and you would suffer so thunderous a headache in the morning that you would wonder why you had not chosen to be aware.'

Judith slanted him a look from her eye corners. 'My mother says that coupling is a duty,' she said uncertainly.

Waltheof returned to the bed, took a single swallow from the brimming cup, then presented it to her. 'Your mother sees everything in the world as a duty,' he said wryly. 'Coupling is a pleasure.'

'But is it not a sin to enjoy it?' Judith said doubtfully and drank. Although she was not aware of the fact, the sweet, strong wine was already working its magic and loosening her tongue.

'Some priests say that it is,' Waltheof admitted, 'but I think that God gave us the means for pleasure as well as pain. I am no scholar, and I leave it for those who are to debate. Perhaps it is better to be continent, but without procreation there would be no children . . .'

'But it is not the reason that men go to brothels – to procreate children.' Judith's tone was acerbic.

Again Waltheof laughed. 'No,' he agreed, 'it is not. And that is why we go to confession.'

She frowned at him. The wine was beginning to spread through her limbs, bringing lassitude and a feeling of well-being. 'But if you confess and then sin again . . .'

Waltheof took the cup from her hands and set it to one side. 'I have no intention of ever sinning again in my life,' he said. 'Well, at least not in matters of the flesh. If we are to speak of duty, then let us speak of your duty to keep me on the straight path.'

'You are mocking me.'

'No, teasing you. There is a difference.' Raising the sheets, he got into bed beside her. 'Your hands are cold,' he said. 'Lie down.'

Somewhat cautiously Judith complied. Waltheof drew the crisp linen sheet, the striped blanket and beaver fur coverlet over their bodies. Taking her hands in his and raising his shirt, he laid her palms against the heat of his breast. She felt the dry warmth of his flesh, the thump of his heart. Strange, unsettling sensations coursed through her, an immodest desire to press herself against him.

He seemed to sense it, for he gathered her close. 'That's it,' he said softly. 'Just for warmth . . .'

She knew it wasn't true. How could it be when the bloody sheet of her taken virginity was expected to be displayed to the entire court on the morrow as proof that any child born nine months from this date would be of Waltheof's begetting? However the lie was soothing and she relaxed against him. He rested his head on one hand and used the other to caress her spine in gentle, rhythmic strokes.

To Judith the sensation was entirely new and blissful. A purr caught in her throat and she had to compress her lips to stifle the sound. Waltheof's hand continued its magic, now gentle and slow, now sweeping and firm. Imperceptibly he moved lower until his fingertips were swirling the small of her back. Judith let out a soft gasp and pushed her hips forward. Waltheof continued caressing her, murmuring gently, reassuring. His hand left her hips, trailed up her ribcage and feathered over her breast. It was the lightest of touches, but rather like a leaf falling into a pool the small ripples spread from the contact and drew a response from all of her body. Her loins were meltingly sensitive. His palm found and lingered upon her nipple, slowly rubbing through the linen chemise; she had to catch back another mew of pleasure. When he replaced his hand with his lips and the flick of his tongue, Judith arched and gasped.

Waltheof pulled on the bow lacing the top of her chemise until it unravelled. And then she felt his touch on her naked skin. His breathing had changed, no longer quiet and even, but ragged and swift. Now he kissed her throat, her jawline, and reclaimed her lips. This time Judith was less passive. She moved her mouth beneath his, and shivered when he explored her lips with his tongue. Her arms encircled his neck and she pressed against him. Thus far he had kept his lower body away from hers, but now he set his arm across her waist, drew her in close and began to rock his hips against hers.

She felt the heat and strength of his body, the firm length of his erect phallus through the cloth of his shirt. Imagining it within her body had been impossible before, something to shy away from, but she was drugged with wine and pleasure now. As he pushed against her he held her steady and tentatively she began to push back, enjoying the pressure. He continued to kiss her and his hand stole beneath her chemise, drawing the linen upwards, baring her legs, her thighs. And the fondling continued, stroking, lulling, leading her onwards.

From the sensitive soft skin of her inner thighs, he moved higher. At first Judith tensed, but he murmured reassurances and love words and stroked so softly that she gasped and parted her thighs. He knew exactly where to touch and she began to writhe and whimper.

Waltheof sat up and removed his shirt. In the dim light from the night candle his hair was the colour of flame and the scattering of hair on his chest sparkled like gold wire. His muscles gleamed with health; his belly was as flat as the planking on a new shield. The bedclothes concealed him from the waist down, and Judith did not know whether to be glad or disappointed.

'Your chemise,' he said hoarsely, 'take it off.'

'I . . .'

'It will bunch between us and be uncomfortable.' He drew her up and tugged the garment off over her head. She watched him cast it to one side, careful even in the intensity of the moment not to send it in the direction of the night candle.

The cold night air struck her flesh and raised small goose chills. He combed his hands through her unbound black hair and watched the tresses slide against his skin. He smoothed her satin shoulders, cupped the heavy weight of her breasts in his palm, and groaned softly.

Pulling her down, he began the slow, stroking process again, until Judith was hot and breathless. The wine and the slow seduction had done their work. Now she gasped openly and made small sounds at each new assault on her senses.

He parted her thighs and began to rub with slow insistence. Judith clenched her fists. She would have bitten her lip too, but he was kissing her, thrusting kisses of his tongue now, moving in time with motion of his hips. A tight sensation was growing and building in Judith's loins, each stroke of his finger bringing her closer. She raised herself against him, wanting to cry out for him to stop so that she could catch her breath, wanting him to go on. Nearer and nearer. He was groaning and she could feel the vibration of his voice through their joined mouths. The sound added to the maelstrom of sensations and excited her further. She was on the brink of discovering something so overwhelming it would shatter her.

He took his hand away and she made a sound of frustration. He cupped her buttocks. Once, twice, she felt the hot jab of flesh, and then he steadied, and thrust into her. Judith cried out at the intrusion. There was a jagged flash of pain, but there was pleasure too. He withdrew a little way and pushed forward again, holding himself still at the deepest point of the surge and pressing his hips flat against hers, then he withdrew, and pushed and held again. His head came up. Judith watched his muscles flex and relax as he held himself over her. His mouth opened. He began to groan with each thrust. Judith let out small whimpers in counterpoint. Each time he pushed into her, she would feel a flash of pain and then a stab of swollen pleasure. And as he moved faster, the two became joined until she did not know where one began and the other ended. She began to thrash and gasp. Part of her was terrified and wanted to escape before she was destroyed, and part of her wanted to leap joyously into that destruction.

'Please . . .' she entreated, not knowing whether she was asking him to stop or go forward. 'Please . . .' Her body was rigid with tension as she held back from the edge.

Without breaking rhythm he reached down between them and stroked. It was the final stimulus to send her crashing into the first climax of her life. She arched against him, her fingers like claws, her teeth clenched, and in the wildness of the moment she threw back her head and screamed. The sound brought an answering roar from Waltheof and he thrust into her so hard that she screamed again. And then his weight came down on top of her and where their bodies were joined she could feel pulsations like a heartbeat, throbbing strongly, then flickering and ebbing away.

Silence fell except for the sobbing gasps of their breath. Judith began to struggle up from the deep well of pleasure into

which she had been cast. She became aware of Waltheof's
weight pinning her to the bed. Her thighs were stretched,
causing a cramping discomfort, and there was a raw burning
in the softness between them.

Slowly Waltheof eased from her body. She clenched at the
pain, and wondered how in the world she had just accepted
that impossible length with screams of delight. Was this the
nature of lust against which the priests counselled?

Waltheof drew her against him and stroked the tangled hair
away from her face. 'I love you,' he murmured. 'If it hurt, I am
sorry. In time it will grow better.'

In time? Judith swallowed. 'I will lose myself,' she said in a
shaken voice.

'That is no bad thing for a while,' Waltheof said. 'I want to
see you smile. I want to see beyond the face you show to the
world. When you cried out in my arms just now . . .' His own
voice shook with tenderness.

Judith hid herself against his chest. She had been unable to
help herself, and now she was chagrined.

'Come now,' Waltheof said softly. 'We should rightly sing
praise for what gives us delight.' Tilting up her face he kissed
her. Judith responded, but with reserve now. She needed time
to assimilate and recover. Against her thigh she could feel his
erection, although it seemed to be softer than a moment since.
Sybille had told her tales of men – and women – who would
indulge their lechery from nightfall until dawn. She hoped that
Waltheof was not one of them. It would be more than she could
bear.

'Truly – did I give you pleasure?'

She heard the need for reassurance in his tone and bit her
lip. 'Yes,' she whispered, 'you gave me pleasure. I had not imagined that it would be like that. Now I understand why the
priests are so often ignored when they exhort people to
celibacy.'

Waltheof snorted. 'More than half the village priests in
England have wives and children,' he said. 'It is only of late

that the Church has taken a different stance. I can see that fornication is a distraction to the spiritual life of monks and nuns, but a common priest should live with his parishioners as they live with him.' He yawned. 'I am glad that you found as much joy in your duty as I found in mine.'

A few moments later he was heavily asleep. Judith eased out of his arms and surreptitiously pushed down the covers. Her inner thighs were stained with blood and there were streaks and smears on the sheets too – proof of her virginity. She pulled the sheets back up and turned on her side away from Waltheof, keeping her distance.

In the morning, he made love to her again, once more coaxing a shattering response that left her dazzled, disorientated and sore. He told her he loved her, that she was his life, and gave her a gift of a gold and garnet brooch and jewelled fillets to thread on the ends of her long dark braids.

The bloodied sheet was displayed in the hall before the entire court as proof of Judith's virginity and the successful wedding night. Adelaide wore an expression compounded of pride for her daughter's bravery and mild distaste at the evidence of what Judith had been made to suffer.

Sybille, ever practical, quietly handed Judith a small pot of soothing salve. 'Until you grow accustomed,' she whispered. Having spent the night rolled in the cloak of Toki, Waltheof's shieldbearer, her own complexion was rosy from the burn of his beard and the satisfaction of being well loved.

Judith took the salve and wondered if she ever would grow accustomed. The sensations roused in her by Waltheof were as disturbing as they were glorious. 'I wish I was like you,' she said almost bitterly to the maid. 'I wish I was like my husband.' Her glanced flickered to Waltheof, who was devouring bread and honey with gusto while he engaged in buoyant conversation with Richard de Rules and her stepfather.

'No use wishing to be like other folks,' the maid said shrewdly. 'You have to learn to live at peace within your own skin.' She squeezed Judith's arm, a gleam of sympathy in her eyes. 'Lord Waltheof's a good man. Just trust in him and you'll be all right.'

Judith said nothing. Trust was the last thing she would yield to anyone.

CHAPTER 13

Summer 1072

Simon rode into Huntingdon on a warm evening in June. He passed townspeople hoeing their garths, women gossiping as they worked distaff and spindle at lightning speed to weave thread from fleece. Others were eating their suppers over outdoor fires. The smell of food and smoke mingled with the green scents of summer and an underlying but not overpowering whiff of midden pits and latrines.

People glanced up as he passed and then ignored him. Simon wondered if they would scowl in hostility behind his back, but he thought not. There was nothing to mark him as overtly Norman unless he opened his mouth. A hood of green linen hid his cropped hair, and his tunic was a sober russet colour with only a narrow trim of decorative braid.

At fourteen years old, Simon was as slender as a birch twig. No matter how much he ate, none of it remained on his wiry frame except by way of stretching his length. His father had jokingly commented that someone must have put manure in his shoes to judge by the speed of his growth. His features were changing too, his nose and jaw lengthening and a smudge of hair downing his upper lip.

A patrol of soldiers came towards him from the direction of the new castle and he turned his roan cob aside to let them pass. Their mail glinted in the evening sun and he heard the rapid French and Flemish of their speech. One of them drew rein and glared at him from beneath the brow ridges of his helm.

'Soon be curfew, boy,' he growled. 'What are you doing out?' He eyed the horse and Simon felt a jolt of fear. He knew that good animals such as this were targets for requisitioning. After the inroads that Hastings and the Northern campaign had made on saddle horses, demand for remounts was ferocious.

'I am travelling to the hall of Earl Waltheof of Huntingdon with messages from the King,' Simon answered more boldly than he felt. 'My name is Simon de Senlis and I am a royal squire and the son of his chamberlain.'

The soldier's eyes narrowed slightly. 'You are young to be entrusted with so important a matter.'

Simon shrugged. 'The King has entrusted me with letters before.'

'Let me see your messages.'

For a moment Simon thought about rebelling, but decided that six against one was not fair odds. Keeping his eyes firmly fixed on the soldier, he reached in his saddle pack and drew out the vellum packet. The man took it, turned it over in his hands, studied the dangling red seal and, with a grunt, thrust the documents back at Simon.

'On your way,' he said gruffly and wafted his arm as if batting at a fly.

With clammy hands and thundering heart, Simon dug his heels into the roan's flanks and made haste to put distance between himself and the soldiers. He knew how intimidated the English must feel with such a watch on their activities. Prisoners in their own land.

In passable if not fluent English, he asked directions to Waltheof's hall of a man returning from the fields, his hoe over his shoulder, and was pointed towards a long building with a roof of wooden shingles and a stockade of pale ash stakes. A soldier guarded the gateway, the westering sun shimmering on the rivets of his hauberk. Seeing Simon approach, he stood to attention.

'Toki,' Simon greeted him with a smile. 'It's good to see you.'

The warrior shaded his eyes with his palm and a sudden grin

spread over his face. 'Master Simon! I didn't recognise you!'

'I've brought letters for the Earl. Is he here?'

'Aye, he's here.' Toki held the cob's bridle while Simon dismounted. 'Saint Winifred's bones, you've grown!' He gave the boy an exaggerated head-to-toe scrutiny.

'I know. I have to duck under the stable lintel at home,' Simon laughed. As he took the weight on his left leg, the familiar pain struck through him, but he had learned not to flinch or grimace. He wanted neither pity nor gentle handling: the less reaction he gave to his pain, the more men treated him as one of their own. Toki summoned a groom to take the horse and Simon told him about the knights he had encountered on the town street.

The smile fell from the Saxon's face. 'They'll be the sheriff's men from the castle,' he growled. 'And the bane of Earl Waltheof's life. King William might have given my lord his own niece to wife, but he has saddled him with a Norman keep and a Norman sheriff who has about as much notion of fair play as a starving wolf has of compassion for a tethered sheep.'

Simon gazed at him, but Toki compressed his lips. 'I've said too much, lad. Go on to the hall. The Earl will be right glad to see you . . . and his lady too,' he added as a diplomatic afterthought.

Simon forced a smile. He was looking forward to seeing Waltheof, but Lady Judith was a different prospect. Nor did he think that she would be overjoyed to greet him.

The arched windows along the length of the great hall were thrown open to admit spars of evening sunlight, gilding the floor rushes and trapping filaments of smoke from the central hearth. Simon caught glimpses of retainers busy assembling trestles for the evening meal and his mouth watered at the tantalising aroma of some kind of meat and onion stew.

On entering the building, he saw that the walls had been recently daubed with white limewash and as yet there were no layers of smoky residue to darken the brightness. Painted Saxon round shields were arrayed down the length of the hall, interspersed with crossed spears and battleaxes. At chair height, several narrow panels of embroidery colourfully divided the expanse of white wall. A lively young soldier by the name of Hrolf escorted him to Waltheof. Although the Earl had no private chamber separate from the hall, there was an area screened off by heavy woollen hangings that served as both apartment and bedchamber.

'Lady Judith likes to keep the curtain across,' said Hrolf. 'She would rather stay at Northampton because they have a private hall of their own, but my lord prefers Huntingdon – he says it is more homely.' Pausing, he raised his voice and craved admittance.

Waltheof answered in a cheerful bellow and, parting the curtain, Hrolf ushered Simon into the private chamber.

Waltheof was seated at a table, poring over a chessboard. One hand was braced on his thigh, the other rubbed his jaw. Judith sat opposite him, her dark braids glossy in the light from the window embrasure, her brow marred by a slight frown that Simon suspected had been caused by his intrusion.

'Simon!' The Earl sprang to his feet in a surge that made the table shake and knocked over several pawns. Beaming from ear to ear, he strode to Simon and swept him into a bone-crunching embrace. 'What brings you to Huntingdon?'

'I have letters from King William, my lord,' Simon replied. 'I asked if I could take this duty.'

Waltheof released him with a hefty slap on the shoulder that almost sent Simon to his knees. 'I'm glad that you did. Judith, look who's here!'

She did not rise but gave a thin smile from her place at the chessboard. 'You are welcome,' she said, her tone holding none of Waltheof's warmth.

Waltheof laughed broadly. 'Pay no heed. My wife is annoyed because she was beating me and you have spoiled her pleasure!'

Dutifully Simon made his obeisance to her. Earl Waltheof's jest had caused Judith's frown to deepen. Simon thought she was lovely, but petulant. He bowed over her shapely, ring-adorned fingers and saw that the hand she did not offer him was laid upon the ripe curve of her belly.

'Our child is due on the feast of Saint Cuthbert,' Waltheof announced, gazing proudly at his wife.

Simon looked blank. He knew many of the saint's days, but he was not familiar with all of them, especially English ones.

'In about two months' time,' Waltheof said with a wave of his hand. 'My lady desires the babe to be born at Northampton, so we are travelling there for the lying in.' Although he spoke with a smile, there was a certain tension at his eye corners, which suggested that the decision was not entirely of his making.

'You said you had letters,' Judith prompted, a flicker of impatience in her tone.

'Yes, my lady.' Simon delved in his satchel and, although Judith was nearer, handed the vellum packet to Waltheof in a show of masculine solidarity.

A look of amusement on his face, the Earl broke the seal and, unfolding the vellum, went to the window where he could read by the light of the westering sun.

'What does my uncle say?' Judith demanded. Her fingers twitched as if longing to snatch the missive from him.

Waltheof shrugged. 'William desires my pledge of assistance in his campaign against the Scots. I am to join him as soon as I may.' He handed her the vellum.

Judith took it and scanned the lines with an almost avid expression.

Waltheof stroked his beard and sighed. 'This comes at a bad time. I had hoped to be with you for the birth of our first child.'

Judith raised her head from the vellum and gave him a narrow look. 'You must do as my uncle requests. If you show reluctance, then you will displease him. There is nothing you can do at the birthing except pace outside the chamber door and get underfoot. It is not as if your presence will affect the outcome.'

Simon felt the tension coiling in the atmosphere, invisible but potent as the heat from a brazier.

'You would rather I went to war?'

'I would rather you did your duty to my uncle,' she said stiffly.

'What about my duty to you and the child?'

'Attending my uncle *is* that duty,' Judith replied tersely. 'You would not want him to seize your lands for your failure to perform your obligations.'

'No . . . but I care about you first . . .'

'Then do as my uncle bids. He is, after all, the King.'

Waltheof glowered and bit the side of his thumb. Judith stared back, her implacable will beating his down.

'Women.' The Earl gave a forced laugh and clapped his hand across Simon's shoulders. 'You never know whether you're going to burn or freeze when you go near them, only that either way you'll lose your ballocks.'

Judith averted her head and Simon could tell by the thrust of her jaw that her teeth were clenched.

Waltheof propelled Simon from the chamber and into the hall. 'Best to let the dust settle,' he murmured. 'My lady can be difficult to handle, but I would not change a hair on her head.'

'Only your own, my lord,' Simon said.

Waltheof ran his hands through his severe crop and smiled rather sheepishly. 'Aye, well, that's of no matter,' he said. 'Tell me what you have been doing.'

So Simon told him about his duties as a squire, about his training and how it was developing apace. Waltheof listened with the genuine interest and concern that made him so well liked by his soldiers, his retainers and the ordinary people of his earldom. Pride he might possess, but unlike his wife there was not an arrogant bone in his body.

'And the leg?' Waltheof glanced down.

Unconsciously, Simon had been putting his weight on his right side to ease the ache. 'It pains me sometimes,' he admitted.

'When I have been standing awhile, or when it is late at night and I have been on duty the day long.' He looked quickly at Waltheof. 'I am not complaining, my lord.'

'I know you are not. It was I who asked.'

'Mostly I do not notice.' It was both the truth and a lie. Simon was always aware of the injury. He was determined that he would not be different, but the path that was straight for others was often more hazardous for him because of the very nature of his handicap. Sometimes he felt bitter and resentful, but he tried to keep such feelings in check. A squire who was surly and uncommunicative received far more kicks and blows than one who was cheerful and swift to please. To avoid the subject of his leg, he told Waltheof about his meeting with the sheriff's men in the centre of Huntingdon.

Waltheof's expression clouded. 'The sheriffs of my lands,' he said in a voice that was now devoid of charity, 'are a thorn in my side. Why the King should give the offices to such wolves as Robert Ilger, William de Caghanes and Picot de Saye is beyond my understanding.'

Simon frowned. A vague memory came to him. He had been a junior squire collecting empty wine jugs in the hall at Rouen on the first night that the English hostages had arrived. He remembered the arm-wrestling contest and Waltheof's prowess against one of William's favoured mercenaries. 'Picot de Saye is a sheriff?' he asked.

'Of Cambridge,' Waltheof bared his teeth. 'And the worst of them, although they are all painted with the same brush. They line their purses at the expense of the people and come down upon them with a mailed fist for the slightest transgression. I may as well not be earl here for they treat me with the utmost contempt.'

'Can you not speak to the King?'

Waltheof shook his head. 'I begin to think that William knows very well how his sheriffs behave and that it is his personal intention to hem me around with such men.'

'I have heard nothing at court,' Simon said, frowning.

'I do not suppose you would. Even you are not permitted into every corner of the King's life.'

Simon shifted uncomfortably, unsure how to respond. At court no one was ever open about their motives or thoughts. 'I think he is pleased to have you for a nephew,' he said diplomatically.

Waltheof smiled bleakly. 'He is pleased to have me where he wants me.'

Simon was spared from finding another reply as Judith's maid Sybille came towards them. A tiny baby was bound in a linen sling at her shoulder.

'Simon!' She embraced him with the side not occupied by the infant and kissed his cheek. 'Saints, boy, you are taller than me now!'

'And you seem to have acquired a baby,' Simon nervously eyed the rosy little face within the depths of the bundle.

'This,' said Sybille proudly, 'is my daughter, Helisende, born on the feast of Saint Winifred.'

Simon murmured congratulations, not quite sure of his ground. He could not ask outright if Sybille had a husband now. Her affections had always been peripatetic in the past and he could think of half a dozen candidates. He was also wary of small babies. For creatures that looked so innocent, they had the ability to make a fearsome noise and even more fearsome smells.

'Do you want to hold her?'

Simon wondered how to decline without seeming churlish.

'He will when she comes of age,' Waltheof rescued him with a twinkle and took the baby expertly into his own brawny arms. 'In the meantime I have to practise.' He smiled at Simon. 'Helisende is my god-daughter,' he said. 'Sybille married Toki last year.'

'Congratulations, mistress,' Simon murmured.

Sybille gave a little preen of her neck like a swan. 'I'm a goodwife now,' she said proudly. 'A fine lusty husband, a baby in the cradle and a mistress about to bear a babe of her own.'

She gave a wry chuckle. 'They serve to keep me well out of mischief!' Plucking her daughter from Waltheof's arms, she bustled on her way.

'She and Toki are very happy together,' he murmured, and for a moment his tone was almost wistful, as if he was gazing upon something he could not have. Then he shook himself like a dog shaking off water, and the look was gone. Simon did not dwell on the moment because at fourteen years old such matters were beyond his experience and of little interest. Besides, the steward had just sounded the dinner horn and Simon was ravenous. Everything but sustenance was suddenly unimportant.

It was a sweltering day at the beginning of August. In the women's bower at Waltheof's hall in Northampton the windows had been thrown open with the view that it would help the woman labouring on the birthing stool to expel the child from her womb.

Judith had begun her travail in the cool of the previous evening's moonrise. Now the sun blazed at its zenith and still the child had not come. Soaked in perspiration, her shift clung to her body, her swollen breasts and distended belly. They had unbraided her hair so that it would not bind the child in her womb, and it hung in sweat-soaked rat-tails to her hips.

Not in her darkest nightmares had Judith imagined the agony and the indignity that childbirth was visiting on her body. Surely this must be akin to the tortures suffered by damned souls in hell. The pains had grown steadily worse as her labour progressed. It was two hours since her waters had broken in an enormous gush of fluid that had soaked the floor rushes and the skirts of the two midwives in attendance.

'Not long, my lady, not long now,' encouraged one of the women, making Judith sip from a cup of honey and water.

Judith's hands tightened on the cup as another pain built to an excruciating pitch and crashed over her. She clenched her teeth and forced down the scream that rose in her throat, her whole body rigid.

'You must not fight it, my lady,' said the other midwife and patted Judith's brow with a cloth soaked in lavender water. 'Let it come.'

The pain receded. Judith sagged on the birthing stool. She wanted to weep, but she would not do so in front of these women . . . and especially not in front of her mother, who was watching the proceedings with a critical eye. Adelaide had already reminded her several times that she was the niece of a king and the wife of an earl and that to scream like a fishwife was unseemly.

She was glad that Waltheof was absent at a parley with her uncle, laying the ground for the campaign against Malcolm of Scotland. Had he been present he would have been pacing outside the room, demanding every few moments to know how she fared. She could not have borne his anxiety on top of her own. Besides, Waltheof and her mother were tepid with each other, and the less they had to share company the better for all concerned.

Another contraction gripped her in its pincers and made her its prey. She writhed and called out to Saint Margaret, protector of women in childbirth. At least by exhorting the saint she could give vent to her pain.

'That's it, my love,' encouraged the senior midwife and knelt beneath the birthing stool to examine how matters were progressing. 'At the peak of the next pain you must begin pushing. We'll have the babe in your arms before the light fades.'

Judith dug her fingernails into her palms at this news and swallowed the sob in her throat. She did not know how much more she could endure.

'You are doing very well, my lady,' the woman encouraged with a smile. 'The child is large and robust.'

'Not too large?' Adelaide queried tersely.

'Oh no, my lady,' the midwife hastened to reassure. 'Just a good size. Your daughter's hips are wide enough to accommodate him, but he is taking his own sweet time to be born.'

'Hah, lazy like his father,' Adelaide sniffed.

Despite her mother's words, Judith founded the slightest glimmer of satisfaction. A healthy boy, she thought. An heir for Huntingdon and Northampton. That would silence her mother, whose first two children had been daughters.

She clung to the notion as the pains surged and she toiled to expel the infant from her womb. He would be named William for her uncle. Waltheof might want to call him Siward, but Waltheof was not here, and the say was hers.

The candle clock had burned down two more notches before the baby's head finally crowned between Judith's thighs. Panting, almost spent, she lolled against the midwife supporting her.

'One more effort, my lady,' the woman crooned. 'One more push.'

Judith heard the words from a distance and summoned her strength for a final thrust. If the child was not born on this last surge, she knew that she would die.

The pain ripped through her in a tearing surge. Judith bore down, the tendons in her throat standing out and her face flushing red as wine. The second midwife cried triumphantly as the baby's head was born. Adelaide moved swiftly to the side of the birthing stool.

'What is it?' she demanded eagerly, looming like a crone over a cauldron.

'Can't tell, yet, my lady. One more little push . . .'

The baby slithered from Judith's body into the swathe of linen that the midwife was holding ready.

'A boy . . .' said Adelaide triumphantly. Her eyes were narrow as she sought to focus.

The baby spluttered, raised a tentative wail, hesitated, then bawled full force.

Looking discomforted, the midwife unwound the bluish, pulsing cord from between the infant's legs. 'No, my lady, your daughter has a girl child,' she said in a low mutter, as if it was her fault.

'A girl?' Adelaide's lips pursed.

'Yes, my lady.' Snicking the cord with a small pair of shears, she swaddled the baby tightly in bands of fresh, soft linen. The bawls subsided to kitten mewings and snuffles.

Judith closed her eyes. She squeezed them tightly shut, but still tears of weakness and disappointment leaked out from beneath her lids. All that effort, all the squalor and pain for a girl child, not the heir of her longing.

'Do you want to hold her?' The midwife brought the wrapped baby to the bedside.

'No.' Judith turned her head aside and refused even to look. 'Take her away. I can bear no more.'

Sybille glanced at Adelaide, and when she did not move stepped forward herself. 'My mistress is exhausted,' she murmured to the midwife. 'I'll hold the babe for now.'

The woman put the infant into Sybille's arms. 'It takes them like that sometimes,' she whispered. 'They sets their heart on a lad, and when the labour goes hard and the child is female they're mortal disappointed. She'll come around soon enough.'

In spite of the lowered voice, Judith heard what the midwife was whispering to Sybille. She did not think that she was ever going to come around to taking joy in the child. All she wanted was for everyone to go away so that she could sleep and forget.

Adelaide came to the side of the birthing stool. 'Look at me, daughter,' she said. It was no coincidence that the last word was emphasised.

Judith gazed at her mother through the spikes of tears and sweat clogging her lashes.

'I know how much the bearing of a girl child is a disappointment. I suffered it myself, twice over, but it is something with which you must learn to live. A daughter will be a companion to you as she grows, and useful in making marriage alliances. Be thankful that the child is strong and safely delivered.' Awkwardly, she pushed a sticky tendril of hair off Judith's brow. 'It is perhaps not the time to talk of such matters, but you might be more fortunate on the next occasion. You can see that I was when I bore Stephen.'

Judith clenched her teeth as her loins cramped and the second midwife set about dealing with the delivery of the after-birth. 'You are right, Mother,' she choked. 'It is not the time to talk of such matters.'

Adelaide let out her breath on an exasperated sigh and went to turn down the bedcoverings.

Through a haze of pain, misery and exhaustion, Judith was aware that on a certain level her mother was relieved. If Judith had borne a son, the balance of power between them would have shifted subtlely in Judith's direction. For the moment, Adelaide continued to have the upper hand.

Sybille jogged the baby gently in her arms. 'Just wait until your papa sees you,' she crooned. 'You'll be the sun and moon to him.'

Judith was assaulted by a vicious pang of jealousy, swiftly followed by remorse. How could she be jealous of her own child? Tears filled her eyes and swelled in her throat until it ached fiercely with the effort of holding the dam.

'Come, my lady, let us make you more comfortable.' Soothing her as if she were a small child, the senior midwife helped Judith from the stool to the bed while the other dealt with the after-birth, which was to be blessed by the priest and buried. A maid set about clearing up the bloody rushes beneath the birthing stool. The stool itself was removed for scrubbing and storing until it should be needed again.

The smooth, lavender-scented sheets and feather mattress felt like heaven beneath Judith's sore body. Her stained and sweat-soaked shift was thrown on the laundry pile. The women washed her in scented warm water, tidied her hair into two long, dark braids, and gave her a fresh shift to wear. Judith's tears retreated as her dignity was restored and she felt the famil-iar mantle of control begin to settle back around her shoulders, cocooning her from harm.

Sybille approached the bed, the baby snuffling gently in her arms. The look of tenderness on her face made Judith feel guilty and a little resentful.

'Here,' said the maid as if reading her thoughts. 'You hold her.' Gently lowering the baby, she arranged Judith's arms so that they supported the delicate skull. 'Doesn't she look like her father?'

Judith stared into the crumpled features unable to see any resemblance at all, except perhaps to a wizened turnip. Its face was red and its eyes had a strange, shiny appearance. The tuft of hair sticking out from beneath the edge of the blanket was stiff with birthing fluid, but the underlying colour shone through – copper gold, like Waltheof's. She had heard women speak of overwhelming love at first sight, but no such emotion resided in her breast. She was surprised; she was curious in a detached sort of way – could not believe that this creature had come from her body. And she was disappointed that she had failed to bear a son. As if sensing her negative thoughts, the baby, who had been settled in Sybille's embrace, began to fret. The red face grew redder and the little face screwed up. A hole opened in its face and an enormous noise emerged.

Judith panicked and pushed the baby away. Leaning over, Sybille swiftly gathered the bawling bundle in her arms and cradled it until the roars subsided into angry hiccups. The infant turned her head and made rooting motions at Sybille's breast.

'I think that she is hungry,' the maid murmured. 'Perhaps if you were to feed her.'

Judith looked horrified. 'I cannot,' she whispered. 'You ask too much. She has taken too much from me already.'

Sybille bit her lip. She turned to Adelaide for guidance. Looking peeved and anxious, the older woman waved her hand. 'You are a new mother yourself, you have milk in your breasts. It will be no hardship to feed the child for now. Your mistress is too distraught.'

'My lady.' Cradling the baby tenderly in her arms, Sybille carried her out to the antechamber. She unpinned her gown, unlaced the drawstring of her chemise and put the child to suckle. As the little jaws worked, she touched the copper bronze curl with a gentle forefinger. Tears of compassion filled her eyes, and love. How could Lady Judith reject such a beautiful, vulnerable little thing? When she had borne her own daughter, she had been unable to wait to hold her in her arms. Regardless of the pain and the exhaustion, she had wept with joy, not chagrin.

Perhaps, she tried to comfort herself, it would be different when Lady Judith had slept. Her labour had been very long and she was clearly at the end of her endurance. Duty would lead her to feed the baby once she had recovered, and from that bonding love would grow. Sybille gnawed her lip. She knew that she was seeking excuses for her mistress's behaviour and that in truth all was not well.

'Never fret, little one,' she whispered, 'I will make sure you do not lack for love, and your papa will adore you. I know he will.'

It was late when Waltheof returned to Northampton from his parley with William. Tired and hungry, he rode into the courtyard, dismounted from his horse and handed the reins to the youth who came running.

'Any news, Brand?' he asked, finding a smile despite his weariness.

'Yes, my lord,' the stable lad said. 'The Countess was safely delivered of a daughter before Compline this very eve.'

Waltheof stood while he absorbed the news, and then, forgetting his exhaustion, he ran.

'Judith is sleeping,' Adelaide said, standing across the bedchamber doorway as fiercely as any armed guard, her expression disapproving. 'The birth was difficult and she is very tired.'

Waltheof struggled with his impatience and the urge to swipe the termagant out of his way. 'Nevertheless, I would see my wife and my child. If Judith is sleeping, I promise I will not waken her.'

With obvious reluctance, Adelaide stepped to one side. Her nose wrinkled. Waltheof looked at her censorious expression, sniffed his armpit, and asked her politely if she would arrange for a bathtub to be prepared. With tightly pursed lips Adelaide stalked away to summon the maids and Waltheof laid his hand to the latch.

There was no sound in the room. Judith was as fastidious in sleep as she was awake. He had never heard her snore or mumble. She lay on her back, the woven coverlet rising and falling as she breathed. Waltheof tiptoed to the bedside and looked down at her in the light from the thick wax candle. There were dark shadows beneath her closed lids that spoke not just of weariness like his own but sheer exhaustion. Her hair had been neatly braided, reminding him of a child. She looked so vulnerable that he wanted to sweep her into his embrace and protect her from everything. He had to fold his hands in his belt and force himself not to touch her

He peered nervously into the cradle at the side of the bed, but it was empty. Indeed, it had never been used, the linen coverings smooth and unrumpled. A slight sound in the doorway caused him to turn.

Sybille was standing on the threshold, a bundle in her arms. Laying her finger to her lips, she beckoned him from the room.

'If she cries, it will disturb her mother,' she whispered.

Waltheof stepped out into the antechamber, his arms already held out to receive the child.

Sybille did not have to tell him how to hold his tiny daughter; he had a natural instinct. His large hand supported her tiny fragile skull and her body lay along the length of his powerful forearm. Tears filled Waltheof's eyes and spilled down his cheeks. He had never set eyes on anything as beautiful, or as moving. A part of himself, a part of Judith, mingled in this perfect, tiny creature. The baby's eyes had been closed, but now they opened and studied him with such owlish solemnity that he laughed brokenly through his tears.

Sybille sniffed too and wiped the back of her hand across

her lids. 'She's been christened Matilda in honour of the Queen,' she said.

Waltheof stroked a tender forefinger upon the incredibly soft little cheek. 'The King and Queen are to be her godparents,' he murmured.

Sybille hesitated. Waltheof looked at her. 'What is it?'

'Naught, my lord. Perhaps it is better that you know that my lady was disappointed not to bear you a son. Countess Adelaide has appointed me as a wet nurse for the moment.'

Waltheof glanced through the crack of the door into the room where his wife slept. 'She will come around,' he murmured. He knew how much store Judith had set on bearing a boy. But how could she fail not to fall in love with the enchanting daughter they had made between them?

The baby snuffled. Waltheof nestled her more securely in the crook of his arm and set off towards the outer chamber door.

'Where are you going?' Sybille's voice rose on a worried note.

Waltheof paused and swung round. 'To show her off to her people,' he said with an exalted smile. 'I want everyone to see her, from the steward to the stable boy.'

'Will the Countess Adelaide approve?' Sybille looked anxiously around as if expecting to see Judith's mother materialise out of the wall.

The relaxed muscles in Waltheof's face suddenly tightened. 'I do not give a fourthing whether the Countess approves or not,' he growled. 'For the moment, this child is my heir, and I want my people to see her, and all the pride and love I have for her.' With determined tread, tear streaks shining on his face, he carried his newborn daughter into the public domain of the great hall.

CHAPTER 14

Abbot Ulfcytel leaned over the cradle and studied the small baby gurgling on the coverlet of soft lambskin. She waved her arms at him and kicked her legs.

'My wife says that she should be swaddled to make her limbs grow straight, but it seems a pity to me not to let her feel the joy of using them,' Waltheof said. 'I cannot see that an hour's freedom will ruin her for life.'

Ulfcytel smiled. 'Nor I,' he said, 'but women are ever protective of their offspring, especially the firstborn.' He prodded the infant with a gentle forefinger and was rewarded by a crow of response and an animated flail of limbs.

Waltheof suspected that Judith's protectiveness stemmed from a desire to order the world as she chose rather than from maternal devotion. His mother-in-law had departed to her own lands in the south a week ago and Waltheof had quietly thanked God for that particular mercy. Judith was always worse when Adelaide was at hand to aid and abet.

He and Ulfcytel were standing in the garden at Northampton. A last flourish of summer had swept the herb beds with sunshine and pointed the sundial to the hour of sext. Nearby the gardeners were harvesting marigold seeds and tidying the straggle of herbs that were tiring as a hot summer wilted towards autumn. On the morrow he was to take his troops and ride north to join King William on the campaign against Malcolm of Scotland.

Waltheof felt apprehensive. Edgar Atheling was sheltering at the Scots court and he had no desire to meet his former ally and companion on the battlefield.

Ulfcytel wrapped his gnarled brown hands around his staff of polished ivory. 'I am pleased to see you settled with lands and a family, my son,' he said. 'I feared for you when you joined the Danes in the North and King William took his revenge.'

Waltheof smiled uneasily and looked away. 'I am going to the North as a Norman now,' he replied, and thrust his fingers through his short, coppery hair as if hoping to discover that its former abundance had grown back. 'It will be hard, but as Judith tells me . . . it is my duty and I have no other choice.'

Judith was polite to Abbot Ulfcytel but vexed by his presence at their table. He spoke very little French, and Judith had no intention of learning the coarse, guttural tongue of the English. There was soil beneath his fingers from tending his garden; the cuffs of his alb were patched and the only possession that reflected his rank was the beautiful staff of yellowed ivory.

Waltheof, however, was so fond of him that he treated the rotund, coarse little abbot as one of his family. Ulfcytel dined at their table more frequently than any other guest, much to Judith's irritation. When she was not enduring Ulfcytel's presence she had to suffer the company of the Breton Ralf de Gael, Earl of Norfolk, whose smooth, bland manner and sly ways she disliked intensely. She could not understand why Waltheof favoured the man other than their shared capacity for drink. Her husband's judgement of others was unsound and a cause for worry.

Making her excuses to Waltheof and Ulfcytel, Judith retired to her chamber. She yearned for the refinement of the Norman court, just as once she had yearned to escape from its stultifying confines. To hear French spoken as a matter of course, rather than mangled haltingly through an English accent. To be accorded the full deference due to her rank. Here she was aware that people bowed to her face and gave her resentful looks behind her back. She was their beloved earl's Norman wife, an intruder, a burden they had to shoulder for their lord's sake. She knew that without her presence in the hall men would be slackening their belts and reaching anew for the ale. The laughter would grow raucous and bawdy, Waltheof's retainers gladly abandoning the notion that they were constrained by Norman rule.

Tomorrow Waltheof would leave for the North and she would become responsible in his absence for the welfare of the earldom. The notion was almost pleasing. She would have work to keep her occupied, she thought, even if it was an uphill struggle to deal with the recalcitrant English. She found that she enjoyed the duties of administration and dealing justice. Waltheof was not so fond of such toil and left much of it to his officials, but Judith would often linger in the hall to observe them at work and provide the necessary overseeing of authority.

Sybille sat in a curule chair near the brazier, suckling baby Matilda at her breast. Judith thanked God that her maid had sufficient milk to feed two infants, for the notion of a baby mouthing her own breast was vaguely repulsive. Some folk said that a child should only drink of its natural mother's milk, that giving a nobly born baby sustenance from a baser source would coarsen the child. Others said that, providing the wet nurse was of good character with abundant milk, it made no difference. Sybille's character had occasionally given cause for concern, but since her handfasting to Toki she had settled down and there was no denying the quality of her milk. Little Matilda was thriving and growing plump.

'She's a greedy one,' Sybille laughed at her mistress. 'I think she is going to be as big as her father when she's full grown.'

Judith winced at the notion of a woman the size of Waltheof. Certainly, Matilda had his hair. The fine wisps on the baby's skull were like threads of gold caught in the light of the setting sun, her complexion the pink and white of dog roses. Folk cooed over her daughter and said that she was beautiful, but to Judith she looked like any other baby. Sometimes she would stand over her and try to find some spark of maternal devotion, but it was as if there was a barrier between her and the child. She felt nothing. It might have been different if Matilda was a son. At least then she would have had pride.

Waltheof doted on the baby and would often fetch her from her cradle and carry her around in the crook of his arm, talking softly to her, showing her the world. Judith had felt emotions then, but none of which she was proud. Indeed, she had prayed on her knees in the chapel for them to be expunged.

Sybille gently prised the baby's jaws off her nipple. 'Asleep,' she said softly, a tender smile on her face that made Judith feel mean and unworthy. She watched the maid expertly change the baby's wet linens then place her snug and replete at the head of the fleece-lined cradle. Little Helisende, Sybille's own daughter, occupied the foot. 'They won't waken again much before the second matins bell – prime if fortune smiles,' Sybille said. Rocking the cradle with a tap of her foot, she removed her wimple and began loosening her thick brown braids.

Judith looked at her askance.

'You have to send your man away to war with a fond farewell,' Sybille said knowingly. 'I don't want Toki getting randy with some red-haired Scottish wench.' Taking her cloak down from a peg set in the wall, she went to the door. 'Besides, you'll be wanting some time alone with your lord.' Winking, not waiting upon a dismissal, the maid left the room, her step light and swift.

Judith flushed. She and Waltheof had not bedded together since Matilda's birth. Her body had needed time to heal, and a man was not supposed to lie with a woman within forty days of childbed, the Church said so; indeed, some Church teachings went further than that. It was six weeks since Matilda's birth. Two and forty days. She went to look down at the sleeping children. The next one would be a boy. That's what everyone told her – as they had told her that Matilda would be a male. And before a child could be born, it had to be begotten, and then forced into the world through a travail of pain.

Shivering, Judith turned away from the cradle and went beyond the curtains into the chamber that she and Waltheof shared. The large bed was the centrepiece of the room, its sides carved with a strange interlacing design of serpents chasing and swallowing each other. It had belonged to Waltheof's father, the legendary Earl Siward, and to his father before him. The hints of pagan religion in the carving filled Judith with distaste and unease. Waltheof, however, had grown intractable when she suggested they be rid of it, and had sworn that while he lived it would remain.

Piled around the room were items of baggage that on the morrow would be loaded onto pack ponies. His mail hauberk, neatly wrapped in a waxed bundle and greased with pig fat to prevent it from rusting; his round shield, which he still preferred over the Norman kite design, the terrible rune-engraved axe, again handed down from his father. She shuddered as she looked at the edge, shining in the candlelight like rippled water. He had killed Normans with that weapon. She was seldom fanciful, but she thought that if she peered too closely in the reflection of the steel she might see scenes from its bloody past flowing across the mirrored surface.

Averting her head from the axe, she sat gingerly on the bed with its coverlet of silver fox pelts and summoned one of her other tiring maids to help her disrobe.

Waltheof arrived a short while later, slightly loquacious with drink but almost sober. She heard him stop in the curtained off antechamber and knew that he had paused by the cradle. He never passed it at night without looking upon his daughter. Judith felt the familiar pang of jealousy, followed by one of guilt. With an irritated gesture she dismissed the maid and sat up in bed, her chemise firmly laced at her throat, her hair combed and smoothly rebraided.

Waltheof parted the door curtain and entered the room. Judith gazed upon her husband and her breath caught with that strange fluttering of panic and desire that she had never been able to reconcile. How could she be so attracted to him, and feel such impatience at the same time?

'Ulfcytel sent me,' he said with a smile. 'He said that I should not be spending my last night before a campaign in the company of an old priest but in the warm arms of my wife.'

Judith raised her brows. 'So you could not come to that conclusion yourself?'

'Well, yes, I was preparing to be polite, but his perception was the swifter.' Waltheof sat down on the edge of the bed and began removing his clothes. 'Besides,' he added softly, 'sleeping in the warm arms of my wife when I cannot make love to her has been a bind almost beyond endurance these past weeks.'

Judith fiddled with the neat lacing of her shift. There was an immodest throbbing in her woman's parts. It was lust, she thought. No matter how she battled to subdue it, her need was always the stronger.

'Some priests say that a woman is not clean to lie with until eighty days have passed from the birth,' she procrastinated.

'Eighty days!' Waltheof looked at her in consternation. 'I have not heard that one before!'

'It happens if the child is a girl. I think it is to do with the sin of Eve.'

He snorted down his nose. 'I would say that "some priests" must hate women beyond all charity,' he said curtly. 'But if the notion of coupling with me disturbs you, I can always fetch Ulfcytel to bless our bed. I am sure he will be delighted to do so.'

Judith shook her head. 'That will not be necessary,' she said in a slightly choked voice. She could imagine nothing worse than having the small, earthy abbot with his ragged tonsure blessing their union. 'I too think that forty days is sufficient.'

'I think it is too long,' Waltheof's voice was heartfelt. He finished undressing and turned to her. Already he was magnificently erect and straining as if he would burst out of his skin. 'Ah, Judith,' he said softly. He reached to unpluck the laces of her chemise. 'You cannot know . . .'

But she did know, and whilst a part of her was shocked another part welcomed him with open arms and wide-parted thighs, and as he lifted her buttocks and thrust into her she coiled her legs around his hips and dug her nails into his broad back. The bed became a Viking ship, rocking on a stormy sea, and she was a slave, tied to the mast and ravished by its sea-wolf master. The imagery tore through her, heightening her lust. She was helpless; what was happening was not her fault, and she was not to blame. When she climaxed she muffled her scream against the polished curve of his shoulder and heard with fierce pleasure the roar of his release and felt the pulse of his seed within her. The next child would be a boy. No girl could possibly be born of such a wild and vigorous mating.

Simon's jaw cracked as he did his best to conceal a yawn. The dawnlight was a low flush on the eastern horizon, but he had been awake and on duty for more than two measures on the time candle. He wondered how the King could be so indefatigable. William had not retired until well past midnight and had risen long before prime. Simon had staggered blearily around the campaign tent, fetching him a ewer of warm water to bathe his hands and face and assisting him to dress. He had attended mass with William in the chapel tent, had knelt among the other battle commanders, barons and squires to receive the body and blood of Christ. Waltheof had been present, looking as bleary as Simon felt, his coppery hair in need of a trim and his stubble thickening into a corn-coloured beard. He had managed a wink at Simon and by swift, silent gestures had intimated that too much ale the night before was the reason for his malaise.

Now Simon was burnishing William's helm. He could have delegated the task to one of the junior squires, but ever since entering the King's employ the duty had been his and it had become a ritual that he guarded jealously. Helm in one hand, cloth in the other, he went to the tent flap, where his gaze was met by ranks of canvas shelters. Soldiers stood around the haze of their morning fires dining on flat bread and ale, and through the wreaths of smoke there was a heather-scented nip in the air. The grooms were readying the horses and Simon could hear the snap of the banners in the stiff breeze that had risen with the dawn.

The Norman army had been on the march for several days, prepared for war but progressing unhindered. No Scots army came raging from the heather to prevent William from entering Lothian, crossing the Forth and marching on into King Malcolm's domain.

Hooves thudded outside the tent and a large chestnut stallion blocked his light. 'I have just been speaking to the King, and he says that you have his permission to ride out awhile,' Waltheof leaned down from the saddle to announce. He looked more awake than he had done an hour since. He had obviously dunked his hair in the burn, for it was sleeked back from his forehead and gleamed like wet rust. His grizzle of beard remained; he had not seen fit to barber it off.

Simon gave the helm another polish. The notion of riding out was a lure too tempting to resist. 'If you but wait a moment while I finish this. It has to be right.'

'Of course it has,' Waltheof said with a straight face, although Simon was sure he detected a twinkle in the deep-blue eyes. 'It would not do for King William to greet the King of Scotland in anything less than royal splendour.'

Simon finished burnishing the helm and set it carefully to one side on a wadded linen cloth. Telling the junior squire to check over the other equipment and make sure that the wine pitcher was full and fresh bread to hand, he left his post and approached the horse line where his roan cob was dozing. Waltheof followed, his huscarls Toki and Siggurd riding a few paces behind with swords at their hips and round shields slung at their backs.

Untethering his mount, Simon grasped a handful of mane and vaulted nimbly across the saddle, showing off a little in front of the men. Waltheof's lips twitched.

'Not only a trusted messenger, but a fine horseman, I see,' he teased.

Simon gave him a self-conscious grin. Then he sobered. 'There was a time when I thought I might never do such a thing,' he said.

'I never doubted it. You have a will the equal of my wife's – formidable.' Waltheof tugged on the reins and set his heels to the chestnut's flanks.

They rode past the sentries and away from the Norman camp, following the rutted cart track through the hardy sheep pasture – although no sheep grazed the turf. All livestock had been spirited away by the locals so that it would not end up as dinner for Scots or Norman soldiers. The nearest settlement was the town of Abernethay, which their scouts had reported as three miles distant and where the Scots army was mustering behind its defensive palisade.

The wind gusted. Waltheof's sleek hair turned wild as it dried and beat around his face. Simon's brown-gold cap ruffled like the layered feathers of a bird. Their horses climbed away from the Norman camp, muscles straining, ears pricked. Simon opened his mouth and let the air blow into him until he felt as if he could take off and scud across the sky like a cloud.

On the crest of a hill they drew rein to let their horses regain their breath. Below them the land was spread out like an elaborate embroidery, moors and mountains, russet and purple, clean scented with heather. Here the bones of the land felt close to the surface, no padding of well-fed flesh to conceal their beauty. The ride and the wild scenery exhilarated Simon, but after a moment he found himself wondering what the blue smudge of the horizon concealed. What lay beyond the ability of the eye to perceive? If only he could climb and see all with the eyes of an eagle.

'The King said to me earlier that it will not come to a fight,' Waltheof murmured, gazing into the distance. 'We are too strong for Malcolm.' He smiled sourly. 'Men begin to think that William of Normandy is unstoppable.' The wind breathed life into his cloak, the white bearskin ruffling as if with a spirit of its own.

Simon said nothing. He heard a great deal, being William's squire of the chamber, but he never spoke of the matters discussed therein. His discretion was a matter of pride, discipline and honour; no one would ever accuse him of braying confidences abroad. Representatives from King Malcolm had arrived shortly after mass bearing messages for William. Simon already knew what was going to happen. He glanced at Waltheof, wanting to speak, constrained not to.

'It isn't true,' Waltheof said softly into Simon's silence. 'We could have stopped him in York if only we had acted together instead of squandering our advantage. I am not advocating treason,' he added quickly, as Simon drew a sharp breath. 'The Danes have gone home and there is no one who possesses the same skills of leadership as William. Edgar Atheling is a weak reed, the sons of Harold are pirates, and after York I know that my own abilities are not up to the task.' He gave a self-deprecatory smile. 'A man should know his own weaknesses. Besides, a child of my blood is William's own great-niece.'

Simon wondered uneasily if there was a crumb of bitterness festering within Waltheof. It was likely, but then from what he had also heard that morning William had a possible cure for it. 'The Scots are coming to parley,' he said, pointing towards a party of horsemen who had appeared on the track below. The new morning sun slanted over their armour and spears, making a brave glitter. A standardbearer carried aloft the banner of King Malcolm of the Scots and close behind him, riding a white horse, was a thickset man of middle years who resembled a peasant but wore a crown at his brow.

Simon reined his horse around. 'I'll be needed for chamber duties, and King William will want you present, my lord.'

Waltheof gave Simon a thoughtful look. 'Will he, indeed?'

'Yes,' Simon answered. 'I can say no more, save that it will be to your advantage.'

Malcolm of Scotland was a little over forty years old with sandy hair turning silver at the temples and narrow light blue eyes.

Last year he had set aside his first wife and married Margaret, the sister of Edgar Atheling, thereby binding his own house of Dunkeld to that of the ancient West Saxon line.

The fact that Margaret desired to enter a nunnery had been ignored. Margaret herself, after some protest, had finally agreed to the marriage. It seemed that she had swiftly become reconciled to her change of direction, for she was already great with child. It was rumoured that her fierce, rambunctious husband doted upon his faery-blonde wife and that he was warm clay in her hands. It was also rumoured that she had embarked on the task of taming and civilising the Scots court. If she was not going to be a nun, then at least she could dwell in an atmosphere conducive to harmony.

There was, however, small sign of that harmony in William's campaign tent. Malcolm of Scotland, known as Caen Mor or Big Head by his own people, was bullish and opinioned. Even if he had come to yield to William of Normandy, he had small intention of doing it with grace.

Simon poured wine and unobtrusively handed it around. Malcolm took the proffered goblet, sniffed suspiciously and then drank. His lips twisted. 'I've tasted better cat's pee,' he said, speaking French but in such a mangled, guttural accent that although the meaning was clear the words themselves were difficult to decipher. Simon was fascinated. Waltheof looked both amused and bemused. William's face wore its customary blank expression, giving nothing away.

'Is ale more to your taste, Lord King?' Simon asked politely.

Malcolm's shrewd warrior's eyes met his. 'Aye,' he snapped. 'Give me ale, although I doot that any o' your Sassenach muck will taste good on my palate.'

'And yet you have put aside your first Scots wife to take a "Sassenach" bride,' William said with deceptive mildness. 'And I understand that congratulations are in order now that she is with child.'

Malcolm scowled and dug his fingers into his beautiful, gilded belt. 'Ye'll nae mock me,' he growled.

'Far from it,' William said smoothly. 'I was merely pointing out that a ruler must act on expediency before instinct – or why are we both here?'

. Malcolm continued to glower. Simon returned with a brimming stone cup. 'It is heather ale, Lord King,' he said, 'of your country's own brewing.'

'Hah, and stolen by Normans,' Malcolm sneered, but he took the cup and sank a long mouthful. 'Och, it will dae,' he said with an irritated wave of his hand.

Simon bowed and retreated. Ever curious about the ways of other peoples, he had sampled Scots fare in the form of a sort of meat and barley pudding boiled in the membrane of a sheep's stomach and served with a thick bread cooked on an open griddle. Compared to the fare of the Norman court it was coarse and strange, but it had been hot and nourishing and had kept out the bitter evening chill. He had to agree with Malcolm that heather ale was preferable to their Norman wine, which had not travelled well. Waltheof seemed to think so too, because he was eyeing Malcolm's cup with a covetous eye. Simon poured another measure of the ale and unobtrusively exchanged it for Waltheof's wine, thereby earning himself a quick smile of gratitude.

The negotiations went forward in fits and starts, mostly caused by Malcolm's mangled accent and his determination to be cantankerous even though he was here to surrender. He had with him his eldest son, a twelve-year-old who was to be given as hostage for his father's good behaviour. The lad, quiet and dark-haired, was a slender contrast to his thickset overbearing father.

'Ye'll treat him well,' Malcolm growled, 'else I'll make garters of every pair o' Norman guts between here and Durham town.'

William inclined his head. 'Providing you keep to your side of the bargain, your son will come to no harm,' he replied.

Malcolm scowled and blustered, but finally agreed to the terms. However neither he nor William were yet prepared to seal them by the ceremony of making the kiss of peace. Both men still had points to settle. William desired the removal of Edgar Atheling from the Scottish court.

'I canna dae that, the man's my brother-in-law!' Malcolm's eyebrows bristled and he folded his arms belligerently.

'The man is a thorn in my side who persists in fomenting rebellion. In yielding to me, you are accepting me as your overlord and you cannot harbour my enemies at your court. Your brother-in-law or not, Edgar Atheling goes.' William spread his hands on the trestle and leaned on them to emphasise his point.

There was a long silence but only one outcome. Everyone knew that Malcolm had no choice. It was one of the prices to pay for peace and the only way that the Norman force was going to withdraw back across the Forth.

'If I dae that for ye, then ye mun dae something for me,' Malcolm said.

William raised his brows.

Malcolm glared with triumphant malice at Earl Gospatric. 'I'll no hae that blethershite Gospatric facing me o'er the border. There'll be more bloodshed than ye've ever seen if he stays.'

Gospatric leaped to his feet, his complexion fire-red and his hand going to his empty scabbard, all swords having been prudently left outside. 'You dare to make such demands!' he spat. 'You're naught but a murdering, primitive heathen with sheepshit for brains!'

'And you're nae more than a runty wee arsewipe who I'll nae entertain as my neighbour.'

Gospatric launched himself at Malcolm and got such a grip on his throat that it took three men to haul him off and then pin him back against the side of the tent. Choking, Malcolm fell to his knees, and Waltheof went to his assistance. With cold fury in his eyes William gestured two guards to carry Gospatric outside.

'Ye see?' Malcolm wheezed. 'What chance is there for peace wi' him on my borders?'

William did not look best pleased. 'You force my hand,' he said, 'and that is something that I do not like.'

'Hah, well I don't like yielding tae you, but I mun dae it to survive,' Malcolm rasped tersely.

William swung round to pace the short length of the tent. Simon watched him. Outside Gospatric could be heard wrestling with the soldiers. There was indeed a bitter enmity between Gospatric and Malcolm. The former had plundered the Scots lowlands last year, serving a warning that Scots raids on English territory must stop. In retaliation Malcolm had brought devastating fire and sword across the border, his attack so savage that William had come harrying north to deal with the situation.

'Very well,' William said, swinging round. 'I will appoint a new earl, and raids on both sides will cease.'

'That depends on who ye appoint,' Malcolm said.

William rubbed his jaw as if deliberating, but Simon knew that his mind was already made up and had long been so. 'I have in mind Earl Waltheof of Huntingdon,' he said. 'He has a natural entitlement to the position, and although he has a Norman wife he is without Norman blood.' A wintry smile curved his mouth corners as he made the last observation.

Waltheof's breath hissed through his teeth and Simon saw the astonishment widen his eyes and brighten his complexion.

Malcolm turned his gaze on Waltheof and eyed him craftily. 'I suppose needs must when the De'il drives,' he pronounced, but he was clearly not displeased by the choice. Why should he be, Simon thought. Waltheof might be a fine warrior in his mid-twenties with an enhanced reputation from the Danish invasion of York, but as yet he was no Siward the Strong, the very mention of his name to be feared. Doubtless the King of Scots thought that he could run rings around him.

Looking dazed, Waltheof first stood up then knelt at

William's feet and bowed his head. 'It is a great honour that you do me, your grace.'

'It is indeed,' William said. 'Make sure you honour the position as much as it honours you.' Stooping he took Waltheof's hands between his own and gave him the kiss of peace on either cheek, thereby conferring on him the earldom of Northumbria that had once been held by his father.

'And what o' Gospatric?' Malcolm demanded with a contemptuous jerk of his head. 'What will ye dae wi' him?'

William stood straight. 'He can be escorted to the nearest shore and put out of these isles with your outlawed brother-by-marriage,' he said curtly.

Malcolm nodded, accepting the fact, then turned to Waltheof, who was slowly easing to his feet, a beatific expression on his face. 'Watch yoursel', laddie,' he said. 'Your king uses men like food. Eats them up and spits oot the bones when he's had the sustenance.'

Simon frowned. Malcolm had it wrong. William did indeed devour men, but if he discarded them it was not because he had no more use for them, but rather that they were unable to live beneath his harsh codes and demands for unquestioning loyalty.

'Since I have never gained so much goodwill from being anyone else's man, I'll take the risk,' Waltheof answered, inclining his head in courtesy to the King of Scots. 'I am sure that you are a gambling man yourself, sire.'

'Aye,' Malcolm said sourly. 'And look where it got me.'

Two weeks later William prepared to leave for Normandy where a border war was brewing with his neighbours in Maine. Waltheof returned home to Judith, bearing with him the momentous news that now, as his father had been, he was Earl of Northumbria.

Judith's pride in his accomplishment glowed out of her eyes. When he kissed her, she kissed him back. In bed her responses were almost feverish and he brought her to pleasure twice before he reached his own. It was as if his new status was a powerful love potion that she was unable to resist.

'Now you are truly a man of influence,' she declared as they lay together in the breathless aftermath of lovemaking, her fingers gently tugging on his coppery chest hair. He had shaved his beard and had the barber return his growing locks to the harshness of a Norman crop in consideration of his wife.

He was aware that his new title meant a great deal to her, but he had not realised how much until he saw her incandescence at the news. He was amused, and also, if the truth were known, a little uneasy. His love for Judith was not bound up in her status as the Conqueror's niece, but it seemed that her regard for him was powerfully influenced by his social standing. But he said nothing. To have done so would have exposed aspects of their relationship that were better kept buried. Besides, he was very tender of her, for she was again with child. The infant had been conceived on the night that he departed for Scotland. At the most there would be eleven months between the new babe and its sister.

'This time it will be a son, for our lands,' Judith said fiercely, and taking his hand, laid it upon her smooth belly. 'I feel it as strongly as a river flowing.'

'Son or daughter, it matters not,' Waltheof murmured, spreading his hand over the pale curve of her flesh. 'There is time enough for both. King William has an equal number of each.'

'No,' Judith said stubbornly, 'it will be a boy.' Her lips became mulish and a little folded inwards, the way they did when she was determined to have her own way.

Waltheof shrugged and smiled, indulging her. 'Very well,' he said with a yawn. 'It will be a boy.'

In the midsummer heat of the following year, Judith gave birth to their second daughter. She wept bitterly and refused to be consoled when the midwife hesitantly delivered the unwelcome news along with the squawling, dark-haired bundle. 'If I had married a Norman,' she hurled at Waltheof, 'he would have given me sons!'

'And if I had taken an English wife, I would not have to suffer the unseemly lash of her tongue!' he had retorted. Shocked at the clash of their mutual bitterness, hurt and angry, Waltheof stormed from their bedchamber and proceeded to get roaring drunk, because apologising was more than he could bear to do. Early on in the session, before he lost his wits in the cool depths of a firkin of ale, Sybille brought him the new baby, still damp from her birth and wrapped tightly in linen swaddling. Holding her in the crook of his arm Waltheof saw his wife clearly in her tiny seashell features and the puff of almost black hair on her brow. It made him want to weep.

'How is she to be named, my lord?' Sybille asked gently.

Waltheof swallowed. 'For her mother,' he croaked. 'Mayhap it will recall her to her duty.'

Sybille said nothing, although she privately thought that naming this second child thus was a bad idea. Every time she looked at the baby, Judith would be reminded of her failure to produce a son.

Waltheof gazed at Sybille. 'How is it possible to begrudge a child its life because of its sex?' he asked in a torn and bewildered voice.

Sybille did not have an answer. Biting her lip to stop it from trembling, she took the baby back into her own arms. 'I'd best go and take her to the new wet nurse,' she said gently. 'I would have nursed her myself, but I don't have enough milk for three.'

Waltheof nodded a dismissal and turned back to the jug of ale with a vengeance.

CHAPTER 15

Palace of Northampton, Spring 1075

The apples had been stored over winter and were slightly wrinkled, but their sweetness was wonderfully concentrated. Sybille peeled one with her small, bone-handled knife, cut it into slivers and divided it between her daughter Helisende and the ladies Matilda and Judith. Lured by a warm flood of April sunshine, she had brought the girls into the garden. Their mother, as usual, was at her prayers. Recently she had been speaking of founding a nunnery on her lands at Elstow near Bedford.

Matilda lingered at Sybille's knee, her eyes on the core.

'You want it, *chérie?*'

'I want to make a tree,' Matilda said. Each word was firm and clear. Everyone agreed that the child was advanced for her years, in both stature and intellect. Already she topped Helisende by a head. Caught back in a blue ribbon, her hair was a mass of coppery-bronze curls, slightly less red in tone than Waltheof's. Her creamy skin was peppered with freckles and her eyes were the same dense shade of blue as her father's.

'A tree, my love?'

Matilda took the core in her chubby hand. 'You put it in the ground,' she said patiently to the maid, 'then you water it, and a tree grows.'

'Ah,' Sybille nodded. 'And who told you that?'

'Edwin.' She announced the gardener's name loudly and looked at Sybille as if she thought her slightly dim-witted. Taking the core, she marched over to a bed of recently dug soil and set about planting her treasure. Sybille thought that she had better inform Edwin about Matilda's endeavour lest he had other plans for the newly turned bed.

Helisende and little Judith came to watch the ceremony of the planting. The latter decided that the soil itself might taste nice, and Sybille had to grab and apprehend the child before she could cram her mouth.

A spectacular tantrum ensued. Helisende looked on admiringly while Matilda ignored the shrieks completely, save to increase her concentration in the burying of the apple core.

'Now water,' she said. While Sybille's back was turned and her fingers busy separating Jude's mouth from the soil she had managed to put in it, Matilda ran over to the well. A heavy wooden lid was held fast to the opening by an iron draw bar. Matilda scowled at the decorative wrought iron bands securing the oak sections and put her hands on her hips. The gesture was an unconscious imitation of Sybille, whom Matilda regarded as her mother. Her true mother was a distant, frowning person who seldom smiled and in whose presence the little girl felt distinctly uneasy. *Her* hands were always clasped in an attitude of prayer. She was always speaking about something called 'duty', and seemed to think that Matilda should know what 'duty' was. Something not very nice, the little girl had decided.

Since the well covering simply would not budge and she needed the water, she looked around for Edwin the gardener or one of the other men who tended the herb and wort beds. Then her eyes lit on someone even better.

'Papa!' Her feet flew on the path and she launched herself

at the large man coming towards her from the wattle gate in the garden's side entrance.

He swung her up in his arms and whirled her around until she squealed with delight. Clinging fiercely to his neck, she nuzzled her cheek against the wiry softness of his golden beard.

'What are you doing out here alone, chicken?' he asked. He spoke in English, and she answered him in the same tongue – something else of which her mother disapproved. Norman was the language of somewhere called the 'court' and nobody there ever spoke English.

'I'm not alone,' she said. 'I'm with Sybille. I want to plant a tree to make apples, but I have to water it.' She pointed to the well cover. 'It's stuck.'

'For a good reason. Someone your size might trip and fall down the well.'

Setting Matilda on her feet, he went to the cover. She watched the strong surge of his muscles as he drew back with ease the bolt that she had been unable to move. Her papa could do anything! He slid the heavy wooden disc aside and pulled on the hemp rope to draw up the wooden bucket from the depths. Matilda peered over the edge into the hole. He watched her with amusement and pressed her gently away when she began to crane too far.

'Here,' he said, and pressed half a silver penny into her hand. 'Throw it to the water elf.'

She looked at him huge-eyed. Sybille often told her stories about the elves and spirits that occupied their world but were seldom seen. Her mother would scold and say that such tales were un-Christian and not true, but that didn't stop Sybille telling them when Lady Judith was not around.

'Is there really an elf?' she demanded.

Her father nodded, seriously. 'Oh yes,' he said. 'And occasionally he has to be paid in silver to keep the water sweet. But he is very shy. He will not come out while the cover is off.'

Enchanted, Matilda tossed the coin. It clinked on the clay

and wattle lining of the well, bounced off, and plinked into the black water far below.

Her father nodded approval, smile lines crinkling around his eyes. 'So,' he said, 'where's this tree of yours?'

Solemnly, her little hand engulfed in his huge paw, she took him to the place where she had buried the apple core. Sybille came running towards them with her other two charges in tow. The maid scolded Matilda for running off and Waltheof greeted little Judith and Helisende. However, as if realising Matilda's need, he curtailed both greeting and scolding with a smile and a word, and gave his attention to the moist churn of soil by his boot.

Crouching, he scooped a handful of water and carefully trickled it over the spot where the core was buried. 'Saint Fiacre of the Holy Furrow, I entreat your guardianship of this seed,' he intoned. 'May it grow into a mature tree as my daughter grows, tall and strong, and bearing many branches of fruit . . . amen.' He crossed himself and Matilda did her best to imitate his gesture before sprinkling her own palmful of water over the patch of soil. She might not yet be three years old but she felt the solemnity of the occasion and knew that something greater than the planting of an apple core had just taken place.

From that moment forth Matilda took to planting seeds with a vengeance. Figs and raisins disappeared off the dining trestle to be buried under mounds of earth, as did costly almonds and peppercorns. She would accompany Edwin the gardener on his rounds, and talk to the elf in the well. She also prayed regularly for her tree and watched anxiously for the first shoots to appear.

'You are as bad as Sybille,' Judith snapped at Waltheof, 'telling her all that nonsense about "elves in the well".' Her tone was hard and disparaging. 'What kind of Christian example is that to set to your daughters?'

'Did you have no sense of fun or imagination as a child?' Waltheof countered, then shook his head and sighed. 'No, I do not suppose that you did – or else that it was "dutied" out of you while you were still very little.'

'It is all nonsense.' She folded her mouth inwards.

Waltheof raised his eyes heavenwards and, without a word, went to the window embrasure to gaze out on the soft glow of a late summer evening.

She looked at his turned back, his forearm braced against the wall, his fist clenched. Lately the gulf between them had grown wider. He seemed to go out of his way to irritate her. She could not bear his ebullient personality, the way he clapped folk on the back whether they were noble or peasant. It was inappropriate to both. His drinking, his loud laughter and childish sense of humour, the way he took nothing seriously and seemed unable to concentrate on any task for long enough to see it through: all of these traits annoyed her to the point of screaming. But looking at him now, quiet, brooding, she could feel his masculinity and her body responded as it had done the first time she set eyes upon him. And when they were in bed, he knew how to make her scream too.

Waltheof sighed and paced back into the room, then crouched at her feet and took her hands in his. 'I don't want to quarrel with you,' he said softly.

Judith swallowed. 'Nor I with you,' she unfolded enough to admit.

He grimaced. 'There are worse things in this world than elves, believe me.'

They went to bed and made love. She muffled her pleasure against his wide, straining shoulder and dug her nails into the smooth, flexing muscles of his back. As usual he pushed her beyond reticence and for a blinding moment she did not care. Then self-awareness returned and she scuttled back into her shell, feeling slightly ashamed.

He withdrew and rolled over on his back, breathing harshly.

'What did you mean about worse things in this world than elves?' she asked after a moment.

Waltheof turned his head on the bolster. 'I meant trolls such as Picot de Saye and the other sheriffs of my counties. This morning Tigwald the currier came to me with a complaint that Picot de Saye had misappropriated a cowhide and three goatskins to his own use.' Waltheof bared his teeth. 'He comes to the market place with his soldiers and he seizes what he wants. If my people protest, they are thrown in gaol or beaten. He's not a sheriff, he's a common thief.'

'Is there nothing you can do?'

Waltheof snorted impatiently. 'Picot de Saye has been appointed by your uncle. I have complained to William on several occasions but without joy. It seems that a common thief is tolerated when he is a tough and brutal soldier into the bargain. I have spoken to Picot myself, but to no avail.' His lips curved in an arid smile. 'I could, of course, take my axe to them, as I took it to their fellows in York, but even I can see the consequences of such an action, and my poor people would be made to pay the price in silver and blood, although what they are paying now is scarcely less.'

Judith said nothing. She knew that De Saye was acting beyond his jurisdiction and that Waltheof's complaint was justified, but she misliked the bitterness in his voice. How easily it could spill out to encompass all Normans. Against her will, she felt defensive.

'I have compensated Tigwald from my own coffers for the price of his hides,' he said, 'but compensation is not justice and I cannot afford to pay everyone from whom De Saye steals.'

'Perhaps you should have complained to my uncle with more vigour,' she suggested.

Waltheof laughed bitterly. 'He would not listen. Picot de Saye is his most trusted servant, and he would see me as a troublemaker. No, he has me where he desires. Earl of Northumbria, Northampton and Huntingdon – mighty titles brought to nothing by the power of his sheriffs.' He punched the bolster.

Judith bit her lip. 'He would listen to you if you made a good enough case.'

'So you think my case not good enough?'

'You are too soft,' she said. 'You melt from argument into anger without standing your ground, and your reasoning comes from the heart not the head.'

'What is wrong with that?' he snapped defiantly.

'Nothing,' she said, 'but my uncle is a man who reasons with his head. He has little time for matters of the heart – as well you should know by now.'

'And God forbid I should ever follow that path.' Waltheof rose from the bed and, drawing on his shirt, padded beyond the hangings that separated their bedchamber from the rest of the long room to look down at his sleeping daughters.

'Innocence,' he said softly. 'What price innocence?'

From the bed Judith watched him. Her appetite sated, she felt only weariness now. A chill draught from the half-open shutters made her shiver and pull the fur coverlet up around her shoulders. 'A price you cannot afford,' she responded in a murmur that disappeared on the air of her breath. He looked around as if he had heard her, but she knew that it was impossible.

Judith laid her hand to her belly. Her flux was a week late, but it had been so on several occasions and she attached small significance to the fact. Perhaps a son would change him, she thought, give that extra bite of iron to his character. Or perhaps he was only capable of siring girls because of the softness at his core. Whatever. She knew that when the time came to choose husbands for their daughters she would be exacting in her selection, and tenderness of manner would not be a consideration.

CHAPTER 16

For Matilda's third year day, Waltheof gave her a pony, bought on his northern lands from a Lothian horse trader. The little beast was little bigger than a large hunting dog, with a shaggy black mane and tail and a hide that was the same golden colour as the sands stretching along the shore by the great keep at Bamburgh. Tiny little bells were stitched around the edges of the red saddlecloth, and the buckles on the bridle were decorated with a pattern of thistles.

Matilda could not believe her eyes. It was love at first sight. She hugged her father, who laughed and swept her up in his arms to receive two smacking kisses. Even her mother wore a smile on her usually severe features. Learning to ride was apparently an important part of becoming a lady.

'She is yours to name,' Waltheof said as he set her down and brought her to the pony. It extended its nose towards her and she felt the sweet gust of its hay-scented breath in her face. Her father produced a crust of bread and placed it in her hand. Steadying and guiding her movements with his own, he offered it to the little mare. She lipped the bread off Matilda's palm with great gentleness, but devoured it greedily and looked for more.

Waltheof laughed. 'Small wonder that she's so plump!'

Matilda laughed too, thoroughly enchanted. Her father lifted her up and set her on the pony's back. She felt the cool leather of the saddle against her thighs and the pressure of the stirrups across her instep as he secured her feet.

'Well,' Waltheof said, 'can you think of a name?' Clicking his tongue, he led the mare around the yard at a gentle walk. Matilda grinned radiantly and preened like a queen.

'Honey,' she said after a moment, 'because she's that colour.'

Her father smiled in that special way he had that was only for her and when he was particularly pleased at her cleverness. 'Very fitting,' he said, 'and much better than "Glutton".'

Matilda screwed up her face at the word and he chuckled deep in his throat, a lovely warm sound that made her feel bubbly with pleasure.

For the next few weeks he continued to teach her to ride. It was a golden time, steeped in honey like the name of her pony, and its memory was to tantalise Matilda for the rest of her life. Everything was perfect. She basked in her father's warmth and attention. Saint Fiacre, aided by the water of the well elf, ensured that her apple tree began to grow, thrusting a single green shoot through the soil. She collected poppy and marigold seeds with the gardener, ready for sowing next year. She played with her little sister and Helisende, and the days seemed to stretch for ever, warm, shining, secure. Nor was the idyll spoiled by her mother, who left the tending of her daughters to Sybille even more than usual. When the reason was revealed, it only added to Matilda's pleasure.

'Your mama is to bear you another brother or sister,' Waltheof told her as he took her out on Honey, a leading rein attached between his mount and the mare like an umbilical cord. 'In the winter time.'

Matilda frowned. It was harvest now. Her papa had promised to take her to his manor at Ryhall on the morrow when he went to oversee the reaping. Winter came after harvest; she vaguely knew that. There were other things she vaguely knew as well. Only last week she had watched a goat drop two kids in the enclosure by the kitchen garden. Sybille had explained that young ones grew inside their mothers until they were ready to be born . . . unless they were chickens, of course . . . or trees.

'I see I have silenced that busy tongue of yours.' Her father's voice was warm with amusement but held the hint of a question.

Matilda looked up at him. Since she was constantly told that she was a gift from God, she assumed that it was God who put the babies inside the mothers to grow. 'Mama will want a boy,' she said.

Her father's eyelids tightened slightly but his smile remained. 'It matters not,' he said. 'It is God who chooses and we should be thankful for his gift of life.'

Matilda nodded, her notion of how babies arrived in the womb reinforced by his words. She liked babies. One of her favourite toys was a doll made of leather, its limbs stuffed with lambs' wool. She would wrap it in linen scraps for swaddling and croon to it, as she had seen the women of the household croon to their own infants.

'Are you pleased?'

Again she nodded. She did not feel as delighted as when she had been given Honey, but the sensation inside her was happy.

When they returned from the ride, her papa had visitors. Matilda recognised his friend, Ralf de Gael, because he often came to visit. They would go away to hunt and play chess and drink a lot of ale. She knew that her mama disliked Ralf de Gael, and Matilda agreed with her. The attention her papa paid to his friend meant he had less time for her. Although De Gael always brought her a present, she had the instinct if not the intellect to understand that she was of no consequence to him – indeed perhaps a nuisance.

Her father flung himself down from his own horse, lifted her carefully from Honey, then strode to embrace his friend and slap him heartily on the back. Matilda watched the greeting with resentful eyes and a pouting lower lip.

'I see your eldest is growing into a pretty little wench,' declared De Gael. He stooped to Matilda and a white grin flashed across his thin, handsome features. 'Looks like her mother at the moment, though, eh?'

Her papa laughed and lifted her in his arms. Matilda clung
to him fiercely and scowled at De Gael.

'Heaven preserve us from jealous women!' De Gael chuckled. 'Never mind, sweetheart. I've brought you a pretty brooch,
all the way from Denmark . . . and since you have Dane blood,
I thought it fitting you should wear it.'

Matilda turned her face into her father's warm, strong neck,
rejecting the visitor. Against her cheek, she felt him tense, but
he did not rebuke her for her rudeness. 'You have been talking
to Danish traders then?' he asked in a strange, flat tone that
she had never heard him use before.

'You could say that.' There was a cautious note in De Gael's
voice too. Matilda wanted him to go away. She clung like a
leech to her father, knowing with a growing sense of dismay
that already she had lost him.

'They bring news that you might find interesting,' De Gael
added as they walked towards the hall.

'I have plenty to interest me these days already,' Waltheof
said, 'and my wife is with child again.'

'Congratulations,' De Gael replied, but not as if he meant
it.

In the hall Waltheof sent a servant to summon Sybille and
inform Judith of De Gael's arrival. 'Although you will excuse
her if she does not attend on us,' he said ruefully. 'She is at the
stage where she is constantly sick.'

De Gael gave a knowing grin. 'And I would only make her
worse,' he said.

Sybille arrived. She curtseyed to the men and reached to take
Matilda from Waltheof. Matilda tightened her arms around
her father's neck until she was almost throttling him and
screamed as Sybille attempted to prise her off.

'Come,' Sybille cajoled, 'your papa will play with you later.'

'No!' screamed Matilda. 'No!' She kicked out, her emotions
so overwhelming and raw that even had she wanted she was
powerless to stop the tantrum.

De Gael winced. Looking astonished and nonplussed, as if

a flower had bitten him, Waltheof unhooked her arms from around his throat and handed her to the maid. Sybille tucked the threshing, screaming Matilda under her arm and struggled out of the hall. Taking her to the stables, ignoring the stares of the grooms and attendants, she threw Matilda down in the clean straw of an empty stall and there let her flail out the storm.

Matilda's voice gave out and the wildness of her emotion drained her body of all its energy, leaving her limp and tearful. Crouching in the straw, Sybille gathered Matilda in her arms and gently rocked her back and forth, smoothing the flushed brow and shushing her. Matilda's eyelids drooped and she fell into an exhausted slumber, her dark gold lashes spiked with drying tears. Tenderly, Sybille lifted the child and bore her back to the women's chambers, where she laid her on a pallet near the window and covered her with a light blanket.

'What is wrong with her?' Judith demanded. 'She looks feverish.'

'She is all right, mistress,' Sybille said quickly to dispel Judith's concern. 'The Earl of Norfolk is here and Mistress Matilda did not want to be parted from her father.'

Judith pressed her hand to the slight curve of her belly. 'Ralf de Gael,' she sniffed, her tone leaving no doubt as to her opinion of their guest. 'Is it just me and my daughter? Does no one else see through his posturing to what he is?'

Sybille lowered her eyes and fiddled with the strap end of her belt. 'He and Lord Waltheof have long been friends.'

'Lord Waltheof does not need "friends" of that ilk,' Judith said scornfully. 'There are men of considerably more character whose company he could seek. If he did as much drinking with my uncle's sheriffs as he does with Ralf de Gael, then he might conduct better business with them.' Turning away, she went to lie down on her own bed. 'My head aches,' she said, closing her eyes. 'I am indisposed – and I believe the malaise will last until that man leaves.'

*   *   *

Ralf de Gael studied the golden liquid in his cup. 'English ale,' he said. 'I have never understood why men have a preference for wine when they could drink nectar like this.'

'It depends on the alewife, and the freshness of the brew,' Waltheof replied, 'but our Wulfhild is the best brewster in the entire earldom.'

Ralf toasted him, then reaching to his tunic, unpinned a fine circular brooch set with irregular globs of polished amber like new, clear honey. 'The brooch for your eldest lass,' he said with a rueful smile. 'I do not think that she was best pleased to see me.'

Waltheof smiled too, albeit with a more pained expression. 'She likes me to herself – not that I mind if I have nothing else to do.' He turned the brooch over in his hand. The Danish silverwork was superb; this would have cost more than a half penny at a huckster's stall. 'Whenever you visit, it is always to take me away for several days' hunting. You cannot blame her for the association.' He pinned the brooch to his own cloak so that he would not lose it.

Ralf drank his ale and replenished his cup from the pitcher set to hand. 'Are you not going to ask me about my news from the Danish trader?'

Waltheof frowned. 'I have small interest in my Danish cousins these days.' It was not entirely true. He could still feel the surge within him like the wash of a wave against a long-boat prow, but he held back. There was too much at stake, and the Danes had proven unreliable allies in the past. 'I cannot see what you would gain from intriguing with them either.'

Ralf gave a shrug that was slightly too nonchalant. 'It is better to be informed on these matters than to hide your head beneath the sheets – or under your wife's skirts and pretend that they do not exist. King Sweyn of Denmark is dead and it is said that his son Cnut intends to send a fleet to England. If we hear these things in Norfolk, then just as surely you must hear them in Huntingdon.'

Waltheof turned his head aside, but he could not ignore the

words. 'They are of no interest to me – save that perhaps I should keep my men in readiness should the King have need of them.'

Ralf gave him a long, thoughtful stare.

Waltheof swallowed. The hair on the back of his neck prickled. 'What are you saying?'

'Nothing.' Ralf spread his hands in an open gesture that to Waltheof rang false. 'My mention of Danish traders was premature and not the reason why I am here.' He forced a smile.

'Then why have you come – to hunt?'

The Earl of Norfolk shook his head and a more natural smile lit his features. 'I came to invite you to my wedding and to a week's feasting and sport afterwards in celebration of my nuptials.'

'Your wedding?' Waltheof's gaze became one of astonishment. 'Jesu, Ralf, I did not realise that you were courting a bride!'

'Ah, well it has not been a long courtship,' he said, 'but the match suits all parties. I am to marry Emma, sister of Roger of Hereford.'

'Congratulations!' Waltheof clapped his friend on the shoulder. 'What's the lass like?'

Ralf laughed and described a curvaceous shape in the air. 'Fair-haired, generously endowed and good-natured. It will be no hardship to do my duty.'

The mention of 'duty' caused Waltheof to wince slightly, for it was the word that most frequently soured his own marriage. He and Judith were miles apart on its meaning. He would see it as his duty to attend his friend's wedding, and he knew that Judith would say that his duty was to remain with her.

'You will come?' asked De Gael, prompted by Waltheof's hesitation.

'Of course I will,' Waltheof said with overdone heartiness and beckoned for another pitcher of ale. 'You danced at my nuptials. It is only fitting that I should dance at yours.'

*   *   *

'You should not go to this wedding,' Judith said when Waltheof joined her in their chamber that evening and told her of his intentions. 'No good will come of it.'

Waltheof's brows drew together. 'What is wrong with the match? Surely, Ralf and Emma FitzOsbern are well suited?'

'Too well suited,' Judith snapped. 'I know that my uncle does not approve of the friendship between their families.'

'Do you?' Waltheof sat down on a bench set against the wall and folded his arms. 'I have heard no rumours. Has William moved to ban the wedding?'

Judith shook her head. 'No,' she said irritably, 'but my mother says that he does not trust De Gael.'

'Your uncle trusts no one whose blood is not Norman,' Waltheof said curtly. 'He gives me honours then hems me around with his own men, he makes sheriffs of his common mercenaries and turns a blind eye to the brutalities that they perpetrate.'

Judith had been lying on the bed. Now she rose and drew a bedrobe over her chemise. Her hair hung down her back in a dark silk curtain. Waltheof loved to run his fingers through its heavy masses, but tonight he knew that it was out of bounds. The flesh around her eyes was puffy and, despite the glow cast by the candlelight, he could see that her complexion was wan and drawn. She was not carrying this child well, and he felt a stab of guilt run through his exasperation.

'I grant that De Gael is of Breton stock and that your uncle has been at war with Brittany, but that is not reason enough to be suspicious of a man.' He narrowed his eyes at her. 'In truth, you have never liked Ralf.'

Going to the small prie-dieu standing in the corner of the room, Judith lit the wax candles either side of the ivory statu-ette of the Virgin Mary. Kneeling on the embroidered prayer cushion, she clasped her hands. 'There are men of far better character whom you could make your friends,' she said. 'And more suited to your standing.'

'Hah!' Waltheof exhaled bitterly and, going to the flagon on the coffer, poured himself some of his wife's wine. It was always wine in the bedchamber. If he wanted ale, he had to send a servant to fetch him some and then suffer Judith's scowling disapproval. 'My standing. Sometimes I think that is all you care about.'

'Someone has to care, because you do not,' she said, flashing an angry look over her shoulder. 'You demean your rank by jesting with grooms and gardeners and kitchen maids. How will folk respect you when you cannot behave fittingly?'

The disdain in her eyes kindled a glowing coal of anger in his belly. 'When I cannot behave like a Norman, you mean?' he threw at her.

'When you cannot behave like a man of noble blood!' she retorted. 'Our daughters are born to high station and yet you bring them to the stables and the outhouses; you encourage them to speak to servants and soldiers as if such people were of their rank – and in English!' She made a gesture of contempt.

Waltheof drew himself up, but even his full height was not large enough to contain his fury. 'So greatness of stature lies in ignorance,' he bit out. 'You are condemned out of your own mouth, my lady. You are nothing. While you are kneeling at your pious devotions, perhaps you might do well to dwell upon the fact that our Lord Jesus Christ came from a family of humble carpenters!' Turning on his heel, he stormed out. He would have been within his rights to strike her, and that made him walk away all the more swiftly. It was common knowledge that William of Normandy was not averse to beating his own wife when she overstepped the bounds of his tolerance. He knew of men who kept hazel switches poked in the thatch for just such a purpose, and others whose belts bore the bloodstains from the welts they had raised on the flesh of their wives and children. But he was not one of them. Even now, he told himself through clenched teeth, he was not one of them.

In the bedchamber Judith closed her eyes and swallowed, fighting the nausea of her pregnancy. She drew slow, deep breaths until her thumping heart slowed and her belly settled to a queasy churn. Turning her attention back to the prie-dieu, she tried to take solace in prayer but was thwarted by Waltheof's words about the Saviour being a common carpenter. Finally she genuflected, rose, and retired wearily to bed.

Matilda watched her father prepare to ride out. It was a cool, September morning with low mist wreathing the ground and dew making clear jewels of the spider webs strung in the eaves and across the wattle fencing that divided the stable yard from the garth. But Matilda had no eyes for the beauties of nature this morning. Only for her papa, who was going away with his friend and leaving her behind.

He gathered the reins, set his foot in the stirrup and swung his leg across Copper's broad back. His thin-legged black hunting horse, Jet, was tethered on a leading rein and there was also a fat, bay packpony laden with baggage. The soldiers of his retinue were mounting up, laughing and talking amongst themselves in close male camaraderie. Ralf de Gael was resplendent in a tunic of flamboyant crimson wool edged with metallic braid. Across his chest he wore a baldric and attached to it was a polished hunting horn, chased with silver.

'Your papa will not be gone for long,' Sybille said soothingly, but her grip was tight on Matilda's hand, ensuring that the little girl did not dash out among the horses.

'I want to go too.' Matilda's lower lip trembled.

'When you are older, *chérie*.' Sybille gently brushed her hand over Matilda's copper-bronze curls.

Waltheof collected his reins. Matilda thought that he was going to ignore her but he raised his glance and his eyes lit upon her and Sybille where they stood against the stableyard entrance. Heeling Copper's flanks, he rode across to them.

'I will take her,' he told Sybille. Leaning down, he scooped Matilda in his arms and drew her onto his saddle before him.

For a wonderful moment, Matilda thought that she was going with him. From the back of the horse her view was altered and she could see everything without having to crane. Her father's arm was strong and warm, holding her in the saddle, and she could smell the sweet, herbal scent emanating from his blue tunic. Leaning back, she nestled her bright head against the thick white fur lining of his cloak.

'I promise to be home soon, sweetheart,' he said, giving her a light squeeze.

'I want to come too,' Matilda pouted.

'This time you cannot, but when I return I promise on my oath to take you out on Honey as often as you want.'

'Now,' Matilda said, and the horrible feeling began welling up in her again as it had done yesterday when she had started screaming and been unable to stop.

'Shall I take her, my lord?' Sybille hastened to the saddle, holding out her arms, her eyes filled with anxiety. Matilda prepared to scream and kick.

Waltheof shook his head. 'It is all right,' he said. 'I will ride a little way down the road with her. One of the men can bring her back in a moment.'

Sybille nodded and, although she was chewing her lip with anxiety, stepped away. Waltheof clicked his tongue to the horse and urged Copper to a trot that took him away from the other riders. When De Gael moved to catch up, Waltheof gestured him back.

'Now then,' he said softly to Matilda, leaning over so that his beard tickled her ear, 'whether you scream or not, I must go. I know that you want me to stay, but I cannot. I am not going to ask if you understand, you are only a baby but . . .'

'I'm not a baby!' Matilda cried and wriggled round in her father's arms to give him an indignant blue glare.

He smiled and gave her a whiskery kiss on the cheek. 'No indeed, you are a big girl,' he said, 'and I want you to be a big girl now and wait patiently until I come home.'

Matilda wrinkled her brow. The dreadful feeling of unrequited rage still lurked in the background, but her father's talk of her being a 'big girl' had given her a device to control it. She folded her soft pink lips into each other in an unconscious gesture that belonged to her mother and managed a nod. The reward was another hug and kiss from her father, and she rode on his saddle all the way through the town. People stood at their doorways to watch them go by. Women curtseyed; men bowed or tugged at their hair. There were several cries of 'God bless you my lord and the young mistress!' and her father responded by shouting a response in English and throwing a small change of silver to the recipients. The warm feeling returned to Matilda's stomach. The silver-throwing ceased as they rode past the castle and the dour-faced guards in their rivet mail hauberks. The salutes were grudging and unfriendly. Her father turned his face away and, even though she had no understanding of why, Matilda knew that something was wrong.

Behind them Ralf of Norfolk had been bowing to the towns-folk and flirting with the women. Now he rode up alongside her father.

'You should do something about those soldiers of De Saye's,' he said. 'I would wring respect out of them with my hands to their throats if I were you.'

Her father's complexion darkened. She knew that he was angry, but she did not know why, or at whom. With a warning look at Ralf, he shook his head. Then he leaned over Matilda. 'Time for you to turn back now, *deorling*,' he murmured. 'Sybille will be wondering where you are, and your mother will be growing anxious.' Lifting her in his strong arms, he handed her across to one of the following escort.

Matilda's chin wobbled but she didn't scream. Her reward was her father's smile. 'There's my brave girl,' he said. 'I'll be back before you know it . . . I promise.'

Matilda craned her head around her escort's strong arm and stared after her father until he was lost to sight. On the way home, although she waved to people and they waved back, it was not the same.

CHAPTER 17

It was late, but Judith was restless and unable to sleep. Leaving the bed she knelt at her prie-dieu and clasped her hands before the figure of the Virgin, but tonight the motions of ritual and prayer had no power to soothe her troubled mind. Waltheof had been gone for ten days, intent on celebrating the marriage of Ralf de Gael to Emma FitzOsbern. He had sent no word, and Judith had sent none to him. For a while the silence had been a blessed relief, but now she was beginning to worry. His nature was such that he had to touch and talk. For him not to communicate at all was unusual. It was true that they had argued before he left, but they had argued before and always he had returned, contrite, bearing gifts, seeking her forgiveness. However, at the back of her mind lay the niggling fear that her approval no longer mattered to him. During the last few months, he had ceased to crop his hair and shave his beard – indications that her influence over him was waning.

Sighing, she rose from the prie-dieu. The statue of the Virgin was just that – a statue carved of oak and painted by the hand of man. Tonight the spirit of the Holy Mother of God chose not to descend and blanket Judith in a silent blue cloak of peace. She poured herself a cup of wine from the flagon on the coffer. One sip caused her lips to pucker. Calling one of the maids on duty, she thrust the flagon into her hand. 'This wine is sour,' she snapped. 'Fetch a clean measure immediately and I will have words with the steward in the morning.'

'Yes my lady.' Bleary-eyed, clumsy with sleep, the girl sham-
bled off on her errand.

Judith paced the chamber, lighting candles in the corner,
chasing the shadows from their hiding places. In the antechamber she heard one of the children cry out in her sleep. Matilda
she thought, with feelings of impatience and guilt. Since
Waltheof had gone the child had not been sleeping well – and
in the daytime she was much quieter than usual. Sulking, Judith
had thought, and had been sharp with her. Yet, as she scolded
the child, she had felt a disturbing awareness of repetition. Thus
had her own mother scolded her.

A masculine voice crooned softly to the child. Judith set her
hand to the curtain but before she could part it to investigate
it was drawn aside by Waltheof, the refreshed flagon clutched
in his hand.

'I met the girl on her way to you with this,' he murmured.
Entering the room, he drew her after him and dropped the
hanging. 'Matilda's settled back to sleep; I don't want to wake
her.'

Judith eyed him in surprise and growing consternation. She
would not have expected him to ride in at such a late hour
unless there was trouble. He looked as if there was. Purple
shadows ringed his eyes and his jaw was tightly grooved above
the beardline. He seemed to have aged ten years since their last
encounter in this room. 'What have you been doing?' she
hissed. 'What's wrong?'

'I should have expected no less a welcome,' he answered
bitterly. Flagon in hand, he went to the coffer and poured the
deep red wine into a goblet. 'I have been doing nothing,' he
said as he took a long drink, 'and I very much suspect that it
will be my downfall.' Abruptly his legs gave way and he sat
down on the bed.

'Meaning?' Judith's hands went to her hips. An unpleasant
smell of stale wine and sweat rose from his body. His tunic was
badly stained and so well worn that it could have stood up on
its own.

'I fear,' he said, 'that I have committed treachery against your uncle.' He drank down the rest of the wine and put his head in his hands.

'What?' Judith's heart began to pound like a drum in a cave.

Waltheof swallowed. He started to look at her, but he could not hold her eyes and his gaze slipped like a footstep on ice. 'Ralf de Gael and Roger FitzOsbern are planning to welcome Cnut of Denmark to our shores and offer him the prize of kingship,' he said. 'They have turned their backs on William for what he has done to the English and Breton people.'

'Jesu!' Judith stared at him in growing horror.

'Even now, there is a Danish fleet assembling to sail to England. Ralf and Roger have overwhelming support from the Bretons both in England and in Brittany.' His throat worked as if swallowing bile. 'They have asked me to bring my own force to the endeavour.'

'It is treason!' A cold knot tightened in the pit of Judith's stomach.

'I know.' Waltheof groaned. 'Roger has gone home to assemble his troops, and Ralf is mustering his. I am supposed to gather my huscarls and join them.'

Judith could not help herself. So great was her anger that she lost control. Snatching up her cup, she dashed the sour wine in his face. 'You fool!' she shrieked. 'You stupid, stupid fool! What in the world possessed you? What is going to happen to us now?'

He had recoiled instinctively as the wine splashed over him. Now he looked at her, pinkish runnels streaming down his face and throat, dark droplets trembling in his hair. 'I thought . . .' his voice cracked and she was horrified to see tears glittering in his eyes. 'You are the strong one. I thought you would know what to do . . .'

The urge to hurl the cup after the wine was almost overpowering. With unsteady hands she set it down on the coffer. Her stomach ached as if he had punched her in the soft part beneath her rib cage. 'Just what did you promise?' she asked in a voice tight with revulsion.

'I do not know . . .' He wiped the back of his hand across his eyes, leaving a grubby smear of tears.

'You do not know?'

'I . . . I was drunk.'

Judith closed her eyes and swallowed. She could imagine the scene. A raucous wedding feast. Copious amounts of wine and ale. A gathering of men possessed of similar interests. Amongst silver-tongued plotters such as Ralf de Gael and Roger of Hereford, Waltheof was as well armed as an infant amidst a pack of wolves. She should have prevented him from going. But 'should have' was too late.

He sniffed loudly. 'I believe I said I would not stand in their way . . . and that if that way went well, then I would join them.'

'So another attempt is to be made on wresting my uncle from England's throne, and you have implicated yourself in it.'

Waltheof nodded. 'It was against my will. I tried to argue against it, but they would not listen.' He gave her a pleading look. 'If I had not agreed to their plan, then Hereford at least would not have let me leave the feasting alive. I was trapped.'

'If you had ridden out the moment that the talk began, you would not be in this predicament,' she snapped. Her upper lip curled back from her teeth in a white snarl. 'Or perhaps you liked the idea. After all, you colluded with the Danes last time, did you not?'

'It wasn't like that!' His complexion darkened with anger and chagrin.

'Then what was it like?' she spat, knowing that she had hit the mark. 'You have always been obsessed by your father's people. We lie in a pagan bed because of it, and you wear that damned cloak all the time as if it is a second skin. It matters not all the honours and greatness that my uncle has bestowed upon you. You would yield it all for some Viking pirate because of his Dane blood. And . . . and for a scheming Breton who has tangled you up in the silken threads of his spider's tongue.'

He had put his head in his hands as she lashed him. Now

he sprang to his feet. 'Hold your venom you bitch!' he roared, raising his clenched fist.

She winced and flinched, but the blow did not descend. In the silence that fell as the ring of his voice faded, a look of pure horror crossed his face. His fist opened, extending instead in supplication. 'Judith, please . . .' He whispered. '*Deorling*, I did not mean . . .'

She stepped away, whisking her gown aside as if his merest touch on herself or her clothing was anathema. 'I wash my hands of you,' she said hoarsely. 'It is finished between us. I may be your wife, but I no longer wish to live as such.' She folded her hands firmly in front of her like a nun at her devotions. 'On the morrow I will go to my manor at Elstow and you will not follow me.'

'Judith, don't leave me . . . I need you . . .'

She tightened her lips and drew herself up. 'You left me first, when you went to Ralf de Gael's wedding in order to plot treason. Go to him for your succour. Doubtless he will furnish you with some willing Danish or Breton whore to slake your lusts. If you are plotting treachery then the last thing you need is a Norman wife.' Her voice trembled and for a terrible moment she had to fight hysterical tears. Unable to face him any longer, she went to her coffer, threw back the lid and began sorting through her gowns, as if choosing those that she would take to Elstow. But it was a ruse. Hand and mind were not co-ordinated.

'I am not going to join them, I swear it.'

His tone was pleading, like a child's begging forgiveness for a prank that had gone wrong. But this was more than a prank.

'If you do not go to my uncle immediately and tell him what is afoot, then you are damned,' she said without looking round. Her hands crumpled a veil of light gold silk, uncaring of the delicate fabric.

'I . . . I gave my word to De Gael . . .'

'You gave your oath to the King!' Nausea churned her belly,

rose up and surged. She only just reached the slop pot in time and hung over it, retching until she thought her gut would tear. 'Go away,' she gasped. 'Go away, you make me ill. I loathe you!'

She heard him stand up and the slow drag of his feet across the chamber rushes, as if they were bound by shackles. Then, mercifully, he was gone. Judith huddled over the slop pot, gagging and weeping. There was pain in her stomach, pain encircling the base of her spine in a tight girdle, and then a sudden gush of water and blood. She had rejected Waltheof. Now her body was rejecting his child.

As she screamed for her maids, Judith found herself hoping that she died.

'What do I do?' Waltheof asked of Ulfcytel. It was a fine autumn morning and they were sitting in the Abbot's parlour, drinking ale and watching the white clouds scud past the open shutters.

The monk sighed and shook his head. 'I wish I could tell you, my son,' he said. 'Doubtless others have already told you how foolish you have been.'

'Only my wife. I have spoken to no one else. A few of my men are aware, but I trust them without reserve.'

Ulfcytel gave Waltheof a severe look. 'Trusting without reserve appears to be part of the reason for your predicament,' he said. 'Only the Lord God is worthy of such faith.'

Waltheof grimaced. 'I know that, Father.' Sighing he rubbed one hand over his face. 'I gave my oath to William, I married his niece, and my own children carry the blood of Normandy in their veins . . . but . . .' He did not complete the sentence.

Ulfcytel sighed too. 'But you let a distant dream, the weakness of drink and the power of another man's tongue lead you away from reality. I know you better, lad, than you know yourself.'

'I should have remained in the cloister and taken holy vows,' Waltheof muttered. 'I do not think I have ever been as content in my life as I was here at Crowland.'

'Yes, perhaps you should have stayed with us,' Ulfcytel said gently, and laid a compassionate hand on Waltheof's shoulder. 'But since you did not, you have to face the storm you have conjured.'

Waltheof tugged at his beard. 'How?' he asked. 'What should I do?'

Ulfcytel was silent for a time. 'It is a matter for your own conscience. I cannot choose your direction.'

'Then advise me.' He gave the Abbot a pleading look. 'I know that my weakness lies in indecision and lack of foresight. What would you do if you found yourself in my position?'

Ulfcytel's grip on Waltheof tightened. 'I would ask myself what mattered most to me in the world. And then I would ask myself how I could best serve and protect it.'

'My children. They are what matter.'

'And how will you safeguard their future?'

Ulfcytel's voice was gentle, but its power was like the smash of a war axe. How indeed was he going to protect his daughters? Already he had lost one. In the aftermath of their argument four nights ago Judith had miscarried of a third little girl. He had seen it before they took it away and buried it – a scrap without a soul, but already its transparent little body perfectly formed. He thought of all the oaths he had given to different men. All of them under duress. And the unspoken promise he had given to his little daughter. That was more important than any oath.

'I . . . I will go to William,' he said. 'I will ask his mercy – beg if necessary.' His expression twisted at the thought.

Ulfcytel's shoulders rose and fell in a sigh of relief. 'It is your decision, but I am glad you have made it,' he said. 'But I would counsel you not to go directly to William of your own accord. You need a mediator. Seek out Archbishop Lanfranc, make your confession to him, and ask him to intercede.'

'You think me incapable of stating my own case?'

The Abbot gave him a steady look beneath which Waltheof was humbled. 'Aye, you are right,' he said. 'I do not have the subtlety of mind to find my way safe.'

'I will write to the Archbishop and tell him of your plight – remind him that you were once intended for the Church and that you have no evil in you – only folly.'

'Great folly,' Waltheof concurred. 'I should have remained in the cloister.' It was not the first time he had said so. At every crisis of his life the cry went up, and he had never meant it more than now. He rose to his feet, but only then to kneel at Ulfcytel's.

A surge of great tenderness and apprehension swelled within Abbot Ulfcytel as he laid gentle hands upon Waltheof's head. The young man was too vulnerable for the wider world, and he feared greatly for him.

Matilda was in her garden examining the small shoot of her apple tree when her papa returned. She heard the creak of the gate, and turned to see him striding towards her. His expression was grim and she thought that he was going to deliver a scolding, but as he drew closer his lips stretched into something that looked like a smile and she realised that he was not angry. Matilda hesitated for a moment and then ran to him, as she had always done. He swung her up in his arms and hugged her so tightly that her breath left her body and she began to struggle with fear. He let her go then and crouched to her level.

'Why are you crying?' She touched the wet streaks on his face. 'Are you sad?'

'A little.' Taking her hands in his, he rubbed his tears off her fingertips. 'I have done something foolish, and now I have to try and set it to rights.'

She frowned at him.

'Ah, you do not understand, and perhaps it is for the best.' He smoothed her tangled curls.

'Do you want to see my tree?' she asked, wanting to break his strange mood. Curling her grip around his thumb and first two fingers, she tugged him to the bed where the small green shoot was growing sturdily.

He admired it, but his eyes filled again and he had to turn

away to wipe them on his cuff. 'It will grow into a fine, strong tree, even as you grow up into a fine and beautiful woman,' he said. 'I am proud of you, and always will be.'

Matilda looked up at him. Something was definitely wrong, but as with most of adult behaviour she was at a complete loss to understand.

'Tomorrow I have to go and visit an important churchman, and then I have to journey to Normandy to see King William, your great uncle. I may not be home for some little while. I want you to think of me when you tend this tree. And when your mama and Sybille bring you to church, I want you to remember me in your prayers.'

Matilda nodded. 'I always pray for you, Papa,' she said solemnly. This time she did not scream and throw herself on the ground in a drumming of heels. Tomorrow was as far away as the stars and she had his attention and company now. 'Can we go and throw a coin to the water elf?'

'Yes, why not,' he said tremulously, and engulfed her small hand in his, a great and tender pain bursting within his heart.

CHAPTER 18

Rouen, Normandy, Autumn 1075

S imon's new falcon was a gift from William in recognition of his squire's exemplary service both in the battle camp and at court. Being pleased with the man emerging from the chrysalis of boyhood, the King had shown it, as was his wont, in a practical fashion.

The young peregrine's wings shone with a slate sheen and her breast was mottled with soft cream and blue herringbone feathers. Simon had called her Guinevere, for to him she was a queen. He was training her to fly as a game hawk rather than to the lure, and for the moment she was taking up all the time he did not spend on duty. She had to be gentled to his fist and so he took her out with him, familiarising her with the sights and sounds of the court, to the presence of dogs and horses and the noise of men. At first she had bated her wings in panic and struggled to be free of her slender leather leashes, but gradually she had grown accustomed to the world outside the mews. Now she perched silently on his wrist, gripping the leather falconer's glove with shining talons like small scimitars of blued steel.

Sabina, the head falconer's daughter, stood beside him at Guinevere's perch. In the sharp-scented dark, her eyes sparkled like black glass. She wore a kerchief for decency over her black braids, but he could remember the feel of her hair beneath his fingers when he had cozened her into loosening it yester eve. Soft and black and deep. The dreams that had visited him later as he lay on his pallet outside William's chamber had been the sort to take to confession.

Crooning softly to the hawk, calling her my love and my beauty, caressing her with his fingers, he lifted her to the perch. All his movements were slow and measured. Swiftness of any kind was forbidden in the mews, where even a stumble or a raised voice could disturb the highly strung birds of prey. She stepped from his fist to the perch, and only briefly bated her wings.

'She does well,' Sabina murmured. 'Soon you will be flying her.'

Simon smiled and agreed. He wanted to say that all the time he had been stroking the bird's breast he had been thinking of Sabina's, but he bit his tongue. It was the sort of trite statement he had heard the other squires make in their efforts to impress the younger women of the Duchess's retinue.

'I wish you could stay.' She looked at him through her thick, black lashes.

Simon glanced around. They were alone, and there was no sign of her father. 'Why should you think I cannot?' he asked and boldly drew her against him, mouth to mouth, hip to hip. He lost himself in the sweetness of the kiss and the heat that rushed from their joined lips to suffuse other parts of his body. He grew as hard as a quarterstaff. Painfully, wonderfully hard, and frustrated; last night's dream had done naught but vent the overspill. He reached to the beguiling softness of her breasts and wondered how they would feel without the barrier of gown and chemise. Sabina made an enthusiastic sound in her throat, and arched against him, but after a moment disengaged from the kiss and gave him a little push. 'I think you cannot because the King has a guest,' she panted. 'You will be sought to serve at the table. They say that there is no one in the King's household who can carve meat like you.'

Simon drew her close again and pressed his lips to the soft pulse in her throat. 'They will find someone else,' he said, nipping flesh, but he knew he was deluding himself. He was one of the senior squires and the junior ones would be looking to him for help and advice, whilst William would indeed expect him to carve at table and serve the food. Of course, that depended on the guest. If it was someone of minor standing, then one of the other young men could see to the task. 'Do you know who it was?'

'Yes.' She threw back her head to give him better access to her throat. 'I saw him many years ago when I was a little girl and the English hostages were at court. I cannot remember his name, but he has hair like beaten copper and a yellow beard.'

Simon stiffened. Now it was he who drew away and looked at her with narrowing eyes. 'Earl Waltheof?'

'Yes, that's him . . . what's wrong?'

Simon grimaced. 'Nothing,' he said, 'I thought this would be the last place he would come.'

'Why?'

'Because there has been some difficulty in England.'

'And you would not tell me what kind even if I tied you to a hawk perch and brought the King's eagle to threaten your eyes,' she said shrewdly.

Simon gave a reluctant chuckle. 'No, I would not,' he agreed. 'Rumours enough abound at court and I make sure that I am not the one who starts them – unless I'm ordered. There is power in knowing what happens in the King's chamber, but I will not smirch my honour or the trust the King has in me by becoming a gossipmonger. I have to go.' He kissed her cheek, his erection subsiding along with the notion of dalliance.

She folded her arms and smiled at him. 'Come back soon,' she said.

Simon nodded. It was part of the game they played. Sabina was clever. She had known that as soon as she told him about the visitor he would have to leave, and therefore she could stop their loveplay before matters went too far. He thought that perhaps her guile was the reason he enjoyed her company as much as he enjoyed the lure of her body. 'As soon as I can,' he said over his shoulder in parting. Whenever that would be.

Making his way towards the tower, Simon's limp was scarcely noticeable. He was well rested, the weather had yet to turn cold, and the muscles he had developed in training and on campaign supported the damaged limb. As he walked, he wondered what Waltheof was doing in Normandy.

William had received letters from Archbishop Lanfranc informing him of the rebellion by the Breton contingent in England, led by Ralf of Norfolk and Roger of Hereford. The letters had assured William that the rebellion was being contained and that there was no immediate cause for the King to return to England. Messengers had continued to arrive at regular intervals. Ralf of Norfolk had fled the country to Denmark to plead for rapid help from the Danes, leaving his young wife under siege at his keep in Norwich. Earl Roger had been captured and flung in prison to await William's pleasure. It seemed that Earl Waltheof, although not participating in their rebellion, had known of their intent and had stood back to let their armies gather. Lanfranc wrote that Waltheof bitterly regretted his action, but Simon wondered if bitter regret was atonement enough. He did not know how he would feel when he saw Waltheof. The man who had saved him from a bolting horse, the man who had sat with and encouraged him, who had pulled him through his darkest days. It seemed ungrateful to call him a fool and a traitor, but those sentiments haunted Simon's mind.

He paused at the entrance to the great hall to wash his face and hands at the laver then made his way unobtrusively along the side of the room towards the dais. William was presiding over the high table surrounded by nobles and officials. Waltheof sat beside him and, although the atmosphere was somewhat strained, the men appeared to be talking amicably enough. Waltheof's hair was Norman cropped again, although he wore a beard, trimmed close to his jaw emphasising the strong Viking bone structure. Two junior squires were serving the lords with wine and dried fruit.

'I have never known a man as brave or as foolish as Waltheof Siwardsson,' muttered Simon's father, pausing briefly beside his son. 'I clearly admit that in his shoes I would have fled to Denmark with Ralf de Gael, not come seeking forgiveness in the lion's den.'

Simon eyed the gathering on the dais. 'Has it been granted?'

His father shrugged. 'I think that William cannot make up his mind. For the moment he bides his time, but again, if I were Waltheof, I would tread very, very carefully.'

Simon made a face. 'He does not know how to do that,' he said.

Advancing to the dais, he took the flagon and linen napkin from the lad who was serving and proceeded to the task himself. As he leaned to replenish Waltheof's cup, the Earl gave him a shadowed, troubled smile.

'It is good to see you, Simon,' he said, but without his usual, hearty ebullience.

'And you, my lord,' Simon replied politely.

'I see you are quite the polished courtier now.'

William refused the offer of more wine by placing his broad swordsman's hand across the top of his cup. 'Simon gives me excellent service, Earl Waltheof,' he said. 'I trust him implicitly, because I know that my trust will never be betrayed.' He spoke without inflection, nevertheless the comment was barbed.

Waltheof flushed. 'I am doing my best to make amends,' he said in a low voice. 'I make mistakes, I admit I do.'

'There are mistakes, and mistakes. It is no use admitting to them if you do not also learn from them. And a mistake such as treason is not the same as dropping a cup or carving a haunch into uneven slices.'

Simon moved down the board. He did not want to appear to be lingering, and it was obvious that the conversation was going to be hard and filled with recrimination. For Waltheof's sake, he knew he should close his ears. Yet, he wanted to hear what Waltheof had to say in his own defence.

'I have not committed treason, sire. Indeed, I have come to you so that you can truly gauge my loyalty.'

'Is that what I am to gauge from your presence here?'

'I would hope so, sire. Indeed, Archbishop Lanfranc has sent you letters to back my plea.'

'Archbishop Lanfranc has sent me letters saying that you confess and repent, which is not the same.'

'I confess to having been foolish -- not to treason, sire. I have brought gold with me, and it is to you that I give it, not to your enemies.'

William grunted. 'Blood money -- isn't that what you English call it? Wergild?' He spat out the word as if it were a piece of gristle.

'It is a peace offering, sire.'

William frowned. 'A peace offering,' he repeated. 'I am cautious of letting you off so lightly. Am I to have this doubt of your character every time that the Danes set out to raid our coasts? Gold does not buy trust or restore innocence.' He rubbed his hand over the blue stubble-shadow on his jaw. 'For the moment you will oblige me by remaining at court while I decide what is to be done with you.'

Waltheof sat upright, his eyes flashing. 'You make me a prisoner?' he bridled. 'I came to you in good faith.'

'Over a matter of bad faith,' William said curtly. 'And be relieved that I am merely putting you under house arrest. Earl Roger of Hereford has a less comfortable captivity that he would willingly exchange for yours.'

The flagon was empty. Simon descended the dais to fetch a fresh one, but he had others to serve and there was no opportunity to hear any more of the conversation.

Later, however, William summoned Simon and told him that for the duration of the Earl's stay in Normandy he would be assigning him to Waltheof's entourage. 'You know him, you are comfortable in his presence, and as I said, I trust you.'

'Yes, sire.' Simon gazed at a wood louse toiling through the deep layer of rushes beneath his feet.

'What is it lad, look at me.'

Simon raised his eyes to meet the King's. 'Earl Waltheof trusts me too,' he said. 'If I had to break his confidence in order to serve you, then I would, but it would leave a bad taste in my mouth.'

William nodded. His lips curved the merest fraction. 'I know your worth, lad, and I am glad of your honesty. Unless Waltheof tells you that he intends to murder me in the dead of night – which I am sure he will not, then you may keep your own counsel as you see fit.' He waved his hand in dismissal.

'Sire.' Simon bowed and, feeling slightly less apprehensive, went on his way. Some young courtiers stood jesting in a group. As Simon passed, Robert de Bêlleme stuck out a leg elegantly encased in red hose and deliberately tripped him.

Simon went sprawling in the rushes and felt a jolt of pain slash through his damaged limb. His assailant's tough, calfhide boot had caught him directly across the area of the old break.

'You'll never be fast enough, De Senlis,' scoffed De Bêlleme. 'I could pull the legs off a crab and it would move better than you.'

His jaw tight with suppressed anger, Simon struggled to his feet. The pain was like the point of a knife blade winkling between his bones, but he refused to show by so much as a blink how much it hurt. The others in the group watched but said nothing. While someone else was being victimised they were safe.

'At least my mind is untainted,' Simon said, knowing that he should hold his tongue but unable to stop himself.

De Bêlleme turned fully towards him, his hand going to the dagger at his hip and a slow smile spreading across his narrow, saturnine features. 'Indeed?' he drawled, 'you seem somewhat of a lackwit to me.'

Simon swallowed. 'Think as you will,' he said, 'that is your undoing.' Turning on his heel, he walked stiffly away. His leg was throbbing fiercely but he forced his will through the pain so that although he limped the impairment was no worse than usual. His shoulder blades twitched and he half expected to feel De Bêlleme's dagger blade prick between them, or a hand on his shoulder, grasping and spinning him round. But there was nothing. De Bêlleme muttered something disparaging to his cronies, though, for a burst of laughter followed Simon from the room and he knew that it was at his expense.

Waltheof was in the small chamber that had been allotted to him. The fact that he was under house arrest meant that a guard hovered nearby. His huscarls had been given space in one of the timber guardrooms in the ward, and their weapons confiscated.

Waltheof welcomed Simon with open gestures and smiles; it was obvious to the youth that they were false and that the Earl had never felt less like smiling in his life. He set down the flagon of wine and the platter of honey wafers he had brought and poured a goblet for the Earl.

'I have been a fool,' Waltheof said bitterly. 'I should never have attended Ralf de Gael's marriage.' He seized on the goblet and drank the contents in several swift gulps. Simon concealed a wince. Drowning sorrows did not make them disappear.

'Then why did you?' Simon trimmed the candle and lit another one beside it to brighten the room.

Waltheof exhaled harshly. 'Because he was my friend. Because his company was better than my wife's. Because he knows what it is to have English blood and be a stranger in your own land . . .' Waltheof shook his head. 'I knew he was ambitious, but I did not realise how high he was aiming until it was too late. He asked me to help him . . . and in my friendship and folly I did not refuse him straightaway. Now I am trapped in a noose of my own coiling and I do not know how to escape.'

Simon said nothing. He admired and liked Waltheof, but not for his political abilities, which were dire.

'Has the King said anything about how long he intends keeping me here?'

'No, my lord. Only that I am to serve as your squire in all things.'

Waltheof studied him closely, as if seeking the truth behind the words. 'And I'm glad to have you,' he said, but his voice was flat and he drank his wine with the swift desperation of a man eager for oblivion. 'I only wish that the circumstances were happier.'

'I too, my lord,' Simon said uncomfortably.

Waltheof rested the cup on his knee. 'I do not think that there has ever been a time when I have not been someone's hostage or prisoner,' he said wryly. 'Save perhaps when I was very young and my father intended me for the Church. After he died I became a ward of the Godwinssons, and when they fell in battle your king took their place.

It was telling to Simon that he said 'your king'. He frowned at Waltheof.

'Why do you look at me like that?'

'I wondered why you did it . . . why you became embroiled in a plot with Ralf de Gael?'

'I was a prisoner trying the door of my cell.' Waltheof smiled humourlessly. 'Someone offered me a key and I took it, only to find that it led to another cell, deeper and darker than the first.' He grimaced at Simon. 'I do not expect you to understand what it is like to live every day of your life like a yoked ox – to have the power of an earl, which is no power at all when versed against that of Norman sheriffs and officials. To be an unwelcome stranger in your own hall.'

'But you are kin by marriage to King William himself,' Simon pointed out. 'Surely that must count for something.'

Waltheof sighed. 'My marriage is like the great battle of Hastings, with no mercy shown and no prisoners taken,' he said bleakly.

Simon shook his head. He had been a party to the clandestine courtship between Judith and Waltheof. Mayhap their marriage had soured, but he knew that they had once been desperate to be lovers.

'Although, I admit I have my daughters,' Waltheof added softly and looked into his cup. 'I would never regret giving them life. And in truth, I once loved their mother, and still do after a fashion, although I doubt that she has anything left in her heart for me but contempt. Ah, enough.' He made an impatient gesture. 'I do not want to talk of the ruin I have made of my life. What of you lad? How soon will you be a fledged knight?'

Simon politely spoke of his own life, but not as eagerly as he would once have done with Waltheof, and although the earl appeared to be listening with eagerness Simon could tell that his inner ear was closed.

CHAPTER 19

In December William prepared to return to England to keep the Christmas feast at Westminster.

Simon was buried under a mountain of preparations; there were errands to run, itineraries to organise, chests to pack. In between dealing with William's demands, he had Waltheof to attend. The Earl was allowed from his chamber but confined to the Tower precincts. The nearest he came to the outdoors was to stand in the window splays and breathe the wind. Simon saw how he bridled at the constraint and sympathised with him. He could still remember with painful clarity how it felt to be hemmed in for weeks on end.

He played chess and dice with Waltheof and advanced his rudimentary knowledge of the English tongue until he was moderately fluent. He brought Guinevere to Waltheof's chamber and let the Earl perch her on his wrist. They spoke of the art of falconry and the beauty of the prized white Norway hawks whose price lay in the realm of kings.

Simon no longer had time for dalliance with Sabina and in his absence she transferred her affections to a young serjeant from the Vexin who was remaining behind in Rouen.

Sometimes the Conqueror's sons and their cronies would visit a brothel in the city, but on the rare occasions that Simon was free of duty he chose not to accompany them, for Robert de Bêlleme was always among their number. The youth baited him at every opportunity, calling him 'lameleg' and 'clodhop'.

Simon refused to show how much he was wounded by the taunts, but shrugging them off became increasingly difficult.

On the day that the court embarked for England, De Bêlleme made one of his barbed remarks and stuck out his foot as Simon was bearing a dish of hot frumenty to the high table. This time, however, Simon was prepared. He avoided De Bêlleme's boot but pretended to stumble and deliberately tipped the steaming dish of stewed wheat over De Bêlleme's head and down the back of his immaculate tunic.

De Bêlleme roared and shot to his feet. The hot, glutinous grains clung to his hair, skin and clothes, making it look as if he were being devoured by maggots, and he danced and flailed as the heat scalded his flesh. Blobs of wheat porridge flew everywhere and the other diners cursed. 'You crippled son of a whore, I'll kill you!' De Bêlleme howled and whipped his knife from its sheath.

Simon flashed his own blade from its scabbard. 'You tripped me. It is your own fault!' he snarled, and knew that although revenge had been sweet it was also short. There was not a chance in hell that he could match the physical prowess of Robert de Bêlleme. Nor could he run.

'Leave him Rob!' cried the Conqueror's son, also named Robert. 'It was an accident.'

'Accident my arse!' De Bêlleme bared his white teeth and made a slashing movement with the knife. By leaping violently backwards, Simon was able to avoid being gutted, but he landed on his unsound leg and went down.

De Bêlleme kicked him, landing him a blow in the ribs hard enough to crack bone. The breath tore out of Simon's lungs on an agonised whoop of air. He told himself without much conviction that he was not going to die. Surely De Bêlleme would not murder him before a hall full of witnesses.

He saw the foot draw back for another assault and prepared to roll away, but the blow never descended. De Bêlleme was lifted off his feet and the knife twisted out of his hand by a furious Waltheof.

'You shame your knighthood!' the Earl roared. 'You so much as go near the lad again and I will rip your head from your neck and use it to kick around for sport on the sward!'

'Hah, since when have you had the right to speak of shame?' De Bêlleme sneered, wrenching himself out of Waltheof's grasp. The brawl had smeared the frumenty deep into the weave of his expensive tunic.

Waltheof rammed the young knight's knife into the trestle. 'Since I witnessed your own shameful behaviour towards one of your own,' he said harshly. 'I meant what I said. Touch him again, and you will reckon with me.'

De Bêlleme's fists opened and closed. He said nothing, but the intensity of his gaze on Waltheof was worth a thousand words.

As the men faced each other there was a flurry at the dais end of the hall and William arrived to break his fast. Amidst the rising and bowing Waltheof dragged Simon to his feet and bore him out of the hall.

'Are you all right, lad?'

Clutching his ribs, Simon nodded. 'I should not have done what I did, but I lost my temper,' he said with self-reproach. 'And you should not have intervened my lord. Robert de Bêlleme is a bad enemy to make.'

Waltheof shrugged as if ridding himself of an irritation. 'One more will make no difference,' he said with a bitter smile. 'He will not touch you again while I am by, I promise you that.'

Simon shook his head. 'No,' he agreed. 'He will bide his time. Robert de Bêlleme does not care whether he sticks a knife in his opponent face to face or in the back.'

'But at least you ruined his tunic,' Waltheof said.

'Oh yes,' Simon said, and suddenly, despite or perhaps because of the shock he had just received, he began to grin. 'I struck him in his vanity, which is his most vulnerable part.'

The sea crossing was cold and uncomfortable, but although the waves were choppy the voyage was swift. From their landing in Southampton, the court rode on to Winchester and the prospect of good hunting in crisp air.

Once they were in England, though, William's mood changed. Before he had only had access to tales of the thwarted revolt against him through letters and messengers. Now he could see and hear for himself, and what he saw and heard was not to his taste. Those of his barons with English interests whispered in his ear, speaking of the need to guard against further treachery and punish wrongdoers. Waltheof was kept under close house arrest, all hopes of returning to his earldom dashed, although the King relented enough to say that there was no reason why the Countess Judith could not come to him at court. To that end Simon was despatched to fetch her.

The weather was sharp and clear, and the roads hard with frost. Simon made good time, arriving in Northampton on the third afternoon of his journey.

He was welcomed to the hall, given food and drink while he waited, and presently was summoned to the Countess Judith's private chamber.

She was seated at a tapestry frame, two vertical lines set between her eyes as she attempted to sew by candlelight. Her daughters sat with her, Matilda labouring over a piece of simple stitchery using a large needle threaded with brightly coloured wool. The child's tongue peeped out from between her teeth as she strove to co-ordinate hand and eye. How old was she? A little beyond three years old, Simon thought, and Waltheof's paternity evident in every curve, line and nuance of her body. Her little sister was occupied in sorting scraps of material into piles of different colour under the watchful eye of Sybille and another maid.

'My lady.' Simon bowed.

Judith beckoned him forward and he came into the ring of candlelight. She was sewing a scene from the life of Saint Agnes, who had chosen martyrdom above marriage. Not an encouraging sign.

'I understand you bear a message for me?' Her tone was

formal, warning him not to expect to be treated as a guest, and her lips were pursed, revealing that she was not delighted at her uncle's choice of messenger.

'The King requests your presence at Winchester,' he said, 'and Earl Waltheof asks that you come also.'

She bent her head to her embroidery, sewing the stitches with a steady hand. 'My husband does not return to Northampton then?'

'No, my lady,' Simon said in a neutral voice. 'The King prefers to keep him by his side.'

'You mean he is a prisoner?' She looked up. 'Wrapping the truth in silk will not make it any prettier. Tell me the whole.'

Simon managed not to recoil at her peremptory tone. 'The King is undecided what to do about the Earl,' he said. 'I think he is keeping him hostage while he makes up his mind. There are those who say that he should be restored to favour, and others who counsel His Grace to have a care. They say it but takes mention of a Danish invasion to send the Earl hurtling into rebellion.' He did not add that those against Waltheof's release had the loudest voices, chief amongst them her own stepfather, Eudo of Champagne, and Roger de Montgomery, who was the sire of Robert de Bêlleme.

The Countess sewed until she reached the end of her thread, snipped it with a set of silver shears, then sat back and sighed. 'These last few months I have been at peace,' she said bleakly. 'I do not think that I could bear the strife.'

'My lady?'

She gave a small shake of her head. 'When I married Waltheof of Huntingdon, I believed that I could change him, but I might as well have been drawing water with a sieve. He is what he is – and I am what I am.' She rose from the tapestry frame and eased the small of her back with the pressure of her palms. 'Very well. I will come to Winchester, and I will have my say.'

'Is Papa coming home?' Matilda demanded, clearly having understood some of the conversation. Her little face was suddenly bright and eager.

'Papa home, Papa home,' echoed her little sister.

'We shall see,' Judith said in a curt tone that put an end to the matter.

In the private royal chambers at Winchester, King William raised his niece from her deep curtsey and formally gave her the kiss of peace. Judith faced him. Although her expression was calm, her stomach was almost clamped to her spine with apprehension. They were not alone. Apart from the usual quota of servants, the room was occupied by her stepfather, her mother, Lanfranc of Canterbury, and several magnates high in her uncle's counsel. A formal gathering . . . or a court preparing to sit in judgement.

William gestured her to be seated. 'Have you seen or spoken to your husband yet, niece?' He gave her an interrogative look as she took her place on the oak bench beside her mother, who drew in her skirts to make room.

She shook her head. 'No, sire, and I do not wish to,' she said.

William eyed her thoughtfully. 'Why not?'

Judith had been debating her reply to this question all the way to Winchester and was still no nearer an answer. If she said that she did not wish to see her husband because he upset her equilibrium, her uncle would think she was being ridiculous.

'Well?' William demanded.

She looked down at her hands. When she had sat down, they had been folded in her lap. Now they were clenched. 'Our marriage ended on the day he returned from Ralf de Gael's bride-ale, and told me what he had done,' she said.

She was aware of her mother's sharp glance, and the sudden heightening of tension among the others.

'And what did he tell you?' William asked gently.

Judith swallowed. She could feel the words sticking in her gullet. Should she speak or hold her silence?

'Your duty is to the house of your birth,' her mother muttered under her breath. 'You betray your blood if you do not speak out.'

Her husband or her blood. It was simple when couched in those terms, but still she hesitated. When she opened her mouth to speak, her voice locked in her throat and she had to cough to clear the way. 'He said that Roger of Hereford and Ralf de Gael were plotting with the Danes to overthrow you and that he had taken an oath not to stand in their way.' Now her hands were not only clenched, but her nails were digging half-moon marks in her skin.

'You are sure of this?' William said.

'Yes, sire, I am sure. I told him that he was a fool and that he had been used, but he did not want to listen. When I took him to task, he threatened to beat me. Even so, I told him that he must come straight to you and seek forgiveness, but he said that he could not because he had given his oath to Ralf de Gael. After that, I knew that I could no longer be his wife.' She bowed her head and felt the heat of tears behind her lids. But she did not shed them. 'It is true that he went to Abbot Ulfcytel of Crowland Abbey and Archbishop Lanfranc in troubled conscience, but I believe that he was also biding his time and waiting to see if De Gael's rebellion would succeed. When it did not, he came to you to confess.'

There was silence except for the soft settling of charcoal in the brazier and a shutter cracking in the wind. Then William slowly exhaled. 'It is as I thought,' he said, 'although I would leif as not believe it.'

'No backbone,' Adelaide declared scornfully. 'I knew that from the beginning. He is like that great bear pelt he wears. All shine and glamour, but no substance.'

'Rather a weak reed, madam, easily led astray.' Lanfranc's tone was conciliatory.

'The words make small difference,' she snapped. 'It is the deeds that count.'

'I have no place for a weak reed.' William rose to pace the chamber, his tread heavy and deliberate. 'Once again he has proven untrustworthy and my patience is frayed.'

'What then will you do with him?' asked Eudo, thumbing

the cleft in his chin. 'Clearly, you cannot restore him to his lands. By all accounts he has committed treason. You cannot hold Roger of Hereford in a dungeon and let Waltheof of Huntingdon go free. From the lips of his own wife, your niece, you have received the words of his guilt.'

Back and forth, William paced, restless with the anger that did not show on his face. 'I have no choice but to punish him,' he said.

'Is that wise?' Lanfranc spoke out. 'He is popular with the English people, and the rebellion has been nipped in the bud. Waltheof claims that he was not intending to be an active participant.'

'Do you take his part?' William rounded on the churchman.

Lanfranc spread his arms, showing the full linen sleeves of his under tunic. 'No sire, I merely point out that you should consider carefully. I do not deny that he has caused you much trouble, and that he should be punished . . .'

'Agreeing to stand aside makes him as guilty as being a participant,' William growled. 'I know full well that if the Danish ships had come sooner, he would have been on the shore helping them to beach their keels.' His regard chopped to Judith. 'Is that not so niece, or do you say differently?'

Judith bit her lip. 'It would depend how much he was swayed by others. I think that he has tried to live by our ways, but has found it very difficult.'

'If Waltheof is so beloved of the English people,' said Eudo silkily, 'then let him be judged by their laws, not our Norman ones. That would show how willing you are to compromise and not impose upon the English way of justice. Of course,' he added, 'Roger of Hereford must be judged by Norman law because he is a Norman.'

William bit on his thumbnail. 'That seems sensible,' he said slowly. 'How does English law deal with such cases?'

Since everyone gathered was Norman, no one knew offhand, although Judith thought that from the gleam in his eyes her stepfather might have an inkling. However he said nothing.

'Then let Earl Waltheof be imprisoned the same as Earl Roger until we have the details,' William said. 'For it is not fair that the one languishes in a dungeon and the other enjoys the hospitality of our court.'

'You could unfasten Earl Roger's shackles and confine him to house arrest,' Lanfranc suggested.

'I think not,' William said curtly. 'Indeed, the more I consider the matter, the less forgiving I become. If this rebellion has not succeeded it is only due to the vigilance of my loyal supporters.'

There was silence, although of the relieved and pleased kind. A decision had been reached, apparently to mutual satisfaction. Guards were sent to apprehend Waltheof and put him in a cell.

'I knew no good would come of this marriage,' Adelaide muttered. She and Judith had retired to the women's quarters, where Judith had ordered her maids to see to the repacking of her travelling chests ready for her return to Northampton.

'You cannot claim outstanding success for your own, Mother,' Judith said tersely.

'At least none of my husbands ever committed treason,' Adelaide retorted. 'Eudo and I understand each other's needs very well. That it involves separate households is by mutual and amicable agreement.'

Judith fought the urge to shriek at her mother. Pre-empting the maid, she snatched a gown off the clothing pole and folded it, giving her hands something to do.

'You are leaving without speaking to your husband?' Adelaide gave her a look that was filled with disbelief.

Judith thrust the folded gown at her maid. 'I have nothing to say to him.' The thought of facing him made her feel queasy – the way she did in the first months of pregnancy.

'If he were mine, I would have much to say. I would tell the traitor what I truly thought of him.'

Judith faced her mother. 'Don't you understand?' she said

impatiently. 'All that is behind me. I have already told him what I truly think. While he is confined, I am free, and that is all that matters.'

Adelaide hitched her arms beneath her breasts. 'That remains to be seen.' Her tone was ominous.

Judith shook her head. 'My uncle will banish him from England as he banished Edgar Atheling. He can do no other.'

'That will depend on whose word prevails with your uncle. Lanfranc is too tender in this matter, and if your uncle listens to him Waltheof may yet be released.'

Judith looked at her mother with burgeoning fear. 'I pray not,' she said. 'I could not bear it.'

'That is foolish talk. You could and you would,' Adelaide made a dismissive gesture. 'I will do what I can to defray Lanfranc's word, and so will your stepfather. It is a pity he did not give you a son,' she said with a glance towards the apple of her eye, who was playing in a corner with a painted wooden horse.

Judith grimaced. It was ground so often covered that it was staler than trencher bread.

'You must be very careful with your own daughters,' Adelaide warned, wagging an instructive forefinger. 'Do not let them yearn after men who are unsuitable. You must mould them while they are young. You must not let the taint of their father's blood gain dominance.'

'No, Mother,' Judith clenched her jaw on her irritation.

'The older one. Already she is too much like her father. She needs a firm hand or you will have cause for regret.'

'Grant me leave to deal with her as I see fit.' Judith knew that if her mother said one more word, she would hit her. Mercifully, Adelaide seemed to realise the danger in which she stood.

'Indeed, daughter. I can only warn. The discipline must come from you.'

Adelaide left, taking her son, and Judith sat down on the small, truckle bed, her legs trembling. The maid pretended not to notice and busied herself securing the hasp on the travelling chest.

Slowly Judith regained her composure. She sent another maid to tell the grooms to ready the horses. The sooner she was gone from Winchester, the better she would feel. It was as if a great dark cloud was engulfing her, robbing her of her faculties. Had anyone suggested it was guilt, she would have denied it furiously, but denial was not enough. She shied from the vision of Waltheof in a cell. He had always so loved the open air and sunlight.

His misfortune was of his own making she told herself sternly – and she was his misfortune as much as he was hers.

'Well?' Adelaide demanded of Eudo as he drew the curtain across their chamber door. 'What did my brother say?' The men had remained to discuss Waltheof's situation and other matters of state after the women's departure.

Eudo hitched his chausses and sat down on the bench squeezed against the side of the room. Their son was asleep on a feather-stuffed pallet on the floor, his small, wiry body covered with a fur-lined blanket and his blond hair softly gleaming. 'Your brother is still of half a mind to let Waltheof go free for that payment in gold.'

'That is foolish!' Adelaide's light brown eyes kindled with wrath. 'Waltheof of Huntingdon cannot be trusted. I won't have my daughter . . . my own flesh and blood yoked to such as he. A traitor once is a traitor for ever!' Her voice was pitched low to avoid wakening their son, but there was no mistaking its venom.

'Lanfranc suggested that Waltheof should be banished from England,' Eudo said, watching her warily. 'Your brother seemed interested in the notion.'

'Lanfranc is an old fool!' Adelaide snapped. 'Waltheof would go straight to Ralf de Gael in Brittany to stir up more rebellion, or to Denmark to rouse his barbarian kinsmen.'

'That is what myself and Montgomery told William.' Eudo rubbed his palms together nervously.

'And?'

'William said he would think on the matter.'

Adelaide made an impatient sound. 'There is naught to think upon. Waltheof is a traitor and should be dealt with as such.'

Eudo looked at her, still rubbing his palms.

'What is it?' she demanded. 'What are you not telling me?'

He cleared his throat. 'I spoke to a cleric versed in English law. He tells me that treason carries the death penalty – so if Waltheof is judged by the laws of his own country . . .' he let the words tail off.

Adelaide stared at him. A red flush began at her throat and crept gradually into her face. 'Does my brother know this?'

'Not yet, but he will do soon.'

They looked at each other, and although nothing was said ambition flared between them like a flash of lightning.

'It is our duty,' Adelaide murmured after a moment, 'to support the decision he makes.' She stooped to watch her sleeping son breathe softly in and out. 'And to make sure that it is the right one for all concerned.'

CHAPTER 20

Winchester, Spring 1076

T he guard took Simon away from the warmth and light of Winchester's hall and brought him into the darker regions where brightness and sunlight did not reach. A single torch flared in a bracket on the wall and a musty smell pervaded everything – like the soil dug from a grave pit. Simon felt the shaved hairs at his nape prickle upright and an involuntary shudder ran down his spine. Behind a door on the right someone moaned, but the guard paid no heed and led Simon further into the darkness until they arrived at another door of iron-bound oak. A narrow grille was cut in the top for observation, and there was an opening at the base to admit and retrieve food bowls and the slop pail.

The guard peered through the grille and, taking a large key from the ring at his waist, turned it ponderously in the door lock. 'Go on, sir,' he said to Simon with an ushering gesture. 'I'll be outside if you have need. Shout when you are ready to leave.'

Simon nodded, pressed a silver penny into the man's hand, and entered the cell. It was large enough to contain several prisoners but confined a single occupant. The floor was thickly strewn with new rushes and instead of a straw pallet the prisoner had a proper bed with linen sheets and a coverlet of red and blue wool. Wax candles burned with a clear, yellow glow, chasing shadows into the deepest recesses of the walls. The prisoner, being an earl, could afford to pay for such luxuries.

'My lord?' The door closed solidly at Simon's back and the key bolt shot home. He advanced into the cell. Waltheof was kneeling before a crucifix that had been nailed into the wall; either side of it, on a narrow bench, two candles flickered, forming a makeshift altar. He turned at the sound of Simon's voice and his features brightened with pleasure. He did not, however, bounce lithely to his feet as once he would have done, but rose rather gingerly, as if he had been kneeling for a long time. 'It is good to see you, lad. What are you doing here?' Hobbling forward, he embraced the youth.

'I asked the King's permission for leave to visit,' Simon replied. In the confines of prison, Waltheof's vigorous musculature had diminished and it was like clasping a gaunt-boned stranger – a man already halfway to the death that was his sentence under English law.

'And I suppose he gave it so that you could bid your farewells to a condemned man.' Waltheof broke from the embrace with a barren smile.

Simon did not reply, for Waltheof had spared him the need.

'Still, all visitors are welcome for whatever reason.' The smile grew bleaker yet. 'Guests to my cell have been somewhat lacking and in truth I have not expected them. Ulfcytel and the Bishop of Winchester of course. My soul has its comfort to take to the next world. I had thought that Judith might . . .' He grimaced and thrust his hands through his hair. Uncropped in captivity it gleamed on a level with his jawline. 'I have not seen her since the day I left for Normandy. I was told that she came to Winchester at Christmastide, and it was about the time of her visit that I was cast in here to rot. I wonder if this is any of her doing. I know her strong enough . . . but I cannot bear to think that she would do this to me . . .'

Still Simon was silent.

'Do you know the truth?' Waltheof demanded harshly. 'You

are a party to much of what is said in the King's chamber.'

Simon lifted his head. 'Indeed I am, but I would not break the King's trust in me by repeating anything that I happened to hear.'

'Even to a man who will take the tale nowhere except to his grave?' Waltheof's expression was bitter. 'Am I not entitled to know who betrayed me?'

'You betrayed yourself at Ralf de Gael's bride-ale,' Simon said. He felt uncomfortable at the turn the conversation had taken, and began to wonder if he should have made this visit at all.

'If I had not been arraigned for my part in Ralf's rebellion, it would have been for something else,' Waltheof retorted. 'I had too much power, too high a standing to be allowed to keep it and prosper. Men are covetous, especially of that which could be theirs for the sake of a push.'

Simon began to feel queasy. The walls of the cell seemed to press in on him. He wondered how Waltheof bore day after day in the gloom, knowing that the only light at the end of the tunnel led to the executioner's sword. 'I can say nothing,' he replied.

'Not even about my wife? Is it because she was responsible that you will not speak? You have to tell me.' He took an agitated pace towards the youth, his hand outstretched to grab at Simon's tunic, but even as he touched cloth a look of misery and self-loathing crossed his face and he spun away. 'I almost struck her,' he whispered. 'And I would not have hurt her for the world.' His shoulders shook.

Simon was at a loss. He had known plenty of pain in his life, and constant challenge. He knew what misery felt like, but when its cause was this deep he was not sure that his arm was long enough to reach down and rescue. 'Lady Judith had naught to do with your imprisonment,' he said. 'It is true that she came to Winchester at Christmastide, but not in order to seek your death.'

'Then for what? Certainly, it was not to see me!' Waltheof said in a grief-drenched voice. 'Not once has she been near . . . nor my daughters.'

The way he spoke the last word left Simon in no doubt as to what was hurting Waltheof the most. 'The Countess came to tell the King what you had said about the bride-ale because he demanded it of her.'

'What else? There must be more.'

Simon drew a deep breath. He knew that he was treading on dangerous ground. Unlike Waltheof, he could dissemble when he had to, but it was not a role that he particularly enjoyed. Probably a gentling of the truth would best serve him now. 'She said that she did not desire to see you because your marriage was over . . . but that was all. And she left your daughters at Northampton – out of a care for them I think, not to slight you.'

'A care for them,' Waltheof repeated and his mouth twisted. 'Oh yes, no one could accuse her of being neglectful in her "duty".'

Simon winced, knowing that whatever he said would not ease Waltheof's torment.

Wiping his eyes, Waltheof made an effort to compose himself. 'I should have remained in the Church and taken the tonsure all those years ago,' he said. 'Of all the mistakes I have made, that is perhaps the worst one.' He bent a reproachful look on Simon. 'Still, I will go to my God with a clearer conscience than those who remain.'

'I am sorry,' Simon swallowed. He had thought himself an accomplished courtier, able to deal with any situation, but knew that he was suddenly out of his depth. 'I came to make my farewell, but I do not know how to do it.'

Waltheof smiled sourly. 'I can lie down on my pallet and we can pretend that it is my deathbed. Would that help?'

'You should not jest, my lord.'

'Why not?' Waltheof shrugged. 'Jesting will avail me more than misery in my hour of reckoning.'

There was an uneasy silence in which Simon cast around for something to say. 'The ordinary folk are disturbed by the rumour that you are to be executed.'

'Are they indeed?' Waltheof's smile broadened and grew a little savage. 'I may yet cause a rebellion then with my dying breath . . .'

'Which William will suppress and swiftly.'

'Oh indeed.' Waltheof paced to the end of the cell and turned. Simon noticed that there was a path worn in the straw. 'Strange how English and Norman rules have suited him,' Waltheof said. 'Roger of Hereford is sentenced to remain the rest of his life in prison because he is a Norman. However since I am English the penalty for me is death, and there is no one willing to stick out their own neck and argue for my freedom.'

'Abbot Ulfcytel has done so, my lord,' Simon objected.

'And he too is English and so his word carries small weight with those who would see me deprived. I should have died in the wasting of the North, fighting with an axe in my hand, not in this dark and shameful way.'

'And I should not have come,' Simon said, and turned to the door. The hand he raised to knock for the guard was trembling violently. Never again, he swore. Never again would he put himself in such a fraught situation.

'No, wait.' Waltheof strode to Simon and grabbed his sleeve. 'I don't want you to leave like this.' Pulling the youth against him, Waltheof smothered him in a second embrace, harder and more desperate than the first. The bone of mortality on bone.

'I know there is nothing you can do. I know that I should not waste my last hours in bitterness, but it is hard,' Waltheof said, his voice tearing. 'Once I gave your life to you. Now live it for me. When you look out on a ploughed field or the women bringing in the May, remember me and see with my eyes as well as your own. When you take a wife and hold your own firstborn child in your arms, think of me.'

'You know I will,' Simon replied, his own voice constricted by the force of the embrace and the emotion that Waltheof was squeezing out of him.

'Do not just say it, swear it.'

'I swear it, on the cross,' Simon gasped as Waltheof's grip tightened.

As if realising that he was asphyxiating the young man, Waltheof relaxed his hold. Simon dragged a deep gulp of air into his lungs and dropped to his knees.

Going to his bed, Waltheof swept the bearskin cloak off the end. 'I want you to have this,' he said. His large hands caressed the thick, white fur.

Simon stared. His throat ached and he could not speak, but he managed to shake his head.

'You always admired it as a child and it will mean more to you than anyone else. I have no doubt that when they sever my head from my body someone will appropriate this garment to themselves in naught but greed. I would rather you had it.' With a final parting stroke, Waltheof handed the cloak to Simon.

The young man took it across his arm and felt its weight settle – almost as heavy as a mail hauberk, for as well as the weight of the pelt the outer layer was thickly woven, fulled wool, and the bordering braid was twined with thread of gold. The garment of a magnate, an earl. He was moved and awed. For as long as he could remember he had admired and coveted this mantle. Now he would have done anything to see it back in its rightful place billowing from Waltheof's shoulders as he strode through his life.

'I will treasure this . . .' he said in a tight voice.

'Do not be so precious as to make of it an object of worship. It is meant to be worn – and worn with pride.' Taking back the cloak, Waltheof opened it out and swung it around the squire's shoulders. It drowned his slenderness and the hem almost swept the floor. Borrowed robes that did not fit, Simon thought with an inward grimace.

'You will grow into it,' Waltheof said, as if reading his mind. His mouth twitched in a painful smile. 'In more ways than one.' He thrust home the enormous silver penanular pin with its thistlehead decoration.

Simon departed shortly after that, and was not ashamed of the tear streaks on his face as the guard led him back through darkness towards the light. He had to hold the cloak above his ankles like a woman holding her skirts to prevent himself from trampling on the hem.

'Worth the meeting then,' the guard said with an envious nod at Simon's acquisition.

'Without price,' Simon said in a choked voice. They passed an alcove redolent with the stink of a latrine hole – a crude wooden seat set over a shaft in the wall. Simon dived sideways and hung over the foul pit, retching dryly. He could have told Waltheof that his betrayers were none other than his mother-in-law and her husband aided and abetted by the Montgomery family, who never forgot a slight, but he had kept that information to himself. He felt as if he had been drinking poison for a long, long time, and finally it had made him sick. Was there a difference between good treachery and bad treachery? Was Waltheof's rebellion against William worse than the calumny practised against him by the venomous tongue of Adelaide of Champagne and Roger de Montgomery? He had no answers, only reaction.

'As bad as that?' the guard said.

'Worse,' Simon gasped, and forced himself upright. His stomach still trembled and he compressed his lips. No matter how much it sickened him, he was a straw on the flood and there was nothing he could do.

In the morning, the final one of May, Waltheof, Earl of Huntingdon, Northampton and Northumberland, was brought from his cell and escorted by mailed guards to the top of a hill outside the city walls. It was a beautiful dawn, a flushed apricot horizon uplighting the growing blue of the new day. Waltheof's last footsteps left their trail in grass that was silver-green with dew and starred with the clenched buds of daisy and dandelion.

Simon stood amidst the small crowd that had followed the

soldiers to witness the execution. Most were Normans and the majority wore the mail and gambesons of knights and soldiers. There was only a handful of English folk, drawn from the community of castle servants. The executioners had deliberately chosen the early hour so that few of the townspeople were about or free of their labours. The Normans did not want a riot on their hands.

Simon saw Waltheof stumble and winced for him. How long it must have been since he had seen the light and stretched his legs. At least they had given him access to clean raiment and he must have washed his hair, for it had a metallic sparkle in the sunshine and the filaments floated on the breeze like the finest threads of copper and gold.

The beheading was to be done with a sword, for he was highly born, an earl, and even those who wanted him dead for their own base reasons, respected the privileges due to his high birth. Simon had watched the swordsman sharpening his blade on a whetstone the night before and the sound of the brightening of the steel had sent chills through him with each long rasp. Had he not owed Waltheof his life he would have fled the slaying, but it was his duty to bear witness so that he could look Waltheof's executioners in the eyes when they could not look him in his.

On the crest of the hill, facing the dawn, the guards thrust Waltheof to his knees. As Walkelin, Bishop of Winchester, prayed over him, the swordsman approached, the blade shining with the reflection of the rising sun.

Waltheof's eyes widened in panic and Simon saw that they were full of the desperate need to live. That even now Waltheof could not believe that he was about to die. 'For the love of Almighty God!' he cried in a choked voice. 'At least let me say the Lord's Prayer one more time . . . for your sake, and for mine.'

The swordsman hesitated and looked round at the gathered soldiers for instruction.

'So be it,' growled Eudo of Champagne with an impatient

flurry of his hand. 'But make haste.' At his side Robert de Montgomery scowled, clearly irritated by the delay. He set his hand to the hilt of his own sword as if contemplating doing the deed himself.

Waltheof spread his hands, bowed his head, and his voice rose above the prelate's in recitation of the Lord's Prayer. '*Pater noster qui es in caelis, sanctificetur nomen tuum. Adveniat regnum tuum . . .*'

Simon prayed too, clearing his throat and raising his strong young voice. Folk either side who had been murmuring their own responses looked at him askance, but he did not care. This was for Waltheof, an affirmation of support and belief.

Waltheof raised his head and followed the sound until his eyes met Simon's across the sward. They held him, nailing him to the promise he had made the night before and filled with a terrible entreaty that Simon was powerless to aid.

'*Et ne nos inducas in temptationem.*' Waltheof's voice died away and his gaze left Simon's and struck on the group of nobles whose pressure had brought him to this place. Roger de Montgomery, Robert of Mortain, Eudo of Champagne. He looked until their image blotted the gold and blue of the new morning from his sight. '*Sed libera nos a malo.* But deliver us from evil.' The crowd around him stirred restlessly and the bladesman's eyes flickered with apprehension. At a nod from Eudo the man laid both hands to the sword, drew back to gain impetus and struck round and down in a lightning movement that clove flesh and vertebrae in one crunching slice.

'Amen!' Simon's voice finished alone, then died in apalled silence. Some members of the crowd turned aside to vomit. Simon had done that yesterday. Now, dry-eyed, he bore witness as Waltheof's crumpled, blood-spattered body was lifted onto a bier and the head placed beside it. Some of the crowd tried to push forwards and the soldiers held them back with spears. Simon, being a royal squire, was permitted through the cordon. Already a servant was swilling the bloody grass with pails of water, removing all trace of the deed. The bier was lined with absorbant hides to soak up the blood that still leaked from the body. The corpse had been covered by a blanket and this too was slowly reddening as the bearers carried it towards the grave that had been made ready.

Simon stood by the deep pit they had dug. Waltheof was permitted neither the dignity of a coffin nor even a shroud, but was tumbled from stretcher to pit in a single motion. One man leaned down to take the head and set it against the severed neck. Immediately labourers began shovelling earth into the grave, their haste as unseemly as the manner of Waltheof's death.

'Is the Earl not to be brought home to Huntingdon for burial?' Simon asked one of the monks attending the Bishop at the graveside.

The man shook his head. 'Our instructions were to bury him at the place of execution,' he said, clasping his hands and joining the others in chanting a litany for the dead.

Listening to their intonation, Simon knew that their prayers were a waste of time. Waltheof's soul would not rest easy in this soil. His ghost would walk and cry out – if not for vengeance, then for proper reverence and peace.

The soil was packed down and covered with fresh green turf. Dry-eyed, burning within, Simon turned on his heel. A small girl and her mother had been watching from a distance. The woman was a servant from the palace kitchens. Her gown of natural brown wool was patched and her braids were bundled up in a simple working kerchief. Her daughter had flaxen braids and deep blue eyes set in a dainty face. Her arms were occupied by a mass of spring flowers, early campion, daisy, dogrose and mingled with them the greenery of young wheat, cut long before its harvesting time. Given a gentle push of encouragement, the child ran over to the raw mound of earth and scattered the flowers on the top. Then she crossed herself, curtseyed and hastened back to her mother.

Simon's throat tightened. He looked at the woman, intending to smile, but encountered naught but hostility in her eyes.

'Norman bastards!' she hissed and, taking her daughter by the hand as if she feared Simon would harm her, she hastened away towards the timber service buildings.

He paced slowly to the graveside. The breeze stirred the petals on the delicate flowers, already beginning to wilt from their untimely cutting. After a while, Simon too, crossed himself, bent his knee, and limped rapidly away.

CHAPTER 21

Crowland Abbey, October 1087

S omewhere a skylark was singing. The bubbling song drew
Simon's gaze away from the space between his horse's ears
and upward to the expansive sky, deep autumn blue swept
with a feathering of high white cloud. After a moment, he
located the tiny warbling speck halfway to heaven. He wondered
what it was like to look down on the world from the height of
angels, to be a bird and feel cool air streaming against feathered
pinions and see everything from a different perspective.

The song ceased and the lark plummeted towards the
pasture, sere-gold at summer's end and autumn's beginning.
Meres and pools glittered like a reflection off armour. Placid
white cattle grazed on the higher ground, taking a final fatten-
ing before the days shortened too far and the grass ceased to
grow. On the still, clear air the bells of Crowland Abbey tolled
the hour of terce, summoning the monks to worship.

Hearing the sound, seeing the church rising from out of the
flat, fenland landscape, Simon felt a flickering in his gut but
whether of anticipation or unease, he could not have said. It
was eleven years since he had made his farewells to Waltheof.
Now he came to don a mantle bestowed upon him by the new
king. But first he had a pilgrimage to make.

William of Normandy, known to some as the Bastard and
to others as the Conqueror, had died in Rouen at the beginning of last month, mortally wounded when his horse trampled on a burning cinder and threw him so hard on to the

pommel of his saddle that his bladder ruptured. During several days of lingering agony he had bequeathed Normandy to Robert, the eldest of his three surviving sons. England went to his middle son, William Rufus, and he had given young Henry five hundred marks of silver from his treasury.

Many thought that Robert, as the eldest, should have inherited England. Robert thought so too, and trouble was brewing faster than yeast froth on new ale. Hence Simon's presence in these parts at the head of a seasoned troop.

As he and his men drew closer to the abbey they passed a steady trickle of folk travelling in the same direction. Some were wealthy enough to be mounted, others rode in ox carts, but the majority were either on foot or had used the extensive waterways surrounding the abbey to arrive by barge and punt. Simon saw a small, golden-haired child walking beside her mother, a bunch of late wayside flowers clutched in her hand. The image reminded him of Waltheof's execution so vividly that his hands twitched on the bridle and his mount danced sideways. The child looked up with sudden fear and the mother's hand shot out in protective alarm. Simon drew the rein in hard, bringing himself and the horse back under control.

'I am sorry,' he said in English.

The mother's eyes flashed and then lowered. He felt the hatred and knew that, despite the passage of time, nothing had changed. Slapping the reins on the dun's neck he rode on at a faster pace. His troop followed, the hooves of their mounts churning the dust. The woman covered her face with her wimple and used the edge of her overdress to shield the child.

Near the abbey gates, hucksters had set up stalls selling chaplets of greenery, small wooden crosses and metal tokens to hang on leather belts. There were pie booths, a baker's counter and even a cobbler, industriously mending shoes that had not stood up to the road. Fascinated, one hand on his swordhilt, the other on the reins, Simon turned in the saddle and stared around.

'What's all this for?' demanded Aubrey de Mar, the serjeant

in command of Simon's troop. He fiddled with the nasal bar of his helm.

'The English have made Waltheof of Huntingdon a martyr,' Simon replied neutrally. 'They say that miracles have happened at his tomb.'

Aubrey grunted. 'Do you believe it?'

Simon shrugged and felt the neck band of his gambeson chafe his neck. 'Stranger things have happened. It is rumoured that when the monks opened his grave at Winchester in order to bring his body back to Crowland, they discovered that his head had been miraculously restored to his torso and that the corpse was as fresh as the day it had been placed in the earth.'

Aubrey curled a sceptical lip. 'I heard a dragon was seen in York last month. Turned out to be a runaway bullock that overset a cauldron of fat and began a house fire.'

Simon gave a wry smile. 'It would be a barren world without wonders. What matters is that the people believe it.'

'Old King William must be rolling in his own grave. Look at 'em all.' Aubrey jerked his head at the pilgrims.

'He knew the risks when he agreed that Waltheof could be brought from Winchester to Crowland. He need not have given his permission for the reburial, but he did.'

'To ease his conscience you think?'

'Quite likely. Even before the Rouen campaign he was ailing. I believe that his past deeds had begun to burden his conscience.' Simon could still remember the morning that Abbot Ulfcytel and the Countess Judith had come to ask William's clemency and beg that Waltheof's body be exhumed and brought to Crowland Abbey for burial. It had been incongruous to see them together; the balding little churchman shabby and farmer-like despite the new robes he had donned for the occasion, and the Countess Judith, sombrely clad in charcoal-grey, her face wan and bloodless. She had knelt at William's feet, kissed his hand and pleaded with him to let her have Waltheof's body for Crowland.

'I thought you would banish him,' she had whispered in a

choked voice. 'I did not believe that you would command his execution.'

'Treason is treason,' William had growled. 'And he was fairly judged by the law of his own land. If I had banished him, where do you think he would have gone? Straight to Denmark or Brittany, to organise more rebellion.'

Ulfcytel had stepped forward and added his own plea to Judith's petition that William at least grant Waltheof the grace of being laid to rest in Crowland Abbey, where once he had been a pupil. After a brief deliberation William had consented. Indeed, Simon had thought that there was a certain degree of relief in his manner, as if he were atoning for a sin and finding the price not too high.

Looking at the gathering around the abbey gates, Simon wondered if William had been right. Waltheof was viewed as an English martyr to Norman ambition and greed. Pilgrims came not only out of hope for a miracle, but as a way of defying their Norman overlords in a manner that could not be contested.

Simon gave his name at the porter's lodge, rode into the courtyard, and dismounted. He had been on the road for several days, and his left leg was aching ferociously. Through long habit he concealed the pain but nevertheless it prodded at him. Turstan, his squire, took the dun in hand, and lay workers arrived from the stables to help with the horses. Lowering his mail coif, Simon thrust his fingers through his cropped hair, and looked around. The abbey was prospering on the proceeds of martyrdom, he thought, studying the fresh, bright paint and the ornate carving over the doorway. The little girl and her mother walked past, following the procession of pilgrims in what was obviously the direction of Waltheof's tomb. Simon ungirded his sword belt, handed it to Turstan, and bidding his men wait, took the path to the church.

The hushed whispers of the pilgrims rose and echoed around the sturdy barrel vaulting of the roof. Geometrical designs were painted on the columns in colours so bright that they almost hurt the eye. Grass green, blood red, lapis blue. Jewelled light from the stained glass window over the altar streamed down upon the pilgrims so that it seemed they were standing at the foot of a rainbow.

Simon's spurs scraped softly on the swept earth floor as he limped up the nave. A young monk was swinging a censer and the spicily scented smoke drifted on the air and settled its heavenly breath on garments, skin and hair.

Waltheof's tomb stood in the Chapter House, the carved wooden housing covered with a pall of dark-red silk bordered with gold embroidery that must have cost someone several marks. The sewing was in the Opus Anglicanum style and exquisitely worked. Above the tomb a ceramic oil lamp supported in brass chains sent out streamers of scented smoke.

Two older monks stood by the tomb, keeping a close watch on those who filed past and lifted the pall to kiss the dark wooden side. Simon supposed that a piece of the silk, surreptitiously cut away by a palmed knife, would fetch a high price from relic seekers. Among the flowers, the silver pennies, prayer beads and lighted candles placed as offerings around the base of the tomb were the sticks, crutches, bowls and cups of the sick who had been cured or improved by their pilgrimage.

The little girl laid her flowers among the other gifts, thus completing the image in Simon's memory. She dipped a curtsey, kissed the pall and with her mother was ushered on by another monk whose task it was to keep the file of pilgrims moving.

Simon knelt on his good leg, crossed himself and said a silent, private prayer over his clasped hands. A part of him half expected the pall to surge or the lamp to come crashing down on his head, but there was nothing, only the shuffle of the people waiting their turn and the soft jingle of the censer as the monk swung it back and forth, fumigating the crowd with its holy fragrance.

Perhaps Waltheof approved of what Simon had come to do. Comforting himself with that thought, he rose to his feet and followed the pilgrims out of a side entrance. His departure took him past another relic in the form of the skull of Abbot

Theodore, who had been martyred in a Danish raid two hundred years before. Stripped of flesh, the cranium bearing the mark of the killing blow, the sockets stared Simon out into the bright morning air where the current abbot was waiting for him, not Ulfcytel, as he had expected, but a taller, thinner monk with patrician features and a neatly clipped silver tonsure.

Once again Simon knelt. He kissed the ring of office on the Abbot's extended fingers. 'Father,' he murmured, managing to keep the note of surprise from his voice.

'I have sent your men to the guesthouse in the company of two brethren who will see to their needs,' the monk said pleasantly as Simon rose. 'I am Abbot Ingulf. Forgive me, it is not often that we see Normans at Crowland.'

Simon thanked him for the care of his men. 'My pilgrimage is a personal one,' he said, adding after a brief hesitation, 'Forgive me if this is a tactless question, but what has become of Abbot Ulfcytel?'

'You knew Ulfcytel?' The Abbot's brows rose towards his tonsure. Simon could see him struggling with the notion of a Norman courtier and soldier having such an acquaintance.

'Not well, but I met him on occasion and he seemed to me a good and holy man.'

'And so he was, God rest his soul.' Ingulf crossed himself and beckoned Simon to walk with him towards the low timber building that housed his private solar.

Simon signed his breast. 'I am sorry.'

'He is buried in Peterborough Abbey, where he finished his days as an ordinary monk.' Ingulf looked sidelong at Simon. 'Three years ago he was removed from the abbacy. His duties were becoming too onerous for his mind and body to perform.'

'It had nothing to do with the way he stood up to the King over Earl Waltheof?' Simon said neutrally.

The Abbot clasped his palms together. 'Yes, that too.' He gave a sorrowful shake of his head. 'Ulfcytel's mind took to wandering and he became outspoken – as a result of senility I believe, not out of any great desire to make mischief, but it was clear he was no longer fit for his duties. They sent him to Glastonbury, but I asked that he be permitted to return to Peterborough, which he knew and loved. He died there shortly after. We pray for his soul every day.'

Ingulf ushered Simon into his private solar and bade him be seated in a cushioned curule chair near an unlit brazier. Sunlight poured through the window arches and shone on the scattered bundles of floor rushes. 'I see that prayers are said daily for Earl Waltheof too,' Simon observed.

'Indeed,' Ingulf's expression was bland. 'He is in our care, and we honour our obligations.'

'Do you think he is at peace?'

Unsealing a leather costrel, Ingulf poured mead into two earthenware cups. 'As I understand, he was always at peace here,' he said gently. 'The difficulties began when he had to leave. Now he is home again – not in the manner that Ulfcytel would have chosen for him, but fitting in its own way.'

Simon took the cup that Ingulf handed to him and drank. The mead was dry and golden, with notes of autumnal crispness.

'And what of the Countess Judith?' Simon tried to make the question casual but saw from the sudden sharpening of the Abbot's gaze that he had failed.

'Despite her estrangement from the Earl in the months before his death, she has mourned him with great dignity and genuine . . . remorse,' Ingulf said.

Simon noted the use of 'remorse' not 'sorrow'. He had not seen Judith in more than ten years. What would she be like now? Although his expression remained unconcerned, his stomach churned.

'The Countess has given much time to the founding of her nunnery at Elstow,' Ingulf continued. 'God has become her solace. She and Waltheof may have had their differences, but they were united in their love of the Church. She has remained a chaste and dutiful widow.'

Simon almost grimaced but managed to lose the expression in his cup.

Ingulf studied him. 'Mayhap it is not my business to ask, but what brings a soldier of the Norman court to these parts? Surely not for the purpose of praying at the tomb of an English earl executed for treason?'

'Is it so obvious?' Simon asked wryly.

Ingulf gave a wintry smile and sipped fastidiously from his cup. 'Not until thought about,' he said. 'If we see Normans at Crowland it is either because they are travellers in need of a night's shelter or sheriff's men keeping an eye on our pilgrims.'

Simon inclined his head in acknowledgement. 'You are right, Father Abbot. Indeed, had I followed my purpose and no other consideration, I would not have come to Crowland at all. What brought me here today was honour and memory.' He hesitated and turned the cup in his hand, contemplating the decorative zigzag design.

Ingulf said nothing, but his silence was one of encouragement. Simon gnawed his underlip. Here in the Abbot's solar it was almost like a confessional and he found himself letting down his guard.

'I loved Waltheof,' he said. 'When I was a child, I thought of him as a heroic warrior. He saved my life and I worshipped him. Even when I grew out of the adoration, I cherished the image of the first time I saw him, striding out as if he owned the world with that red hair flowing and that cloak of his pinned at his shoulder with silver and gems. That is how I remember him. I have seen him with feet of clay many times, but those are not the occasions that hold my mind.'

Ingulf smiled and nodded gently. 'Ulfcytel told me that he always saw Waltheof as a young boy, learning his Psalter with the other lads in his care. He said that he saw the child standing at the side of the tomb, staring in bewilderment at what became of the man.'

'A vision you mean?'

The Abbot shrugged. 'So some would say, and I would not deny them.'

Silence fell again. Simon gently swirled the mead in his cup.

'You asked my purpose, Father. When I leave Crowland, my journey is to Northampton . . . to the dowager Countess,' he said. 'On the new king's command.'

'Ah,' Ingulf said, and the way he spoke told Simon that there was no need to say more; the Abbot understood perfectly. 'You will not necessarily find a welcome,' he warned. 'The Lady is strong-willed and accustomed to governing by her own hand. Nor has she made a pig's ear of the task. Harsh she may be, and not well loved as Earl Waltheof was, but she is fair. And she has the support of her family . . .'

'I have not been remiss in asking about such matters,' Simon said evenly.

'Then you will know what to face, my son.' The Abbot gave him a look that was almost pitying.

The last two words made Simon feel gauche and juvenile. For a seasoned courtier and battle commander it was ridiculous. He set his mead cup on the Abbot's trestle. 'I should be returning to my men,' he said abruptly, and rose to his feet. A pain, sharp and dull by turns, throbbed across his shin.

'Of course.' Ingulf saw him to the door and when he refused the services of a lay brother to show him the way to the guesthouse pointed him in the direction. 'You are always welcome here,' he said.

Thanking him, Simon joined the stream of pilgrims, easing his way through them until he came to the guesthouse situated near the porter's lodge. He sluiced his face and washed his hands in the laver provided. His men had made themselves beds along one wall with the straw palliasses provided. Listening to them joke as they assembled and sorted their gear, Simon briefly wished that he was one of their number, with nothing more pressing on his mind than obeying simple orders and looking forward to the next meal. And then he thought of the prize and realised that being one of their number had never been his destiny.

CHAPTER 22

The tree was heavy with apples, green flushing with pink and gold as they ripened, and the size of a strong man's clenched fist. In the thirteen years since Matilda had planted the pip it had grown into a sturdy tree, kept compact and shapely by careful pruning and loving attention. Matilda had grown with it. She towered above Sybille and Helisende and had a good handspan advantage over her sister and mother. From the latter's barbed comments, it was clear to Matilda that her mother wished her daughter was a bush to which she could apply the pruning shears.

Stooping to the water jug at her feet, Matilda poured a silver libation around the base of the tree and murmured a blessing. The water elf still dwelt in his well, but now she was old enough to draw the lid herself. She always carried a quarter penny in her pouch to pay him. Her mother would have called the custom pagan and bid her cease, but what her mother did not know could not be a source of friction.

The garden belonged to Matilda. Ever since the planting of her first apple pip in small childhood, it had been her source of pleasure and refuge. She relished the feel of the crumbly dark loam in her hands. There was nothing more satisfying than setting seeds and watching them thrust their way into the light, in nurturing them and harvesting their fruit.

Her mother would take her to task for spending so much time among her plants, but she never sought to prevent her.

The tending of the garden was a suitable task for a female, and since Judith did not enjoy the pursuit herself she was glad to leave it to her daughter. Matilda delighted in the solitude and the breathing space, much preferring the vagaries of the elements to the hencoop of the women's chamber.

She scattered the final glistening droplets around the roots of the tree and watched them soak into the ground. The garden gate squeaked, announcing Helisende's return. Matilda had sent the young woman who was both maid and companion to the solar with a basket of lavender for strewing among the rushes, thus giving each of them the excuse for a few moments alone.

'We have visitors,' Helisende announced, cheeks pink and eyes sparkling with excitement. 'A whole troop of them.'

Visitors to Northampton were frequent. Northumbria had been taken away on her father's death and given to the bishop of that diocese to administer, but Huntingdon and Northampton remained beneath her mother's vigorous rule. However, while stewards and administrators, merchants and soldiers came and went in a constant trickle, an entire troop was a different matter.

'Do you know who they are?' Matilda's first thought was that they were her grandfather Eudo's soldiers from his lands of Holderness. He brought them to Northampton several times a year, usually with his son Stephen in tow. But then Helisende would have said so.

'No,' Helisende shook her head, 'but I saw my father and their leader giving each other a handclasp and smiling as if they were old friends. They were speaking English too.'

Matilda's curiosity sharpened. English noblemen were rare these days. What one was doing at Northampton, where Norman ways were encouraged, was intriguing. Glancing down, she realised that there was soil on her hands and bits of leaf and twig festooning her gown, which was her oldest one of plain grey homespun. Hardly the garb in which to greet a visitor whatever his status. Whilst not overly vain, Matilda well knew that first impressions were often lasting ones. Nor with her mother's strictures ringing in her ears could she fail to be aware of her duty to keep up appearances.

Leaving the garden, she hastened towards the women's solar. There was no sign of the visitors, although several fine horses were being turned out in the paddock beside the stables. 'Was he old or young, this lord?' she asked the maid.

Helisende's flush deepened. 'There was no silver in his hair,' she said.

Hastily Matilda exchanged her old grey gown for one of sky-blue linen with a yoke and sleeve trim of darker blue that picked up and highlighted the colour of her eyes. Although as an unwed daughter of the house she was not forced to wear a wimple, her mother preferred her to cover her braids in formal company. Matilda settled a veil of plain cream linen over her copper-bronze braids and secured it with a woven band stitched with tiny seed pearls.

'You've a smut of soil on your cheek.' Helisende dabbed it away with the end of a kerchief she had dipped in the laver jug. 'You should pinch your cheeks and bite your lips to give them colour.'

Matilda laughed and waved a hand in dismissal. 'Why should I do that?' she demanded. 'Whoever our visitor is, I doubt that he's come courting.'

'You never know,' said Helisende.

Matilda shook her head. 'No,' she said. 'My mother does not like men. She founded the nunnery at Elstow for her spiritual comfort, and she wants this place to be like a nunnery too.'

'She will never manage that,' Helisende replied stoutly.

'It does not stop her from trying.' Matilda smoothed her palms over her gown and adjusted the side lacings so that they flattered her trim waist and full bosom.

'Perhaps you should elope,' Helisende suggested.

'Find me a suitable mate and I will,' Matilda retorted, going to the door.

When she arrived in the hall, it was to find the visitor's troop supping at trestle tables with the soldiers of her mother's guard. Her sister Jude was seated at the dais table in their mother's place, playing host to a quartet of knights. Matilda assessed them. Two were grey, one was going bald and the other had a beard. There was also a handsome squire, but he was in mid-adolescence and in no wise a man.

'He's not here,' muttered Helisende out of the side of her mouth.

'Neither is my mother,' Matilda said. Jude had seen her and was making frantic eyes for help. Lifting her chin, Matilda walked down the length of the hall and tried to remember to keep her steps small. Her mother was always taking her to task for striding out like a warrior.

The men rose to greet her and she inclined her head and smiled graciously. Jude stammered out introductions. She had a quiet nature and playing hostess was daunting.

The men all had Norman names, none of which Matilda recognised, and they spoke French, not English. 'You are most welcome to our hospitality,' she said formally as she took the high-backed chair her sister had vacated. 'Has my mother greeted you also?'

'Indeed, Lady Matilda, she has,' said the one named Aubrey de Mar. 'If the Countess is not here now, it is because our lord desired to have words of a private nature with her.'

'Your lord?'

'Simon de Senlis, my lady. He is here on the orders of King William.'

'For what purpose?' The question was surprised out of her before she could think better of asking it.

The men looked at each other and she could see their thoughts clearly. Countess Judith's daughter was cast in the same autocratic mould as her mother, and still only a chit of a girl.

Outwardly calm, inwardly quaking, she signalled an attendant to refresh the goblets and directed another servant to place a dish of honey cakes before the men. Food and drink always served to appease and mellow.

'Forgive me if I was brusque,' she said. 'But it is not every day that we receive a visitor with orders from my cousin, the King.'

She saw grudging humour light in the eyes of Aubrey de Mar as she reminded them of her rank while apologising for her lapse of grace.

'Not at all, my lady,' he responded in a hoarse voice that sounded as if he had eaten the road rather than ridden on it. 'Indeed, you will learn my lord's purpose soon enough. But it is only mete that he informs your mother first.'

Matilda inclined her head and took a sip of wine from her cup while she recovered from that particular exchange and prepared herself for the next. Simon de Senlis. The name echoed in the halls of her memory, but was too distant to be more than the merest distortion. If she had met him, it must have been a long time ago.

'Tell me,' she said, 'Does your lord speak English?'

'He does, my lady, and taught by your late father.'

Matilda's stomach leaped and she looked at the knight with widening eyes. 'He knew my father?'

'Aye, my lady, he did. It was before I entered my lord's service, so I know few details, only that they were master and pupil. Doubtless, my lord will tell you himself. He prefers to do his own speaking.'

Matilda's hand shook slightly as she took another drink of the wine. She might not be able to remember Simon de Senlis, but the image of her father was still as sharp and clear as the day on which he had ridden out and not come back. Shining hair of deep copper-red, a soft golden beard, the smile that was for her alone, and the sadness behind it. She had prayed so hard for him to return – and eventually he had. Now he lay in his shrine in the chapter house at Crowland. So near and yet so far. They never spoke of him in this household – or at least not in front of her mother, who would not stand to hear the mention of his name. Sometimes she and her sister would whisper together, or Sybille would talk of him, or Toki spin memories, but all in a clandestine fashion to avoid detection by Judith. The ordinary folk had more access to her father than she had ever done. Now, with this visitor from the past, this Simon de Senlis, she had a chance to strengthen the fragile memories and build a solid edifice worthy of him.

'Do you know how long you will be staying?' she asked when she was sure that her voice was steady. 'I need to ensure that the household is provisioned.'

'No, my lady.' De Mar spread his huge hands. 'My lord has not told us, and it will depend on how matters progress . . . If it helps you, I would say that you could plan for a sennight at least.' He reached for a honey cake, bit into it, and smiled. 'Mayhap longer if this is any judge of the fare on offer.'

Matilda returned the smile, but in a slightly preoccupied manner. It was all she could do not to leap from the table, rush to her mother's apartment and seize hold of this Simon de Senlis. The knight said they would be staying at least a week. There was time enough. She just wished that it were now.

Simon stood in Countess Judith's private chamber, and took in his surroundings with a feeling of unease that raised the hair on his nape. An embroidered frieze depicting the lives of various female saints relieved the plainness of the limewashed wall. There was also a wooden crucifix nailed above a small prie-dieu. The Countess's bed spanned a scant body-width and was made up with coarse blankets, not a fur in sight. She was living the life of a secular nun, he thought, and that did not bode well for what was to come.

The Countess did not invite him to sit. Nor did she offer him wine. Both should have been courtesies extended to a guest, but it was already clear that she viewed him as an intruder.

Facing him, she lifted her chin. 'Well, my lord, are you going to inform me of the reason for your visit and why it is better told in secret than in the open company of the hall?'

At six and thirty she was still an attractive woman, although her features, like her nature, had sharpened with the years and he could see that in old age she would be a replica of her fearsome mother.

'Not in secret,' he said, refusing to be intimidated. 'But in private. Since the matter is somewhat delicate, I thought it best discussed between us without an audience.'

'I cannot see that I have anything to discuss with you, witnesses or not,' she said gracelessly.

She had not offered him a seat but he took one anyway, settling himself on the cushioned bench that ran along the far wall. Irritation and resentment sparked in her eyes and Simon sighed. He could see that his purpose was already doomed. She might listen, but she was determined not to hear. He reached into his tunic. Secured between it and his shirt, held in place by his belt, was a letter bearing the royal seal. 'King William Rufus has entrusted me with the care of the earldom of Northampton and Huntingdon,' he said. 'His instructions are here.'

She stared at him, her body stiffening as if she was turning to stone. 'I am the Countess of Northampton and Huntingdon,' she said icily. 'He cannot do this.'

'The dowager Countess,' Simon corrected, 'and the lands are within the King's gift. He can bestow them where he chooses.'

Her complexion was ice-white. 'It is ten years since my husband's death. I have ruled these lands competently. He has no reason to issue such a command.' She almost snatched the packet from him.

'The King needs them to be held with military strength.'

'Hah!' she snapped. 'If that is so, then why has he sent a cripple?'

The words were intentionally cruel. Simon had learned in boyhood not to flinch, and he matched her gaze stone on stone. 'That is unjust of you, my lady. I thought you above casting cheap insults.'

Her cheeks reddened and her dark eyes glittered. She was beautiful in a strange, hard way that made Simon want to shiver. How many brittle layers had she grown since Waltheof's death, each one more frozen than the last?

'And is it not "unjust" of you to come and take these lands when I have ruled them competently since my husband's death?' she demanded. 'Is it not an insult to me, to my governance?'

'No my lady, it is not,' Simon said evenly. 'No one is disputing your administrative abilities or your judgement. But you cannot lead men in war or make military decisions based on the training of experience. You can only appoint deputies.' Even as he spoke, he knew that his words must sound like the greatest insult of all. How could he not offend her when he came to remove her authority?

'Neither can you, my lord,' she said, sweeping his slight build with a disparaging look.

'In that you are wrong, Countess,' he said quietly, for he had long since learned that keeping his temper was more than half the battle. 'If I were a boastful man, I could present you with a list of campaigns and military services to the house of Normandy that would take the day to recite. I may not be capable of swinging a battleaxe like your late husband, but no one has ever found me lacking. You are a wealthy widow of childbearing age and you have young daughters. This earldom is a plum, and in plain terms the King wishes to secure it to a man of his choosing rather than those who would profit at his expense – including your mother and stepfather and their son. I am sorry for your distress, but rail as you will, Countess, you can change nothing.'

'The people will never accept you,' she spat.

'They accepted you,' he pointed out, 'despite the rumours that you had connived at your own husband's death.'

That blow hit a soft part and Judith recoiled. 'I did not!' she gasped and drew herself up. 'I went to my uncle on bended knees to beg that my husband's body be allowed to rest at Crowland.'

'But that is guilt,' Simon said softly, 'not sorrow. You may not have connived at your husband's death, but neither did you plead for his life.' Suddenly he felt as exhausted as if he had fought a daylong battle. Making the effort, he rose to his feet and forced himself to go to the door. Each step burned, but his pride would not let him limp.

The maidservant Sybille was seated outside on a stool, await- ing her mistress's call, her ear inclined towards the heavy, studded oak. 'I would appreciate a flagon of wine,' Simon said courteously.

Sybille curtseyed. A smile curled her mouth corners. 'You have changed since last I saw you, my lord,' she ventured.

Simon returned the smile and felt some of his tension dissi- pate beneath the warmth in her tone. It had always astonished him that someone as proper and glacial as Judith could have a maid who was earthy, mischievous, and completely lacking in the propriety of which the Countess seemed so fond. 'Whether for the better I do not know,' he murmured ruefully, 'and I could say the same for your mistress.'

'She is hard on everyone.' Sybille darted a glance at the door to make sure that Judith was not within hearing range, 'and twice as hard on herself.' She looked at him. 'I do not think that you are here to cushion that hardness, my lord.'

'I am here,' Simon said, 'because the King has given me orders, and because I would have to be without ambition to ignore them. I cannot help your mistress if she will not help herself.'

'I doubt that she knows how,' Sybille said. Her eyes gleamed with curiosity – too much of it.

'Will you go and bring wine, or do I have to summon one of my men to do so?' Simon said, more curtly than he had intended.

A glimmer of resentment flared in Sybille's eyes. 'No,' she said, 'I will fetch it. But just remember that I once swatted you around the ears for filching fig pastries from Countess Adelaide's table.' Her nose in the air, she left on her errand.

Rubbing his brow where a headache was beginning to throb, Simon turned back into the room.

Judith was standing near the embrasure, gazing down at the sheets of vellum in her hand. She had obviously read the contents for her expression would have crusted hell's cauldron in ice.

'It is not to be borne,' she said with controlled fury.

Simon lowered his hand and wrapped it round his belt. It would not do to show her how tired he was. 'I can see that this news has come as an unwelcome shock, my lady,' he said. 'But I urge you to reconcile yourself to what has to be.'

'Never,' Judith said vehemently.

Simon knew it was futile, but still he spoke out, because he had promised. 'If you wish to remain in your position, there is nothing to prevent you, should you consent to be my wife.'

The words struck the air like fiery brands and Simon could almost feel their heat scorch his face. Rufus had set the condition when bestowing the earldom. See the women safe and provided for. Give Judith the opportunity of remarriage while there was still sap in her body, while she was still young enough to bear more children.

'Should I consent to become your wife?' she repeated, and looked him up and down as if he was some loathsome thing that had just crawled out from under a stone. 'If you are not jesting, then your wits are deranged.'

'I am neither in jest, nor lacking in wit,' Simon said quietly. 'Marriage to me would vouchsafe your status and enhance mine. You are still of childbearing age. I can fulfil the military obligations that Rufus requires. It would suit us both, if you could find it within you to swallow your pride and be civil.'

'I can find nothing within me but contempt,' Judith said. In her face he saw a revulsion so strong that it cut him to the quick. He was not accustomed to that look from women.

'You think me beneath you?' he asked. 'You think me damaged goods and lacking in the esteem by which you set so much store?'

Judith's lip curled. 'I swore when my first husband betrayed me that I would not wed again. I lusted after Waltheof Siwardsson, and it gained me naught but grief. No man is worth the price. I put my faith in God.'

'So you refuse my offer?'

The curve of her smile was thin as a whip. 'I throw it in your face,' she said.

Sybille entered the room bearing a flagon and two cups. 'Here we are,' she said cheerfully.

'Sir Simon is leaving,' Judith said without looking at her maid.

Simon narrowed his eyes. Crossing to Sybille, he took one of the cups and the flagon and poured himself a measure of wine. 'When I am ready,' he said, 'and only as far as the hall. What you do is your decision, my lady, but what I do is your cousin's. By all means keep this chamber, I will find one of my own, but let us be in no doubt as to who has the reins of governance here from now on.'

Judith glared at him and he knew that if looks could have killed he would have died there and then. He returned her stare, his expression impassive, but he could feel the heavy, swift bumping of his heart in his throat. Without taking his gaze from hers, he raised the cup to his lips and drank with slow, symbolic deliberation.

Judith held her ground, but he could see that she was trembling with the effort – or perhaps it was just with anger. He finished the wine, set the cup down on the coffer and sauntered to the door. 'Think on what I have said, my lady,' he said. 'Swallowing pride may be difficult, but living off it will be more difficult still.'

'You have my answer,' Judith said stiffly. 'I would rather go forth in rags than pledge myself to you.'

'Let us hope it does not come to the test,' Simon said with a sardonic curve of his lips and left the room.

Her control had the strength of iron. He was half expecting to hear a cup or a candlestand crash against the doorpost or whistle past his head, but there was only silence.

As Simon walked away he was hit by the same reaction that came upon him after facing the danger of battle. His legs turned to water and his vision blurred. Pivoting from the walkway, he braced himself against the wall and vomited until his throat was on fire and his stomach aching, but although he had rid himself of the wine the sensation of malaise remained and intensified.

Gasping, he leaned against the wall and closed his eyes. He would have slumped down against the welcome support of the painted timber, but he dared not lest Judith emerge from her chamber and find him thus. He knew he was in no condition to face the crowd in the great hall and impose his will. First, he needed to gather that will go and hold it together.

A cool draught blew across his face, chilling the sweat on his brow. He opened his eyes and glanced out of the narrow embrasure. The walkway faced an inner courtyard and he could see the greenery and floral colours of a well-tended garden. With lurching steps, one hand pressed to his aching stomach, Simon sought the respite of its sanctuary.

CHAPTER 23

atilda was beginning to feel anxious. There was still no sign of her mother and she had exhausted all topics of conversation with their visitors. The flagons had been replenished and the griddlecakes were a memory of crumbs. There was no sign of Simon de Senlis either, and the knights at the high table were growing restless.

What should she do? Matilda had no precedent. She also had no idea why Simon de Senlis was here. Amid the polite conversation, there had been no hints beyond that first comment that they would be in Northampton for at least a week.

She turned to Aubrey de Mar. 'If you and your lord are to remain here for a sennight, then sleeping arrangements must be prepared. By your leave I will go and attend to the matter.'

The knight made an open-handed gesture. 'By all means my lady.' His expression was an odd mingling of relief and anxiety. She could see that he was glad to relinquish the burden of polite conversation and plainly concerned by the absence of his lord.

As she left Jude scrambled from her own place on the bench, agitated at the notion of being left behind to continue the entertainment. 'Where's Mama?' she hissed, seizing Matilda's arm. 'What is she doing?'

Matilda shook her head. 'Likely in her chamber talking to Simon de Senlis about the matter that has brought them here,' she said.

'What do you think it is?'

'I do not know, but it must be important. From what I could glean from Sir Aubrey, Simon de Senlis is one of the new king's most trusted men.' She gave Jude's hand a reassuring squeeze, as much for her own benefit as her sister's. 'If these men are to spend several nights here, the most important will need beds making up. I must have the keys to the linen coffer, and Mama keeps them on her belt.'

'She will be angry if you disturb her,' Jude warned nervously.

Matilda shrugged. 'She is always angry for one reason or another. What difference will it make?'

They had been passing a window embrasure as they spoke. Matilda stopped abruptly and took a back step. There was a stranger in her garden, seated on the turf bench beneath her apple tree. Even from a distance she could see that he was wearing mail and a sword. His head was thrown back in a posture of utter weariness and his arms were folded across his chest. A pang of resentment shot through her that he should be in her place but mingled with it were anticipation and sudden breathlessness. It had to be Simon de Senlis. He was no longer with her mother, but for some reason had chosen the solitude of her garden above the company of the hall.

Matilda gave her sister a gentle push in the direction of their mother's chamber. 'Go to Mama, and ask her about the linens,' she said. 'I will join you presently.'

Jude looked alarmed. 'Why? Where are you going?'

'To speak with Simon de Senlis,' Matilda replied, and, before the impulse could desert her, she turned towards the steps that led down to the courtyard.

Her sister gnawed her lip, hesitated, and then continued towards their mother's chambers, where the very worst that could happen was a scolding.

At the garden gate Matilda hesitated. The need that had carried her thus far suddenly flickered and threatened to turn into a feeling of foolishness. She should not become embroiled. She should be a dutiful daughter of the house and seek her mother's bidding. What was she going to say to the man who was occupying the shade of her apple tree?

However, the double measure of stubbornness and courage she had inherited from both parents renewed her impetus. She opened the gate and fastened the rope latch behind her with resolution.

Her tread was purposeful but it was also quiet, for she wanted the advantage of observing him before he should notice her. She brushed past the lavender bushes, leaving a trail of scent in her wake, and walked along the paths that led to a second, smaller gate and the inner garden with its turf seats, rose trellis and vine arbour.

Simon de Senlis had not stirred from his position on the bench beneath the apple tree. His arms were still folded and his legs were stretched out, barring the path. She noticed that the waxed thread on one of his shoes was coming unstitched and that his chausses, although of excellent quality, bore the dusty appearance of hard travel. Whatever had happened between him and her mother, the Countess had not seen fit to offer him the courtesy of refreshing himself.

His eyes were closed, the lids lined with dense brown lashes tipped gold at the ends. Matilda could not tell if he were asleep or just resting, but she took the opportunity to examine the thin, clever features. His jaw was outlined in dark stubble and his brown hair was sun-bleached to blond on top, revealing that he had spent the summer months outdoors. Unlike the sheriff and the blunt men of his garrison, he did not resemble a Norman reaver. There was evidence of neither bulk nor breadth. A courtier, perhaps, she thought. But he was not dressed like a courtier either.

It was only after she had perused him thoroughly that she noticed he was sitting on his cloak and belatedly realised at what she was looking. The lustre of white fur against a background of blue wool trapped her eyes and filled them until they overflowed. Through a blur of moisture, she remembered being wrapped in the warmth and security of that cloak, remembered being encompassed in her father's love. It was a memory as sharp as it was distant, and made all the more powerful in her life by the fact that it was one of the few she had of him.

She must have made a small sound, for De Senlis stirred and opened his eyes. His arms unfolded and he instinctively groped for his sword, then relaxed as he realised there was no danger.

Matilda swallowed against the tightness in her throat. De Senlis stood up, and through her tears she caught the hint of pain in his expression before it was schooled to a careful neutrality. A trifle hazy, but clearing fast, his eyes were a lucent fox-gold.

'My lady, you surprised me.' Given the slightness of his build, his voice was deeper and more certain than she expected. One hand rested on his swordhilt, but she thought it was a customary gesture rather than a sign that he was about to draw it on her. It spoke oceans of her mother's reception that he had not removed it, though. She saw that he leaned on one hip, slightly favouring his left leg.

'Your men are wondering where you are, my lord,' she said rather breathlessly.

He raised a thin, interrogative brow. 'They sent you to find me?'

From the way he was studying her, Matilda knew that he was trying to place her within the household hierarchy – maid or mistress. 'No, my lord. I was seeking my mother for the keys to the linen chest when I looked from the embrasure and saw you seated here.'

'Ah.' He gave a half-smile. 'Would I be right in assuming that your mother is the Countess Judith?'

'Yes, she is.'

'And yet you diverted to talk with me rather than going directly to her?' He spoke as much to himself as Matilda and seemed to be weighing something in his mind.

'My sister was with me. Our mother will give her the keys.' She licked her lips, suddenly feeling nervous beneath his scrutiny.

'And which sister are you?' Without taking his gaze from her, he reached to a low hanging apple, cupped it in his hand and gave a gentle tug. The fruit came away with scarcely a bending of the bough. Dappled green, gold and red, it shone in his hand, reflecting the late glow of the sun.

'I am Matilda. My sister is Jude,' Matilda said faintly.

He nodded, as if she had confirmed something that he already knew. 'You were named for King William's queen, God rest her soul,' he said and crossed himself. 'I saw you once when you were a small child – little more than a babe in arms. I was a squire in the King's service then.'

Matilda's gaze darted to the cloak on the bench and her stomach turned over. 'Your men said in the hall that you knew my father.'

He shrugged. 'I thought I did, but now I believe that only God truly knows any of us and what we will or will not do.' His coppery gaze was assessing. 'You resemble him.'

'I remember him wearing that cloak,' she said in a choked voice. 'I always wondered what had happened to it . . .'

'He gave it to me when he was imprisoned in Winchester.' He turned the apple in his hand, lightly running his thumb over the glossy surface.

Matilda lowered her eyes from his and fought the wave of jealousy that swept her. This man was a link with her father. It should not matter that the cloak had been given to him, not her. Even had it been returned to Northampton, she knew that her mother would never have allowed her to keep it. She longed to reach out, to thrust her hands into the thick, white pelt, to press her nose against the tickly fur and be four years old again. But not in front of De Senlis.

'Why are you here?' she asked brusquely. She wanted to snatch the apple out of his hand too.

If he was taken aback by her tone he concealed it well,

although he hesitated before he spoke. 'King William Rufus has bidden me take the earldom of Huntingdon and Northampton into my custody.' He glanced towards the embrasure of the Countess's apartments. 'Your mother has no choice but to yield.'

Matilda stared at him. The words played across the surface of her mind, too new and strange to be absorbed on the instant. 'You are to take my father's lands?' she heard herself ask.

'His Midland shires, yes,' he said. 'I am under royal orders to do so . . . and I will brook no resistance.' His voice grew harsh on the last statement.

It was on the tip of her tongue to ask what resistance he expected to receive from mere women, but from his manner it was plain that he had not emerged unscathed from the meeting with her mother.

She raised her chin. 'What is to become of us? Are you under royal orders in that matter too?'

He gave her a brooding look. 'Yes, I am under orders,' he said curtly, 'and in truth I am of half a mind to disobey them.' Raising the apple, he bit into it. His teeth were sound, for there was no hesitation, no attempt to find good ones with which to chew.

Matilda stared at him, afraid to ask what he meant and filled with indignation.

He inclined his head to her in the barest deference and, without clarifying his statement, left the garden.

She gazed after him. His walk was slightly lop-sided and she could see that he was striving not to limp heavily in her sight. He had left the cloak strewn on the bench and she wondered if it had been as deliberate a ploy as taking and biting the apple. Matilda sat down upon the pelt, and, as she had been longing to do, filled her hands and buried her face in the cool, glossy fur.

The feel brought the distant memories of her father flooding back. She could see the laughter in his dark blue eyes and sunlight sparkling on his ruddy hair. She could hear the rumble of his voice, speaking in English, and experience the delight tingle through her body as he swung her aloft in his arms. Tears burned her lids. Wrapping herself in the folds of the cloak, she was both comforted and desolated. An odour clung to the wool – of sun-warmed fabric and dust, and something else. The individual scent of the man to whom the cloak now belonged. The hair rose softly on her nape and she gazed in the direction of the garden gate, her lips slightly parted.

Hearing the click of the latch, she thought for a moment that he had returned to claim the cloak, but it was Sybille who came hurrying down the path, cheeks flushed and wimple askew.

'Your mother wants you immediately,' the maid panted.

Matilda rose and the older woman's eyes widened at the sight of the blue mantle.

'Sir Simon left it behind,' Matilda explained. 'I was about to return it to him.'

Sybille shook her head. 'No time for that, sweeting. And best not take it into your mother's presence,' she counselled. 'She's already fit to burst.'

'Sir Simon told me that he is here to take the earldom into his hands.' Matilda removed the cloak and draped it over her arm. It was almost as heavy as a mail shirt.

'Did he tell you anything else?'

Matilda smoothed her hand over the soft, midnight-blue wool. 'Should he have done? Is there more?'

Sybille gave her a dark look. 'Enough to shake the walls to their foundations,' she said with a certain grim relish. 'I won't say more. The mood your mother's harbouring, one word out of place would be cause for a whipping.'

Outside her mother's chamber, Matilda paused to lay the cloak in a coffer that stood against the wall. Straightening her skirts, tucking a stray wisp of hair inside her wimple, she braced herself and entered the room.

Judith was pacing the floor, a deep frown scored between her brows. Her mouth was tucked in upon itself, making her look shrewish and old. When she saw Matilda, she ceased pacing and faced her, fury brimming in her eyes.

'Your sister informs me that you went to speak to Simon de Senlis,' she said icily. 'Do you want to tell me why?'

Matilda cast about for an explanation that would satisfy her mother. 'I saw him in the garden and from the way he was sitting I thought perhaps he was injured.'

'Well, he is not,' Judith snapped, 'and you are to keep away from him. He is a wolf in sheep's clothing.' Her voice shook on the pronunciation. 'What did he say to you?'

'Very little,' Matilda said, beginning to feel resentful of her mother's stance. 'Only that he had come to take my father's lands into his care.'

'Your "father's lands",' Judith sneered. 'Your beloved, blessed father could keep neither his lands nor his head. It is I who have maintained them through all the years of your life, and I will not be replaced by some upstart knight.' The tremble in her voice increased.

'But if it is the King's command . . .' Matilda said.

'I will appeal against it. William Rufus is a fool, and Simon de Senlis is no more an earl than I am a serf. I will not wed him and let him make of me his chattel.'

Matilda gasped and clapped one hand involuntarily across her mouth.

'Oh yes,' declared her mother with a vicious nod. 'He wants to legitimise his claim by marriage, the traitorous thief. I knew Simon de Senlis when he was a snivelling brat. I will not be subject to his rule now.'

Matilda's stomach roiled with shock, anger and a strange unsettling stab of feminine jealousy. When she had stood in the garden and looked upon the vulnerable figure of Simon de Senlis, she had certainly not viewed him in the guise of step-father.

'At first light we will leave and take refuge at Elstow while I decide what is to be done,' Judith said grimly.

'But if we leave, surely that will be granting him the victory.'

'No. It will show that we spurn him, and his authority will be diminished.' Judith curled her lip. 'My family will not stand quietly by and see this happen to me, and nor will the people of these shires. I am Waltheof's widow, and not without influence.'

And I am Waltheof's daughter, Matilda thought, but she held her tongue. Across the room she caught her sister's eye. Jude looked frightened. It was obvious that the keys to the linen coffer had not been given and that there was no point asking for them. The only beds that her mother intended Simon de Senlis and his men to lie upon were made of thorns.

It was late evening. The Countess and her daughters had appeared in neither the hall nor the guest chamber. Not that Simon had expected them to do so. The mother hen had swept her chicks beneath her wing and was cooped up in the women's bower clucking in high dudgeon. The notion brought the slightest of smiles to his lips, but it did not linger. Countess Judith was not a hen and he did not believe that she would sit and cluck for long.

Rubbing his leg, he eased himself down on to the bench and lifted the cup of wine that his squire had left to hand. Since the Countess had originally had the chamber built to house important guests, it was spacious and well appointed – which he doubted she would have wished for him. A cosy burial casket was probably the accommodation she currently had in mind.

He thought of his encounter with the daughter in the garden. The girl possessed her father's strong bones, although the features were refined to feminine delicacy. There was a look of Judith about the arch of her brows, but instead of being glossy black they were a rich, copper-bronze and made him want to smooth his thumb across them, and then down the line of her cheek to the soft curl of her mouth corner.

It was many years since he had played at love and lust with Sabina the falconer's daughter. Long too since he lost his virginity in a hayrick with a cowherd's young widow. He knew about attraction, the excitement of the chase, the pleasure of gorging on the kill. Knew also about the brothels that Waltheof had once warned him against. The thought brought a grim smile to his lips.

How old was the girl? He was tired, his leg was paining him, and his mind was woolly. Fifteen, sixteen summers? Of an age to be bedded, and she had Waltheof's blood in her veins.

His musings were disturbed by the return of Turstan his squire and several attendants bearing a large oval bathtub and pails of hot and cold water. Late it might be, but Simon could not bear to lie another night in his own sweat and dirt. It was not that he was particularly fastidious, but there came a time when the itch and prickle of unwashed skin and hair became unpleasant. Besides, a hot tub would soothe the ache in his leg.

The attendants, albeit that they belonged to the Countess and kept their heads down, were swift and efficient. He laboured to his feet so that Turstan could help him unarm. On retiring to this chamber, Simon had removed the grinding weight of his mail hauberk, but he still wore his padded gambeson and swordbelt. A show of constant vigilance was prudent.

Once the tub was filled the attendants were dismissed. The last one out closed the door but did not latch it, and as the squire knelt to unfasten Simon's hose bindings it swung open on a draught of air that sent the flames guttering in the two hanging lamps. Instinctively Simon reached for his sword, and the squire flashed his knife from its sheath.

Matilda paused, looking from one to the other, alarm flaring in her eyes.

'My lady.' Simon uncurled his grip from the hilt of his sword and motioned the squire to put up his knife. 'You are brave to enter the lion's den,' he remarked, the imagery suggested to him because she seemed like a young doe, poised for flight.

She coloured, but advanced into the room, although he noticed that she did not close the door. There was no sign of her maid; she was without a chaperone.

'I am not brave at all, my lord,' she replied. 'I know that you are honourable and that you will not harm me.'

Simon gave a humourless smile. 'I doubt you have imbibed such sentiments from your lady mother,' he said. 'And I wonder if you are right to trust your source of information. Any man can turn from his honour in the dark of night if given the opportunity.'

'You are not any man, my lord,' she said.

Her answer surprised a snort of genuine amusement out of Simon. What might have sounded arch and flirtatious coming from an older woman in a different tone was made comically touching by the plain innocence of the girl's. 'Am I not?' he said.

'The King would not have sent "any man" to this task.' She gave him a clear, steady look that burned him like a flame. 'You knew my father. He would not have given you his cloak unless he thought highly of you.' She held out her arms like a handmaiden, the garment draped across them. 'Since we are leaving in the morning, I am returning this to you now.'

With a gesture and a nod Simon dismissed the squire, following him to the door and ensuring the latch fell behind the lad. Then he approached Matilda and removed the cloak from her outstretched hands.

'Do you still trust me, girl?' He could not control the hoarse note that had entered his voice, nor the speed of his breathing.

'Yes, my lord.' She stared back at him and he saw that although her gaze was steadfast her breathing was as rapid as his own.

'Well, you should not. Even a tame beast will turn wild of tooth and claw if provoked.'

'Have I provoked you, my lord?'

He went to lay the cloak on the coffer, giving himself time to gather his wits and his control. 'In ways you cannot begin to know,' he said with a short laugh. When he was more certain of himself, he turned to her. 'It is courteous of you to inform me that you are leaving on the morrow. I suspect that your mother does not know you have done so – or that you are here in my chamber.'

'No,' she said with pinkening cheeks. 'She does not know. Will you prevent us from going now that I have told you?'

He steepled his hands beneath his chin. 'Where does your mother intend to take you?'

The girl hesitated and licked her lips.

Simon had seen those sorts of gestures before. Dwelling at court, observation of expressions and bodily actions became second nature. 'Lies may help you get over a small slope, but eventually you will come to a mountain and the burden you have accumulated will be your ruin.' He studied her through narrowed lids. 'The truth or nothing.'

Her chin jutted. 'I was not going to lie to you,' she said. 'If I paused it was because I was unsure how you would respond to my answer.'

'Which is?'

'To the nunnery at Elstow, and then to my stepgrandfather's estates in Holderness.'

'Ah,' Simon said, and lowered his clasped hands. 'I thought that your mother might seek her sanctuary there. After all, your stepgrandfather has a vested interest in these lands – and a son.'

She looked nervous, but not surprised, and she made no attempt to deny the implication of his words. Her reaction pleased him.

Unlatching his swordbelt, he turned to lay it across the coffer beside his discarded hauberk. 'Do you want to go with your mother?'

Although his back was to her, he felt her surprise at the question. The breath she drew was audible.

'Do I have a choice?'

The tone of her response told him that she was already ahead of the conversation, that she knew where it was going – and perhaps that was why she had come to him in the first place.

'I think you know the answer to that,' he said. Facing her again, he bent double and extended his arms. 'If you could help me, it will save me calling my squire . . . unless you wish me to do so.'

She shook her head and, coming to him, peeled the gambeson off with nimble efficiency. 'We keep to the custom in this household that honoured guests should be served by us personally,' she said, and a rueful smile lit in her eyes. 'Most of the time, at least.'

'Your mother considers me neither honoured, nor a guest,' Simon replied, equally rueful. Then his nostrils flared. 'God's Sweet Death, I stink like a midden pit,' he said apologetically. 'Too many days in the saddle and on the road.'

She looked at the gambeson in her hands, its outer layer streaked greasy black from his hauberk and its inner layer giving off a staggeringly concentrated aroma of man. 'I'll put a broom pole through the sleeves and hang it to air in the wind,' she said. 'The laundrymaids can tend to your linens if you have fresh raiment in your baggage. I will see that your tunic is brushed and aired.'

He nodded, both amused and impressed by her efficiency. He wondered if she was using it as a shield. Or perhaps she was showing him how advantageous it would be for him to let her remain.

He pondered for a time as she folded his tunic to one side and cast his shirt into an open willow basket for taking to the maids. Chausses and leg braids followed. With great diplomacy, or perhaps a sense of self-preservation, she ensured that her back was turned as he removed his braies and cast them into the same basket as his shirt.

Simon stepped into the water. It was still hot and sufficiently deep to reach to his mid-chest. 'You still have not answered my question,' he said to Matilda's back. 'Do you want to go with your mother?'

She turned around, a dish of soft soap in one hand and a linen washcloth in the other. From pink, her cheeks had turned to red. 'You said that I had no choice.'

'Not exactly.'

'In so many words.' She came to the tub. A servant had left a jug at the side. She filled it with water from a spare pail and doused his head.

Simon spluttered beneath the deluge. Twice more she did it and then he felt the coldness of the soap and the kneading touch of her hands as she lathered his hair. 'No,' she said. 'I do not want to go with my mother. Why do you think I came to your chamber? It would have been as easy to leave your cloak in the hall.'

The pressure of her fingers set up opposing sensations of languor and lust. It might be the family tradition for the women of the household to bathe honoured guests, but usually it would be in full public with servants present. He doubted that she had ever been in this situation before. Raising his knees, he concealed his arousal.

'I asked your mother to marry me,' he said.

Again she doused him, this time to sluice the soap from his hair. 'I know,' she replied. 'And she refused you.'

He took the cloth that she handed him and dried his face. The water rippling around his torso was rapidly turning a scummy grey. 'My own fault for asking the wrong woman.' He put deliberate emphasis on the last word and heard her small gasp of response. 'I always thought of Waltheof's daughter as a little girl, but while my imagination has remained still, the reality has moved on.' He gave a wry shrug. 'Your mother has made it plain what she thinks of a match with me. Indeed, if we were to wed, I think that it would be a marriage made in hell for both of us.' Reaching back, he took her arm in a wet grip and drew her round to the side of the tub where he could look at her. 'If I ask you now, it is not because you are second best, but that I had not seen you then and I did not realise.'

Her complexion might be flushed but she was in full control of her mental faculties. 'I know that in many ways I have lived a sheltered life,' she said, 'but my mother is a dowager count- ess and she has raised neither me nor my sister in ignorance. I know that to truly make yourself lord of my father's lands you must seek a marriage alliance either with his widow, or with one of his daughters, who bears his blood in their veins. I recognise that this is a bargain of the market place, not of the scented bower.'

He gave her a pained smile. 'That is a speech inspired by your mother and delivered with the honesty of your sire.' He extended a hand to touch her cheek. 'You are right in most of what you say, but even in a market place there is space for a seller of rare jewels.'

She rose to her feet and moved away, but only to fetch more soap. 'And if I refuse you, will you go to my sister and ask the same of her?'

He heard the challenge in her voice and had to bite back a smile for fear of offending her. 'I might,' he admitted, 'but it would be a great pity. But I say again, you would not be here in this chamber except by your own will. And I have not forced you to perform the services of a bath maid.'

'No, my lord, you have not,' she agreed.

'So, what say you? Shall I send Turstan to fetch my chaplain while I dress?'

She looked startled and a little apprehensive – as if a game had suddenly become reality.

'There is no stepping back from this point,' he said softly. 'Either go now, or remain the night – as my wife. That is my ultimatum.'

Although she trembled like a leaf in the wind, she held her ground. 'I will remain,' she said stoutly.

He nodded. 'Good. I hoped you would agree.' Taking the dish of soap, he washed himself, not trusting his reaction should she offer to perform the task. After all, he thought with grim humour, they were not yet wed, and it would not be proper.

Matilda's stomach was queasy with fear, but she knew that she had made the right decision. It had been her choice to come to him in his chamber, no other's. To do so she had crept from the room where her mother and sister were sleeping with a murmur that she was visiting the privy. She had lied and used subterfuge. She had not screamed and pounded upon the door that he closed, and of her own volition she had ministered to him in the bathtub. Come hell or high water, she was not going to lose her courage now. He needed her, if not for herself then for her blood; she was Waltheof's daughter and the Conqueror's great niece. From the moment she saw her father's cloak, she had known that whatever happened she was bound and beholden to Simon de Senlis.

To keep her apprehension at bay and occupy her hands, she fetched the rough linen towels that had been warming on a stool near the brazier. Laying one on the floor, she held the other out to him. He rose to his feet in a surge of dirty water and took the towel from her. He was slender and wiry, but there was muscle nevertheless, firm and compact, closely following the line of bone. His chest and stomach were flat and hard, and a crucifix of curling dark hair ran from nipple to nipple and from the hollow of his throat to his genital area. The latter he covered smartly with the towel before she had taken more than a startled glimpse.

Taking a third towel from the stool to dry his hair, he went to the door and pulled it open. The squire was leaning against the wall, arms folded, but immediately came to attention.

'Fetch Father Bertulf and Aubrey de Mar,' he told the lad and looked back at Matilda. 'Do you have a female companion you wish to stand witness?'

Matilda frowned in thought. 'My maid Helisende, if you can rouse her without waking my mother,' she said.

The squire nodded and without question quietly disappeared on his errand.

Simon closed the door and, rubbing his hair, came back into the room. 'I am sorry it is to be like this,' he said. 'Most women like to have a fuss made of their wedding day. I promise you a full mass and a feast to follow as soon as I can.'

Matilda shrugged. 'I have never been very fond of ceremony,' she said.

'No?' he sounded sceptical. 'Not of wearing fine clothes and being the centre of attention?'

She shook her head. 'I enjoy celebrating. I like great gatherings, and it is true that fine clothes are appealing. But the glitter swiftly tarnishes when you are forced to it day in and day out. My mother says that I should never forget my rank. I am the great niece of a king and the daughter of an earl and I should live accordingly.' She screwed up her face. 'In truth I am happiest on my hands and knees in my garden, with a piece of sacking tied around my waist and my hands dark with soil. The importance lies beneath. When we are dead, we become naught but bones, and then who is to tell the difference between a beggar and a king?'

It was grave wisdom for one of such tender years and Simon was touched, intrigued, and almost saddened. 'Indeed,' he said. 'However for my own sense of ceremony and to show the value I set by your consent, I will still give you a wedding day to remember . . . and, I hope, a wedding night.'

Matilda was immediately flustered. Her mother's protection meant that to a great extent men were an unknown territory. Helisende, giggling, had told her what happened on a wedding night and Matilda believed her because, although protected, she was not blind to what went on around her. She had often pondered the matter. What it would be like. How it happened. Thoughts she had kept to herself because they were immodest and unseemly and if her mother had known of them she would have marched her straight to confession.

She went to a wooden coffer against which his large green and gold kite shield was propped. 'Is this your baggage?' she asked a little too swiftly.

He told her that it was and, although her back was to him, she did not miss the note of rueful amusement in his voice. 'You need not be afraid,' he said. 'I will not harm you.'

'I am not afraid,' Matilda said stoutly, and it was almost

true. Her greater fear was that this was all a dream and that in the morning she would be forced to go to Elstow with her mother, and from there to Holderness and the tyranny of her grandmother's household. That thought led on to another. 'If my sister wishes to stay here too, will you let her?' she asked with a swift look over her shoulder. 'Jude is quieter than me, more likely to do my mother's bidding, but out of obedience and duty rather than desire.'

'Of course,' Simon said gravely. 'I will be pleased to offer her my protection.'

'Thank you,' she murmured and turned to his baggage again before she was trapped in that knowing, vulpine gaze. He did not have many garments, but those he possessed were of excellent quality. There were two shirts of soft linen chansil, bleached in the sun to the colour of ripe barley. His braies were of chansil too – both luxurious and sensible since the fabric was soft and would not chafe.

Simon's spare hose were fashioned from wine-red wool in close-woven diamond twill with bindings of red and blue braid. He had two tunics, one blue, one soft tawny, and both trimmed with the red and blue braid at neckline, hem and cuffs, garments that would take him from palace to castle to manor and be appropriate for all.

He donned the braies and shirt and sat on a stool to draw on the legs of the hose. Matilda saw him wince as he pulled the left one up his leg.

'What's the matter?'

'Nothing. An injury I have had since boyhood. It pains me now and again.' A slightly defensive note entered his voice.

From the way he had been limping earlier, and his grimace now, Matilda thought perhaps that it was more than nothing. 'We have some marigold salve if that will help,' she offered.

'There is no need,' he dismissed. 'It is only painful because I have been standing on it for too long. If I support it with leg bindings, it is not so bad.' As he spoke, he rapidly wound the length of braid from ankle to calf and tucked it neatly in the top. Matilda sensed that he was vulnerable, that he did not wish to pursue the matter.

She took a hesitant breath. 'Will you . . . will you tell me about my father,' she said.

He raised his head. His eyes were as clear as the best mead, but totally unreadable. 'What do you want to know?'

She clasped her hands, looked down at them, then up at him. 'Is it true that he was a wastrel and a drunkard?'

He considered her for so long that she began to grow afraid that he would confirm her mother's opinion, but as she was about to break the silence and say that it did not matter, she would rather keep her dreams intact, he spoke.

'Your father was a man with faults like any other,' he said. 'Not a saint, even if that is what folk are trying to make of him now. Yes, he could drink an alehouse dry, and yes, he would rather go out hunting than sit down with his steward and a heap of tally sticks, but there are worse failings than that. He had generosity and courage in abundance – and if I am here now, it is because of him.'

Matilda listened with rapt attention as he told her how Waltheof had saved his life in Fécamp. She could see the scene vividly in her mind and the image of her father snatching Simon to safety and wrestling a wild horse to a standstill, gave her a queasy feeling of pride and pleasure. 'He was always so strong,' she murmured, tears prickling her lids. 'I knew what my mother said of him wasn't true.'

Watching her, Simon wondered if by telling her the tale of Waltheof's prowess he had tipped the balance too far the other way. Then again, he suspected that she would be selectively deaf. For the moment she only wanted to hear the good and heroic things. And who could blame her?

There was a light tap on the door, heralding the return of his squire with Father Bertulf, Aubrey de Mar, and a wide-eyed Helisende.

Simon gestured to the maid. 'Attend your mistress,' he said.

Matilda had few preparations to make. Helisende helped her

to remove her wimple and hair net. Her braids were unpinned and her hair combed down until it shimmered at her hips like a river of molten bronze shot through with fire.

'Are you sure you know what you are doing?' Helisende whispered. There was fear in her voice, but also an incorrigible glint of relish.

Matilda gave a tremulous laugh. 'Not in the least,' she whispered back, 'but I know that it is right.' She was still resonating from Simon's words about her father. She felt elated and dizzy.

'Your mother will not see it in the same light.'

Matilda's expression grew stubborn. 'That is my mother's choice,' she said, 'not mine.' As the words left her lips, a sense of power stirred in the pit of her belly. Her choice. Hers. Mayhap brought about by circumstance, but she had selected the path . . . and the manner of its treading.

With head high, she went to join Simon and the waiting chaplain.

CHAPTER 24

The ring Simon had given her fitted Matilda's finger perfectly. It was one of his own, for he had small hands and hers were a feminine version of her father's, large and square. She examined it by the light of the night candle, for it was unlike any ring that she had seen before; set in the gold band was a circle of blue-grey stone that had been expertly worked to show two clasped right hands surrounded by a border of leaves.

'I believe it is Roman,' Simon said, looking over her shoulder and handing her a cup of wine. 'I bought it from a trader in Rouen who had it from a man who found a cache of coins and jewels buried in a field. There is not another like it . . . that's why I wanted it to be your marriage ring, for you also are a rarity.'

Matilda blushed at the compliment, unused to such flattery. Her mother was always telling her how large and clumsy she was.

She moved away from the heat of the candle flame. Once again, they were alone. The chaplain had officiated at the taking of their wedding vows. Simon's squire, his knight and Helisende had borne witness. Now all that remained to make the marriage indissoluble was the consummation.

For a second time Simon started to undress in front of her. She averted her glance, but he caught her arm and gently turned her around.

'No,' he said softly, 'do not look away. I want you to know my body as familiarly as I will know yours. Since we are united in marriage, it behoves us to be two halves of one whole from the beginning.'

Matilda swallowed. 'I do not know what to do,' she whispered. He had unfastened his belt and removed his tunic. Shirt, hose and braies remained.

Capturing a handful of her loose hair, he drew her towards him. 'It is an easy thing to learn,' he murmured.

She was almost as tall as he, and when he set his arm around her waist and pulled her against his body they were a match. Matilda caught her breath. She had never been this close to a man in her life before, except her father. No one until now had had the right or the audacity to touch her as Simon de Senlis was touching her. She could smell the soap of his recent bathing, and mingled with it the masculine tang of his skin. Her heart pounded at twice the speed of his.

'Be my squire,' he said softly, bringing his face close to hers, so that their lips were almost touching but not quite. 'And in return I will be your maid.' Taking her hand, he set it against the tied lacing of his shirt.

Matilda felt weak and hot. She was afraid, and at the same time she was intoxicated. With trembling fingers she unfastened the knot, and was fascinated to watch her own hand at the task, adorned by the new wedding ring. The shirt fell open exposing the wiry curl of hair at his throat and an expanse of summer-tanned skin.

'Now my turn,' he murmured and unpinned the round silver brooch securing the neck opening of her gown. With hands that were as steady as hers were trembling, he gently unplucked the drawstring of her chemise. Matilda shivered but raised her arms obediently so that he could draw her overgown over her head.

'Now you.' He placed her hands on his waist. For a moment Matilda was unsure what he meant, but then she realised and tugged his shirt out of his braies and off over his head. The scent of freshly washed linen and the warm smell of his body beguiled her senses. He was naked to the waist, and she was a mere breath from his flesh. A crucifix of garnets set in gold glittered on his chest, the jewels and metal flashing each time he inhaled.

He took her lightly by the hips and pulled her against him, angled his head and nuzzled beneath her ear. 'Now me,' he said huskily, and while one hand held her against him the other moved up her body and cupped her breast.

Matilda gasped at the sudden jolt of sensation that shot from nipple to groin. He was holding her firmly in the small of her back, keeping her steady, and since they were much of a height, she could feel a distaff-shaped solid heat pressing against the juncture of her thighs. He nipped and sucked at her throat. The amalgam of sensations both unnerved and excited her. It was like the occasional dreams from which she had woken panting and wet between the legs, dreams that she had confessed neither to her mother nor the priest. Without stopping what he was doing, he guided her to the fastenings that held his hose to his braies. 'Now you.'

Matilda fumbled, unsure without looking, and the back of her hand brushed against the crown of his erection. Simon hissed through his teeth and Matilda recoiled, torn between a worry that she had done wrong and her fear of the unknown. But he drew her back and placed her palm and fingers against the fabric-covered column of flesh.

'It is how all men are made,' he said, and there was a smile in his voice. 'Granted you may not have encountered one in quite this condition before, but there is nothing of which to be afraid. And your touch does not hurt . . . Indeed, it is a source of great pleasure.'

Matilda swallowed. It was half as long again as the span of her hand and had the feel and thickness of a drop spindle full of woven yarn, springy, yielding, but bone-hard at the core. How in God's name it was going to fit inside her she did not know. Yet, since all animals did this to mate, it was obviously possible. She dared to close her fingers around its length. He hissed again and thrust against her hand. And now he kissed her on the mouth.

His lips were warm, smooth, not in the least how she had imagined a man's lips to be. They took her breath and, rather like the touch of his hand on her breast, their movement sharpened the sensation in her loins. His tongue circled her lips and then thrust gently back and forth, echoing the motion of his hips. He slipped the loosened chemise from her shoulders and it slipped to the ground, leaving her clad only in her knee-length hose and a pair of linen braies like his own.

Matilda shivered at the cool air on her naked skin, and at the same time was scorched by the look in his eyes as he drew back to look at her. 'I am dazzled by your beauty,' he said hoarsely.

No one had ever told her that she was beautiful. Everyone considered Jude the pretty one with her daintier size and bones. 'Truly?' she whispered.

'Truly . . .' His hand followed his eyes in a slow caress down the length of her body and Matilda trembled beneath his touch. Her nipples rose in peaks of chill and excitement. He drew her to the bed and, laying her down upon it, gently removed her hose and completed the unfastening and removal of his own. Matilda felt the coolness and warmth of fur at her back, and realised that she was lying across the bearskin cloak. She dug her fingers into the gleaming pelt and wondered if he had placed it there deliberately.

Simon lay down beside her and all thought was sublimated by feeling. His hand moved on her thigh, circling upwards beneath the wide leg of her braies. At first his touch tickled and made Matilda want to recoil with a giggle, but that sort of sensitivity very swiftly gave way to another that made her gasp and arch. Higher still. Her eyes widened. She was not quite certain where his fingers were now, but she didn't want him to stop, and if that was being wanton she did not care.

When he drew her hand to the bulge in his braies, she was

more eager to touch and stroke this time. He slipped his thigh between hers, nudged them apart and mounted her. Matilda gasped and gasped again as he moved upon her. He twisted his body and kissed and sucked her breasts, and the first cry was torn from her. She dug her fingers into the flesh of his arms. Her legs widened and she returned his rocking motion in a rhythm that came from instinct. His own breathing was ragged now, his heartbeat swift. Lifting himself from her, he was in haste to untie the drawstring of her braies and pull them off. Then his own, and for the first time Matilda was gifted with a view of a man in a full state of arousal.

'It is not as frightening as it looks, I promise you,' he said somewhat breathlessly.

'I am not afraid,' Matilda replied, half of her speaking with false courage like a child determined not to be frightened in the dark, and half of her needing to know the full truth. With great daring she willed herself to touch him and found the feel not unpleasant. Smooth and warm, hard and yielding.

'I am,' Simon gave a congested laugh. 'If you continue to do that, I might gain great pleasure, but not the consummation we need to make this marriage binding.'

She looked at him curiously, not having the least idea what he meant.

He pushed her hand aside and moved over her. She felt the solid hot nudge of his flesh, felt him enter a fraction, then held her breath. There was so much of him; he was bound to hurt. But he went no further. She heard him swallow and through her own body felt the tremors of his restraint. He fondled and stroked her until she clutched at him. Instinctively she bore down and he eased further inside. And still he held off, continuing to pleasure and caress. The stimulation became unbearable. Matilda felt a swelling tightness in her loins. Suddenly she didn't care about anything but the feeling building within her pelvis. Whimpering, uttering little cries, she bore down on the pain of his invasion, because behind and above it there was a pleasure so huge that she would do anything to be a part of it.

His hands delved to her buttocks, tilted them upwards, and with a groan he thrust into her full measure, once and then again. The pain blossomed in a raw, red starburst, but so did the pleasure and she sobbed, her body drawing each pulse of his seed deep within her womb.

He groaned softly against her throat and continued to rock gently upon her, the first violent surge spent. Gentler waves of pleasure followed each other through Matilda's loins and she shifted, seeking the echoes of the wild delight she had just known.

Slowly, with much greater effort than it had taken to mount her, Simon withdrew. 'I am sorry if I hurt you,' he said. 'I would have given you greater joy but . . .' He made a shrugging gesture serve for the rest.

Greater joy? So there was more than this? The bed, being intended for guests, was large enough for them to lie side by side and not even have to touch unless they wanted to, but Matilda wanted to. She needed the closeness. 'It is true that I am sore,' she said. Indeed, now that the throb of pleasure had diminished, she was aware of the tenderness of bruised tissues, 'But I do not know how you could have given me greater joy than you did just now.'

He faced her and the faintest of smiles curved his narrow mouth. 'By not giving you pain,' he said. 'I am not accustomed to deflowering virgins.'

Matilda raised her eyebrows at that. 'No?'

'Very few men are, whatever tales you hear,' he said wryly. 'The only virgins that have come my way have either been heavily chaperoned by their families or spoils of war. And since I am not a man given over to rape and debauchery, the latter fruit has never appealed to me – unlike some.'

'So all the women you have known have been experienced?' Matilda felt a pang of jealousy, followed by fear. How was she, who knew nothing, ever going to measure up?

'That is so.'

'Have there been many?'

His lips twitched. 'One or two. Several in my youth who were more use to me than I was to them.'

Matilda lowered her gaze from his face, not wanting to read his expression. Her eyes happened upon his erection. Before it had seemed an enormous thing, quivering with a life of its own; now it was much diminished, curving towards his thigh, the taut sheath wrinkling. The sight fascinated her and she realised anew how ingenious God was.

'What?' he said, tilting her face on his forefinger so that she had to meet his gaze.

She caught her underlip in her teeth. 'I was thinking that it is a good thing that a man's part is able to diminish as it does,' she said. 'Otherwise it would be a great hindrance to every activity but mating.'

He roared with laughter at that, and Matilda's heart fluttered. This morning she had not known of the existence of this slender, unprepossessing man. Now she wore his ring on her finger, was naked by his side, and had taken his seed into her womb. Already she could be with his child.

'A man would say that it is a good thing for both sexes that it is able to rise as it does,' he commented. Pillowing his hands behind his head, he yawned hugely. 'Not that mine will do any more rising this night, unless you are truly a worker of miracles.' He glanced at her, his lids heavy and dark smudges beneath them. 'However that is because weariness outstrips lust on this occasion. It will not always be so.'

She was not sure what he meant so she just gave him a smile and made a resolution to find out as much as she could from Helisende. Sybille was the usual font of such wisdom, but being her mother's maid was unavailable to ask. The thought of facing her mother in the morning caused a small jolt of trepidation to run through her and she moved closer to her new husband, seeking the comfort of his body.

His eyes had closed, but with obvious effort he opened them. 'You will never regret this marriage, I swear to you,' he mumbled, and tucked a wild strand of her hair tenderly behind her ear.

'You need give me no assurances,' she whispered in reply and pressed herself against his naked warmth. 'I know in my own heart that I could have done no better for myself than this.'

'Mayhap,' he said and kissed her fingers. Moments after that he was asleep, his breathing deep and even, with a slight catch at the top of each breath. Matilda lay against him, watching the glitter of the garnet cross in the light from the single candle. She whispered his name like a talisman. Girls dreamed of love and talked of it with their maids and companions. They flirted with the squires and knights of their fathers' retinues; they set their fancy on passing troubadours. But love had come to Matilda in a single hammer blow, and its image was not that of a tall, fair young man bearing gifts and songs, but of a slightly built soldier with a damaged leg and a baggage wain full of cares.

Laying her cheek against the smooth curve of his bicep, feeling beneath her the soft prickle of her father's bearskin cloak, she was content.

CHAPTER 25

The instant Judith opened her eyes she knew that something was wrong. Too overwrought to rest, she had dozed throughout the night, such sleep as she had managed beset by dark, unpleasant dreams. Now, jerked to awareness by a stealing sensation of unease, she sat up. The large night candle had burned low on the wrought iron pricket, but more lights were blossoming in the doorway and she could hear Sybille's swift murmur.

Judith flung back the covers and stood up. Whatever was happening, she would go to meet it, head on as she always had. She more than half expected the disturbance to be that of Simon de Senlis' soldiers, coming to imprison her. It would be their shame, not hers, if they were to take her in her chemise, her hair uncovered.

'What is happening?' She raised her voice imperiously. Hearing it cut across the air, as it had always done, gave her a boost of confidence. And then she saw Matilda and she froze. The girl was wearing yesterday's blue gown. Her hair was decorously concealed beneath her wimple and, at first glance, there was nothing untoward about her appearance. However the fact that she was entering the room gave Judith cause for concern because she could not recall her leaving. She must have crept from the chamber very circumspectly indeed. A swift glance at Matilda's pallet revealed the girl's subterfuge; the bedclothes were mounded in the shape of a sleeping body. What disturbed

Judith most, though, was the look on her daughter's face. The heavy lids, the flushed cheeks told their own vivid story.

'Where have you been?' she demanded. 'If you have been conniving behind my back, I will never forgive you.'

Matilda lifted her head in defiance and Judith saw Waltheof clearly in the line of jaw and thrust of chin. 'I have done no more conniving than you, Mother,' she said defensively. 'Simon de Senlis knows of your plans, but he will not stand in your way if you wish to leave.'

Judith gave her daughter a look filled with disdain. 'I do not need his yeasay to do as I please.' Her voice was deadly with control. 'I am mistress here yet.'

Matilda drew a deep breath and clasped her hands against her breasts. 'No, Mother, you are not. Last night I was married to Simon de Senlis. I wear his ring on my finger and the match has been witnessed and consummated.'

The words poured over Judith like an icy drench. 'That is impossible. I have given no consent to the match.'

'But I gave mine,' Matilda said. 'Our vows were taken in the presence of Father Bertulf. He's not only Simon's chaplain, but also an ordained priest of St Stephen's in Caen. I was not forced. I agreed to the marriage of my own will.'

'You have been duped!' A red mist hazed Judith's vision. 'All that Simon de Senlis wants is the sanction of your blood to bolster his position. This marriage would not stand up for one moment in a court of law.'

'Why don't you test it and see, my lady.' Simon emerged from the gloom of the doorway. He was wearing a fresh tunic of tawny wool that reflected his eyes. His sword was girded at his hip, and his left hand lightly grasped the buckskin grip. 'I doubt you will find it other than watertight.' He went to stand beside Matilda and possessively took her hand. He raised his bride's hand to his lips, pressed a kiss in the palm and curled her fingers over it.

Judith felt sick. 'You have betrayed me!' she hissed at her daughter. 'In truth, you have your father's blood, for he was

weak and unsteady of purpose too. It was his downfall, and
now it will be yours.'

'No, Mother, you were *his* downfall,' Matilda retorted.

'You were just a child, how could you know?' Judith spat
bitterly. 'All you had were his kisses and adoration. You did
not see his indecision and the way that he would take refuge
from it in drink. You did not see the times I had to follow him
like a parent, clearing away the debris of his mistakes.' She
stabbed her forefinger. 'You did not see his fecklessness and
stupidity. It was I who had to live with that.'

Matilda had flushed beneath Judith's onslaught as if each
word were a slap across the face. 'No,' she said in a trembling
voice, 'I did not see, because he was my father and I loved him.
But I do not believe he ever received love or even respect from
you, Mother. Sometimes . . .' she swallowed. 'Sometimes I
think that you hated him.'

'I hated his weakness.' Suddenly Judith's eyes were sting-
ing. 'Think what you will of my feelings for your father. It will
not alter the truth.'

De Senlis laid his hand on Matilda's shoulder. 'Enough,' he
said gently. 'You will tear each other to pieces. Lady Judith, if
it please you, my men will escort you wherever you wish to go.
I do not think it appropriate that you remain here for the
moment.'

Judith flashed him a glare of utter loathing, which was met
by an implacable shield wall of courtesy. She had spoken of her
husband's errors of judgement, but now she wondered if she
had made one of her own in refusing him. It had been an
instinctive choice, born of the memory of seeing him as a child
at the royal court, and then as an invalid, his handicap the in-
direct result of her carelessness. She had not wanted the humiliation of yielding her personal governance to De Senlis. If
she had quashed her pride she could at least have had half a
loaf. Now there were not even crumbs, and in one fell swoop
her daughter had snatched the title of Countess for herself.

'I would not stay even if this was my last place of refuge,' she said scornfully. 'At least her father, whatever his faults, did not come like a thief in the night.'

The remark bounced off his blank expression like a blunt spear off a hardwood shield. It was her daughter who flinched as if wounded. De Senlis was right. They were tearing each other apart.

She turned to summon Jude, who had been watching the proceedings with widening eyes, but De Senlis pre-empted her.

'I am desirous that your younger daughter remain with her sister,' he said in that same, quiet tone that left room for neither discussion nor argument. 'She is more easily protected under my jurisdiction – and I believe that she will be the happier for remaining here.'

Judith's knees almost gave way. 'And if I refuse to yield her?'

His shoulders twitched in the slightest of shrugs. 'There is little you can do to gainsay my will, my lady. Accept it with a good grace, and in return I will be gracious too.'

Nausea churned Judith's stomach and the taste of defeat was in her mouth. He was right. She could do little until she reached her family – save perhaps salvage her dignity.

'You have stolen my daughters from me,' she said, lowering her own voice to match the tone of his. 'And the lands that I have cared for since my husband's death. Perhaps it is God's way. Perhaps this is my penance for that day of heedless pride in the stableyard at Rouen. I will pray God to forgive my many sins, and I hope that I can find it in my heart to pray that he forgive you yours . . . for I am mortal, and I cannot.'

She did not have to push past Matilda and De Senlis, for they stood aside to let her go and neither spoke to call her back. Judith stumbled in the darkness of the corridor. Her cheeks were wet with the first tears she had shed since Waltheof's body had been borne to Crowland. If this was God's will then she did not know how she was going to reconcile herself. She desperately needed somewhere to go and lick her wounds.

Biting her lip, Matilda made to go after her mother, but Simon gripped her arm. 'No,' he said. 'Leave her. You have come to a parting of the ways and whatever you said now would only make things worse. Let her grieve awhile in peace. There will be time enough later to make things right between you.'

'Things have never been right between us,' Matilda said desolately. 'As my mother says, I am my father's daughter, and that alone is unforgivable in her eyes.'

'Then it is she who must change, not you.' He gave her arm a small shake to bring her attention fully to him. 'You are chatelaine of this place now. The care of its people falls to you.'

Meeting his gaze Matilda encountered a will as implacable as her mother's but differently channelled.

'I need you by my side, not just as a decoration or a seal to my rule, but as a true wife and helpmate.' He claimed her lips in a kiss that drew a collective gasp from the Countess's women.

Simon raised his head and glanced at them. 'Those of you who wish to follow your mistress are free to go with her,' he announced. 'Those who wish to remain may do so.' His arm around Matilda, he left them to their decisions and withdrew to the hall.

While Simon was speaking to his knights, Jude grabbed Matilda's arm. 'It is true then?' she whispered, her glance darting towards Simon.

Matilda's lips twitched. 'Is what true?' she teased.

'That you and he are married – is it binding?'

'As a piece of thrice woven braid. There will be no annulment.'

Jude lifted Matilda's hand to the growing light from the shutters to look at the ring.

'He tells me that it is Roman, and very rare.' Matilda's smile deepened.

Jude looked over her shoulder to make sure that Simon was not listening and gave her sister a little nudge. 'What was it like?'

'What was what like?'

Jude dug her in the ribs again. 'You know . . . Are the things that Sybille says true?'

Matilda giggled. 'I am not sure that it is decorous for me to tell you!' she declared. She cast her own gaze towards Simon and viewed him through modestly downswept lashes. 'But if you were to press me, I would say that Sybille was restrained.'

Jude's eyes sparkled with curiosity. 'Did it hurt?'

'Not beyond bearing,' Matilda said, and gave a small shiver, thinking that what had been almost beyond bearing was the pleasure and the alchemy between man and woman that changed everything in its wake. Gold was dross. Dross was gold. The burden of love was light as a feather and heavy as lead – if love it was, and not the glamour of the night dazzling in her eyes. She could not explain such things to her sister. Instead she smiled and squeezed Jude's hand.

'My heart is gladdened,' she said. 'I cannot pretend to be cast down when I am not . . . although I could wish that the circumstances were different.'

'You mean Mother?' Jude caught her full underlip in her teeth. 'I . . . I did not want to go with her,' she confessed. 'When Lord Simon said I was to stay, I felt glad . . . and then I felt guilty because I was glad.'

Matilda embraced her sister. 'I feel that way too; but if we had gone with her it would have been to no avail. Simon would have sent men after us before we had gone half a mile. Indeed, I doubt he would even have allowed us out of the gates.'

'Is that what you were thinking when you went to him?' There was a note of admiration and a tinge of envy in Jude's tone. 'That it was better to play by his rules than Mother's?'

Matilda looked down at her hands, and then at her new husband. Her heart swelled. 'No,' she said softly. 'I went to return his cloak . . . and it became my marriage bed.'

CHAPTER 26

Northampton,
November 1087

A cold winter rain slashed against the walls of the palace. It had been dark all day, for the shutters had been closed against the inclement weather and the only chinks of light came from angled windows high up near the roof beams of the hall.

In their private chamber Matilda approached the bed where Simon lay. Beneath his left leg was a linen cloth to protect the winter coverings of Norwegian furs. The cold, wet weather and his own restless energy had caused his old injury to trouble him. Not that he had admitted as much, but after two months of marriage Matilda was becoming slightly more adept at reading the language of his body. It was difficult, because he gave so little away. He was either good-humoured or impassive – as controlled as her mother, but without the coldness. She took the glimpses of his true self he yielded to her, but was unsatisfied and ravenous for more.

She did at least know that he abhorred being confined. He refused to stay abed longer than it took his body to rest in sleep, or to lie with her in the act of love and procreation. She was also discovering that the latter might as easily take place in a stable, under a tree in the woods, or in the arbour of her garden as in their chamber.

Today's vicious weather had confined them to quarters, though, and she had insisted that rubbing his leg with a soothing balm made from the herbs in the garden would give him ease.

'I ought to be out on the walls,' he said.

Matilda hiked up her skirts to climb on the bed, making sure that he got a glimpse of thigh above her gartered hose. 'Why?' she asked. 'No one else is. It is true that folk can work in the rain, but not when it comes down like arrows and is so cold it is almost ice. One day will make no difference.'

He gave an impatient grunt. 'But one day will become two, then three, then four. I promised the King that I would make all haste to secure this place with a keep and strong walls to protect the town. I want to give him a good report of the work's progress.'

'And so you shall, but not if you push yourself beyond your endurance and become too sick to make your answer.' Straddling him she took a dollop of balm onto her fingers and applied it to his leg. There was a misshapen lump where the broken edges of bone had fused together. She knew that he suffered more pain from the old injury than he was prepared to admit. Late in the day, if he had been particularly active, she would see the tension in the skin around his eyes and his gait would become progressively uneven and stilted. A comment that he should rest would draw forth the reply that he was not an invalid. If she pushed further, he would become quiet and self-contained, effectively shutting her out.

With firm pressure, she rubbed the balm into his leg. He had condescended to remove his hose, so she knew that while his conscience dictated that he should be elsewhere it was not strong enough to override other considerations. The aromatic tang of chamomile, meadowsweet and warm undertones of bay filled the chamber as she pressed and smoothed with long strokes of her thumbs. She felt his body relax beneath her ministrations. His lids grew heavy, but they did not close.

A fresh burst of rain spattered against the shutters like a handful of flung shingle. He pushed his hand beneath her skirt and stroked her thigh with a languid hand. Matilda gasped at his touch then gasped again as he quested further.

'I fear,' he murmured lazily, 'that in trying to ease me you have only made the situation worse.'

'I have?' The last word rose with Matilda's hips in response to what he was doing.

'Indeed, much worse.' Cupping her buttocks he pulled her up his body and at the same time raised his tunic. 'The stiffness has moved, and if you do not relieve it then I will go mad.'

She discovered that when removing his chausses he had removed his braies too, and that he was huge and hard and ready. He filled her with such heat and strength that she felt as if she were riding upon a burning brand. Her mother would have been horrified at the notion of fornicating in almost broad daylight, when anyone could have walked in on the scene, but Matilda cared not. It was not a holy day when the priests said that a couple must not join, and if it were a sin to take her pleasure above her husband she would confess later.

It did not take long, for both of them were fired by the piquancy of what they were doing. In moments, Matilda was shuddering in the throes of pleasure, her teeth clenched to muffle the cry that might bring Jude or Helisende hastening in upon them. Beneath her the tendons in Simon's neck stood out like whipcords. Seizing her hips, he lunged up into her body, and she felt the frantic throb of his release.

For some time there was no sound but the harshness of their mingled breathing. Then Matilda sat up, pushed loose strands of hair from her face, and giggled. 'Have I then saved your sanity?' she demanded, and rocked on him, enjoying the flickers of after-pleasure.

He chuckled and she felt the humour tremble through his

body into hers. 'No, you have rendered me witless.' The rigidity of lust had departed his expression in exchange for a softening of tenderness. He ran his hands up the long bones of her thighs and stroked her skin gently.

Matilda shivered. 'I think it would take more than this to render you witless,' she murmured. 'Indeed, I am the one who is in danger of losing myself.'

He gave a shrug, conceding the point with a lascivious curl to his lips. 'More than in danger,' he said softly. His hands moved further, teasing, stroking, until she began to writhe beneath a new onslaught of sensations.

Matilda gasped incoherently and clutched at his tunic. Outside the weather lashed at the shutters, emphasising the fact that there was no escape, abetting the maelstrom between her and Simon. He watched her narrow-eyed and intent, holding her on a brink until she bared her teeth in frustration. Rolling over, he pushed her down on the bed, drew her legs around his hips and thrust into her, damming her scream of completion with his mouth until she went limp under him.

'Jesu!' Matilda half sobbed as he kissed the thundering pulse in her throat. 'I could die of this!'

'It would be glorious,' he admitted with a smile. His eyes were bright and opaque with lust-haze.

'Imagine if you had married my mother,' she said as she regained her breathing. It was a thought that visited her on odd occasions – usually ones like this. Judith had retired to her nunnery at Elstow and they seldom spoke of her, but her shadow lingered.

He caressed her braid and dipped his head to nip her throat where a love flush was rising in strawberry blotches. 'I do not dwell on it,' he said quietly, 'because I married you. I openly admit that from the moment I saw you in the garden at Northampton, I wanted you in my bed. I did not have the same reaction to your lady mother.'

'But if she had said yes, you would have taken her to wife?'

'Yes, I would have done it,' he said, and, withdrawing from

her, rolled over and drew her side to side against him. 'I doubt we would have made each other happy, but we would soon have arranged separate households.'

'And do I make you happy?' She played with a loose thread on the throat decoration of his tunic.

'Have I not just given you the proof of that?' he said and kissed her again.

It was an answer and it was an evasion. But she was afraid to push him, lest his pleasure in her was indeed no more than masculine lust for a nubile female body. What she had was enough. It was greedy to seek more. But she had never been good at suppressing her appetite.

The next morning the rain had stopped and the work could go forward again on the new walls and castle of Northampton. Matilda rode out with Simon to observe the progress of the builders. Workmen's huts and shelters were clustered on the site and straw had been thrown down to absorb the worst of the slurry from yesterday's heavy rain. The sky was grey and there was a cutting wind from the north. Matilda blew on her fingers and watched Simon go among the men. He had a way with them, was swift to comprehend, and allowed neither his rank nor his disability to stand in his way – especially the latter. She winced as he began climbing the scaffolding with one of the masons. Small wonder that his leg required so much tending when he would not rest it. Indeed, he seemed determined to prove that he had more power of endurance than any man in his retinue.

What her father would have made of the Norman keep rising above Northampton town, or of the encircling walls, she did not know. In the ten years of her mother's widowhood, Northampton had grown as the presence of the dowager Countess and the frequent visits of her illustrious family attracted traders. It had been much smaller when Matilda was a little girl and her father alive. Now the place warranted a castle. Simon said that the King had sanctioned its building because he did not feel secure on the throne and was ensuring that men loyal to him had every means of holding their lands. Castles were the Norman method of exerting control over each other and the English. They were here to stay, no matter the opposition to their building. At least, she thought, Simon had compensated the occupants of the twenty-three houses that had been pulled down to make space for the foundations of the keep. She had made sure of that by encouraging him when he had seemed in doubt. He had accepted the conscience-nudging with patience, the sexual bribery with enthusiasm and finally admitted with a grin that both were superfluous since he had been intending to compensate the people from the start.

Matilda spoke to her groom and he helped her to dismount. Holding her gown above the mud, she moved among the workmen at the foot of the scaffolding. One eye cocked to the antics of her daredevil husband, she joined the mason's wives who were standing around the warmth of a cooking fire. Broth and a pease pudding in a cloth were boiling in the same cauldron over the flames, and one of the women was frying griddle cakes. The savoury, smoky aroma made Matilda's stomach growl. Tentatively one of the women offered her a cake, and seemed both delighted and surprised when Matilda gratefully accepted.

At first Matilda was puzzled by the woman's attitude, but when she thought about it realised that until recently her mother had been the highest female authority here and would not have deigned to dismount from her horse, let alone join a group of artisans' wives at their domestic fire. Matilda, however, had an affinity for such gatherings. They gave her a sense of companionship, of belonging. All the affection she had ever received in her life had come from folk of lesser degree than her exalted mother and she instinctively gravitated towards them.

The griddlecake was smoking hot with a crisp brown outer crust and a tender white centre. Matilda did not think she had ever tasted anything so wonderful, lest it be the fried fat bacon and toasted wheaten bread that the gardeners shared with her on early summer mornings outside their hut.

'The changes come quickly, my lady,' ventured a woman whose husband was one of the trench diggers. She spoke in English but Matilda understood her well enough, for she had her father's ear for language and although her mother had disapproved of Matilda speaking the tongue she had recognised the usefulness of comprehension.

'Indeed they do,' Matilda said between mouthfuls.

'Your mother was a fair mistress, I'll give her that,' the woman said, holding her hands out to the warmth of the fire. 'Exacted every penny that was her due, but we always received justice.' She tilted her head to one side and studied Matilda out of rheumy eyes. 'But it was your father we loved, God rest his martyred soul.' She crossed her scrawny bosom. 'And since you are his daughter, we love you also.'

Matilda had crossed herself too at the mention of her father. Now she blinked to stem a sudden rush of tears. 'You are my people. I will do my best for you . . . and so will Lord Simon.'

The woman pursed her lips. 'He will do his best for himself,' she said boldly but without insolence. 'But a woman of English blood who can gentle him and who understands us is a boon. Some say as you are overly young to the task, but you have been well schooled, and you have learned to shoulder burdens early.'

'And what do the people say of my husband, other than that he will do his best for himself?' Matilda asked, a note of challenge in her voice. She was almost but not quite offended.

Her companion shrugged. Taking an iron poker leaning against the spit bar, she riddled it among the flames. 'That he is a Norman and one of the new king's supporters. That he is like a cat and that folk should not think that just because he treads softly he has the gentle ways of the old lord.'

Matilda thought that the assessment was probably right, although she was stung by the way the woman said 'Norman' as if the word alone was an insult. She drew herself up and dusted the griddle cake crumbs from her hands. 'My father loved Lord Simon as a son,' she said. 'He gave to him his own cloak on the eve before he died, and it is a sign of my husband's right to this earldom that he has brought it back to me. Lord Simon will make this place great and prosperous. The town walls will protect you all. More people will come and trade will flourish.'

The woman smiled and rested the poker back against the spit bar. 'Aye, my lady,' she said. 'I am sure that it is fitting. May you always look upon him the way that you do now.'

Was that a word of warning? Matilda narrowed her eyes, but the woman had lowered her gaze and would not meet Matilda's scrutiny.

There was a sudden flurry of curtseying among the other women. Turning, Matilda found Simon standing at the entrance to the shelter. His hands and clothes were muddy, stone dust smeared one cheek and his eyes were bright with relish.

'Well?' she said, holding out her arm so he could curve his around it and lead her out among the buildings. 'What will you have to report to the King?'

He looked smug. 'That this town will be the equal of York in size when it is done – which is fitting, since York bears tribute to your ancestors, does it not?'

'My grandfather Earl Siward is buried there,' Matilda said. 'Your white bear cloak was originally his.'

'Well then, I will lay another York at your feet.' He glanced at her sidelong. 'Why do you smile like that?'

Matilda walked carefully through the mire, trying not to slip while keeping the hem of her gown from trailing in the mud. 'Because I have never seen York to know what it would look like at my feet.'

Simon's gaze widened in astonishment. 'Never?'

She shook her head. 'Indeed, I have never seen any place larger than Huntingdon or Northampton. When I was a child, if my mother travelled to Winchester or London she would leave Jude and I with our nurse. This is our world.' A defensive note crept into her voice. She knew how strong Simon's desire was for new experiences and places. The only time he was still was immediately after making love. Even in sleep he was restless and as often as not would steal all the covers. Matilda, however, was as happy toiling in the tranquillity of her garden as she was going about grander business. 'You have been the companion of kings,' she murmured. 'You are accustomed to the large towns and grand palaces. I may be the daughter of an earl, but my life has been simpler.'

'Mayhap so,' Simon said, 'but I would enjoy showing you different places.'

'And I would enjoy seeing them,' Matilda said, and felt a qualm of excitement and a larger surge of misgiving at the notion.

He smiled. 'Good, then you can attend the Christmas court at Westminster with me.'

'The court!' Matilda's voice became a squeak.

'Why not? It is true that the King is a bachelor and keeps other bachelors around him, but at Christmastide there will be barons present with wives and daughters. After all, you are the King's kin within the third degree. It is only fitting that you should be seen at court . . . and Jude too.' He gave her hand a squeeze. 'It is time you saw something of the world around you.'

'Well?' Simon grinned. 'What do you think to the royal palace of Westminster?'

Matilda's eyes were at full stretch and still she laboured to take everything in. They had arrived as a frosty winter dusk was falling over the city, whitening the buildings with a glitter of silver rime. The cold weather had gripped for several days, and the air burned as she drew it into her lungs.

'It is big,' she said inadequately, as she faced the many buildings that made up the precincts of palace and church. Here the Saxon King Edward was buried in the cathedral that had been frowned on them, saying that vanity was not to be encouraged. She was still unaccustomed to dealing with praise and to seeing open appreciation in men's eyes. Her growing awareness of her feminine power was only matched by the fear that she was climbing too high too swiftly. Her husband said, 'Dare.' She obeyed him, and then was terrified to look down.

'And he did not tell me that he had such gallant friends to call upon,' she responded, finding the words from the uncertain depths of her new confidence.

Ranulf de Tosny laughed. 'Mayhap he does not want too many rivals,' he said. Then his gaze fell upon Jude, who was standing modestly at Matilda's side. And the focus of his attention changed.

'This is my younger sister, Jude,' Matilda murmured.

Jude dipped a curtsey and De Tosny bowed. 'You didn't tell me that your wife had a sister either,' he said softly to Simon.

'A good shepherd is always prudent when wolves are sniffing around.' Simon was smiling, but there was a warning note in his voice.

'Is that an insult?'

'Common sense when I remember some of our days and nights at court – or should I say some of your days and nights?' Simon retorted.

Ranulf snorted. 'Then you do not remember your own now that you stand on the other side of the stockade?' He winked at Matilda and Jude. 'I could tell you some tales.'

Simon cleared his throat. 'Tales would be all they would be,' he said, although Matilda was fascinated to see that his colour was high. Thinking of their marriage bed, knowing his penchant for exploration, she was certain that there was no smoke without fire.

Ranulf de Tosny fiddled with the handsome buckle of his . 'Tales are the language of the court,' he said. 'A whisper an insinuation there. Always in the background, no matter loudness of what you hear on the surface.'

his life's work. Here too were his royal apartments, now the domain of King William Rufus, blazing with torches to light the way of visitors and guests.

Simon grinned. 'Is that all you can say?'

She dug her elbow in his ribs. 'Does it have a garden?' she asked sweetly.

'I . . . umm . . .'

'You don't know,' she pounced, and her own lips curved at having jolted him out of his smugness.

'I was always too much occupied on my lord king's business,' he said loftily.

Matilda laughed and wagged her finger at him. 'In that case you might as well have been anywhere, and you have no advantage over me.'

Simon was spared from finding a suitable answer by the arrival of the grooms to attend to their horses and a steward to show them where to pitch the tents they had brought with them. The sward outside the King's hall was already a mass of coloured canvas, but a space had been reserved among the ranks that were closest to the hall.

As Simon's men set to work with canvas, rope and tent pegs a fair-haired knight emerged from one of the erected tents. H genial expression was compounded by large hazel eyes ar wide, good-natured mouth.

He greeted Simon with a hefty slap on the back and to ear smile. 'Well, my lord,' he said, 'is an English to your taste?'

'Very much,' Simon replied and, drawing Matil introduced her to Ranulf de Tosny. 'A friend in wine cups,' he said ruefully.

'My lady.' The knight bowed to her, and ℕ tered admiration and amusement in his eyes managed to land on his feet. I had hea marriage, but not that his wife was quite

Matilda reddened. Until she had we had seldom come her way, and when t' his life's work. Here too were his royal apartments, now the domain of King William Rufus, blazing with torches to light the way of visitors and guests.

Simon grinned. 'Is that all you can say?'

She dug her elbow in his ribs. 'Does it have a garden?' she asked sweetly.

'I . . . umm . . .'

'You don't know,' she pounced, and her own lips curved at having jolted him out of his smugness.

'I was always too much occupied on my lord king's business,' he said loftily.

Matilda laughed and wagged her finger at him. 'In that case you might as well have been anywhere, and you have no advantage over me.'

Simon was spared from finding a suitable answer by the arrival of the grooms to attend to their horses and a steward to show them where to pitch the tents they had brought with them. The sward outside the King's hall was already a mass of coloured canvas, but a space had been reserved among the ranks that were closest to the hall.

As Simon's men set to work with canvas, rope and tent pegs, a fair-haired knight emerged from one of the erected tents. His genial expression was compounded by large hazel eyes and a wide, good-natured mouth.

He greeted Simon with a hefty slap on the back and an ear to ear smile. 'Well, my lord,' he said, 'is an English earldom to your taste?'

'Very much,' Simon replied and, drawing Matilda forward, introduced her to Ranulf de Tosny. 'A friend in arms and in wine cups,' he said ruefully.

'My lady.' The knight bowed to her, and Matilda encountered admiration and amusement in his eyes. 'Simon has ever managed to land on his feet. I had heard rumours of his marriage, but not that his wife was quite such a beauty.'

Matilda reddened. Until she had wed Simon compliments had seldom come her way, and when they had her mother had frowned on them, saying that vanity was not to be encouraged. She was still unaccustomed to dealing with praise and to seeing open appreciation in men's eyes. Her growing awareness of her feminine power was only matched by the fear that she was climbing too high too swiftly. Her husband said, 'Dare.' She obeyed him, and then was terrified to look down.

'And he did not tell me that he had such gallant friends to call upon,' she responded, finding the words from the uncertain depths of her new confidence.

Ranulf de Tosny laughed. 'Mayhap he does not want too many rivals,' he said. Then his gaze fell upon Jude, who was standing modestly at Matilda's side. And the focus of his attention changed.

'This is my younger sister, Jude,' Matilda murmured.

Jude dipped a curtsey and De Tosny bowed. 'You didn't tell me that your wife had a sister either,' he said softly to Simon.

'A good shepherd is always prudent when wolves are sniffing around.' Simon was smiling, but there was a warning note in his voice.

'Is that an insult?'

'Common sense when I remember some of our days and nights at court – or should I say some of your days and nights?' Simon retorted.

Ranulf snorted. 'Then you do not remember your own now that you stand on the other side of the stockade?' He winked at Matilda and Jude. 'I could tell you some tales.'

Simon cleared his throat. 'Tales would be all they would be,' he said, although Matilda was fascinated to see that his colour was high. Thinking of their marriage bed, knowing his penchant for exploration, she was certain that there was no smoke without fire.

Ranulf de Tosny fiddled with the handsome buckle of his belt. 'Tales are the language of the court,' he said. 'A whisper here, an insinuation there. Always in the background, no matter the loudness of what you hear on the surface.'